PENGUIN BOOKS

MIRROR, MIRROR

Jane Yolen is an internationally known poet, writer, and story-teller. The author of more than two hundred books, she has won the Nebula World Fantasy Award, Christopher Medal, and the National Jewish Book Award. She and her husband live in Hatfield, Massachusetts, and St. Andrews, Scotland. She can be found at www.jane-yolen.com.

Heidi E.Y. Stemple is Jane Yolen's daughter and the coauthor of two of her children's books. She has also published children's poetry and adult fiction. She lives in Myrtle Beach, South Carolina, with her husband and two daughters. She can be reached at http://members.aol.com/heidieys/.

Mirror, Mirror

FORTY FOLKTALES FOR
MOTHERS AND DAUGHTERS TO SHARE

Edited and Discussed by
Jane Yolen and Heidi E. Y. Stemple

PENGUIN BOOKS

PENGUIN BOOKS

Published by the Penguin Group

Penguin Putnam Inc., 375 Hudson Street,
New York, New York 10014, U.S.A.
Penguin Books Ltd, 27 Wrights Lane, London W8 5TZ, England
Penguin Books Australia Ltd, Ringwood, Victoria, Australia
Penguin Books Canada Ltd, 10 Alcorn Avenue,
Toronto, Ontario, Canada M4V 3B2
Penguin Books (N.Z.) Ltd, 182–190 Wairau Road,
Auckland 10, New Zealand

Penguin Books Ltd, Registered Offices:
Harmondsworth, Middlesex, England

First published in the United States of America by
Viking Penguin, a member of Penguin Putnam Inc. 2000
Published in Penguin Books 2001

1 3 5 7 9 10 8 6 4 2

THE LIBRARY OF CONGRESS HAS CATALOGED
THE HARDCOVER EDITION AS FOLLOWS:
Mirror, mirror: forty folktales for mothers and daughters to share
[compiled by] Jane Yolen and Heidi Stemple.
p.   cm.
Includes bibliographical references.
ISBN 0-670-88907-5 (hc.)
ISBN 0 14 02.9835 5 (pbk.)
1. Mothers and daughters.   2. Tales—History and criticism.
3. Women—folklore.   I. Yolen, Jane.   II. Stemple. Heidi E. Y.
HQ755.85.M57 2000   99–046891

Printed in the United States of America
Set in Stempel Schneidler and Centaur
Designed by Betty Lew

To Our Motherline

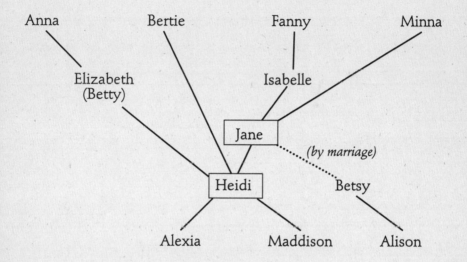

Anna Bertie Fanny Minna

Elizabeth (Betty) Isabelle

Jane

(by marriage)

Heidi Betsy

Alexia Maddison Alison

Everything's got a moral, if only you can find it.
—Duchess in Lewis Carroll, *Alice in Wonderland*

Mothers are a biological necessity; fathers are a social invention.
—Margaret Mead

Oh, what a power is motherhood, possessing
A potent spell. All women alike
Fight fiercely for a child.
—Euripides, *Iphigenia in Aulis*

All women become like their mothers.
That is their tragedy. No man does.
That's his.
—Oscar Wilde

Daughter am I in my mother's house,
But mistress in my own.
—Rudyard Kipling, *Our Lady of the Snows*

CONTENTS

INTRODUCTION

MOTHER LINES

JANE: "Don't touch it, you don't know where it's been."
"Clean your plate. Think of the poor starving Armenians."
"Your face is going to freeze that way."

Those are three pieces of mother wisdom, or "mother lines" as I like to call them, that my own mother, Isabelle Berlin Yolen, passed on to me.

Isn't it odd that my mother—a well-educated, articulate, dedicated reader who created crossword puzzles and double acrostics—should fall back on such old saws?

Being the daughter of my mother, I am certain I have said similar things to my own daughter and granddaughters. But perhaps because I am a writer, I have managed to couch the adages in slightly more surprising ways. Certainly no one thinks of the "poor starving Armenians" anymore. ("Name three!" had been my sassy answer when I was six). These days mothers are more likely to point to the poor starving Cameroonians, or Croats, or Kosovars or anyone in a number of ex-Soviet satellites. Alas, there is always a populace in a nation on the edge of malnutrition that a marginally politicized mother can use to browbeat her children into eating what they would not otherwise want to eat.

But the mother tongue is in my mouth. And as my daughter has remarked on more than one occasion: "I open my lips and your voice comes out."

Do all mothers and daughters respond this way? My sons do not tell me these things. Well, my sons actually tell me very little without prodding. They talk more to their father—about fishing, about birding, about football, politics, computers, golf—though rarely about emotional issues. They tell each other jokes.

Anne Sexton wrote in a poem to her own daughter:

> *Now that you are eighteen*
> *I give you my booty, my spoils,*
> *my Mother & Co. and my ailments.*

We mothers pass on to our girl children our Mother & Co. all right. We emerge from between our mother's legs and then spend a lifetime trying to return or to turn (or not turn) into her. As women we see in our mothers the body that will be ours: breasts, genitals, blood, even the bending of bone in old age. We pattern on her voice, on her walk, on her way of relating to others. Begun as shadow women, we spend the rest of our lives trying to get out from under that shadow.

I remember thinking my mother was beautiful. A child's notion, of course. In the beginning all our mothers are beautiful. But the several photographs I have of my mother in her youth actually confirm this. She had a subtle beauty, dark and mysterious, with eyes that turned down at the edges, which meant she looked in a perpetual state of mourning. Her mouth was a perfect bow. I used to be fascinated by her putting on lipstick. She never used a mirror. She was also what was once called a "pocket Venus," for she was not quite five feet tall yet beautifully proportioned.

However, she always saw herself as plain. She cultivated the mind, thinking she had no reason to cultivate the body. And she had a quick, cynical, Dorothy Parker wit, as if getting in the first jab meant winning the fight.

I wanted to copy her, though we looked little alike except for those down-turned eyes. Where she was small—hands, feet, breasts, thighs—I was large. Where she was quiet, I was loud. Where she was audience, I was center stage. Where she was happy to follow, I always wished to lead. But the cynical mouth, the passion for print, the lack of body confidence—those were my inheritance.

I understood about part of this inheritance for the first time when a boy I had known slightly in high school slipped into the seat next to mine on the train riding back home during some college vacation. He roused me from my book with the line "Hi, Jane—going home for the holidays? Say something sarcastic." I opened my mouth—and *my* mother's voice came out.

This story from Aesop seems so appropriate:

THE CRAB AND HER MOTHER

Said an old Crab to a young one, "Why do you
walk so crooked, child? Walk straight!"
"Mother," said the young Crab, "show me the
way, will you? And when I see you taking a
straight course, I will try and follow."

My mother and I talked about everything except how we felt about Daddy, my brother, each other. Those confidences remained hidden, as if we feared that knowing the truth would break the family apart. The 1950s was not a time of truth-telling.

We gossiped happily about relatives and friends. We discussed politics—she watched the Kefauver investigations on television and during the hearings knit innumerable items which we inevitably called her "Estes sweaters." We shared a love of mystery novels and recommended books to one another. And we traded baseball stats because she was a major Giants fan and I was for the Dodgers. (Daddy liked the Yankees, so we didn't talk to him about baseball at all.) She also read my stories in manuscript and commented on them. But we did *not* talk about emotions.

Until—that is—her granddaughter was born. And then, as if her daughter's daughter had opened some kind of door, we began to tell one another how much we loved and admired each other, enjoyed being together. Much that had been covert and hidden in our relationship became open. It was an amazing transformation. We practically wore out the hinges on that door, running back and forth with our confidences.

We left it till it was almost too late. She died when my daughter Heidi was four. Except that Heidi is five-foot five, she reminds me of her grandmother, especially in looks and in the generous way she treats unfortunates. She also has that same cynical mouth. But we have made a conscious effort all of her life to talk about our feelings ("ad nauseam," as the men in our families often charge). But in both cases—mother to daughter—there were two taboo subjects.

Sex and death.

My mother never knew—or at least never admitted to knowing—that my husband and I had lived together for a year and a half before we were married. Those were the days before such arrangements were the norm. David and I lived in Greenwich Village on Commerce Street, in a fifth-floor walk-up above the Cherry Lane Theater, though he kept his old apartment a few blocks away, just in case. Mother would always call ahead when she and Daddy were coming to visit. We had plenty of time to hide the razor, the hairbrush, the men's clothes.

I knew—but never admitted to knowing—that my father had not been faithful to my mother. And that she had repeatedly forgiven him.

So much for sex.

My mother and I never talked about her impending death either. Except once, within the context of a fairy tale. Our conversation—if one can call a single line a conversation—revolved around a children's picture book I was writing, called *The Bird of Time*. ("Fakelore" the great folklorist Alan Dundes calls such stories, meaning a tale that looks and smells like folklore but is an original or art tale created by a specific and identifiable author.)

I had begun writing the book on the very day I'd been told my mother had incurable cancer and had only six months to live. My father had begged my brother and me not to tell her, to support his fabrication that she had a nonlethal form of Hodgkin's disease. He said it was for her sake, but we both knew he couldn't bear to face her death head-on.

We agreed to do as he asked. But clearly my heart was telling me something else. What I could not say aloud, I said in story, which has always been my way. The book I was writing was about a miller's son who finds a bird that can magically speed time up or slow time down or stop time altogether. As *I* wanted to. As I desperately wanted to—to save my mother.

Six months went by. Mother and I talked every day on the phone, about almost everything except her advancing death. I counted each extra month as a blessing, though I could not possibly talk about that with her. Even bad promises are sacred.

And then she came up to Massachusetts for a visit. She was still mobile while I—seven months pregnant with my third child and with a torn cervix and a doctor's warning not to travel very far afield—was not.

It was the last time I saw her alive.

Sitting in our great brown leather chair, she read the manuscript of *The Bird of Time*. She was so shrunken with her illness that the chair practically enveloped her. When she was done reading, she looked up and smiled that wry Dorothy Parker smile.

"Intimations of mortality, eh?" she said.

She had known all along that she was dying. She was letting me know—through story—that she knew I knew, too.

Sex and death.

Heidi and I do not discuss these things either.

My mother and I never cooked together or sewed together, those traditional mother-daughter occupations. She was a lousy cook, blending the worst of Jewish and Southern cookery.

Her mother, Fanny Morewitz Berlin, was also a terrible cook, at least according to my aunts and cousins. But I remember with great vividness and longing my grandmother's cozy kitchen in Hampton Roads, Virginia. What I recall most is sitting on top of the table, my chubby little legs tucked under me, helping chop apples in a big wooden bowl for Grandma's applesauce.

I have no such cooking memories with my own mother. The family joke was that she could ruin hamburgers. My childhood was filled with dinners to accommodate my skinny brother's food preferences—hamburgers, mashed potatoes, peas from a can—and thinking about those poor starving Armenians.

Children did not eat with the grown-ups often in those days, but earlier and at a different table. Maybe that is why I have no mother/food memories. But really, I think that food simply did not matter to my mother, except that a dinner party was a place where interesting people could gather to make interesting conversation.

However, she went through a ghastly period for about ten years in which she felt it was incumbent upon her to sew all my clothes. She was awful at it, but she persevered, as if the act of sewing made her more motherly. The blouses she made had sleeves that were never set in properly; the skirts were style-less, with flawed waistbands. I never got to pick out the materials and hated her every choice.

I put my foot down when it came to a homemade prom dress. Since by the time I was ready to go to my first prom, my mother was at the end of her sewing period anyway, I didn't have to suffer the embarrassment of her working up some little number in peau de soie or tulle. Her time was all taken up with running a secondhand clothing shop for the

Staples High School PTA. So instead of a homemade prom dress, I got a secondhand one. Even in the 1950s, Westport, Connecticut, hand-me-downs were nothing to sniff at, though I was terrified some sophisticated super-rich high school girl would identify my dress as one she had recently given away. From the distance of forty-five years, a secondhand prom dress seems a strange choice for the daughter of a vice president of the largest public relations firm in America, but of course my father had nothing to do with it. And as far as I remember, the dress was neither a political nor an ecological statement by either my mother or me. The only thing I can think of is that it was a protofeminist, fist-raised stance by a woman asserting her independence from her husband.

Or perhaps not. Sometimes, Dr. Freud, a prom dress is just a dress.

Still, I remembered my embarrassment when Heidi began getting ready for her first prom. At my insistence, we drove the three hours from our home in Massachusetts to New York City and I bought her a dress at Bloomingdale's after a full day of looking. Sometimes we learn different lessons than the ones our mothers meant to teach.

Here's another apropos story from Aesop:

THE MOON AND HER MOTHER

The moon once asked her Mother to make her a
little cloak that would fit her well.
"How," replied she, "can I make you a cloak to fit
you, who are now a New Moon, and then a Full
Moon, and then again neither one nor the other?"

Astonishing to me, my daughter cooks well enough to be thinking of a possible other career in catering, and she sews well, too: costumes for her little daughter, handmade blankets and pillowcases for the older one. She also produces handmade baby baskets for her pregnant friends as well as curtains and wall hangings. I have to remind myself that she is not just made up of Berlin/Yolen genes, that she has an entire patrilinear side, which includes a great-grandmother who was an award-winning West Virginia quilt maker.

My mother trained as a psychiatric social worker, as did her three sisters. She was working in New York City when she met my father, who was a hotshot young journalist. She continued to work until I came along, five years after they were married, and then she never held a paying job again.

When my brother and I were in high school, mother began doing volunteer work, heading up a Fairfield County social work organization. She ran the PTA boutique. She created crossword puzzles and acrostics. In fact, if I were to take the perfect picture of my mother, she would be sitting in an armchair, cigarette in her mouth, reading a mystery novel and working on a double acrostic at the same time. The acknowledged breadwinner, around whose schedule and whims the entire family revolved, was my father.

I did *not* marry my father. In fact, I probably did a reverse turn. My professor husband has always encouraged my writing, my career. He has cheered me every step of the way. Since I had a home office, I was able to be around to raise the children. Whenever I needed to go off to a conference, to give a speech, to be an FA (a Famous Author)—as the children used to call it—he stepped in and played Dr. Mom.

My daughter has done a bit of both. She has worked and not worked. She has written, bartended, waitressed, done a few years as a probation officer and as a private detective. As a child and then a young woman, she had always talked about wanting to teach. But in her sophomore year in college she called to ask if we thought it strange that she wanted to change her major midstream to social work. Not strange at all, I told her, given her grandmother and those three great-aunts! Now she is a stay-at-home mom who writes and works tirelessly for the foster parenting group in her region.

What is it, then, that we give one another, mother to daughter, besides body image, besides a rota of mother lines, besides snapshots that are like a crazy quilt of a past that we lived together but that neither of us remembers in the same way?

If we are lucky, we get and we give unconditional love.

I remember being overwhelmed by that love when, standing by the hospital bed, I watched my daughter give birth to her daughter, my first grandchild.

The doctor began laughing at something Heidi said (for she was amusing even in extremis) and he looked away for a moment. I reached out, ready to catch the already-crowning child. The doctor recovered. Heidi's husband—whey-faced in the doorway from the sight of all the blood—was relieved.

But I would have been happy to haul my grandchild, red with blood, from the birth canal. If necessary I would have bitten through the umbilical cord with my teeth. We daughters, we mothers, we mothers of mothers— we are tough when we have to be, tender when we need to be.

Lisel Mueller, who often uses folkloric themes in her poetry, puts it this way, recalling the mother in the Grimm's "Cinderella":

THE VOICE FROM UNDER THE HAZEL BUSH

> *I died for you. Each spring*
> *I wake in my house of roots;*
> *my memory leafs out*
> *into a rich green dress*
> *for you to dance in. The moon*
> *turns it to silver, the evening sun*
> *to gold. Be happy, my daughter.*
> *You think I have magic powers,*
> *others call it love.*
> *I tell you it is the will*
> *to survive, in you, in the earth.*
> *Your story does not end*
> *with the wedding dance, it goes on.*

OUT OF THE SHADOWS

HEIDI: I am a mother of two daughters. But I begin in this collaboration as a daughter in the shadow of my mother's introduction. Strangely, I find myself not fighting to get out from under that shadow. Though I am a control freak, for once I am enjoying being on the second string.

I can't imagine any better footprints to walk in. I am hardly a child, but at thirty-three years old, next to my mother I am still the newcomer in writing, and also in life. My mother is wise and witty. Talented, too. And, in my view, all-knowing. I look up to her and look to her for advice, judgment, and approval. When she comes to me for advice on the few subjects in which my knowledge surpasses hers, I feel unworthy and at the same time complimented.

We are not the same type of thinkers. In that I take after my scientist father. Where my mother is fantasy and faerie, I am reality and fact. If I can't see it, it is not so. If she cannot find it on this earth, she makes it up.

Each of the million times as a child (and even into early adulthood) when asked if I wanted to be a writer just like my mommy, I replied with an adamant no. I wanted to be anything but. I wanted to be a gymnast. I wanted to be an actress. I wanted to be a teacher. And finally, I wanted to work in the law.

Now I write. Go figure.

I find it amusing that in order to become my mother, I had to reject everything that she was until—as an adult mother of two daughters—I have come full circle, aspiring to be exactly like her, though sometimes I feel a pale copy.

"Look with your eyes, not with your hands." One of her mother lines. Much more poetic than some. She passed that one on to me and now I use it with my own grabby little girl.

Freud believed that little girls relate early on to their father as a sexual figure and come to resent and fear their mothers because they want to take their mothers' place in their fathers' life. Eventually, Freud theorized, girls develop gender identity by rejecting this jealousy and identifying with the same-sex parent. This theory, sometimes called the Electra complex (after the Greek tragic heroine who kills her mother at her brother's insistence) is generally considered a bit far-fetched by today's psychological standards, which tend to lean less on the classic "all problems stem from issues with your mother" and more on taking control. Shifting views.

Still, as the mother of a teenage daughter, Lexi, I find that while the theory is perhaps off-center, it still has some validity. I tell Lexi that it is all right to be mad at me because in order to become a woman, she must separate herself from me, to find which pieces of me she wishes to discard and which pieces she will take on as her own. This irritates her; she cannot understand why she is angrier at me when she considers me right than when she honestly believes I am being unreasonable.

I remember my own teenage response to this same problem. Standing at the bottom of the steps in our house, I wailed to my mother, "I *hate* it when you're so reasonable!" Okay, she was right. She knew she was right. I knew she was right. And that made me miserable.

During my college years, I was asked to write a paper—"My Socialization Autobiography"—for one of the many psychology classes I took. While writing this paper I discovered myself through my names.

I had been given the name Heidi Elisabet followed by my father's surname, Stemple. My mother has successfully retained her maiden name, Yolen, for professional purposes and used her married name only for motherhood. She is still, in my eyes, two separate people: Dr. Jane Yolen, the author, and Mrs. Jane Stemple, my mom.

At approximately 3:00 a.m., as I was finishing the paper, I realized that I was a joint effort of both parents. It felt unfair that Yolen was not part of my official name—both the person who was my mother and all who came before her. In those early hours I became Heidi Elisabet Yolen Stemple. I announced it on my paper. It is in my college records and on my graduation certificate.

When I married, I played the name game again, and I came to the conclusion that dropping any of my names would be an injustice to the woman that I had become. So I dropped not a one. On my crowded driver's license I am known as Heidi Elisabet Yolen Stemple Piatt. A mouthful—but me.

As for mothering daughters, I am becoming quite an expert. While my mother raised a daughter and two sons, I am raising two girls.

My first daughter, Maddison Jane (more mother name games) was born on a beautiful March afternoon in Atlanta. Things had been going too slowly, the water breaking early the evening before but labor not advancing. My doctor wanted to induce, but I begged him to hold off until the following morning because my mother was not due to arrive until then. When the labor became too painful—and eventually danger-ous—I called my mother for permission to induce even if it meant her missing the birth of her first grandchild. She laughed. "Do what's best for you and the baby," she said. Did I remember then that I hated it when she was so reasonable?

Luckily, she made the actual birth (due to an earlier flight and a crazy cab driver who broke all of Georgia's speed limits) with exactly two hours to spare.

Could I have delivered Maddison without her there? Probably. But did I want to? It wouldn't have felt right.

Less than an hour after Maddison's birth, I looked up from her big blue eyes to see my mother's eyes—the mirror of my own brown ones—and apologized to her.

"You loved me this much," I said, "and I treated you so badly. I am sorry." We both laughed and cried there in the delivery room as we entered a new phase in our relationship.

My second daughter was an easier delivery. I met Lexi by pure coincidence the day before my thirty-first birthday when she was fourteen years old and in need of a new home. Separated from her birth mother and eventually from her first foster mother, she spent time with us on the weekends and after school for six months while we all waited, none too patiently, for our foster care license to be approved. Finally, Lexi came to live with us as a temporary foster daughter. She is not leaving. We are adopting her.

Two years later, when I am yelling at Lexi for putting off her homework until the eleventh hour or missing curfew and making me worry, my mom commiserates with me on the phone, or via e-mail, and I apologize again for my own long-past teenage antics, knowing full well that I was much more of a handful than Lexi. But I think that this is my mother's reward for all the heartache that I caused.

Someday I will be a grandmother. Someday my girls will call and apologize to me.

Until I started doing the research for this book, I had been largely annoyed with fairy tales. Yes, I had grown up on the classics (how could I avoid them living with the Queen Mother of the Fairies), but all those old tales seemed passé. With my feet, as always, firmly planted on the ground, I wondered: What do these stories tell us about now? Besides, the classic tales had been largely replaced by the ubiquitous Disney movies, which I hated—tidy versions easily acquired on video, in which the heroines were no longer strong-willed young women surviving on their wits but Barbies waiting for rescue.

I complained to anyone who would listen about the pencil-thin waists of Disney's women and their childlike features. "Waif women," I called them. I ranted about Disney's *Beauty and the Beast* as a classic case of a battered woman enabling her batterer. I even wrote an angry short story for adults called "Brittany and the Beast," about a beauty queen, fueled in part by my living in South Carolina, home to many child beauty pageants.

Against my better judgment, I allowed my daughters to watch the Disney movies, trying to find lessons—both positive and negative—to discuss with them. At last, I tried to remember the classics and talked about those as well.

Now through this book, I have rediscovered the old tales with a vengeance. And—no surprise to my mother—I found that they are not always as I remembered them. In fact, they are hardly ever what I remember.

"Rapunzel" is a good example. I had thought of it as the story of a horrible witch who had locked up an innocent girl and never wanted to let her out. Talk about a grounding! This time, as the mother of a teenager, my take on that story has shifted a full 180 degrees. I read it today as a tale about a woman who has adopted a baby, lavishing years of love and care. And that baby—now grown into a spoiled teenager—sneaks out and gets pregnant by the first rich and equally spoiled prince who compliments her.

Ah, if we could all just lock up our teenage girls in tall towers. How much easier life would be.

And seeing some of the boys who have come to visit my too-beautiful-for-her-own-good teenage daughter, I would surely not make the same mistake as the old woman in "Rapunzel." Besides, short hair is very in right now.

When Maddison at age four tells me I am the best mommy in the world, she has no other frame of reference. It is simply a heartfelt statement of love.

When Lexi tells me the same, I know that there is competition out there. After all, I am her third mother. Mother-daughter relationships are difficult enough in a normal (whatever that is) situation, but what Lexi and I have is unique.

I will be forever compared—for better or for worse—to Lexi's biological mother and her first foster mother. I even encourage this, where possibly other foster and adoptive mothers may not be able to. I am forever indebted to the woman who gave birth to my daughter. I love her in a way I didn't know was possible, for without her, I could not have Lexi. But the competition between us—fought only in our daughter's heart—is also painful.

Through no fault of my own, I lost fourteen years with Lexi. There is no way for me to get back that mother-daughter time, no way to describe that feeling of loss. With my younger daughter I experienced birth and breast-feeding. Being up all night with colic and ear infections. Then those first real smiles that bound us one to the other. The first words that touched on her world: Momma, Dadda, Nana, Papa . . . All lost with Lexi.

But we build on what we have now. *Now.* Like the shifting views in psychoanalysis, I had to revise my opinions on mothering to include a past of which I was not part.

Sex and death.

Now there are two subjects I talk about a lot. I talk about both with my older daughter (more than I would like to, actually). My younger daughter isn't much interested in sex yet (thank goodness for small favors), but we are very involved in death conversations since I recently had to put my fourteen-year-old dog (my first daughter) to sleep. Maddison is trying very hard to understand but can't quite get a handle on it yet.

My mother would like to talk about these two things with me, but I am the one who resists. At parties where we are both guests, she warns her friends that sex is not to be a topic because her daughter doesn't want to talk about it.

Not true. I just don't want to talk about sex with *her.*

In fact, I learned that she had not been married to my daddy when they first moved in together only when I read her draft of this introduction! I should have suspected something, perhaps, when she never said a word when my daughter was born without benefit of a marriage license. But, two and a half years later, when Maddison walked down the aisle throwing rose petals at my wedding to her father, I know my mother breathed a huge sigh of relief.

As for death, I am somewhat of an expert there, having worked for a grief and death counselor. My friends—and even Lexi's friends—turn to me for counseling in matters pertaining to death. Death of parents, grandparents, friends.

But my own mother's death? I refuse to think about it, let alone discuss it. Maybe as my mother turns sixty, I will be able to grow up and talk about it. Her birthday marks the end of her fifty-ninth year, the year in which her own mother died, so it has been a potent and difficult year for her. Maybe I will give her that conversation as a birthday present.

Or maybe not.

While my mother so eloquently quotes Aesop, I'd like to fall back again on my psychology books. The "Mother Mandate" contends that little girls are pressured by society to become good mothers and feel unfulfilled as women if they are not.

Now, I do not work outside the home (with heartfelt thanks to my husband, who makes this possible) in order to raise our girls. I have taken on writing projects to fill in the gaps. It turns out I'm good at writing and enjoy it as well—a bonus, certainly. But my primary job is to be a good mother. I was taught by an expert. So I *do* feel the pressure to live up to my mother's standard of mothering. And, more important, to pass on to my girls—who are my immortality, if you will—how to be a good mother. Could there be anything more important?

Recently I have been reading the introduction to a collection of Grace Paley stories my father gave me for Christmas. In one partial sentence I recognized myself (that shock that good writing can give you). Ms. Paley wrote about "history that happens to you while you're doing the dishes."

That is my history, my life. Raising my girls is of primary importance right now. Everything else—even writing—takes a distant back seat for me. My mother has to call me twelve times a day to remind me of a deadline.

Paley went on to say that she has "two ears, one for literature and one for home."

Right now, both my ears are tuned to the sounds of home. And when everything else is quiet, I can listen to stories as well.

HEART-TO-HEART

JANE: No one likes to read long introductions. But we all like to eavesdrop on private conversations. So the rest of this book is filled with mother-daughter folktales and the heart-to-hearts Heidi and I have had over them.

We have held these conversations over the course of almost two years. In that same time Heidi had meningitis and was in the hospital, I was on crutches from a blown knee which eventually necessitated several cortisone shots, my husband retired. Heidi's oldest daughter got a driver's license, I turned sixty, a new baby girl (brother Adam's daughter) was born into our family. Heidi's husband's job expanded, I won the Nebula Award twice and had a TV movie made from one of my books, Heidi's youngest started nursery school. Another foster daughter entered the scene for the winter holidays only and left amid tears. The president of the United States was impeached. Bombs fell on Belgrade. Two teens killed almost a dozen classmates in Colorado. A mass killer rode the rails.

In other words—life happened.

The folktales we were both reading for this book became an organizing principle around which we could speak of things other than the immediate day-to-day crises that afflict any family. "Rapunzel" started us off on the whole world of nature versus nurture, "Snow White" on beauty versus brains. "Cinderella" got us talking about "lookism." The Eskimo story "Tuglik and Her Granddaughter" had us musing about dirty words. And "Diamonds and Toads" made me bemoan the problems of making a living as a writer. We expanded our normal conversations because of the stories we were reading.

Most of us, so caught up in day-to-day minutiae, have phone calls with our mothers or daughters that sound something like this:

Hi.

Hi.

Wanted to tell you that the baby is awfully croupy.

You were like that.

I was?

Yep.

What did you do?

Lots of fluids and held you a lot.

Doing that already. Oops—she's crying. Gotta go.

Bye.

We all hold compressed, even coded conversations with our mothers and daughters. We send smoke signals or signal with flags. But do we really *think* about our relationships, the ones that began in the womb and end up—if we are lucky—woman to woman? Do we really talk to one another? Or do we—like the bad girl in the French folk story "Diamonds and Toads"—snub the old woman and her needs, shortcutting her wisdoms and ending up with amphibians instead of gems dropping from our lips?

These folktales from our collective past are really signposts. They tell us, "Begin talking here." And if we are smart, we do just that. However, in these days of movies, television, the World Wide Web, who really gives those old stories mouth-to-ear resuscitation anymore? And what have we lost if we forget them and all that they have held in sacred trust for us these hundreds of years?

We have lost those tales that have the power of transformation at their core, where happy endings come at great cost, where wisdom is won only when something else is given up. As Gertrude Mueller Nelson says in *Here All Dwell Free,* the old stories are really about "anguish and darkness" and—we'd like to add—they are also about the one true path through the tangled wood to the castle door.

WHY THIS BOOK?

HEIDI: This book was created to meet a perceived need. By recording our conversations on the stories, we hope to offer them as models for other mothers and their daughters. Take these stories yourselves and do what we have done. Dredge up moments from your pasts—separate and together—long forgotten or never discussed. Look for synchronicities you never knew existed. Find the changes that have occurred over time and space that define you and bind you together.

In fact, this book and the stories herein have already begun to work as we had hoped. And not just to us.

Lexi was putting together an anthology of stories and poems for a school assignment, stories that were meant to help define how she saw herself. I offered her a look at a number of the folktales we were working with. She chose "The Serpent Mother" because she saw how immediate it was to her situation, even though it was a story that had first been told centuries ago, in a country far from where she lives.

Read a story and open a life.

Even if you never talk about sex. Or death.

BEYOND THE MAGIC MIRROR

BOTH: There is an interesting trend in America these days for mother-daughter reading groups. This book is—and is not—designed to be part of that.

Most of the books the reading groups tackle are novels or works of nonfiction. The main thrust within the groups is to discuss the books read, to have a shared cultural experience.

We are suggesting something a bit more radical than that. We feel that by reading folktales with one another, mothers and daughters can use the core motifs to open up conversations that have been long delayed or never before ventured.

These tales are mirrors reflecting back our deepest, most hidden selves. We hope our own conversations—posted after each group of stories—can serve as guides to other mothers and daughters.

Folktales are by nature short, archaic, culture laden. They have a dreamlike quality. Often within the borders of a folktale animals speak, queens dance in red-hot iron shoes, high towers are constructed in tangled woods without recourse to architects or masons. A traveler in these lands knows that she is not in downtown Chicago or uptown Manhattan or even in Kansas.

She is in Wonderland. She is in Once Upon A Time.

Because these tales have been polished by centuries of tongues, they encapsulate all that is human and therefore are the perfect form with which to open a conversation.

So read the stories, and see where we have gone—mother to daughter and back again. Then try your own conversations. Very quickly you will discover that Once Upon A Time becomes your own time: time past, time present, and time future.

Cinderella

Cinderella

GERMANY

The wife of a rich man fell sick, and as she felt that her end was drawing near, she called her only daughter to her bedside and said, "Dear child, be good and pious, and then the good God will always protect thee, and I will look down on thee from heaven and be near thee." Thereupon she closed her eyes and departed. Every day the maiden went out to her mother's grave and wept, and she remained pious and good. When winter came the snow spread a white sheet over the grave, and when the spring sun had drawn it off again, the man had taken another wife.

The woman had brought two daughters into the house with her, who were beautiful and fair of face, but vile and black of heart. Now began a bad time for the poor step-child. "Is the stupid goose to sit in the parlor with us?" said they. "He who wants to eat bread must earn it; out with the kitchen-wench." They took her pretty clothes away from her, put an old gray bedgown on her, and gave her wooden shoes. "Just look at the proud princess, how decked out she is!" they cried, and laughed, and led her into the kitchen. There she had to do hard work from morning till night, get up before daybreak, carry water, light fires, cook and wash. Besides this, the sisters did her every imaginable injury—they mocked her and emptied her peas and lentils into the ashes, so that she was forced to sit and pick them out again. In the evening when she had worked till she was weary she had no bed to go to, but had to sleep by the fireside in the ashes. And as on that account she always looked dusty and dirty, they called her Cinderella. It happened that the father was once going to the fair, and he asked his two step-daughters what he should bring back for them. "Beautiful dresses," said one. "Pearls and jewels," said the second. "And thou, Cinderella," said he, "what wilt thou have?" "Father, break off for me the first branch which knocks against your hat on your way home." So he bought beautiful dresses, pearls and jewels for his two step-daughters, and on his way home, as he was riding through a green thicket, a hazel twig brushed against him and knocked off his hat. Then he broke off the branch and took it with him. When he reached home he gave his step-daughters the things which they had wished for, and to Cinderella he gave the branch from the hazel-bush. Cinderella thanked him, went to her mother's grave and planted the branch on it, and wept so much that the tears fell down on it and watered it. It grew, however, and became a handsome tree. Thrice a day Cinderella went and sat beneath it, and wept and prayed, and a little white bird always came on the tree, and if Cinderella expressed a wish, the bird threw down to her what she had wished for.

It happened, however, that the King appointed a festival which was to last three days, and to which all the beautiful young girls in the country were in-vited, in order that his son might choose himself a bride. When the two step-sisters heard that they, too, were to appear among the number, they were delighted, called Cinderella and said, "Comb our hair for us, brush our shoes and fasten our buckles, for we are going to the festival at the King's palace." Cinderella obeyed, but wept, because she, too, would have liked to go with them to the dance, and begged her step-mother to allow her to do so. "Thou go, Cinderella!" said she. "Thou art dusty and dirty, and wouldst go to the festival? Thou hast no clothes and shoes, and yet wouldst dance!" As, however, Cinderella went on asking, the step-mother at last said, "I have emptied a dish of lentils into the ashes for thee; if thou hast picked them out again in two hours, thou shalt go with us." The maiden went through the back-door into the garden, and called, "You tame pigeons, you turtle-doves, and all you birds beneath the sky, come and help me to pick

"The good into the pot,
The bad into the crop."

Then two white pigeons came in by the kitchen window, and afterwards the turtle-doves, and at last all the birds beneath the sky came whirring and crowding in, and alighted amongst the ashes. And the pigeons nodded with their heads and began pick, pick, pick, pick, and the rest began also pick, pick, pick, pick, and gathered all the good grains into the dish. Hardly had one hour passed before they had finished, and all flew out again. Then the girl took the dish to her step-mother, and was glad, and believed that now she would be allowed to go with them to the festival. But the step-mother said, "No, Cinderella, thou hast no clothes, and thou canst not dance; thou wouldst only be laughed at." And as Cinderella wept at this, the step-mother said, "If thou canst pick two dishes of lentils out of the ashes for me in one hour, thou shalt go with us." And she thought to herself, "That she most certainly cannot do." When the step-mother had emptied the two dishes of lentils amongst the ashes, the maiden went through the back-door into the garden and cried, "You tame pigeons, you turtle-doves, and all you birds under heaven, come and help me to pick

"The good into the pot,
The bad into the crop."

Then two white pigeons came in by the kitchen window, and afterwards the turtle-doves, and at length all the birds beneath the sky came whirring and crowding in, and alighted amongst the ashes. And the doves nodded with their heads and began pick, pick, pick, pick, and the others began also pick, pick, pick, pick, and gathered all the good seeds into the dishes, and before half an hour was over they had already finished, and all flew out again. Then the maiden carried the dishes to the step-mother and was delighted, and believed that she might now go with them to the festival. But the step-mother said, "All this will not help thee; thou goest not with us, for thou hast no clothes and canst not dance; we should be ashamed of thee!" On this she turned her back on Cinderella, and hurried away with her two proud daughters.

As no one was now at home, Cinderella went to her mother's grave beneath the hazel-tree, and cried,

"Shiver and quiver, my little tree,
Silver and gold throw down over me."

Then the bird threw a gold and silver dress down to her, and slippers embroidered with silk and silver. She put on the dress with all speed, and went to the festival. Her step-sisters and the step-mother, however, did not know her, and thought she must be a foreign princess, for she looked so beautiful in the golden dress. They never once thought of Cinderella, and believed that she was sitting at home in the dirt, picking lentils out of the ashes. The prince went to meet her, took her by the hand and danced with her. He would dance with no other maiden, and never left loose of her hand, and if any one else came to invite her, he said, "This is my partner."

She danced till it was evening, and then she wanted to go home. But the King's son said, "I will go with thee and bear thee company," for he wished to see to whom the beautiful maiden belonged. She escaped from him, however, and sprang into the pigeon-house. The King's son waited until her father came, and then he told him that the stranger maiden had leapt into the pigeon-house. The old man thought, "Can it be Cinderella?" and they had to bring him an axe and a pickaxe that he might hew the pigeon-house to pieces, but no one was inside it. And when they got home Cinderella lay in her dirty clothes among the ashes, and a dim little oil-lamp was burning on the mantel-piece, for Cinderella had jumped quickly down from the back of the pigeon-house and had run to the little hazel-tree, and there she had taken off her beautiful clothes and laid them on the grave, and the bird had taken them away again, and then she had placed herself in the kitchen amongst the ashes in her gray gown.

Next day when the festival began afresh, and her parents and the step-sisters had gone once more, Cinderella went to the hazel-tree and said—

> "Shiver and quiver, my little tree,
> Silver and gold throw down over me."

Then the bird threw down a much more beautiful dress than on the pre-ceding day. And when Cinderella appeared at the festival in this dress, every one was astonished at her beauty. The King's son had waited until she came, and instantly took her by the hand and danced with no one but her. When others came and invited her, he said, "She is my partner." When evening came she wished to leave, and the King's son followed her and wanted to see into which house she went. But she sprang away from him, and into the garden behind the house. Therein stood a beautiful tall tree on which hung the most magnificent pears. She clambered so nimbly between the branches like a squirrel, that the King's son did not know where she was gone. He waited until her father came, and said to him, "The stranger maiden has escaped from me, and I believe she has climbed up the pear-tree." The father thought, "Can it be Cinderella?" and had an axe brought and cut the tree down, but no one was on it. And when they got into the kitchen, Cinderella lay there amongst the ashes, as usual, for she had jumped down on the other side of the tree, had taken the beautiful dress to the bird on the little hazel-tree, and put on her gray gown.

On the third day, when the parents and sisters had gone away, Cinderella once more went to her mother's grave and said to the little tree—

> "Shiver and quiver, my little tree,
> Silver and gold throw down over me."

And now the bird threw down to her a dress which was more splendid and magnificent than any she had yet had, and the slippers were golden.

And when she went to the festival in the dress, no one knew how to speak for astonishment. The King's son danced with her only, and if any one invited her to dance, he said, "She is my partner."

When evening came, Cinderella wished to leave, and the King's son was anxious to go with her, but she escaped from him so quickly that he could not follow her. The King's son had, however, used a stratagem, and had caused the whole staircase to be smeared with pitch, and there, when she ran down, had the maiden's left slipper remained sticking. The King's son picked it up, and it was small and dainty, and all golden. Next morning, he went with it to the father, and said to him, "No one shall be my wife but she whose foot this golden slipper fits." Then were the two sisters glad, for they had pretty feet. The eldest went with the shoe into her room and wanted to try it on, and her mother stood by. But she could not get her big toe into it, and the shoe was too small for her. Then her mother gave her a knife and said, "Cut the toe off; when thou art Queen thou wilt have no more need to go on foot." The maiden cut the toe off, forced the foot into the shoe, swallowed the pain, and went out to the King's son. Then he took her on his horse as his bride and rode away with her. They were, however, obliged to pass the grave, and there, on the hazel-tree, sat the two pigeons and cried,

"Turn and peep, turn and peep,
There's blood within the shoe,
The shoe it is too small for her,
The true bride waits for you."

Then he looked at her foot and saw how the blood was streaming from it. He turned his horse round and took the false bride home again, and said she was not the true one, and that the other sister was to put the shoe on. Then this one went into her chamber and got her toes safely into the shoe, but her heel was too large. So her mother gave her a knife and said, "Cut a bit off thy heel; when thou art Queen thou wilt have no more need to go on foot." The maiden cut a bit off her heel, forced her foot into the shoe, swallowed the pain, and went out to the King's son. He took her on his horse as his bride, and rode away with her, but when they passed by the hazel-tree, two little pigeons sat on it and cried,

"Turn and peep, turn and peep,
There's blood within the shoe,
The shoe it is too small for her,
The true bride waits for you."

He looked down at her foot and saw how the blood was running out of her shoe, and how it had stained her white stocking. Then he turned his horse and took the false bride home again. "This also is not the right one," said he; "have you no other daughter?" "No," said the man. "There is still a little stunted kitchen-wench which my late wife left behind her, but she cannot possibly be the bride." The King's son said he was to send her up to him; but the mother answered, "Oh, no, she is much too dirty; she cannot show herself!" He absolutely insisted on it, and Cinderella had to be called. She first washed her hands and face clean, and then went and bowed down before the King's son, who gave her the golden shoe. Then she seated herself on a stool, drew her foot out of the heavy wooden shoe, and put it into the slipper, which fitted like a glove. And when she rose up and the King's son looked at her face, he recognized the beautiful maiden who had danced with him and cried, "That is the true bride!" The step-mother and the two sisters were terrified and became pale with rage; he, however, took Cinderella on his horse and rode away with her. As they passed by the hazel-tree, the two white doves cried,

> *"Turn and peep, turn and peep,*
> *No blood is in the shoe,*
> *The shoe is not too small for her,*
> *The true bride rides with you."*

and when they had cried that, the two came flying down and placed themselves on Cinderella's shoulders, one on the right, the other on the left, and remained sitting there.

When the wedding with the King's son had to be celebrated, the two false sisters came and wanted to get into favor with Cinderella and share her good fortune. When the betrothed couple went to church, the elder was at the right side and the younger at the left, and the pigeons pecked out one eye of each of them. Afterwards as they came back, the elder was at the left, and the younger at the right, and then the pigeons pecked out the other eye of each. And thus, for their wickedness and falsehood, they were punished with blindness as long as they lived.

Cinderella
FRANCE

Once upon a time there was a worthy man who married for his second wife the haughtiest, proudest woman that had ever been seen. She had two daughters, who possessed their mother's temper and resembled her in everything. Her husband, on the other hand, had a young daughter, who was of an exceptionally sweet and gentle nature. She got this from her mother, who had been the nicest person in the world.

The wedding was no sooner over than the stepmother began to display her bad temper. She could not endure the excellent qualities of this young girl, for they made her own daughters appear more hateful than ever. She thrust upon her all the meanest tasks about the house. It was she who had to clean the plates and the stairs, and sweep out the rooms of the mistress of the house and her daughters. She slept on a wretched mattress in a garret at the top of the house, while the sisters had rooms with parquet flooring, and beds of the most fashionable style, with mirrors in which they could see themselves from top to toe.

The poor girl endured everything patiently, not daring to complain to her father. The latter would have scolded her, because he was entirely ruled by his wife. When she had finished her work she used to sit among the cinders in the corner of the chimney, and it was from this habit that she came to be commonly known as Cinder-clod. The younger of the two sisters, who was not quite so spiteful as the elder, called her Cinderella. But her wretched clothes did not prevent Cinderella from being a hundred times more beautiful than her sisters, for all their resplendent garments.

It happened that the king's son gave a ball, and he invited all persons of high degree. The two young ladies were invited among others, for they cut a considerable figure in the country. Not a little pleased were they, and the question of what clothes and what mode of dressing the hair would become them best took up all their time. And all this meant fresh trouble for Cinderella, for it was she who went over her sisters' linen and ironed their ruffles. They could talk of nothing else but the fashions in clothes.

"For my part," said the elder, "I shall wear my dress of red velvet, with the Honiton lace."

"I have only my everyday petticoat," said the younger, "but to make up for it I shall wear my cloak with the golden flowers and my necklace of diamonds, which are not so bad."

They sent for a good hairdresser to arrange their double-frilled caps, and bought patches at the best shop.

They summoned Cinderella and asked her advice, for she had good taste. Cinderella gave them the best possible suggestions, and even offered to dress their hair, to which they gladly agreed.

While she was thus occupied they said:

"Cinderella, would you not like to go to the ball?"

"Ah, but you fine young ladies are laughing at me. It would be no place for me."

"That is very true, people would laugh to see a cinder-clod in the ballroom."

Anyone else but Cinderella would have done their hair amiss, but she was good-natured, and she finished them off to perfection. They were so excited in their glee that for nearly two days they ate nothing. They broke more than a dozen laces through drawing their stays tight in order to make their waists more slender, and they were perpetually in front of a mirror.

At last the happy day arrived. Away they went, Cinderella watching them as long as she could keep them in sight. When she could no longer see them she began to cry. Her godmother found her in tears, and asked what was troubling her.

"I should like—I should like— "

She was crying so bitterly that she could not finish the sentence.

Said her godmother, who was a fairy:

"You would like to go to the ball, would you not?"

"Ah, yes," said Cinderella, sighing.

"Well, well," said her godmother, "promise to be a good girl and I will arrange for you to go."

She took Cinderella into her room and said:

"Go into the garden and bring me a pumpkin."

Cinderella went at once and gathered the finest that she could find. This she brought to her godmother, wondering how a pumpkin could help in taking her to the ball.

Her godmother scooped it out, and when only the rind was left, struck it with her wand. Instantly the pumpkin was changed into a beautiful coach, gilded all over.

Then she went and looked in the mouse-trap, where she found six mice all alive. She told Cinderella to lift the door of the mouse-trap a little, and as each mouse came out she gave it a tap with her wand, whereupon it was transformed into a fine horse. So that here was a fine team of six dappled mouse-gray horses.

But she was puzzled to know how to provide a coachman.

"I will go and see," said Cinderella, "if there is not a rat in the rat-trap. We could make a coachman of him."

"Quite right," said her godmother, "go and see."

Cinderella brought in the rat-trap, which contained three big rats. The fairy chose one specially on account of his elegant whiskers.

As soon as she had touched him he turned into a fat coachman with the finest mustachios that ever were seen.

"Now go into the garden and bring me the six lizards which you will find behind the water-butt."

No sooner had they been brought than the godmother turned them into six lackeys, who at once climbed up behind the coach in their braided liveries, and hung on there as if they had never done anything else all their lives.

Then said the fairy godmother:

"Well, there you have the means of going to the ball. Are you satisfied?"

"Oh, yes, but am I to go like this in my ugly clothes?"

Her godmother merely touched her with her wand, and on the instant her clothes were changed into garments of gold and silver cloth, bedecked with jewels. After that her godmother gave her a pair of glass slippers, the prettiest in the world.

Thus altered, she entered the coach. Her godmother bade her not to stay beyond midnight whatever happened, warning her that if she remained at the ball a moment longer, her coach would again become a pumpkin, her horses mice, and her lackeys lizards, while her old clothes would reappear upon her once more.

She promised her godmother that she would not fail to leave the ball before midnight, and away she went, beside herself with delight.

The king's son, when he was told of the arrival of a great princess whom nobody knew, went forth to receive her. He handed her down from the coach, and led her into the hall where the company was assembled. At once there fell a great silence. The dancers stopped, the violins played no more, so rapt was the attention which everybody bestowed upon the superb beauty of the unknown guest. Everywhere could be heard in confused whispers:

"Oh, how beautiful she is!"

The king, old man as he was, could not take his eyes off her, and whispered to the queen that it was many a long day since he had seen anyone so beautiful and charming.

All the ladies were eager to scrutinize her clothes and the dressing of her hair, being determined to copy them on the morrow, provided they could find materials so fine, and tailors so clever.

The king's son placed her in the seat of honor, and at once begged the privilege of being her partner in a dance. Such was the grace with which she danced that the admiration of all was increased.

A magnificent supper was served, but the young prince could eat nothing, so taken up was he with watching her. She went and sat beside her sisters, and bestowed numberless attentions upon them. She made them share with her the oranges and lemons which the king had given her—greatly to their astonishment, for they did not recognize her.

While they were talking, Cinderella heard the clock strike a quarter to twelve. She at once made a profound curtsy to the company, and departed as quickly as she could.

As soon as she was home again she sought out her godmother, and having thanked her, declared that she wished to go upon the morrow once more to the ball, because the king's son had invited her.

While she was busy telling her godmother all that had happened at the ball, her two sisters knocked at the door. Cinderella let them in.

"What a long time you have been in coming!" she declared, rubbing her eyes and stretching herself as if she had only just awakened. In real truth she had not for a moment wished to sleep since they had left.

"If you had been at the ball," said one of the sisters, "you would not be feeling weary. There came a most beautiful princess, the most beautiful that has ever been seen, and she bestowed numberless attentions upon us, and gave us her oranges and lemons."

Cinderella was overjoyed. She asked them the name of the princess, but they replied that no one knew it, and that the king's son was so distressed that he would give anything in the world to know who she was.

Cinderella smiled, and said she must have been beautiful indeed.

"Oh, how lucky you are. Could I not manage to see her? Oh, please, Javotte, lend me the yellow dress which you wear every day."

"Indeed!" said Javotte, "that is a fine idea. Lend my dress to a grubby cinder-clod like you—you must think me mad!"

Cinderella had expected this refusal. She was in no way upset, for she would have been very greatly embarrassed had her sister been willing to lend the dress.

The next day the two sisters went to the ball, and so did Cinderella, even more splendidly attired than the first time.

The king's son was always at her elbow, and paid her endless compliments.

The young girl enjoyed herself so much that she forgot her godmother's bidding completely, and when the first stroke of midnight fell upon her ears, she thought it was no more than eleven o'clock.

She rose and fled as nimbly as a fawn. The prince followed her, but could not catch her. She let fall one of her glass slippers, however, and this the prince picked up with tender care.

When Cinderella reached home she was out of breath, without coach, without lackeys, and in her shabby clothes. Nothing remained of all her splendid clothes save one of the little slippers, the fellow to the one which she had let fall.

Inquiries were made of the palace doorkeepers as to whether they had seen a princess go out, but they declared they had seen no one leave except a young girl, very ill-clad, who looked more like a peasant than a young lady.

When her two sisters returned from the ball, Cinderella asked them if they had again enjoyed themselves, and if the beautiful lady had been there. They told her that she was present, but had fled away when midnight sounded, and in such haste that she had let fall one of her little glass slippers, the prettiest thing in the world. They added that the king's son, who picked it up, had done nothing but gaze at it for the rest of the ball, from which it was plain that he was deeply in love with its beautiful owner.

They spoke the truth. A few days later, the king's son caused a proclamation to be made by trumpeters, that he would take for wife the owner of the foot which the slipper would fit.

They tried it first on the princesses, then on the duchesses and the whole of the Court, but in vain. Presently they brought it to the home of the two sisters, who did all they could to squeeze a foot into the slipper. This, however, they could not manage.

Cinderella was looking on and recognized her slipper:

"Let me see," she cried, laughingly, "if it will not fit me."

Her sisters burst out laughing, and began to gibe at her, but the equerry who was trying on the slipper looked closely at Cinderella. Observing that she was very beautiful he declared that the claim was quite a fair one, and that his orders were to try the slipper on every maiden. He bade Cinderella sit down, and on putting the slipper to her little foot he perceived that the latter slid in without trouble, and was molded to its shape like wax.

Great was the astonishment of the two sisters at this, and greater still when Cinderella drew from her pocket the other little slipper. This she likewise drew on.

At that very moment her godmother appeared on the scene. She gave a tap with her wand to Cinderella's clothes, and transformed them into a dress even more magnificent than her previous ones.

The two sisters recognized her for the beautiful person whom they had seen at the ball and threw themselves at her feet, begging her pardon for all the ill-treatment she had suffered at their hands.

Cinderella raised them, and declaring as she embraced them that she pardoned them with all her heart, bade them to love her well in future.

She was taken to the palace of the young prince in all her new array. He found her more beautiful than ever, and was married to her a few days afterward.

Cinderella was as good as she was beautiful. She set aside apartments in the palace for her two sisters, and married them the very same day to two gentlemen of high rank about the Court.

The Wonderful Birch

RUSSIA

Once upon a time there were a man and a woman, who had an only daughter. Now it happened that one of their sheep went astray, and they set out to look for it, and searched and searched, each in a different part of the wood. Then the good wife met a witch, who said to her:

"If you spit, you miserable creature, if you spit into the sheath of my knife, or if you run between my legs, I shall change you into a black sheep."

The woman neither spat, nor did she run between her legs, but yet the witch changed her into a sheep. Then she made herself look exactly like the woman, and called out to the good man:

"Ho, old man, halloa! I have found the sheep already!"

The man thought the witch was really his wife, and he did not know that his wife was the sheep; so he went home with her, glad at heart because his sheep was found. When they were safe at home the witch said to the man:

"Look here, old man, we must really kill that sheep lest it run away to the wood again."

The man, who was a peaceable quiet sort of fellow, made no objections but simply said:

"Good, let us do so."

The daughter, however, had overheard their talk, and she ran to the flock and lamented aloud:

"Oh, dear little mother, they are going to slaughter you!"

"Well, then, if they do slaughter me," was the black sheep's answer, "eat you neither the meat nor the broth that is made of me but gather all my bones, and bury them by the edge of the field."

Shortly after this they took the black sheep from the flock and slaughtered it. The witch made pease-soup of it, and set it before the daughter. But the, girl remembered her mother's warning. She did not touch the soup, but she carried the bones to the edge of the field and buried them there; and there sprang up on the spot a birch tree—a very lovely birch tree.

Some time had passed away—who can tell how long they might have been living there?—when the witch, to whom a child had been born in the meantime, began to take an ill-will to the man's daughter, and to torment her in all sorts of ways.

Now it happened that a great festival was to be held at the palace, and the King had commanded that all the people should be invited, and that this proclamation should be made:

> "Come, people all!
> Poor and wretched, one and all!
> Blind and crippled though ye be,
> Mount your steeds or come by sea."

And so they drove into the King's feast all the outcasts, and the maimed, and the halt, and the blind. In the good man's house, too, preparations were made to go to the palace. The witch said to the man:

"Go you on in front, old man, with our youngest; I will give the elder girl work to keep her from being dull in our absence."

So the man took the child and set out. But the witch kindled a fire on the hearth, threw a potful of barleycorns among the cinders, and said to the girl:

"If you have not picked the barley out of the ashes, and put it all back in the pot before nightfall, I shall eat you up!"

Then she hastened after the others, and the poor girl stayed at home and wept. She tried to be sure to pick up the grains of barley, but she soon saw how useless her labour was; and so she went in her sore trouble to the birch tree on her mother's grave, and cried and cried, because her mother lay dead beneath the sod and could help her no longer. In the midst of her grief she suddenly heard her mother's voice speak from the grave, and say to her:

"Why do you weep, little daughter?"

"The witch has scattered barleycorns on the hearth, and bid me pick them out of the ashes," said the girl; "that is why I weep, dear little mother."

"Do not weep," said her mother consolingly. "Break off one of my branches, and strike the hearth with it crosswise, and all will be put right."

The girl did so. She struck the hearth with the birchen branch, and lo! the barleycorns flew into the pot, and the hearth was clean. Then she went back to the birch tree and laid the branch upon the grave. Then her mother bade her bathe on one side of the stem, dry herself on another, and dress on the third. When the girl had done all that, she had grown so lovely that no one on earth could rival her. Splendid clothing was given to her, and a horse, with hair partly of gold, partly of silver, and partly of something more precious still. The girl sprang into the saddle, and rode as swift as an arrow to the palace. As she turned into the courtyard of the castle the King's son came out to meet her, tied her steed to a pillar, and led her in. He never left her side as they passed through the castle rooms; and all the people gazed at her, and wondered who the lovely maiden was, and from what castle she came; but no one knew her—no one knew anything about her. At the banquet the Prince invited her to sit next him in the place of honour; but the witch's daughter gnawed the bones under the table. The Prince did not see her, and thinking it was a dog, he gave her such a push with his foot that her arm was broken. Are you not sorry for the witch's daughter? It was not her fault that her mother was a witch.

Towards evening the good man's daughter thought it was time to go home; but as she went, her ring caught on the latch of the door, for the King's son had had it smeared with tar. She did not take time to pull it off, but, hastily unfastening her horse from the pillar, she rode away beyond the castle walls as swift as an arrow. Arrived at home, she took off her clothes by the birch tree, left her horse standing there, and hastened to her place behind the stove. In a short time the man and the woman came home again too, and the witch said to the girl:

"Ah! you poor thing, there you are to be sure! You don't know what fine times we have had at the palace! The King's son carried my daughter about, but the poor thing fell and broke her arm."

The girl knew well how matters really stood, but she pretended to know nothing about it, and sat dumb behind the stove.

The next day they were invited again to the King's banquet.

"Hey! old man," said the witch, "get on your clothes as quick as you can; we are bidden to the feast. Take you the child; I will give the other one work, lest she weary."

She kindled the fire, threw a potful of hemp seed among the ashes, and said to the girl:

"If you do not get this sorted, and all the seed back into the pot, I shall kill you!"

The girl wept bitterly; then she went to the birch tree, washed herself on one side of it and dried herself on the other; and this time still finer clothes were given to her, and a very beautiful steed. She broke off a branch of the birch tree, struck the hearth with it, so that the seeds flow into the pot, and then hastened to the castle.

Again the King's son came out to meet her, tied her horse to a pillar, and led her into the banqueting hall. At the feast the girl sat next him in the place of honour, as she had done the day before. But the witch's daughter gnawed bones under the table, and the Prince gave her a push by mistake, which broke her leg—he had never noticed her crawling about among the people's feet. She was *very* unlucky!

The good man's daughter hastened home again betimes, but the King's son had smeared the door-posts with tar, and the girl's golden circlet stuck to it. She had not time to look for it, but sprang to the saddle and rode like an arrow to the birch tree. There she left her horse and her fine clothes, and said to her mother:

"I have lost my circlet at the castle; the door-post was tarred, and it stuck fast."

"And even had you lost two of them," answered her mother, "I would give you finer ones."

Then the girl hastened home, and when her father came home from the feast with the witch, she was in her usual place behind the stove. Then the witch said to her:

"You poor thing! what is there to see here compared with what *we* have seen at the palace? The King's son carried my daughter from one room to another; he let her fall, 'tis true, and my child's foot was broken."

The man's daughter held her peace all the time, and busied herself about the hearth.

The night passed, and when the day began to dawn, the witch awakened her husband, crying:

"Hi! get up, old man! We are bidden to the royal banquet."

So the old man got up. Then the witch gave him the child, saying:

"Take you the little one; I will give the other girl work to do, else she will weary at home alone."

She did as usual. This time it was a dish of milk she poured upon the ashes, saying:

"If you do not get all the milk into the dish again before I come home, you will suffer for it."

How frightened the girl was this time! She ran to the birch tree, and by its magic power her task was accomplished; and then she rode away to the palace as before. When she got to the courtyard she found the Prince waiting for her. He led her into the hall, where she was highly honoured; but the witch's daughter sucked the bones under the table, and crouching at the people's feet she got an eye knocked out, poor thing! Now no one knew any more than before about the good man's daughter, no one knew whence she came; but the Prince had had the threshold smeared with tar, and as she fled her gold slippers stuck to it. She reached the birch tree, and laying aside her finery, she said:

"Alas! dear little mother, I have lost my gold slippers!"

"Let them be," was her mother's reply; "if you need them I shall give you finer ones."

Scarcely was she in her usual place behind the stove when her father came home with the witch. Immediately the witch began to mock her, saying:

"Ah! you poor thing, there is nothing for you to see here, and we—ah: what great things we have seen at the palace! My little girl was carried about again, but had the ill-luck to fall and get her eye knocked out. You stupid thing, you, what do you know about anything?"

"Yes, indeed, what can I know?" replied the girl; "I had enough to do to get the hearth clean."

Now the Prince had kept all the things the girl had lost, and he soon set about finding the owner of them. For this purpose a great banquet was given on the fourth day, and all the people were invited to the palace. The witch got ready to go too. She tied a wooden beetle on where her child's foot should have been, a log of wood instead of an arm, and stuck a bit of dirt in the empty socket for an eye, and took the child with her to the castle. When all the people were gathered together, the King's son stepped in among the crowd and cried:

"The maiden whose finger this ring slips over, whose head this golden hoop encircles, and whose foot this shoe fits, shall be my bride."

What a great trying on there was now among them all! The things would fit no one, however.

"The cinder wench is not here," said the Prince at last; "go and fetch her, and let her try on the things."

So the girl was fetched, and the Prince was just going to hand the ornaments to her, when the witch held him back, saying:

"Don't give them to her; she soils everything with cinders; give them to my daughter rather."

Well, then the Prince gave the witch's daughter the ring, and the woman filed and pared away at her daughter's finger till the ring fitted. It was the same with the circlet and the shoes of gold. The witch would not allow them to be handed to the cinder wench; she worked at her own daughter's head and feet till she got the things forced on. What was to be done now? The Prince had to take the witch's daughter for his bride whether he would or no; he sneaked away to her father's house with her, however, for he was ashamed to hold the wedding festivities at the palace with so strange a bride. Some days passed, and at last he had to take his bride home to the palace, and he got ready to do so. Just as they were taking leave, the kitchen wench sprang down from her place by the stove, on the pretext of fetching something from the cowhouse, and in going by she whispered in the Prince's ear as he stood in the yard:

"Alas! dear Prince, do not rob me of my silver and my gold."

Thereupon the King's son recognised the cinder wench; so he took both the girls with him, and set out. After they had gone some little way they came to the bank of a river, and the Prince threw the witch's daughter across to serve as a bridge, and so got over with the cinder wench. There lay the witch's daughter then, like a bridge over the river, and could not stir, though her heart was consumed with grief. No help was near, so she cried at last in her anguish:

"May there grow a golden hemlock out of my body! perhaps my mother will know me by that token."

Scarcely had she spoken when a golden hemlock sprang up from her, and stood upon the bridge.

Now, as soon as the Prince had got rid of the witch's daughter he greeted the cinder wench as his bride, and they wandered together to the birch tree which grew upon the mother's grave. There they received all sorts of treasures and riches, three sacks full of gold, and as much silver, and a splendid steed, which bore them home to the palace. There they lived a long time together, and the young wife bore a son to the Prince. Immediately word was brought to the witch that her daughter had borne a son— for they all believed the young King's wife to be the witch's daughter.

"So, so," said the witch to herself; "I had better away with my gift for the infant, then."

And so saying she set out. Thus it happened that she came to the bank of the river, and there she saw the beautiful golden hemlock growing in the middle of the bridge, and when she began to cut it down to take to her grandchild, she heard a voice moaning:

"Alas! dear mother, do not cut me so!"

"Are you here?" demanded the witch.

"Indeed I am, dear little mother," answered the daughter. "They threw me across the river to make a bridge of me."

In a moment the witch had the bridge shivered to atoms, and then she hastened away to the palace. Stepping up to the young Queen's bed, she began to try her magic arts upon her, saying:

"Spit, you wretch, on the blade of my knife; bewitch my knife's blade for me, and I shall change you into a reindeer of the forest."

"Are you there again to bring trouble upon me?" said the young woman.

She neither spat nor did anything else, but still the witch changed her into a reindeer, and smuggled her own daughter into her place as the Prince's wife. But now the child grew restless and cried, because it missed its mother's care. They took it to the court, and tried to pacify it in every conceivable way, but its crying never ceased.

"What makes the child so restless?" asked the Prince, and he went to a wise widow woman to ask her advice.

"Ay, my, your own wife is not at home," said the widow woman; "she is living like a reindeer in the wood; you have the witch's daughter for a wife now, and the witch herself for a mother-in-law."

"Is there any way of getting my own wife back from the wood again?" asked the Prince.

"Give me the child," answered the widow woman. "I'll take it with me to-morrow when I go to drive the cows to the wood. I'll make a rustling among the birch leaves and a trembling among the aspens—perhaps the boy will grow quiet when he hears it."

"Yes, take the child away, take it to the wood with you to quiet it," said the Prince, and led the widow woman into the castle.

"How now? you are going to send the child away to the wood?" said the witch in a suspicious tone, and tried to interfere.

But the King's son stood firm by what he had commanded, and said: "Carry the child about the wood; perhaps that will pacify it."

So the widow woman took the child to the wood. She came to the edge of a marsh, and seeing a herd of reindeer there, she began all at once to sing—

> "Little Bright-eyes, little Redskin,
> Come nurse the child you bore!
>   That bloodthirsty monster,
>   That man-eater grim,
> Shall nurse him, shall tend him no more.
>   They may threaten and force as they will,
>   He turns from her, shrinks from her still,"

and immediately the reindeer drew near, and nursed and tended the child the whole day long; but at nightfall it had to follow the herd, and said to the widow woman:

"Bring me the child to-morrow, and again the following day; after that I must wander with the herd far away to other lands."

The following morning the widow woman went back to the castle to fetch the child. The witch interfered, of course, but the Prince said:

"Take it, and carry it about in the open air; the boy is quieter at night, to be sure, when he has been in the wood all day."

So the widow took the child in her arms, and carried it to the marsh in the forest. There she sang as on the preceding day—

> "Little Bright-eyes, little Redskin,
> Come nurse the child you bore!
>   That bloodthirsty monster,
>   That man-eater grim,
> Shall nurse him, shall tend him no more.
>   They may threaten and force as they will,
>   He turns from her, shrinks from her still,"

and immediately the reindeer left the herd and came to the child, and tended it as on the day before. And so it was that the child throve, till not a finer boy was to be seen anywhere. But the King's son had been pondering over all these things, and he said to the widow woman:

"Is there no way of changing the reindeer into a human being again?"

"I don't rightly know," was her answer. "Come to the wood with me, however; when the woman puts off her reindeer skin I shall comb her head for her; whilst I am doing so you must burn the skin."

Thereupon they both went to the wood with the child; scarcely were they there when the reindeer appeared and nursed the child as before. Then the widow woman said to the reindeer:

"Since you are going far away to-morrow, and I shall not see you again, let me comb your head for the last time, as a remembrance of you."

Good; the young woman stript off the reindeer skin, and let the widow woman do as she wished. In the meantime the King's son threw the reindeer skin into the fire unobserved.

"What smells of singeing here?" asked the young woman, and looking round she saw her own husband. "Woe is me! you have burnt my skin. Why did you do that?"

"To give you back your human form again."

"Alack-a-day! I have nothing to cover me now, poor creature that I am!" cried the young woman, and transformed herself first into a distaff, then into a wooden beetle, then into a spindle, and into all imaginable shapes. But all these shapes the King's son went on destroying till she stood before him in human form again.

"Alas! wherefore take me home with you again," cried the young woman, "since the witch is sure to eat me up?"

"She will not eat you up," answered her husband; and they started for home with the child.

But when the witch wife saw them she ran away with her daughter, and if she has not stopped she is running still, though at a great age. And the Prince, and his wife, and the baby lived happy ever afterwards.

· *Conversation* ·

JANE: Poor Cinderella. Reading these three stories over, I realized anew what a bum rap she has gotten over the years, specifically since the 1950s, when Walt Disney got hold of her.

She is a much more able young woman than Disney would have us believe. She dissembles, works magic, tends her mother's grave, offers assistance to her godmother, is a capable seamstress, hairdresser, and cook. And in the Grimm's version, she even directs the birds to help her.

In two of the stories we have printed here, Cinderella is quite bloody-minded as well. You don't see her bending down to help that poor distressed Russian stepsister under the table, with the broken arm, broken leg, and poked-out eye. Nor in the Grimm's version does she stop her wedding march to call an ambulance for her stepsisters when her pet doves peck out their eyes. Only in the French version, written for the aristocrats of the French court by Charles Perrault, does she forgive her sisters and make them good marriages.

The ancient storytellers realized for themselves what G. K. Chesterton would remark centuries later—that children know themselves innocent and demand justice, while we fear ourselves guilty and prefer mercy.

And in at least two of the stories—the Grimm's and the Russian—Cinderella's mother helps her from beyond the grave.

Now I don't expect to shower gold dresses and glass slippers on you after I am dead. But you know there will be a little something in the will . . .

HEIDI: There you go. Trying to sneak death into the conversation at the very start!

And you took the wind out of my Disney argument. I have always felt that Disney's *Cinderella* was the worst teaching tool for children, especially girls. I watched it with my jaw dropped open while this strong-willed girl of the Grimm's tale melts into a simpering wimp (or is that a whimpering simp?) who watches teary-eyed while cute singing bunnies and birdies make her dress and clean up after her.

JANE: Actually I believe they are mice, not bunnies. But your point is well taken. In fact, the majority of the Cinderella figures are strong-willed young women. And a couple of Cinderlads, too.

Would you believe I wrote an article about this, first published in 1977—when you were eleven—called "America's Cinderella." I had been equally jaw-dropped by Disney's portrayal of Cinderella, which has for all practical purposes eclipsed the others. His Cinderella is a spun-sugar caricature of her hardier European and Oriental forebears. (As a side note, there are some five hundred variants of the Cinderella story in Europe alone.)

I still stand by what I wrote then: "Since [Disney], America's Cinderella has been a coy, helpless dreamer, a 'nice' girl who awaits her rescue with patience and a song . . . The wrong Cinderella has gone to the American ball." Or as editor Terri Windling describes her in an article in the magazine *Realms of Fantasy,* Cinderella is "a timid, passive girl whose lovely face wins her the 'happy ending' of a wealthy marriage." It's that Disney dreaming patience, that semi-comatose, feckless state, that has set feminist teeth on edge.

Still there is a mythical take on the story that should be mentioned. Irish philosopher Aarland Ussher, writing in *World Review* in 1951 (and reprinted in *The Cinderella Casebook*), said of the English version of the tale that it is about "the Soul's discovery of its Image—that Image which lives hidden, like an invisible spark among ashes, in the humdrum hours and tasks." Ussher sees those hours in the chimney corner as Cinderella's learning time, where she has a chance to grow into her future. And he feels that it is the prince's story most of all, for Cinderella is the prince's "sought-after image" and because in the end the prince "will find, in dreams, *one* slipper on the stair." Of course I utterly reject the idea that the story is the prince's. I mean, that prince is no more than a shoe salesman. Or perhaps a shoe fetishist. Where was he when our girl was toiling away in the chimney corner? It feels as if men are once again trying to co-opt a quintessential woman's story.

But it's the Marxists who should have a shot at the generic Cinderella, not the feminists. After all, the story in all its earlier incarnations is not about a poor girl making good through marriage, but a rich girl who fights to win back her rather impressive patrimony. A debutante scrapping to go to the coming-out ball.

Her stepmother and stepsisters have literally stolen what should have been hers. No wonder she goes after them with a vengeance. Not only is she not sweetly forgiving to them at the end of most of the tellings, but she also does not share.

Is this a good story to tell our girls? *Do not share. Do not be fair. Fight for what is yours.* I don't know. A lot of mixed messages.

HEIDI: I *do* know. What I tell my girls is that as they grow to be women, they need to develop their own list of things that they refuse to compromise on. Usually I have this conversation with my older daughter and generally it refers to boys. But I believe the lesson is valid for all ages.

Any relationship—friend, family, spouse—is going to be full of compromises. For example, I do not lose part of myself by compromising with my husband on the dropping-clothes-on-the-floor rule, but I refuse to give up other things, such as friendships with people my loved ones do not especially like.

JANE: The friendship thing is a tough one all right. I have a couple of long-term friends your father cannot abide. And he has several I don't like much. We have done major compromises on all of them over the years.

HEIDI: I think it's fair for every girl to choose those things that are fight-to-the-death issues and refuse to compromise on them. Compromise on the rest. Why shouldn't birthright be on Cinderella's list of fighting principles?

JANE: How did you get to be so smart? As I recall, I regularly lost that don't-leave-your-clothes-on-the-floor fight with you. Now you are neater than I am, regularly doing a drawer-cleanup for me each winter holiday visit.

And what about the famous "It's-not-fair" fight?

HEIDI: You mean "Who ever told you life was fair?" How many times did I hear that as a daughter? And how many times have I said it as a mother? A ubiquitous mother line.

We all try to make sure that everything is fair and equal for our children, but life is not that easily quantified, as Cinderella knows.

It used to seem strange to me that you always justified your gift-giving by saying, "Now I gave your brother a new thingamajig, but don't forget, I gave you that expensive whatzit last year." In fact, I thought this was ridiculous until my second daughter arrived. Now I count Christmas and birthday presents, total the receipts, and pray that no one feels slighted.

Perhaps it's no surprise that I found the fairness issue as one central to the Cinderella stories, because—like Cinderella and her sisters—my two girls don't share a biology. By that I mean that one was born to me, and one was not. In a way, I am a stepmother. The favoritism issue is a heavy weight on my shoulders, especially when—on occasion, in Lexi's eyes—I fit right into the "evil-stepmother" role.

JANE: Well, we *all* slip into the evil-stepmother role on occasion, whether the child is a birth child or other. Just deny your daughter something she wants—or thinks she is due—and there you are! Evil incarnate. In fact, one psychological theory about folktales is that the stepmother is merely a displacement in the story for the actual mother. And in some stories—like a number of "Snow White" variants—stepmother and mother really are interchangeable. (Though the really evil stepmother in the Cinderella canon is one from a Persian story in which the stepmother is first a female friend who helps convince the child to drown her mother in a vat of vinegar, even providing instructions. After that the woman marries the child's father and treats the child badly.)

Psychologist Maria Van Franz, a Jungian who has done a lot of work with fairy tales, points out that the mother's death in "Cinderella" is the "beginning of the process of individuation." In other words, Cinderella cannot become the woman she is to be, cannot be separate from her beloved mother, without that death. Still, we do get rid of the mother awfully quickly and efficiently in the first paragraph of the German story. She gets one sentence of dialogue and then departs, to be set down in the garden for later use in the story.

However, I hate to think that girls need their mothers to die before they can grow up. A good, hardy conversation might suffice.

My mother used to tell me that at age seven I was furious with her for something I felt I had been denied, and I wrote her the following letter:

> Dear Mommy—
> I hate you, I hate you, I hate you.
>
> Love, Janie

How she used to laugh at that. It took me a long while to find the humor in that letter, but now I understand its double-weightedness, the ironic duality. The moment I wrote the letter, my mother was the wicked stepmother. At the same time I knew that at the deepest level she was still the mother I adored.

But at least I knew I adored her.

Recently I was reading Adrienne Rich's *Of Woman Born,* and came upon the term "matrophobia," which is the fear of becoming one's mother. Rich comments on it this way: "Thousands of daughters see their mothers as having taught a compromise and self-hatred they are struggling to win free of, the one through whom the restrictions and degradations of a female existence were perforce transmitted."

I see that kind of hatred and self-loathing manifested in many of my friends, but I never felt it myself, and have to thank my mother for that. She never set her life of volunteerism as the pattern for mine. It was *her* encouragement, rather than my father's (who never actually read any of my books), that kept me happily productive.

HEIDI: Another issue that re-reading these Cinderella stories brought up for me was the whole dress thing.

JANE: You mean Cinderella's gold and silver dresses? The ball gowns? Especially all the details in the French version of the story.

HEIDI: Exactly. Why is it that we women have to dress up in the most beautiful gowns—tiara and all—before we can feel better about ourselves?

JANE: A coinage I particularly dislike but use anyway is "lookism," where one is afraid of not being pretty enough. Where one is willing to hurt oneself (cut off a heel, a toe?) to look beautiful.

HEIDI: Or pluck an eyebrow? Or shave a leg?

JANE: I remember once when I was complaining about the difficulties of dressing up—remember this was the day of incredibly tight girdles, and garter belts that left welts on your thighs—my mother brought out a classic mother line: "You have to suffer for beauty."

What I wanted, of course, was beauty without the suffering. Or I wanted inner beauty. Or I wanted . . . I don't know what I wanted except that I wanted to go to the ball.

I am not sure how different things are today—except for those girdles and garter belts. In Mary Pipher's book *Reviving Ophelia: Saving the Selves of Adolescent Girls,* one girl was described this way: "A part of Rosemary hated the pressure and another part was obsessed with looking right."

Obsessed . . . with . . . looking . . . right. Who makes the rules about what is the right look anyway? And why do we slavishly follow those rules? As a five-foot, three-inch woman of, shall we say, abundant proportions, I find little in the current "right look" categories that I can wear.

HEIDI: I've always found that my body type (athletic, slim, small breasted) goes in and out of fashion. When "voluptuous" women grace the covers of magazines, I have to wait until my size is "in" again.

JANE: I don't remember ever being obsessed with looking right as a teen, except when forced to wear the clothes my mother had sewn. But certainly there were some girls in my high school who could wear a paper bag and look good, and I was aware of them.

Sally Campbell. I remember that she was always perfect. She had those perky cute blonde cheerleader looks that seemed to go with everything in the fifties. I didn't come into my own till the beatniks and hippies made what I was already wearing a kind of uniform.

As I recall, though, clothes and makeup were a big part of *your* adolescent life.

HEIDI: Don't get me started on the makeup thing, because I know that you'll insist on telling the story of my teenage love affair with makeup. Now that I take a minimalist stance on cosmetics and give the same "You look better with less goop on your face" speech to my teenage daughter, it embarrasses me to remember that 1980s eye shadow.

JANE: [Laughing.] You used to look like a teen hooker. Or a wannabe Goth. All that black mascara and blue eye shadow. There is a Moorish proverb that I adore: "Every beetle is a gazelle in the eyes of her mother." You were my little beetle with gazelle legs—and raccoon eyes.

HEIDI: Maddison at age three and a half is now insisting on wearing dresses to nursery school instead of the overalls I prefer. I have tried to make her into a tomboy because I just don't want her trapped in that whole beauty versus brains mentality. But she wore a tiara to our lawyer's office the other day. And just last week she told me she didn't like something because it was a "boy color." Where does she pick that up? Not at home.

And once I let Lexi try on my wedding dress (shoes, veil, push-up bra and all) and she and Maddison sat together on the sofa dressed as princesses, watching Disney's *Cinderella*.

Does every girl want to be a princess?

JANE: Actually I wanted to be King Arthur. Or, failing that, Merlin. Guinevere had such a stupid role in what was my favorite story.

But you also insisted on wearing dresses to school—long dresses, because you were a child during the seventies. Your gym teacher complained to me that you had a lot of trouble running the bases in your outfit. "You tell her," I said. "I've tried and gotten nowhere." He couldn't change your mind either.

But I would say—yes, even today, after years of feminism—most little girls want to dress up as princesses. As long as they also get to carry swords. And they would wear glass slippers, too, if they weren't afraid of cutting their feet.

By the way—that glass slipper is most often credited to Perrault's version of the tale. Actually he wrote about a fur slipper, but a mistranslation into English changed that, since "variegated fur" and "glass" in French are but a single letter apart.

HEIDI: Does the problem with lookism start with the Cinderella story? Is that our first glimpse into the fairy-tale world of "Everything will be better when I am beautiful"? Or does Cinderella remain a popular story because it speaks to the way we were feeling, even before reading or hearing the tale?

JANE: I don't know the answer to that, but it leads into a question of my own: How early does lookism take hold anyway? Do we worry about Maddison dressing as a princess—or is that just little-girl play? Does giving her a dress-up box filled with princess items constitute promoting lookism, or just encouraging imaginative play?

Recently Germaine Greer was photographed biting the head off of a Barbie doll. She was quoted as saying, "Barbie has been instrumental in teaching broad-shouldered women, short-legged women, wide-bodied women, real women the world over to despise their bodies." It may be worse than Greer realizes. There are stores in America that sell only Barbies. You found one in the Mall of America. And in great Britain there is a new chain of stores called Girl Heaven which sells—according to an article in *The Guardian* of June 9, 1999—"virtually every item a mother has ever thought of banning—from Barbies and nail polish to the 'shop till you drop' doll, outdated nurse's outfits, and full bridal regalia."

I shudder at pictures of the JonBenet Ramsey girl/women and the rampant sexualization of the pre-adolescents in movies, on TV, in ads. The girls there are always pretty, pretty, pretty, slathered with inappropriate makeup and as stuffed into unsuitable clothing as those stepsisters into the Grimm's Cinderella shoes.

HEIDI: I worry that we can never get rid of the idea of girls fitting into only one of two categories: the pretty one or the smart one. I always thought I was in a third category: the funny one.

JANE: A size three and she thinks she's the funny one! I went from rompers to size twelves with no intervening steps.

But if you think you are funny, you certainly come by it naturally. Grandmother to mother to daughter. All by way of Dorothy Parker.

HEIDI: Reading our conversation about Cinderella, a reader might think that we have the greatest relationship in the world: no hostility, no animosity, no rivalry. This is, indeed, the case—now.

But there were bumps along the road to this great relationship. Not great mountains, maybe not even foothills. But definitely speed bumps as I went barreling along into my adult life.

However, since we started working together—in co-authorship as well as separately but in the same field—we have been able to connect as peers as well as mother and daughter.

But there is more to our strong relationship than just being fellow authors. The bond began to strengthen with the birth of my first daughter and strengthened again with the addition of Lexi to our family. There is the old cliché that teenagers are the grandparents' revenge. No one adds the corollary that teenagers can also serve to bind the matriarchs together.

I have already—after a single fairy-tale conversation—learned more about you and my grandmother (whom I only remember with a four-year-old's eyes) than I ever knew before. And knowing the two of you, I therefore know more about myself.

This is actually fun. Well, work too, but with some fun rolled up in it. Less like psychoanalysis, more like a late night in a college dorm.

Shall we continue the once-upon-a-right-now?

Good Girls/
Bad Girls

One-eye, Two-eyes, and Three-eyes

GERMANY

There was once a woman who had three daughters, the eldest of whom was called One-eye, because she had only one eye in the middle of her forehead, and the second, Two-eyes, because she had two eyes like other folks, and the youngest, Three-eyes, because she had three eyes; and her third eye was also in the center of her forehead. However, as Two-eyes saw just as other human beings did, her sisters and her mother could not endure her. They said to her, "Thou, with thy two eyes, art no better than the common people; thou dost not belong to us!" They pushed her about, and threw old clothes to her, and gave her nothing to eat but what they left, and did everything that they could to make her unhappy. It came to pass that Two-eyes had to go out into the fields and tend the goat, but she was still quite hungry, because her sisters had given her so little to eat. So she sat down on a ridge and began to weep, and so bitterly that two streams ran down from her eyes. And once when she looked up in her grief, a woman was standing beside her, who said, "Why art thou weeping, little Two-eyes?" Two-eyes answered, "Have I not reason to weep, when I have two eyes like other people, and my sisters and mother hate me for it, and push me from one corner to another, throw old clothes at me, and give me nothing to eat but the scraps they leave? To-day they have given me so little that I am still quite hungry." Then the wise woman said, "Wipe away thy tears, Two-eyes, and I will tell thee something to stop thee ever suffering from hunger again; just say to thy goat,

> 'Bleat, my little goat, bleat,
> Cover the table with something to eat,'

and then a clean well-spread little table will stand before thee, with the most delicious food upon it of which thou mayst eat as much as thou art inclined for, and when thou hast had enough, and hast no more need of the little table, just say,

> 'Bleat, bleat, my little goat, I pray,
> And take the table quite away,'

and then it will vanish again from thy sight." Hereupon the wise woman departed. But Two-eyes thought, "I must instantly make a trial, and see if what she said was true, for I am far too hungry," and she said,

> "Bleat, my little goat, bleat,
> Cover the table with something to eat."

And scarcely had she spoken the words than a little table, covered with a white cloth, was standing there, and on it was a plate with a knife and fork, and a silver spoon; and the most delicious food was there also, warm and smoking as if it had just come out of the kitchen. Then Two-eyes said the shortest prayer she knew, "Lord God, be with us always, Amen," and helped herself to some food, and enjoyed it. And when she was satisfied, she said, as the wise woman had taught her,

> "Bleat, bleat, my little goat, I pray,
> And take the table quite away."

Immediately the little table and everything on it was gone again. "That is a delightful way of keeping house!" thought Two-eyes, and was quite glad and happy.

In the evening, when she went home with her goat, she found a small earthenware dish with some food, which her sisters had set ready for her, but she did not touch it. Next day she again went out with her goat, and left the few bits of broken bread which had been handed to her lying untouched. The first and second time that she did this, her sisters did not remark it at all, but as it happened every time, they did observe it, and said, "There is something wrong about Two-eyes, she always leaves her food untasted, and she used to eat up everything that was given her; she must have discovered other ways of getting food." In order that they might learn the truth, they resolved to send One-eye with Two-eyes when she went to drive her goat to the pasture, to observe what Two-eyes did when she was there, and whether any one brought her anything to eat and drink. So when Two-eyes set out the next time, One-eye went to her and said, "I will go with you to the pasture, and see that the goat is well taken care of, and driven where there is food." But Two-eyes knew what was in One-eye's mind, and drove the goat into high grass, and said, "Come, One-eye, we will sit down, and I will sing something to you." One-eye sat down and was tired with the unaccustomed walk and the heat of the sun, and Two-eyes sang constantly,

"One-eye, wakest thou?
One-eye, sleepest thou?"

until One-eye shut her one eye, and fell asleep. And as soon as Two-eyes saw that One-eye was fast asleep, and could discover nothing, she said,

"Bleat, my little goat, bleat,
Cover the table with something to eat,"

and seated herself at her table, and ate and drank until she was satisfied. And then she again cried,

"Bleat, bleat, my little goat, I pray,
And take the table quite away,"

and in an instant all was gone. Two-eyes now awakened One-eye, and said, "One-eye, you want to take care of the goat, and go to sleep while you are doing it, and in the meantime the goat might run all over the world. Come, let us go home again." So they went home, and again Two-eyes let her little dish stand untouched, and One-eye could not tell her mother why she would not eat it, and to excuse herself said, "I fell asleep when I was out."

Next day the mother said to Three-eyes, "This time thou shalt go and observe if Two-eyes eats anything when she is out, and if any one fetches her food and drink, for she must eat and drink in secret." So Three-eyes went to Two-eyes, and said, "I will go with you and see if the goat is taken proper care of, and driven where there is food." But Two-eyes knew what was in Three-eyes' mind, and drove the goat into high grass and said, "We will sit down, and I will sing something to you, Three-eyes." Three-eyes sat down and was tired with the walk and with the heat of the sun, and Two-eyes began the same song as before, and sang,

"Three-eyes, are you waking?"

but then, instead of singing,

> *"Three-eyes, are you sleeping?"*

as she ought to have done, she thoughtlessly sang,

> *"Two-eyes, are you sleeping?"*

and sang all the time,

> *"Three-eyes, are you waking?*
> *Two-eyes, are you sleeping?"*

Then two of the eyes which Three-eyes had, shut and fell asleep, but the third, as it had not been named in the song, did not sleep. It is true that Three-eyes shut it, but only in her cunning, to pretend it was asleep, too, but it blinked, and could see everything very well. And when Two-eyes thought that Three-eyes was fast asleep, she used her little charm,

> *"Bleat, my little goat, bleat,*
> *Cover the table with something to eat,"*

and ate and drank as much as her heart desired, and then ordered the table to go away again,

> *"Bleat, bleat, my little goat, I pray,*
> *And take the table quite away,"*

and Three-eyes had seen everything. Then Two-eyes came to her, waked her and said, "Have you been asleep, Three-eyes? You are a good care-taker. Come, we will go home." And when they got home, Two-eyes again did not eat, and Three-eyes said to the mother "Now I know why that high-minded thing there does not eat. When she is out, she says to the goat,

> *'Bleat, my little goat, bleat,*
> *Cover the table with something to eat,'*

and then a little table appears before her covered with the best of food, much better than any we have here, and when she has eaten all she wants, she says,

'Bleat, bleat, my little goat, I pray,
And take the table quite away,'

and all disappears. I watched everything closely. She put two of my eyes to sleep by using a certain form of words, but luckily the one in my forehead kept awake." Then the envious mother cried, "Dost thou want to fare better than we do? The desire shall pass away," and she fetched a butcher's knife, and thrust it into the heart of the goat, which fell down dead.

When Two-eyes saw that, she went out full of trouble, seated herself on the ridge of grass at the edge of the field, and wept bitter tears. Suddenly the wise woman once more stood by her side, and said, "Two-eyes, why art thou weeping?" "Have I not reason to weep?" she answered. "The goat which covered the table for me every day when I spoke your charm, has been killed by my mother, and now I shall again have to bear hunger and want." The wise woman said, "Two-eyes, I will give thee a piece of good advice; ask thy sisters to give thee the entrails of the slaughtered goat, and bury them in the ground in front of the house, and thy fortune will be made." Then she vanished, and Two-eyes went home and said to her sisters, "Dear sisters, do give me some part of my goat; I don't wish for what is good, but give me the entrails." Then they laughed and said, "If that's all you want, you can have it." So Two-eyes took the entrails and buried them quietly in the evening, in front of the house-door, as the wise woman had counseled her to do.

Next morning, when they all awoke, and went to the house-door, there stood a strangely magnificent tree with leaves of silver and fruit of gold hanging among them, so that in all the wide world there was nothing more beautiful or precious. They did not know how the tree could have come there during the night, but Two-eyes saw that it had grown up out of the entrails of the goat, for it was standing on the exact spot where she had buried them. Then the mother said to One-eye, "Climb up, my child, and gather some of the fruit of the tree for us." One-eye climbed up, but when she was about to get hold of one of the golden apples, the branch escaped from her hands, and that happened each time, so that she could not pluck a single apple, let her do what she might. Then said the mother, "Three-eyes, do you climb up; you with your three eyes can look about you better than One-eye." One-eye slipped down, and Three-eyes climbed up. Three-eyes was not more skilful, and might search as she liked, but the golden apples always escaped her. At length the mother grew impatient, and climbed up herself, but could get hold of the fruit no better than One-eye and Three-eyes, for she always clutched empty air. Then said Two-eyes, "I will just go up, perhaps I may succeed better." The sisters cried, "You indeed, with your two eyes, what can you do?" But Two-eyes climbed up, and the golden apples did not get out of her way, but came into her hand of their own accord, so that she could pluck them one after the other, and brought a whole apronful down with her. The mother took them away from her, and instead of treating poor Two-eyes any better for this, she and One-eye and Three-eyes were only envious, because Two-eyes alone had been able to get the fruit, and they treated her still more cruelly.

It so befell that once when they were all standing together by the tree, a young knight came up. "Quick, Two-eyes," cried the two sisters, "creep under this, and don't disgrace us!" and with all speed they turned an empty barrel which was standing close by the tree over poor Two-eyes, and they pushed the golden apples which she had been gathering, under it, too. When the knight came nearer he was a handsome lord, who stopped and admired the magnificent gold and silver tree, and said to the two sisters, "To whom does this fine tree belong? Any one who would bestow one branch of it on me might in return for it ask whatsoever be desired." Then One-eye and Three-eyes replied that the tree belonged to them, and that they would give him a branch. They both took great trouble, but they were not able to do it, for the branches and fruit both moved away from them every time. Then said the knight, "It is very strange that the tree should belong to you, and that you should still not be able to break a piece off." They again asserted that the tree was their property. Whilst they were saying so, Two-eyes rolled out a couple of golden apples from under the barrel to the feet of the knight, for she was vexed with One-eye and Three-Eyes, for not speaking the truth.

When the knight saw the apples he was astonished, and asked where they came from. One-eye and Three-eyes answered that they had another sister, who was not allowed to show herself, for she had only two eyes like any common person. The knight, however, desired to see her, and cried, "Two-eyes, come forth."

Then Two-eyes, quite comforted, came from beneath the barrel, and the knight was surprised at her great beauty, and said, "Thou, Two-eyes, canst certainly break off a branch from the tree for me." "Yes," replied Two-eyes, "that I certainly shall be able to do, for the tree belongs to me." And she climbed up, and with the greatest ease broke off a branch with beautiful silver leaves and golden fruit, and gave it to the knight. Then said the knight, "Two-eyes, what shall I give thee for it?" "Alas!" answered Two-eyes, "I suffer from hunger and thirst, grief and want, from early morning till late night; if you would take me with you, and deliver me from these things, I should be happy."

So the knight lifted Two-eyes on to his horse, and took her home with him to his father's castle, and there he gave her beautiful clothes, and meat and drink to her heart's content, and as he loved her so much he married her, and the wedding was solemnized with great rejoicing.

When Two-eyes was thus carried away by the handsome knight, her two sisters grudged her good fortune in downright earnest. "The wonderful tree, however, still remains with us," thought they, "and even if we can gather no fruit from it, still every one will stand still and look at it, and come to us and admire it. Who knows what good things may be in store for us?" But next morning, the tree had vanished, and all their hopes were at an end. And when Two-eyes looked out of the window of her own little room, to her great delight it was standing in front of it, and so it had followed her.

Two-eyes lived a long time in happiness. Once two poor women came to her in her castle, and begged for alms. She looked in their faces, and recognized her sisters, One-eye and Three-eyes, who had fallen into such poverty that they had to wander about and beg their bread from door to door. Two-eyes, however, made them welcome, and was kind to them, and took care of them, so that they both with all their hearts repented the evil that they had done their sister in their youth.

The Good Girl and the Ornery Girl

NORTH AMERICA, OZARKS

One time there was an old woman lived away out in the timber, and she had two daughters. One of them was a good girl and the other one was ornery, but the old woman liked the ornery one best. So they made the good girl do all the work, and she had to split wood with a dull axe. The ornery girl just laid a-flat of her back all day and never done nothing.

The good girl went out to pick up sticks, and pretty soon she seen a cow. The cow says, "For God's sake milk me, my bag's about to bust!" So the good girl milked the cow, but she didn't drink none of the milk. Pretty soon she seen a apple tree and the tree says, "For God's sake pick these apples, or I'll break plumb down!" So the good girl picked the apples, but she didn't eat none. Pretty soon she seen some cornbread a-baking, and the bread says, "For God's sake take me out, I'm a-burning up!" So the good girl pulled the bread out, but she didn't taste a crumb. A little old man come along just then, and he throwed a sack of gold money so it stuck all over her. When the good girl got home she shed gold pieces like feathers off a goose.

Next day the ornery girl went out to get her some gold too. Pretty soon she seen a cow, and the cow says, "For God's sake milk me, my bag's about to bust!" But the ornery girl just kicked the old cow in the belly, and went right on. Pretty soon she seen a apple tree, and the tree says, "For God's sake pick these apples, or I'll break plumb down!" But the ornery girl just laughed, and went right on. Pretty soon she seen some cornbread a-baking, and the bread says, "For God's sake take me out, I'm a-burning up!" But the ornery girl didn't pay no mind, and went right on. A little old man come along just then, and he throwed a kettle of tar so it stuck all over her. When the ornery girl got home she was so black the old woman didn't know who it was.

The folks tried everything they could, and finally they got most of the tar off. But the ornery girl always looked kind of ugly after that, and she never done any good. It served the little bitch right, too.

Sukhu and Dukhu

BENGAL

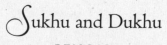

A man had two wives and had a daughter by each of them. Dukhu was the daughter of the elder wife and Sukhu was the daughter of the younger. The man loved his younger wife and her daughter Sukhu more than the older wife and her daughter Dukhu.

The daughters' natures were just like their mothers'. Sukhu was as lazy and ill-tempered as Dukhu was active and lovable. Furthermore, Sukhu and her mother hated the other two and treated them badly anytime they had the chance.

The man took ill, and died in spite of every kind of treatment. The younger wife inherited all his property, and she drove Dukhu and her mother out of the house.

Dukhu and her mother found an empty hut outside of town and occupied it. They made a living by spinning thread.

One day when Dukhu was spinning outside her hut, the wind blew hard and carried away her wad of cotton. She ran after it but couldn't catch up with it. When she began to cry in desperation, she heard a voice in the wind. "Don't cry, Dukhu, come with me. I'll give you all the cotton you want."

So she followed the wind.

On the way, she met a cow, which spoke to her: "Not so fast, Dukhu. My shed is covered with dung. Wash it clean for me, and I'll help you later." Dukhu drew water from the well and got herself a broom and washed the cowshed clean as clean could be.

The wind was waiting for her to finish. As soon as she finished, she went with the wind again. They came to a plantain tree, which stopped her and said, "Where are you going, Dukhu? Can't you stop a minute and pull down all these creepers from my body so that I can stand up straight? It's hard to stand bent down like this all day and all night. Please."

"I'll be glad to do that," said Dukhu, and she tore down all the creepers that were smothering the tree.

The tree said, "You're a good girl. I'll help you some other time."

"I didn't do anything special, really," said Dukhu and hurried on, for the wind was waiting for her.

Next she met a horse and it said, "Where are you going, Dukhu? This saddle and bridle cut into me. I can't bend down to eat the grass. Will you please take them off for me?"

Dukhu took off the saddle and bridle. The horse was grateful and promised her a gift.

The wind said, as they moved on, "Do you see that palace there? That's where the Mother of the Moon lives. She can give you as much cotton as you want."

With that, he left her there.

Dukhu walked towards the palace. It seemed deserted. She felt afraid and lonely. She stood there in front of it for a while and then decided to go in. Timidly, step by step, she walked through the rooms. Not a mouse stirring, not a living soul anywhere. Suddenly she heard a noise behind a closed door. She went up to it and knocked softly. A voice said, "Come in."

Dukhu pushed the door open and saw an old lady working at a wheel. She was luminous as if the moon was specially shining on her.

Dukhu bowed to her, touched her feet and said, "Granny, the wind blew away all my cotton. If I don't spin, my mother and I will starve. Will you give me some cotton?"

"I'll give you something better than cotton," said the old Mother of the Moon, "if you are deserving. Do you see that pond out there? Go to that pond and dip in it twice. Only twice, not three times, remember."

So Dukhu walked out of the palace and went to the pond and took a dip. When she rose out of the water, she had been changed into someone very beautiful. When she took a second dip, she was covered with silks, pearls, and gems. Her sari was muslin, and she had gold necklaces so heavy that they weighed her down. She couldn't believe what was happening to her.

When she ran back to the palace, the old woman said, "Child, I know you are hungry. Go to the next room. I've food there for you."

The next room had food of every kind, the best rice, the finest curries, sweets beyond her dreams. After eating her fill, she went back to the old woman, who said, "I want to give you something more," and showed her three caskets, each bigger than the next. "Choose one," she said. Dukhu chose the smallest one and said good-bye to the old woman and left the palace.

As she retraced her steps, she met the horse, the plantain tree, and the cow. Each wanted to give her a gift to take home with her. The horse gave her a young colt of the finest *pakshiraj* breed; the tree gave her a bunch of plantains yellow as gold and a pot full of old gold coins called *mohurs;* and the cow gave her a tawny calf whose udders would never be dry.

Dukhu thanked them all for their wonderful gifts, seated herself on the colt with the pot of gold and the plantains, and found her way home, with the calf walking close behind her.

Her mother, meanwhile, had made herself sick with anxiety, not knowing where Dukhu had gone and when she would come back. She was beside herself with joy when she heard Dukhu's voice call out, "Mother, where are you? Look what I've got!"

When the mother had recovered from her shock of joy, she couldn't believe her eyes. The muslins, the jewels, the gold coins, the plantains, the horse, and the calf—she looked at every one of them over and over. She was speechless.

After a while she found her voice and asked her daughter how she came by all these fabulous things. Dukhu told her the whole story about the wind, the cow, the tree, the horse, and the old Mother of the Moon, and ended by saying, "That's not all. Here's something else she has given me: this casket!"

She then showed her mother the casket. They thought it would be full of more jewels, pearls, gold, and silver. But when they slowly opened it, out of it stepped a most handsome young man dressed like a prince.

"I've been sent here to marry you," he said to Dukhu, without wasting an extra word.

Soon a date was fixed, kith and kin were invited, and a great gala wedding was celebrated. The only people who did not come to the wedding were Sukhu and her mother.

Now, Dukhu's mother was a good woman. Though she had suddenly come into wealth and status, it hadn't gone to her head. She still wanted to be friends with Sukhu and her mother. So she offered Sukhu some ornaments, as they now had heaps of them. But Sukhu's mother was offended. She put her fist to her cheek and hissed, "Why should Sukhu take your leftovers? She's not going begging for jewels! If God had wanted to give my daughter jewels, he would have kept her father alive. My Sukhu is lovely as she is. She needs no ornaments. Only girls who are ugly as owls need fine saris and necklaces to make them look good."

But she didn't forget to make discreet inquiries to find out how Dukhu had come by her great good fortune. Once she learned where Dukhu had gone and how she found the Mother of the Moon, she said to herself, "I'll show her! She is trying to rub her good luck in my face. I'll make my Sukhu a hundred times richer."

Then she brought Sukhu a spinning-wheel and made her spin in the outer yard where the wind was blowing. "Listen to me carefully, Sukhu, my dear," she said. "The wind will blow away your wad of cotton. Then don't forget to howl and wait until the wind asks you to follow it. Be courteous to anyone you meet on the way. Go wherever the wind takes you till you meet the Mother of the Moon."

"I'll do exactly as you say, Mother," said Sukhu and began to spin.

Soon, as expected, a big wind swept away all her cotton, and she began to howl and cry as if someone in the house had died.

"Don't cry, Sukhu, just for a wad of cotton. Come with me. I'll get you all the cotton you want," said the wind.

Sukhu then followed the wind, just as Dukhu had done earlier. She too met the cow, who asked her to clean its shed. But she tossed her head and said, "Clean your stinking shed? Me? Fat chance! I'm on my way to see the Mother of the Moon."

When she met the tree, she said, "I've better things to do than take your creepers down. I'm in a hurry. I'm going to meet the Mother of the Moon."

She was just as insulting to the horse. "You stupid nag, who do you think I am? Your groom's daughter or something?"

They said nothing, but they were hurt. They bided their time.

It was a long way to the palace, and Sukhu was sick and tired of walking. She arrived at the palace in a foul mood. Forgetting her mother's instructions, she burst into the old woman's room and screamed, "The wind has blown away all my cotton. You'd better give me some at once or else I'll break things! And don't take too long about it."

The old woman didn't raise her voice. She said to the young woman quite gently, "Don't be impatient. I'll give you something better than cotton. But you must do as I say. Do you see that pond through the window? Go out there and take two dips in it. Only two dips, no more, or you'll be sorry."

Sukhu ran to the pond and jumped into it. And it made her a beauty. She dived into it a second time, and she came up covered with silks and jewels. She was beside herself with joy and couldn't stop looking at herself in the water. Then she thought, "If I take one more dip, I'm sure I'll get much more than Dukhu did. The old woman doesn't want me to have more than she gave Dukhu. That's why she asked me not to take more than two dips. But I'm going to do it." And dip she did, a third time. But when she rose from the water, she was grief-stricken to see that her jewels and finery were gone, her nose had grown long as an elephant's trunk, and her body was covered with blisters and boils.

She ran to the Mother of the Moon, white with rage, shaking her head and fists at her. "Look what you've done to me!" she screamed.

The old woman looked at her from top to toe and said, "You didn't listen to me. You dipped in the pond more than twice, and this is what you get for not listening to me. You've yourself to thank for the mess you're in . . . But I've one more thing to offer you."

Then she showed her the three caskets, each one bigger than the next, and asked the young woman to choose one for herself. Sukhu had eyes only for the largest of them and chose it.

Meanwhile her mother was impatiently pacing to and fro in the yard, worrying about her girl not coming home. "When is she going to be back and when can I feast my eyes on all the jewels?" she cried. Suddenly she heard her daughter's voice from behind the bushes: "Mother!"

The mother ran out to greet her but nearly died of shock when she saw what she saw. Her daughter's nose was as long as an elephant's trunk. Her body was covered with boils, not jewels. "What's happened to you? Sukhu, what's happened to you? Why? What did you do?" she cried in despair.

But Sukhu showed her the casket. "The old crone asked me to choose, and I chose the biggest of them!"

The mother thought, "The old woman must be playing tricks. She has some surprise waiting here. She's going to make up for the way she treated my Sukhu." Anxiously, with beating hearts, they opened the casket, and out came a long black snake, hissing angrily. It pounced on Sukhu and swallowed her whole, as a python swallows a goat.

Her mother went raving mad and died soon after.

The City Where People Are Mended
NIGERIA

One morning all of the girls in the village went into the forest to pick herbs. They had no sooner gotten there than it began to rain and they quickly ran to a baobab tree and climbed into a hollow in its wide trunk. While the girls were in the tree, the devil caused the hollow to close over. In order to release them, the devil said that each girl must give him her necklace and cloth. All of the girls but one gave the devil her necklace and cloth. The one who refused to do this remained enclosed in the hollow when the others ran back to the village.

On arriving at the village, the girls told the mother of the girl who had been left in the tree what had happened. Knowing that the tree had a small hole near the top, the mother prepared the evening meal and took it to the tree where her daughter was captive. She called out to the girl, "Daughter, daughter, stretch out your hand and take this food." The daughter did as she was instructed, and she took the food from her mother and ate it. After she was finished, her mother returned home.

A hyena, who had been hunting for game in the nearby bush, heard the mother talk to the girl and saw the girl take the food. When the mother left, the hyena went to the tree and called out, "Daughter, daughter, stretch out your hand and take this food."

The daughter was not fooled. "That does not sound like my mother's voice," she said, and she would not stretch out her hand.

Frustrated, the hungry hyena went to a blacksmith and asked him to alter his voice to make it sound like that of a human being. The blacksmith agreed to do so, but he warned the hyena that if it found any food along the way, it should not eat the food before returning to the tree.

As the blacksmith had foretold, while the hyena was returning to the baobab tree he saw a centipede, which he ate. "After all, does one ignore food when it is found?" he said. He then finished his trip to the tree, where he called out, "Daughter, daughter, stretch out your hand and take this food." However, eating the centipede had affected the sound of the hyena's voice. Again the girl replied, "That does not sound like my mother's voice." Once more she refused to stretch out her hand.

The hyena returned to the blacksmith's shop very angry about what had happened. "My voice does not sound like a human's," he said. "Therefore, I am going to eat you." The blacksmith insisted that if the hyena did not eat him, he would make the hyena's voice sound like a human voice.

For a second time the hyena traveled back to the baobab tree. When he got there, he called out, "Daughter, daughter, stretch out your hand and take this food." This time the hyena's voice sounded like that of a human, and the girl stretched out her hand. When she did so, the hyena seized it in his strong jaws and pulled the girl out of the tree. For his meal he ate the girl entirely, leaving only the bones.

That evening when the girl's mother brought food for her daughter, she saw the bones lying on the ground and realized what had happened. She gathered up the bones, put them in her basket, and began walking to the city where people are mended.

After some time the mother came to a place where food was cooking itself. "Oh food, where is the road to the city where people are mended?" she asked.

The food answered, "Why worry about traveling such a long distance? Just stay here and eat me."

The mother replied, "I am not hungry, and I do not wish to eat you."

To this answer the food said, "After you have traveled awhile, you will come to two roads. Take the road on the side of the hand with which you eat and ignore the road on the other side."

The mother returned to her journey, and soon she came to some meat that was cooking itself. "Oh meat, where is the road to the city where people are mended?" she asked.

The meat answered, "Why worry about traveling such a long distance? Just stay here and eat me."

The mother replied, "I am not hungry, and I do not wish to eat you."

To this answer the meat said, "After you have traveled awhile, you will come to two roads. Take the road on the side of the hand with which you eat and ignore the road on the other side."

The mother returned to her journey once more, and soon she came to a *fura* that was mixing itself in a pot. "Oh *fura*, where is the road to the city where people are mended?" she asked.

The *fura* answered, "Why worry about traveling such a long distance? Just stay here and eat me."

The mother replied, "I am not hungry, and I do not wish to eat you."

To this answer the *fura* said, "After you have traveled awhile, you will come to two roads. Take the road on the side of the hand with which you eat and ignore the road on the other side."

Leaving the *fura*, the mother continued her journey until she finally arrived at the city where people are mended. When she got there the people asked why she had come. "The hyena has eaten my child," she said.

"Did you bring her bones with you?" the people asked. When the mother showed them the basket with her daughter's bones in it, they said, "Tomorrow we will mend your daughter."

The next morning, the people of the city asked the mother to tend to their cattle. The mother took the cattle from their enclosure and herded them into the fields to feed. The only food that was available for the cattle was the fruit of the *adduwa* tree. The mother picked the fruits of the tree and gave the ripe ones to the cattle, saving the green ones for her own food. All day she gathered the fruits and fed them to the cattle until it was time to return to the city in the evening. When she returned home with the cattle, the largest bull of the herd cried out, "This mother has a good heart; mend her daughter well."

The people of the city, therefore, mended the daughter well, and the next day the mother and daughter returned to their home.

When they got back to their village, the mother's rival wife, who also had a daughter, was jealous because her own daughter was very ugly. Thinking that she might improve her daughter's looks, she devised a plan whereby she would kill her daughter and then go to the city where people are mended, as her rival had done.

The rival wife put her daughter in a pestle and pounded her to death. Then she took out her daughter's bones, put them in a basket, and headed down the road to the city where people are mended.

After she had traveled awhile, she came to the place where the food was cooking itself. "Oh food, where is the road to the city where people are mended?" she asked.

The food answered, "Why worry about traveling such a long distance. Just stay here and eat me."

The wicked mother replied, "You do not have to invite me to eat you twice," and she quickly ate the food.

She then continued on until she came to the place where the meat was cooking itself. "Oh meat, where is the road to the city where people are mended?" she asked.

The meat answered, "Why worry about traveling such a long distance? Just stay here and eat me."

The wicked mother replied, "You do not have to invite me to eat you twice," and she quickly consumed the meat.

Continuing on her journey, she came to the *fura* that was mixing itself in a pot. "Oh *fura*, where is the road to the city where people are mended?" she asked.

The *fura* answered, "Why worry about traveling such a long distance? Just stay here and eat me."

The wicked mother replied, "You do not have to invite me to eat you twice," and she quickly ate the *fura*.

On she traveled until finally she came to the city where people are mended. When she got there, the people asked why she had come. "My daughter is dead, and I wish that she be mended," she said.

"Did you bring her bones with you?" the people asked. When the mother showed them the basket with her daughter's bones in it, they said, "Tomorrow we will mend your daughter."

The next morning, the people of the city asked the mother to tend to their cattle. The mother took the cattle from their enclosure and herded them into the fields to feed. As she gathered the fruit of the *adduwa* tree, she set aside all of the ripe pieces, which she ate, giving the cattle only the green fruit to eat. When she returned home with the cattle, the largest bull of the herd cried out, "This mother has a bad heart; mend her daughter ill."

When the mended daughter was brought to her mother, the daughter had only been mended halfway. She had half a nose, one ear, one leg, one hand, and so forth. When she saw her daughter, the distraught mother said, "I am not your mother," and she ran away and hid.

The daughter followed her footprints until she found her mother. "Why do you run from me, mother?" she asked.

"Go away. You are not my daughter."

"No, it is you who say that you are not my mother, and it is true that it was someone else who brought me back to life. But you are the one who gave birth to me, and you are the one who is responsible for my misshapen body."

The horrified mother ran off again and she ran until she came to her hut. She hurried in and closed the door behind her. When the daughter arrived at the hut, she called out, "Mother, I am home." When the mother did not answer her, the daughter opened the door and went in to her mother. The rival mother and her hideous daughter lived the rest of their lives together. For as long as they lived, the wicked mother was haunted by the fact that her own daughter was so ugly while the daughter of her rival was so beautiful.

$\mathcal{D}$iamonds and Toads

FRANCE

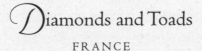

There was once upon a time a widow, who had two daughters, the eldest was so much like her in face and humour, that whoever looked upon the daughter saw the mother. They were both so disagreeable and so proud, that no body could live with them. The youngest who was the very picture of the father for civility and sweetness of temper, was withal one of the most beautiful girls that ever was seen. This mother loved even to distraction her eldest daughter, and at the same time had a frightful aversion for the youngest. She made her eat in the kitchen and work continually.

Amongst other things, this poor child was forced twice a day to draw water above a mile and a half off from the house, and bring a pitcher full of it home. One day as she was at this fountain there came up to her a poor woman, who begged of her to let her drink: "O ay with all my heart, Goody," said this pretty little girl; and rinsing immediately the pitcher, she took up some water from the clearest place of the fountain, and gave it to her, holding up the pitcher all the while that she might drink the easier.

The good woman having drank what she had a mind to, said to her, "You are so very pretty, my dear, so good and so mannerly, that I cannot help giving of you a gift" (for this was a Fairy, you must understand, who had taken upon her the form of a poor countrywoman to see how far the civility and good manners of this pretty girl would go). "*I will give you for gift,*" continued the fairy, "that at every word you speak there shall come out of your mouth either a flower or a jewel."

When this pretty girl came home, her mother scolded at her for returning so late from the fountain. "I beg your pardon, mamma," said the poor thing, "for staying so long," and immediately upon speaking these words there came out of her mouth two roses, two pearls, and two large diamonds. "What is it I see there?" said her mother all astonished. "I think I see pearls and diamonds come out of her mouth: How comes this, child?" (This was the first time she ever call'd her child.) The poor creature told her plainly all that had happen'd, not without dropping out of her mouth an infinite number of diamonds. "Truly," said the mother, "I must send thither my daughter. Come hither, *Fanny,* see what comes out of your sister's mouth when she speaks: Would not you be glad to have the same gift given to you? You have nothing else to do but go and draw water out of the fountain, and when a certain poor woman comes to ask to drink a little, to give it her very civilly." "It would be a very pretty sight indeed," said this brute, "to see me go to draw water." "I will have you go," said the mother. So she went, but grumbled all the way, taking along with her the best silver tankard they had in the house. She was no sooner at the fountain than she saw coming out of the wood a lady most richly drest, who came up to her and asked to drink. Now you must know, that this was the very fairy that appeared to her sister, but had now taken upon her the air and dress of a Princess, to see how far the rudeness and ill manners of this girl would go. "Am I come hither," said the proud brute, "for nothing else but to give you to drink? I have just now brought a silver tankard on purpose for my lady. You may drink out of it, I think, if you will."

"You have not a grain of civility or good breeding in you," reply'd the Fairy, without putting herself into a passion. "Well then, since you have so little manners and are so disobliging, *I give you for gift,* that at every word you speak there shall come out of your mouth a snake or a toad." As soon as her mother saw her coming she cry'd out, "Well, daughter." "Well, mother," answer'd the brute, and at the same time there came out of her mouth two snakes and two toads. "O, mercy!" cry'd the mother, "what is it I see! It is her sister that has been the cause of all this; but she shall pay for it." And immediately she ran after her to beat her. The poor creature fled away from her and went to hide herself in the forest that was hard by.

The King's son, who was returning from hunting, met her, and seeing her so very pretty, asked her what she did there alone, and why she cry'd! *"Alack-a-day! Sir, my mamma has turned me out of door."* The King's son, who saw five or six pearls and as many diamonds come out of her mouth, desired her to tell him whence this happen'd. She accordingly told him the whole story; upon which the King's son fell in love with her; and considering with himself that such a gift as this was worth more than any marriage portion whatsoever in another, conducted her to the palace of the king, his father, and there married her. As for her sister, she made herself so odious that her own mother turn'd her out of doors, and the unhappy wretch having wandered about good while without finding any body to take her in, went to a corner of a wood and died.

· *Conversation* ·

JANE: Of these five reward-and-punishment tales, as Professor Maria Tatar calls them, the one I knew as a child was "Diamonds and Toads" (also called "The Fairy"). But as there are more than a thousand variants on the tale worldwide, I must have known others, for I was an avid reader of fairy stories. The Andrew Lang color fairy books were my favorite bedtime reading.

Certainly it was borne home to me early on that if I remained a good girl, diamonds would drop from my mouth, and if I became a bad girl, all I would get was toad spit.

The warnings were straightforward, and if you read a lot of these particular "kind and unkind girls" stories, you will be surprised—as Tatar says—"by the emphasis on blunting the will of stubborn children and punishing disobedient ones." Those punishments are endless and awfully inventive. I took them to heart and I really was a goody-goody, even into college. ("Goody-goody" was a term applied to me by a number of boyfriends as I remember, and I wore that badge proudly.) I bit back bad behavior till I was well out of my mother's sight. She was so patient and helpful (as long as we weren't dealing with matters of sexuality) that I didn't have the heart—or the guts—to be bad.

I remember one particular small party at our house when I was sixteen that got completely out of hand. It was crashed by the entire (winning) Staples High School football team. Probably because my then-boyfriend was on the varsity and had told them all. (That's when I developed my rule: every girl is allowed one dumb jock per adolescence. But only one.)

Some boys sneaked in drinks and what had started as a quiet party turned into a rout. My father threatened to call the police when the fifth boy landed in the fish pool in front of our house. But it was my mother who helped me clean out my boyfriend's car when he threw up all over the front seat, because—as he weepingly confessed after Mom had made an entire pot of hot coffee just for him—he had to take his mother to early mass the next morning.

It never occurred to my mother to blame me for what had clearly been beyond my control, though my father didn't speak to me for a week. After all, I really was a good girl. I would have milked the cow who was bursting, or pulled down the creepers from the tree, or helped the old lady without caring if she was a fairy or a witch. I was so good, in fact, that I didn't even get my ears pierced till I was forty-two. After all, when I was growing up, only the fast girls put holes in their ears. I didn't do any heavy petting till I was in college.

So of course I expected good-girl behavior from you.

The behavior bar—that which distinguishes good girls and bad girls—has shifted. Lowered, some might say. Raised, according to others. Certainly it has changed.

What would my mother have made of navel and labial piercings, for example? Or girls with tattoos? A recent *Newsweek* article estimated that "our painted population" is at 20 million, and a good number of those are female. Possibly my mother would have judged the girls doing such things as "bad."

What my maternal grandmother would have said about Dykes on Bikes I think I can guess, since when told a certain famous violinist whom she adored was a homosexual, she said, "No—he's a Russian." After the term was explained, she raised her eyebrows and said, "There's no such thing."

However, mothers responding to their own daughters and granddaughters' good/badness can often surprise us. And, I suppose, surprise themselves as well.

My friend Leslea Newman wrote about finally coming out to her grandmother, a traditionalist. This happened after Leslea and her partner, Mary, became engaged. The old woman's first response was: "Lezel, darling, you're ruining your life." They parted in anger and tears. But the next morning at 6:00 a.m. there was a call from her grandmother, saying, "If you're happy, I'm happy, too. . . . You could sleep with a dog and I wouldn't care, I would still love you." In the end *good*-ness is defined by those who love us, not necessarily by society.

Would I ever judge you or your daughters as bad girls? I suspect only if you behaved as outspoken racists or became ax murderers or abused children.

Of course, now that I am old and wise—if not wicked and wild—I realize that the diamonds-and-toads story is a perfect metaphor for a writer. Always hoping for diamonds to fall from my mouth and always afraid that instead (as the *Kirkus* reviewers often tell me) I have a mouthful of toads.

HEIDI: I find it interesting that you begin our conversation about good girls versus bad girls with this discussion about how "good" you were as a child.

Not that I dispute the facts. You were, and still are, the quintessential good girl.

It must have been tough to raise me. Under your definitions, I definitely fit into the other category. I had my ears pierced at fifteen and had sex before college. But I'd like to point out that in the stories in this section, "bad girl" is defined by traits such as "lazy and ill-tempered," "ugly," and "ornery." Not one of these stories mentions relations, or lack thereof, with boys. Or wild parties.

Since we live in a media-driven society today, our bad-girl cues come from sex, drugs, and rock and roll, not so much from kindness to others and hard work.

So where did I fit in? I was into all of the former, but also was committed to helping others, and I wasn't in the slightest bit lazy (okay, maybe a little bit lazy when it came to cleaning my room and getting my schoolwork in on time). Was I a teenage good girl? Bad girl? A little of both?

I'd also like to say in my defense that I did not lose my virginity when you thought I did, but almost two years later. And I watched all of my friends do drugs but wasn't much involved with them except for a little cannabis. But, everyone thought I did these things even when I did not. Including you.

I felt then—and I feel now—that if you are okay with the label you have, then do what you want. But if what people say about you bothers you, then make a change. I was all right with what was being said, and even started a few rumors myself. I wanted to be good, but not to be labeled as such.

JANE: A part of me would have loved to be bad, but not labeled as such. Even today I have that problem.

Recently I heard of a book called *Slut! Growing Up Female with a Bad Reputation,* by Leora Tanenbaum. It is about sexual harassment among preteens and adolescents, often initiated by girls and not boys, against girls who differ from the norm (sometimes early developers, or other races).

As a full-bodied teen, I actually had some of this nastiness sent my way early on, because I transferred into the school system in ninth grade. However, I was so clearly naive that after a while I was left alone. But one girl in my class—who went on to become a Hollywood starlet and indeed was infamous for the car-washing scene in *Cool Hand Luke*—had a terrible time in high school. Not for anything she actually did, but for the way she looked. She was much less sexually precocious than a lot of girls in our class, but she was the one everyone picked on.

I was not immune to doing some finger-pointing myself. One of my best friends started dating a young woman in my college dorm. He asked me what I thought of her and I passed on some not-so-nice sexual gossip, which I believed. And he said, "I've been thinking of marrying her." He did, too. It was the end of our friendship and I never got to ask their forgiveness and tell them what a sorry spectacle I had made of myself. Jane Austen would have loved the moment but regretted—as I did—the lack of closure. From all accounts they had a wonderful marriage, full of mutual love and intelligent friendship. She nursed him throughout a long and horrible illness. That conversation is the one thing I ever did of which I am thoroughly ashamed.

I am still pretty naive about sexual matters, but I don't tattle anymore. I don't consider it my business.

Speaking of naive—I never told you this story, but once I spoke at a conference in North Carolina and afterward, my hostess—a well-known children's literature scholar—gave me my choice of going to a movie, a male strip club, or a drive-in funeral home.

HEIDI: If you went to the funeral home, I'm gonna clobber you!

JANE: Part of me wanted to go to see the male strippers. But a greater part was too embarrassed. Besides, the writer in me was dying to visit a drive-in funeral home.

HEIDI: Mother! Now I am going to have to take you to a strip club.

JANE: I've actually been to one. The stripper turned out to be a male dressed as a female. I was so embarrassed I could hardly watch.

HEIDI: I have been to a number of strip joints, though the men were always dressed as men and women dressed as women. Or, I suppose, I should say "undressed." I've even held conversations with friends who had naked gyrating women "performing" in their laps. If you don't consider it a big deal, it isn't. But, I have to say, my new favorite mental image is going to be of you watching a female impersonator take his clothes off. If I had a picture, I'd put it on my next Christmas card.

JANE: But that's exactly what I mean about the changing bar. I was embarrassed by the stripper, you are not. My mother would never have considered entering such a place, though having lived in Hollywood for a year she knew a number of show girls. My grandmother wouldn't have believed any such places existed. And so forth.

I grew up idolizing Audrey Hepburn and Deborah Kerr, quintessential good girls. But today the bad girls are the superstars and role models. The popular culture is full of them. On TV we have Xena and her sidekick Gabrielle, as well as Buffy the Vampire Slayer and Le Femme Nikita. In the comics, characters like Ricky Carrakero's China and Jazz in *Double Impact,* and Neil Gaiman's Death in the *Sandman* series. In the movies, Ripley in the *Alien* series rules. Pop music has brought us Madonna and the Spice Girls and other spike-bra babes. All terribly pleased at playing bad. Not exactly what the fairy-tale tellers had in mind when they recited these good-girl/bad-girl stories, some of them going back well into the fifteenth century.

Do you know the Lucille Clifton poem "To My Last Period"? It ends like this:

> *. . . I feel just like*
> *the grandmothers who,*
> *after the hussy has gone,*
> *sit holding her photograph*
> *and sighing,* wasn't she
> beautiful, wasn't she beautiful?

And suddenly I remember a literature conference where you met me for dinner before heading off to a dance club. You were wearing a skin-tight black dress with cutouts and I said, "You look adorable." Your mouth twisted wryly. "Adorable was not what I was going for, Mom." But you were also with your roommate and planning to drive home together. You both liked dancing and weren't looking for dates.

Well, I didn't expect you to be my kind of good. Pierced ears was my definition, not yours. And though your father and I had lived through changes in sexual perceptions, we always joke that two days after we got married the sexual revolution broke out.

Still, I wanted you to be good in an amorphous and ill-defined way. "Good" meaning that you would bring something to society, and not just take from it. Remember, my first actual presidential vote was for Jack Kennedy. We took that "Ask what you can do for your country" business seriously. I joined a Quaker meeting when you were four years old after thinking about it for a long time.

Of course, my mother's good girl was different from mine. She expected good grades of me, hoped I might enjoy a bit of popularity but not too much, desired college as a definite, and sex as a definite no-no till marriage. She did, in fact, use the line about "What will the neighbors think?" when I wanted to go off to visit a boyfriend at Williams College for the weekend. I remember retorting loudly: "What business is it of theirs?" I never understood how the neighbors were going to know that I was in Williamstown, Massachusetts, if she didn't tell them.

Her mother's good girl was different, too. Grandma's definition would have been: stay pure, marry a nice Jewish boy, and be a model citizen. In fact, my mother and father had already been married secretly at City Hall for several months when they were at a Yolen family gathering. Dad's younger brother made a pass at her saying, "Will isn't the marrying kind. Why don't you go out with me?" The truth never came out to either set of parents, though their siblings eventually all knew. They went through a religious ceremony four months later which—as long as all the grandparents were alive—was the date they celebrated their anniversary.

But what kind of good-girl definition do you have for your own daughters? And are they different definitions—since you became Lexi's mom when she was fourteen, but are raising Maddison from tadpole on up?

HEIDI: Let me first vent a bit about a word: "ladylike." I remember blowing a gasket one day when a friend of mine told two-year-old Maddison that she shouldn't spit because it wasn't ladylike. I agreed that since we were in a car, spitting was rude, disgusting, and extremely unhygenic. But I also wanted Maddison to know there were more important reasons not to spit than what's ladylike and what is not. I guess the point here is that I want to raise Maddison to be a good girl for the right reasons, to appreciate her femininity, but not to have it forced upon her.

As for my expectations for the girls, I am sure they will be different for each of them. I don't believe it is fair to change the rules in the middle of the game, so when Lexi came to us with some rules already in place (by other foster parents, by the state, etc.) we chose to start from there and build. Although I have to admit that one of my favorite mom things to say is that it's my right to change the rules whenever I please, so I guess I contradict myself a bit here.

But Maddison will not be allowed to date as early as Lexi, or wear the same kind of clothes she does, or stay out until 11:00 p.m., and a host of other things I'll come up with as age demands it.

JANE: [Laughing.] Good luck! You will no doubt have as much success with her as I did with you in the cosmetics struggle and the black leather skirt struggle.

HEIDI: You may be right. And I'm sure to make Maddison crazy. Though she'll probably agree it's better than her other option, which is convent school. But this also makes Lexi nuts since she knows she doesn't have much wiggle-room when arguing for extended privileges.

My expectations for my girls have less to do with each being a good girl and more with being a happy girl, something that I learned from you. You always told me (and my brothers) that we should do what we love. Of course, out of the three of us, there's not a doctor or lawyer in the house. You wound up with a writer, a musician, and a photographer. We're all happy and broke.

Just ask Maddison what her full name is and she'll tell you it's "Maddison Jane Piatt, M.D." I want her to be happy *and* rich.

Jokes aside, in these good-girl/bad-girl stories, the good girls are rewarded with diamonds, muslins, gold coins, a horse, fine food. On the other hand, the bad girls spit toads, are disfigured by hot tar, and get eaten by snakes.

The lesson is pretty obvious. Good equals happy and bad equals—well, bad equals disfigurement, ugliness, unhappiness, and death. No room for any middle ground.

JANE: Or as Maria Tatar frankly notes, these "fairy tale plots begin to resemble blueprints for enterprising young capitalists rather than for self-sacrificing do-gooders."

Bad Seeds

$\mathcal{G}$boloto, the River Demon

LIBERIA

Once long ago in the Kpelle country there was a village surrounded by a river. In this river there lived a demon, called Gboloto, who swallowed people who lied. Anyone suspected of lying was placed on the river in a skillet. Gboloto would swallow those who had lied.

Now, a mother, her two daughters, and their cat lived in this village. Every day when the big sister cooked, she would place her mother's rice, peppers, and cassava food on the table. They were a happy family and things were going well, when something happened that spoiled the peace of their home. One day when the mother came home from work, some of the food had disappeared from the bowls.

The mother asked what was happening to the food, but the girls both said that they didn't know.

One day the little girl's mouth was all covered with oil. The mother called the girl to her and asked if she had been taking the food. "No, no," the girl exclaimed, "it is big sister who takes the food-o!" Naturally, the big sister swore that she knew nothing about her mother's missing food.

The next day the mother pretended to go to work but stayed at home. After the older girl had dished up the dinner, the mother stood behind the dining room door to see who would steal some of the food. As she stood there, the older girl came, took some meat, and ate it. The mother went out and returned in the evening. She called the older girl and questioned her again. Still the big sister denied even touching the food.

"I know what I'll do. I'll take you all to Gboloto," said the overwrought mother.

Early the next morning they all went to the waterside where the small girl was the first to get into the frying pan. When the pan was pushed onto the water, she began singing this song:

Ma, if that is me eat
the rice and the soup, fry pan
must carry me down and
Gboloto must swallow me.

After singing this song three times she was removed from the skillet. Then the big sister was put into the pan. As the older sister sang, the skillet began to sink in the water, carrying her down. When the water reached her waist, her mother asked her if she was willing to confess, but she still denied that she had stolen the food. She started singing again. The water covered her up to her throat. Still, she would not tell the truth, so the water covered her completely. Gboloto had again caught its victim.

The mother and the little girl turned and went up the hill to their home, where they lived happily ever after. They may still be there, if you want to check for them.

The Greedy Daughter

ITALY

There was a mother who had a daughter so greedy that she did not know what to do with her. Everything in the house she would eat up. When the poor mother came home from work there was nothing left.

But the girl had a godfather-wolf. The wolf had a frying-pan, and the girl's mother was too poor to possess such an article; whenever she wanted to fry anything she sent her daughter to the wolf to borrow his frying-pan, and he always sent a nice omelette in it by way of not sending it empty. But the girl was so greedy and so selfish that she not only always ate the omelette by the way, but when she took the frying-pan back she filled it with all manner of nasty things.

At last the wolf got hurt at this way of going on, and he came to the house to inquire into the matter.

Godfather-wolf met the mother on the step of the door, returning from work.

"How do you like my omelettes?" asked the wolf.

"I am sure they would be good if made by our godfather-wolf," replied the poor woman, "but I never had the honour of tasting them."

"Never tasted them! Why, how many times have you sent to borrow my frying-pan?"

"I am ashamed to say how many times; a great many, certainly."

"And every time I sent you an omelette in it."

"Never one reached me."

"Then that hussy of a girl must have eaten them by the way."

The poor mother, anxious to screen her daughter, burst into all manner of excuses, but the wolf now saw how it all was. To make sure, however, he added: "The omelettes would have been better had the frying-pan not always been full of such nasty things. I did my best always to clean it, but it was not easy."

"Oh, godfather-wolf, you are joking! I always cleaned it, inside and out, as bright as silver, every time before I sent it back!"

The wolf now knew all, and he said no more to the mother; but the next day, when she was out, he came back.

When the girl saw him coming she was so frightened that she ran under the bed to hide herself. But to the wolf it was as easy to go under a bed as anywhere else; so under he went, and he dragged her out and devoured her. And that was the end of the Greedy Daughter.

The King of the Mineral Kingdom
CZECHOSLOVAKIA

Once upon a time, and a long, long time ago it was, there lived a widow who had a very pretty daughter. The mother was a good and honest soul, and was quite happy with her station in life, but her daughter was otherwise. She, like all spoiled beauties, looked down with contempt at her many admirers. She was full of proud and ambitious thoughts, and the more lovers she attracted, the prouder she became.

One beautiful moonlit night the mother awoke, and unable to sleep, she began to pray that God bring happiness to her only child, although she often had made her mother's life miserable. The woman looked lovingly at the daughter lying next to her, and she wondered, as she saw her smile in her sleep, what happy dream had visited her. She finished her prayer, and laying her head on her pillow, soon fell asleep.

The next day she said, "Come here, Daughter, and tell me what you were dreaming last night. You looked so happy smiling in your sleep."

"Oh, yes, I remember what it was. I had a very beautiful dream! I thought a rich nobleman came to our house in a splendid carriage of brass, and gave me a ring set with stones. How it sparkled like the stars in heaven! When I entered the church with him it was full of people, and they all thought me as beautiful, divine and adorable as the Blessed Virgin herself!"

"My child, what sin! May God keep you from having such dreams!"

"Oh, pooh!" The daughter kissed her mother on the cheek, and ran away singing. That same morning a handsome young farmer drove into the village in his cart and begged them to come and share his country bread. He was a kind and respectable fellow, and the mother liked him very much. But the daughter refused his invitation, and insulted him in the bargain. "Even if you had driven in a carriage of brass, and offered me a ring set with stones shining as the stars in heaven, I would never have married you! You are nothing but a mere peasant!"

The young farmer was terribly upset and returned home a saddened man. The mother turned to her daughter and scolded, "How dare you put on such airs! You yourself come from a humble home!"

The next night the woman again woke, and taking her rosary prayed even more intensely that God would bless her child. This time the girl laughed in her sleep.

"What can the child possibly be dreaming about?" the woman said to herself. Sighing, she finished her prayers, laid her head upon the pillow, and tried in vain to sleep. In the morning as her daughter dressed, the mother said, "Well, my dear, you were dreaming again last night, and laughing like a maniac."

"Was I? I suppose it's possible. I dreamt a nobleman came for me in a silver carriage, and gave me a golden diadem. When I entered the church with him, the people admired and worshipped me more than the Blessed Virgin."

"What a terrible dream that was! What a wicked dream! Pray God not to lead you into temptation." She scolded her daughter severely, and then stomped out of the house, slamming the door behind her.

That same morning a carriage drove into the village, and some gentlemen invited the mother and daughter to share the bread of the lord of the manor. The mother curtsied low—she knew this was a great honor—but the daughter sniffed and said, "Even if you had come to fetch me in a carriage of solid silver and presented me with a gold diadem, I would never have consented to be the wife of your lord."

The men could not believe their ears, and they turned away in disgust. The mother rebuked her daughter for having so much pride.

"Miserable, wretched, foolish girl!" she cried. "Pride is a breath from hell. It is your duty to be humble, honest and sweet-tempered—not a spoiled brat!"

The daughter only laughed at her mother.

The third night the daughter slept soundly, but the poor woman at her side could not even close her eyes. Butterflies flew about her stomach, and she feared that some misfortune was about to happen. She counted her beads, praying all the while. All at once the sleeper beside her began to sneer and laugh.

"Merciful God in Heaven!" cried the old woman. "What are these dreams that plague the brain of my beautiful daughter?"

In the morning she was almost afraid to question the girl. "What made you sneer so frightfully last night? You must have had bad dreams again, poor child."

"Don't start with me, Mother. You look all set to begin preaching again."

"No, no; but I do want to know what you were dreaming about."

"Well, if you must know, I dreamt someone drove up in a golden carriage and asked me to marry him, and he brought me a mantle of cloth of pure gold. When we came into the church, the crowd shoved and pressed forward to kneel before me."

The mother wrung her hands, and the girl quickly left the room to avoid another scolding. That same day three carriages entered the yard, one of brass, one of silver, and one of gold. The first was drawn by two white horses, the second by three, and the third by four swan-white horses. Gentlemen wearing scarlet gloves and green mantles got out of the brass and silver carriages, while from the golden carriage alighted a prince who, as the sun shown on him, looked as if he were dressed in gold. They all made their way to the widow and the prince asked for her daughter's hand.

The old woman curtsied so low her nose touched the ground, and when she spoke her voice shook, "I . . . I fear we are not worthy of so much honor." But when the daughter's eyes fell on the face of the prince, she recognized in him the lover of her dreams, and she withdrew into the house to weave an aigrette of many-colored feathers. In exchange for this aigrette which she offered her bridegroom, he placed upon her finger a ring set with stones that shone like the stars in heaven, and over her shoulders he threw a mantle of gold cloth. The young bride, beside herself with joy, retired to the house to gather her remaining things. Meanwhile the anxious mother, eaten away by the blackest forebodings, said to her son-in-law, "My daughter has agreed to share your bread, only tell me of what sort of flour it is made?"

"In our house we have bread of brass, of silver, and of gold; I am a generous man, my wife shall be free to choose."

Such a mysterious reply astonished the poor woman, and made her still more unhappy. The daughter asked no questions, and was, in fact, content to know nothing, not even what her mother suffered. She looked magnificent in her bridal dress and golden mantle, and she left her home with the prince. She did not even say goodbye to her mother or to any of her friends. Nor did she ask for her mother's blessing, although the old woman wept and prayed for her safety.

After the marriage ceremony, the pair mounted the golden carriage and set off, followed by the attendants of silver and brass. The procession moved slowly along the road without stopping until they reached the foot of a high rock. "But where is your palace?" asked the girl. "I do not see anything." Here, instead of a carriage entrance, was a large cavern which led out onto a steep slope down which the horses went lower and lower. The giant Zémo-tras (he who makes earthquakes) closed the opening with a huge stone. They made their way in darkness for some time, and the terrified bride sought to be reassured by her husband. "Where are we going? Will you answer me, please?"

"Fear nothing," he said, patting her hand. "In a little while it will be clear and beautiful. You'll see."

Grotesque dwarfs, carrying lighted torches, appeared on all sides. "Welcome, welcome King Kovlad!" they shouted as they illumined the road for him and his attendants. "You have brought us a queen!"

For the first time the girl realized the one she had married was named Kovlad, but this mattered little to her. On coming out of the gloomy passages into the open they found themselves surrounded by large forests and mountains—mountains that seemed to touch the sky. And, strange to relate, all of the trees—no matter what kind—and even the mountains were of solid lead. When they had crossed these marvelous mountains, the giant Zémo-tras closed all of the openings in the road they had passed. They then drove out upon a vast and beautiful plain, in the center of which stood a golden palace covered with precious stones. The bride was weary with looking at so many wonders (who would have thought!), and gladly sat down to the feast prepared by the dwarfs. Meats of many kinds were served, roasted and boiled, but lo! they were of metal—brass, silver and gold. Everyone ate heartily and enjoyed the food, but the young wife, with tears in her eyes, begged for a piece of bread.

"Certainly, my dear, with pleasure," answered Kovlad, but she could not eat the bread which was brought, for it was of brass. Then the king sent for a piece of silver bread. Still she could not eat it. Again he asked for a slice of bread, and the girl was brought a slice that was made of gold. She was unable to take even the tiniest bite. The servants did all they could to get something to their mistress' taste, but she found it impossible to eat anything.

"I would be most happy to satisfy you," said Kovlad, "but I don't have any other kind of food."

Then the girl realized the extent of the situation in which she had placed herself, and she began to weep bitterly and wished she had heeded her mother's advice.

"It is no use to weep and regret," said Kovlad. "You must have known the kind of bread you would have to break here. Your wish has been fulfilled."

And so it was, for nothing can recall the past. The wretched girl was obliged henceforth to live underground with her husband Kovlad, the God of Metals, in his golden palace . . . and all this because she had set her heart upon nothing but the possession of gold, and had never wished for anything better.

What became of her in the end? What becomes of anyone who has no food to eat . . .

· *Conversation* ·

JANE: Sometimes no matter how much a mother tries, a daughter is no good.

There, I have said it, though I have a hard time believing it. Perhaps I have been lucky. Not a smart or perfect mother, but a lucky one. I have loved you since the moment you, pink and perfect, were put in my arms.

No—I loved you from the moment I first felt the flutter kick that announced your presence in my belly.

But surely Lizzie Borden's mother felt that way some of the time, too. And Lucretia Borgia's mother. And Jezebel's mother. And the mothers of Eva Braun, Bloody Mary Tudor, and the lady pirates Anne Bonny and Mary Reade.

So is there such a thing as a bad seed? Or are we into the old nature/nurture argument for real?

I read stories like "The Greedy Daughter" (a "Red Riding Hood" variant) and wonder that such abnormal behavior couldn't have been solved in a less violent manner. Or that the ambitious, dreaming girl in "The King of the Mineral Kingdom" might not come to such a miserable end. Or I hope each time that the lying daughter in Gboloto's frying pan repents and tells the truth before it is too late.

Of course, these are moral tales. They are meant to show the worst of what can happen when a truly bad girl does not change her ways. However, I wonder that the mothers in these stories don't step in and save their erring daughters.

Yes, I know that Lizzie Borden's mom was already long dead when Lizzie axed her stepmother and father. And Lucretia Borgia's mother had never really taught her to temper her inclinations toward poisoning. Mothers of queens rarely perceive bad behavior as a problem. At least in traditional tales they encourage a sense of entitlement.

Are these bad girls simply the product of bad mothering? Or were they born evil?

HEIDI: Ah, the eternal question of nature versus nurture. Somewhere between the concept of original sin, which states that children are born evil and that baptism (or, as Victoria Secunda points out in her book *When You and Your Mother Can't Be Friends,* some believe a "healthy" amount of beating) washes the evil away, and the concept of tabula rasa, that states that children are born with a blank slate that is filled in by experiences, we might find the answer to the nature versus nurture question.

And, even if mothers believed a recent study by some crazy woman (my own opinion here) that says parents have no influence at all on how their children turn out, we mothers would still have mother guilt.

We did too little. We did too much. We weren't strict enough. We smothered and didn't let them spread their wings enough.

Definitely a no-win situation.

Certainly in these three stories, the mothering was not the apparent cause of the greedy and lying daughters' shortcomings. I think that one line from "The King of the Mineral Kingdom" says it all: The mother "began to pray that God bring happiness to her only child, although she often had made her mother's life miserable."

JANE: I remember you phoning me three weeks after giving birth to Maddison and crying, "I'm sorry. I'm sorry. I'm sorry." And when I asked what for, you replied, "For everything!" And as bad girls go, you were hardly on the graph paper, much less the graph.

I wish these girls in the stories had had a chance to live longer and repent in leisure. They make me very sad.

HEIDI: I have to say that the three stories fit into the category of "just desserts." The three bad-seed daughters don't have any happily-ever-after. One drowns, one starves, and one gets eaten by a wolf. Greedy liars beware!

I complain a lot about violence in the media—on television, in films, and in cartoons—but I tend to forget how violent the old classics were.

JANE: Dance in red-hot iron shoes till you drop down dead. Get shoved into an oven. Or rolled down the hill in a barrel full of snakes. Living in a fairy-tale world was definitely not for wimps.

HEIDI: But, perhaps, herein lies the true reason for these tales. While the young daughters are sitting on Mama's knee during the telling of these tales, they get a story *and* a reason for being good. I believe that the Bible was written for just this. A lesson is more easily explained by saying, "Because God said so, and if you don't, then you could go to Hell."

Action—consequence. Lie—drown in a frying pan. Be greedy—starve to death. Simple.

JANE: Well, having minored in religion in college, I think I need to point out that telling moral stories is only one of may reasons the Bible was written. Some of it was done for historical reportage, some to revise and remake history, some for kinship lines, some for literature's sake, and a great deal was about a marginalized religion laying claim to its vision of the beginnings of the universe and to set out completely and clearly its belief system.

So endeth the lesson.

HEIDI: As usual, you're right. And as usual, I'm oversimplifying. I actually didn't mean to imply that the only reason the Bible was written was to teach lessons. Although I did say that, so I'm guilty as charged.

But I do believe that its most essential tool is in the teaching of children. Although I am trying to raise Maddison without falling back on the Bible as a crutch, it's not always easy either. (I'd like to note that Lexi practices her own religion separately from, but supported by, the family.)

I tried to supply Maddison actual reasons in her early "why" stage. She would repeat, as every small child does, "Why?" after every answer that my thirty-year-old mind found logical. This went on for months until I discovered that "Because Mommy says so" actually made her nod and move on.

There is no consequence for "You can't rip the pages out of Mommy's book because then Mommy won't be able to read it." But "You should not lie because a wolf will eat you" sure hits home.

JANE: Even if there are no wolves in Myrtle Beach?

HEIDI: Even if there are no wolves in urban Myrtle Beach in 1999.

Sex and . . .

Maroula

GREECE

Now the story begins—good evening to your worships.

Once upon a time there was a woman who had no children and every day she asked God to give her a child. One morning, as she stood at her window, she turned to the Sun, and said, "Good Master Sun, Master Sun, give me a child and when it is twelve years old, you can come and take it."

The Sun heard her plea and gave her a pretty little girl, as pretty as the morning star. She called her Maroula and she was full of joy that she had a child. The more Maroula grew, the prettier she became, and soon she was twelve years old. One day, as she was going to the spring for water, the Sun saw her and turned himself into a brave young lad and went up to her and said, "Ask your mother when she'll give me what she promised."

"But who are you?" Maroula asked the lad.

And he answered, "You tell your mother what I said, and she'll know who I am."

"Very well, I'll tell her," said Maroula, and picked up her pitcher and went home, and said to her mother, "Mother, when I was at the spring, I saw a lad, but what a lad! He was so handsome, he shone like the Sun. And his face! And he told me to ask you when you will give him what you promised him? I asked him who he was, and he told me you'd know who."

And her mother sighed, and said, "I know the lad, my lass. But tell him, when he finds you again, that you forgot to tell me."

The next day, when the lass again went to get water, the Sun came down, and asked her, "Did you tell your mother what I said?"

"I forgot to tell her," she told him.

Then the sun gave her a golden apple, and said to her, "Take this apple and put it in your headdress. This evening, when your mother undresses you before bed, the apple will fall out and you'll remember to tell her."

Maroula went straight home, and said to her mother, "The lad who told me to ask you when you would give him what you promised, found me again and gave me this apple, telling me to put it in my headdress so that when you undress me this evening, it will fall out and I'll remember to tell you."

"When he finds it, he may take it," said her mother, and made up her mind not to send her little girl any more for water.

For a long while she did not send Maroula for water and then she grew bolder and sent her. But, when the Sun saw her, he turned into a young lad again and came down and asked Maroula what her mother had said to her about the promise she had made.

"Ah," said Maroula, "she said, when you find it, you may take it."

Then the Sun took Maroula by the hand and took her far away to his palace, which had a beautiful garden before it. The Sun was away all the day and left Maroula in the garden to play, and in the evening he came round to his palace again. But poor Maroula, however much she was given in the Sun's palace, thought of her mother and sat all day in the garden and wept, and said:

> As my mother's heart withers and colder grows,
> So will the Sun's lettuces fade in their rows:
> Fell yourself, tree, fell yourself.

And she would put up her hands and tear her cheeks. And the lettuces faded and the trees fell with Maroula's tears.

In the evening the Sun would come and see Maroula with swollen eyes and scratched cheeks.

"Who did this to you, Maroula, my dear?"

"The neighbor's cockerel came and fought with ours and I went to part them and they scratched me."

The next day, Maroula sat in the garden and wept again and tore at her cheeks, and said:

> As my mother's heart withers and colder grows,
> So will the Sun's lettuces fade in their rows:
> Fell yourself, tree, fell yourself.

The Sun came that evening and again saw her with her cheeks torn.

"Who has done this to you again, Maroula, my dear?"

"The neighbor's cat came over to ours and they fought and I went to part them and they scratched me."

Maroula went again the next day to the garden, and when she sat down, she remembered her mother and again made her cheeks run with blood, and wept, and said:

> As my mother's heart withers and colder grows,
> So will the Sun's lettuces fade in their rows:
> Fell yourself, tree, fell yourself.

So all the lettuces withered and all the trees fell and the garden was strewn with logs and tree stumps.

The Sun came that evening and saw Maroula, all bloodstained.

"Who has done this to you again, Maroula, my dear?"

"I got caught in a rosebush," said Maroula to him, "and it tore me with its thorns."

But when he got out the next day, the Sun said to himself, "What if I went to see what Maroula does in the garden?" So he turned back and what should he see but Maroula, weeping and clawing at her cheeks.

He drew close to her, and said, "Why are you crying, Maroula, my dear? Can it be you are unhappy here?"

"No," said she, "I'm not unhappy."

"Then why are you weeping? Can it be you want to go back to your mother?"

"Yes, I want to go back to my mother," said Maroula.

"Well, since you want to go to your mother," said the Sun to her, "I will send you home."

So he took her by the hand to the edge of the garden, and there he began to call, "Little lions, little lions!"

Up came the lions.

"What is your will, Lord?" they said to him.

"Will you take Maroula to her mother?"

"We will."

"And on the road, what will you eat if you hunger, and what drink, if you thirst?"

"We'll eat her flesh and drink her blood."

"Run away, and quickly, too," said the Sun to them. "You will not do for me."

Then he called, "Little foxes, little foxes!"

Up came the foxes.

"What is your will, Lord?" they said to him.

"Will you take Maroula to her mother?"

"We will."

"And, on the road, what will you eat if you hunger, and what drink, if you thirst?"

"We'll eat her flesh and drink her blood."

"Get away from here, and quickly," said the Sun to them.

Then, once more, he called, "Little deer, little deer!"

Up came the deer.

"Will you take Maroula to her mother?"

"We will."

"And, on the road, what will you eat if you hunger, and what drink, if you thirst?"

"Fresh, fresh grass, and clear, clear water."

"Go with my blessing," said the Sun to them, and he lifted Maroula up and sat her on the antlers of one of the deer, adorned her with gold coins, and sent her home to her mother. On and on went the deer, and it grew hungry.

It came across a cypress tree, and said to it, "Bend, cypress, and I'll set Maroula down."

The cypress bent over and the deer set Maroula down upon it.

"Now I'll just go and graze a little," said the deer to her, "and then I'll come for you. But don't call out, unless you chance to need me, so that I can eat."

"Very well," said Maroula, "go."

Under the cypress tree there was a well, and nearby lived a *drakaena* who had three daughters, and she had sent one of her daughters to bring water from the well. So when she bent over to lower the bucket into the well, she saw Maroula's face reflected in the water and thought it was her own. So she threw down her bucket and danced back home.

"Did you bring the water?" her mother asked.

"Would you send a girl the likes of me for water?"

Her mother bided her time and sent the second daughter to the well, but as soon as she saw Maroula's face in the water, she, too, took it to be her own. So she, too, threw the bucket away and went running home to her mother.

"Would you send a girl the likes of me for water?"

Then she sent the third daughter to the well, but the same thing happened. Then the mother herself up and went to the well. She bent and looked into the water and saw Maroula's face. She looked up, saw the girl, and burst out laughing.

"Oh, my dear young woman," the *drakaena* said to her, "it was you that my daughters saw in the water and that turned their heads, and it was for you I left kneading my dough. Come down and I'll eat you."

"Make your bread first," said Maroula to her, "and then come back and eat me."

The *drakaena* ran home and kneaded her dough in a hurry and then ran back to Maroula.

"I've kneaded the dough," she told her, "so now come down and I'll eat you."

"Make your bread first," said Maroula, "and then come."

So she ran and made her bread and came running back.

"I've made it," she said, "now come down and I'll eat you."

"Run and heat the oven first and then come and eat me."

The *drakaena* went and heated the oven and came back.

"I heated it," she told her. "Come down and I'll eat you.

"First put your bread in, before the oven goes cold," Maroula bade her, "then come and eat me."

The *drakaena* went off to put the bread in the oven, and then Maroula called out, "Little deer, little deer!"

The deer heard and came running.

"Quick," Maroula told it, "the *drakaena* wants to eat me."

Then the little deer said, "Bend, cypress tree, and I'll take Maroula."

The tree bent and the deer took Maroula and began to run. On the way, they met a mouse, and the deer said, "Mouse, if the *drakaena* meets you and asks if you've seen us, tell her some story and keep her from following us."

After a while, the *drakaena* came along, and said to it, "Here, mouse, have you seen a girl on a deer?"

The mouse said, "I did find a tress of hair."

The *drakaena* said, "That's not what I asked you. Have you seen a girl on a deer?"

"Just wool-gathering!" said the mouse.

"That's not what I asked you. Have you seen a girl on a deer?"

"Just yarn-spinning!" said the mouse.

"That's not what I asked you. Have you seen a girl on a deer?"

"Just cloth-cutting!" said the mouse.

"That's not what I asked you. Have you seen a girl on a deer?"

"I have," said the mouse. "Hurry, and you'll catch her."

As the deer ran and drew closer to her mother's house, the dog sensed that it was Maroula and began to bark, "Bow-wow! It's Maroula coming! Maroula's coming!"

And her mother said, "Sh! Naughty dog! Would you have me die of grief?"

Then the cat on the rooftop sensed it was she, and mewed, "Miaow, miaow! Here's Maroula coming!"

And her mother said, "Shoo! Naughty cat! Would you have me die of grief?"

Then the cockerel sensed her coming, "Cock-a-doodle-doo! Cock-a-doodle-doo! Here's Maroula coming!"

And her mother said, "Hush, naughty bird! Would you have me die of grief?"

Just as the deer came to the house, the *drakaena* caught them up, and, as the deer was going in at the door, the *drakaena* was able to catch it by the tail.

"Ouch, my tail, my tail!" cried the deer.

As it came inside the house, Maroula's mother got up to welcome it, "Welcome, welcome, and, as you have brought me my Maroula, I'll put on your tail for you," and she got a little wool and put on its tail.

And she lived happily ever after with her little girl, and may we live even happier.

The Water Snake

RUSSIA

There was once an old woman who had a daughter; and her daughter went down to the pond one day to bathe with the other girls. They all stripped off their shifts, and went into the water. Then there came a snake out of the water, and glided on to the daughter's shift. After a time the girls all came out, and began to put on their shifts, and the old woman's daughter wanted to put on hers, but there was the snake lying on it. She tried to drive him away, but there he stuck and would not move. Then the snake said:

"If you'll marry me, I'll give you back your shift."

Now she wasn't at all inclined to marry him, but the other girls said:

"As if it were possible for you to be married to him! Say you will!" So she said, "Very well, I will." Then the snake glided off from the shift, and went straight into the water. The girl dressed and went home. And as soon as she got there, she said to her mother,

"Mammie, mammie, thus and thus, a snake got upon my shift, and says he, 'Marry me or I won't let you have your shift'; and I said, 'I will.' "

"What nonsense are you talking, you little fool! as if one could marry a snake!"

And so they remained just as they were, and forgot all about the matter. A week passed by, and one day they saw ever so many snakes, a huge troop of them, wriggling up to their cottage. "Ah, mammie, save me, save me!" cried the girl, and her mother slammed the door and barred the entrance as quickly as possible. The snakes would have rushed in at the door, but the door was shut; they would have rushed into the passage, but the passage was closed. Then in a moment they rolled themselves into a ball, flung themselves at the window, smashed it to pieces, and glided in a body into the room. The girl got upon the stove, but they followed her, pulled her down, and bore her out of the room and out of doors. Her mother accompanied her, crying like anything.

They took the girl down to the pond, and dived right into the water with her. And there they all turned into men and women. The mother remained for some time on the dike, wailed a little, and then went home.

Three years went by. The girl lived down there, and had two children, a son and a daughter. Now she often entreated her husband to let her go to see her mother. So at last one day he took her up to the surface of the water, and brought her ashore. But she asked him before leaving him,

"What am I to call out when I want you?"

"Call out to me, 'Osip, Osip, come here!' and I will come," he replied.

Then he dived under water again, and she went to her mother's, carrying her little girl on one arm, and leading her boy by the hand. Out came her mother to meet her—was so delighted to see her!

"Good day, mother!" said the daughter.

"Have you been doing well while you were living down there?" asked her mother.

"Very well indeed, mother. My life there is better than yours here."

They sat down for a bit and chatted. Her mother got dinner ready for her, and she dined.

"What's your husband's name?" asked her mother.

"Osip," she replied.

"And how are you to get home?"

"I shall go to the dike, and call out, 'Osip, Osip, come here!' and he'll come."

"Lie down, daughter, and rest a bit," said the mother.

So the daughter lay down and went to sleep. The mother immediately took an axe and sharpened it, and went down to the dike with it. And when she came to the dike, she began calling out,

"Osip, Osip, come here!"

No sooner had Osip shown his head than the old woman lifted her axe and chopped it off. And the water in the pond became dark with blood.

The old woman went home. And when she got home her daughter awoke.

"Ah! mother," says she, "I'm getting tired of being here; I'll go home."

"Do sleep here to-night, daughter; perhaps you won't have another chance of being with me."

So the daughter stayed and spent the night there. In the morning she got up and her mother got breakfast ready for her; she breakfasted, and then she said good-bye to her mother and went away, carrying her little girl in her arms, while her boy followed behind her. She came to the dike, and called out:

"Osip, Osip, come here!"

She called and called, but he did not come.

Then she looked into the water, and there she saw a head floating about. Then she guessed what had happened.

"Alas! my mother has killed him!" she cried.

There on the bank she wept and wailed. And then to her girl she cried:

"Fly about as a wren, henceforth and evermore!"

And to her boy she cried:

"Fly about as a nightingale, my boy, henceforth and evermore!"

"But I," she said, "will fly about as a cuckoo, crying 'Cuckoo!' henceforth and evermore!"

Daughter, My Little Bread

INDIA

There was a mother and a daughter. The mother, poor thing, would go off to work in other people's houses. After earning something, she'd bring it home and give it to her daughter saying, "Cook this up." Then the two of them would eat.

Bas. The daughter would roll out and cook up two breads: a big one and a small one. She'd give the small one to her mother and eat the big one herself. But when she grew more mature, some wisdom came into her head. "Look, my mother goes from house to house to earn something. She brings home whatever she earns and gives it to me. Then I eat the big bread myself and give my mother the small one. What am I doing?"

That day she ate the small bread herself and left the big one for her mother. When her mother came home, the daughter gave her the big bread. But the mother wouldn't eat it. She cried, "Daughter, my little bread!" She understood that her daughter had taken the little bread. Now a mother, if she's sane, would hardly feel upset about this! But she began to search everywhere, "My bread! I must eat that very piece of bread."

The daughter had already eaten it up, so how could she give it back? When the mother said, "Give me my little bread," she said, "I've eaten it." But the mother said, "I must eat that very one." There was nothing else stored in the house: after all, every day food would be brought home by going out, then cooking, then eating, then going again the next day and eating that, and doing the same the day after. There was nothing else in the house. But the mother kept on reciting, "Daughter, my little bread. Daughter, my little bread."

The daughter slipped off with a clay water pot and went to the spring nearby. When she got there, she placed her water pot to fill under the jet of water, and she sat down beside it. Just then, the King's servant arrived with a brass pot. He too wanted to fill water. The brass pot was filthy. So the girl took the pot from the servant's hands and gave it a good scrub until it gleamed. Then she filled the pot and returned it to him saying, "Take this, take it to the King to drink."

When the servant gave the water to the King, he asked, "Why does this brass pot shine so much? This isn't your doing, for you only fetch water. Yet this brass pot has been transformed. It's become really beautiful."

The servant said, "King, there's a girl sitting there by the spring. She took the brass pot from my hand and scrubbed at it."

"Let's go," the King said. "I must take a look at her."

When they went there, he saw that the girl was very beautiful. "Come along, you must marry me," said the King.

Now she was unhappy at home anyway. So the King took her. She went off with him.

When she went off with the King, the mother went really crazy. She kept repeating this one line: "Daughter, my little bread. Daughter, my little bread. Daughter, my little bread."

Bas. Repeating this line, the mother set out searching for her daughter.

Who knows how many years had passed before the mother reached the King's palace. She arrived there, still crying out, "Daughter, my little bread. Daughter, my little bread."

The Queen's serving maid came in from outside and reported, "These days there's this woman who's come to town. She wanders everywhere calling, 'Daughter, my little bread. Daughter, my little bread.' "

When she said this the Queen remembered her mother, "Oh-ho! If she makes her way here I'll be dishonored. This is a catastrophe. Where is a King, and where is she: covered in dust, unkempt? The poor thing, in her mad state. . . ."

So the Queen called for someone, and who knows, she probably gave them some money too. "Discreetly kill that woman and bring her to me." So that person finished the mother off. In the past we had huge trunks. She put her mother in the trunk and thrust it high up in the beams.

Bas. The Five Days of Fasting came around. Where the Queen slept, there the King probably slept too. All of a sudden, his gaze fell on that trunk. "What do you keep in that?" he asked.

She said, "Women's things, like rags that I've put away."

"Bring it down," demanded the King. "Open it up!" Some sort of obstinate whim had come over him.

She, poor thing, didn't want to bring it down. "What am I going to show him now?" She lit the lamps, and she began to pray to them, "Oh God, protect my honor." Who knows what she'd planned to do with the contents—maybe float it downstream or something—but she hadn't yet had the chance.

Bas. She bowed before the lamps.

"Eternal Goddess Lamps, keep my honor!" Then she brought the trunk down and set it on the ground. She opened it up.

Inside, there was a necklace worth nine hundred thousand. An incredibly gorgeous, fabulous necklace studded with gems and diamonds.

"Where is this from?" asked the King.

She said openly, "This was a gift from my parents."

The King's eyes grew big. "If you have parents that give such a precious necklace, then they must be wealthy and powerful people. I want to visit your parents' place. I must see where they live!"

So the poor thing was filled with anguish. After all, what was there to see, what was there to show? Once again, she bowed before the lamps. "Oh Eternal Goddess Lamps, keep my honor."

Then the King issued the command for a certain date: "On this date we will go to your parents' place." He was such an important person, with such enormous wealth, he traveled with a whole army of attendants to make his arrangements: hordes of men. And she kept burning the lamps, making the vow. "Just as you preserved my honor here, do this there too. You must definitely keep my honor for me."

Bas. So they all got ready and set off. Her heart was thumping: "What am I going to show as my parents' place when we arrive? Who knows what the grace of the lamps is, and what we will find there?"

When they arrived, there was a huge palace! She led the King into it. A huge, huge palace with a kitchen filled with workers and all kinds of arrangements for the King, arrangements for his horse-riders and for their horses, arrangements for his elephant-riders and their elephants. There was room for all the attendants: places to sit, places to wander. There were arrangements made for everything.

Bas. Now the Barber had accompanied the group. Everyone ate and drank, they did this and that. And the Barber hung from a hook his satchel with all his things for shaving. Then after much eating and drinking, they all turned back.

As they were proceeding, when they were halfway home, the Barber said, "Oh no! My satchel has been left behind." All of his things were in it. "It was left behind," he said.

Now she had asked for a parent's place for just two-and-a-half days. Before the two-and-a-half days were up, they had all set off. The Barber returned along that same path. But there was not even a blade of grass there. There was a withered tree that had been a window, and there hung his satchel. Otherwise, not even a blade of grass.

When the Barber came back with his satchel, he told the King, "This is a hugely astounding matter!"

The King said, "What?"

The Barber said, "It's an enormous puzzle."

"What?"

"When I went to fetch my satchel there wasn't even a blade of grass: just one tree with my satchel hanging on it. Otherwise, nothing, not even a blade of grass."

The King said, "You're lying."

"No, sir, come along and take a look. What would I get out of telling a lie? There's not even a blade of grass there."

Then the King asked her, "What is this? What's going on? Tell me the full truth."

She said, "Just don't ask me the truth about this matter. Otherwise, that will be the end of me. I'll die."

He said, "Whether you live or you die, I must know the truth of this matter. Tell me, what illusion did you set dancing?"

Bas. Then she told him everything that had come to pass for her. How she had such and such a mother, how there was nothing to eat, how the mother would fetch materials and they would eat. How she had thought that if the mother recognized her, they would have to go out collecting food all over again. "I had my mother killed. Then I put her in a trunk, but you wanted to see it. I prayed to the lamps that I light, making a vow, asking them to protect my honor. When you opened the trunk there was a necklace worth nine hundred thousand inside. You asked me 'Who gave this to you?' and I said that my parents had. Then you were possessed with the whim: 'We must go there.' I made a vow to the lamps, asking them to give me that place for two-and-a-half days."

Bas. She told him the whole story, and that was the end of her.

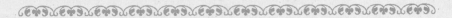

The Girl Made of Butter

BAHAMAS

Once was a time, a very good time,
Monkey chew tobacco and spit white lime.

There was a woman. She had a daughter who was made entirely of butter. Tom and William used to come courting her, and they didn't know this about her. So the woman never let those boys near her daughter, lest she melt with the heat. But, one day, she got so busy cooking for these two boys, the woman forgot to keep watch, and the boys saw their chance. They came and sat down next to the girl. The girl started singing while the woman was in the kitchen cooking, trying to remind her.

Momma, come wash my skin,
Momma, come wash my skin!
Move off, Tom! move off, William!
Till my momma has washed my skin.

The girl started melting because her mother wasn't there to wash her skin with cool water. She melted from her head down to her shoulders.

Momma, come wash my skin,
Momma, come wash my skin!
Move off, Tom! move off, William!
Till my momma has washed my skin.

She started melting more. She melted from her shoulder down to her waist. She started singing again:

Momma, come wash my skin,
Momma, come wash my skin!
Move off, Tom! move off, William!
Till my momma has washed my skin.

She melted from her waist down to her knees. All that time the woman was in the kitchen cooking, while her daughter was melting. The girl started singing again:

> Momma, come wash my skin,
> Momma, come wash my skin!
> Move off, Tom! move off, William!
> Till my momma has washed my skin.

She melted from her knees down to her feet. When the woman did remember, she cried out, "Oh, my butter daughter! Oh, my butter baby!" She had forgotten all about her daughter. When she did go back in the house, she only found a pile of melted butter but no one else. Tom and William were gone.

The bow bended, my story ended.

· *Conversation* ·

JANE: What to do when it is *that* time in your girl child's life:

1. Sit down calmly and explain sex to her?
2. Buy her a book, video, or CD that gives her the details?
3. Buy her condoms and put her on the pill?

Or do as many mothers before you did—just stick your head in the sand and hope she joins a convent.

Of course these days your child may know much more about sex than you did at her age, what with in-school health lessons, and out-of-school R-rated movies easily accessed on the TV, not to mention the Starr Report!

In the days of the fairy tales, sex was dangerous because so many women died in childbirth. Today sex is again dangerous because of diseases like AIDS. So what do we say?

Can we still be as innocent as my friend Patricia Maclachlan's mother when Patty came home wanting to know what the word "fuck" meant.

And her mother said, "Oh, Patty, it's a fine and wonderful thing that will happen to you one day. One of the finest things. But perhaps it's best if you don't say it in public because it offends some people. Maybe you can write it down on a piece of paper and look at it until you are older."

My mother was never so creative. She simply left pamphlets from Kotex about "What Every Girl Should Know" in my room. And from them I learned how birds and bees and fish did it. I thought that fish sounded the cleanest, and I really hoped that was what humans did, too, swimming over a lovely spot in the river and depositing eggs. Because we were then living in Westport, Connecticut, near Long Island Sound, it wasn't as far-fetched an idea to me then as it seems now.

And I never quite got what those books like *Forever Amber*—which we passed around Bedford Junior High School from sweaty hand to sweaty hand—were all about, though I faithfully read the "dirty" parts while sitting in my bathroom at home, the water in the sink running, as my friend Stella had told me to do.

Dirty parts! Even Young Adult books these days have more sex in them than those old cherished trash books of yore.

HEIDI: I was twenty-eight when I found myself pregnant with Maddison. I was living with her father in the house that I owned; I was an adult. But admitting to you on the phone that I was pregnant was the first time I had to truly admit that I had sex.

On the other hand, Brandon simply called his mother and said, "Hi Grandma!" She knew weeks before I got up the courage to tell you. And you had to tell Daddy. There was no way I was admitting the whole sex thing to him.

As a teen, you gave me the option of talking about it or getting a book. I, of course, chose the book.

But I talk to my girls with no problem. I guess it's easier to be the expert than the inquisitive kid. And, as you said, it is more important now than ever to talk about these things. AIDS didn't even become an issue until I was in college.

JANE: These folk stories, however, come from an even simpler time than the fifties, when I grew up, or even the eighties, when you did. They come from an age when a good girl was taught what she needed to know by her mother in a few swift sentences on her wedding night. Or a bad girl learned the same lessons for herself in the hayloft.

But except for those who went directly to the convent as infant oblates, or otherwise pledged themselves to the life of a spinster, that time always came sooner than mother was ready, even in fairy tales.

So in the first story, Maroula's mother, fearing that the worst may happen, decides not to send her daughter out where she may meet any more handsome boys. And after an adventure with the handsome boy (and what do you make of that blood running down her face, eh? or have I been reading too much Freud?), Maroula's happy ending is to stay back home with her mother forever.

The mother in "The Water Snake," though, first tries to save her girl child from snakes. (Snakes—oh Dr. Freud would really love this one!) And in the end, Mama bobbits him. Surprisingly—or maybe not—her daughter is not pleased.

In "Daughter, My Little Bread," sex, marriage, murder, and guilt are all rolled up into one big ball. But I think the daughter was feeling guilty long before she got around to killing her mother. Clearly Mom forgave her—see all the gifts she got from the corpse. But husbands are not so easily pleased.

I guess the moral of this whole sex-and-the-single-girl-child group of stories is murky. And even when a mother tries to do the right thing, like the mother in "The Girl Made of Butter," it is the girl who gets burned.

HEIDI: I see these stories as "coming-of-age" tales. There is a point in time where a girl becomes a woman (be that legally, sexually, or simply in her own mind) and then the relationship shifts between herself and her mother. I tell Lexi that being a teenager is like being pregnant. All those hormones running your body and very little control over it. "Mother" becomes synonymous with "idiot."

In "Maroula," the mother promises to give her child back at twelve. Although we now "give our daughters back" at the legal age of eighteen, the moral here to me is the same. Daughters grow up too quickly. You blink, and the sun—or some guy in a tuxedo—is coming for her or waiting to marry her at the front of the church. And that grown woman is the same person you held and fed and cared for on the day she was born.

This coming of age is seen quite literally in "Daughter, My Little Bread." The girl chooses to eat the smaller bread, which shows she has shifted from being taken care of by to caring for her mother. The change in relationship is too much for her mother, sending her spiraling into madness. The daughter, of course, runs off and marries the first kind man with a nice water pot. The quote "Now she was unhappy at home anyway. So the King took her" says it all.

In "The Water Snake" the mother takes the action that we mothers would all like to take when our daughters' virtue is compromised by a snake, Freud's cigar, or any other phallus. I know of several boys who—if I were a fairy-tale mom—would be dead in the water.

JANE: This is the moment I hold my hand firmly over my mouth and try not to laugh, remembering your old boyfriends. But it's hard. Oh, my—it is hard.

HEIDI: [Patently ignoring you.] As for the butter girl, I take this as a warning: Mothers, keep a close eye on your daughters.

JANE: So you see—we have talked about sex. Maybe not as much as we should. Certainly more than you would like. But every conversation has to start somewhere.

And as you said to me back in those days when I was trying to sit you down to talk about it—"Just get me a book, Mom!"

Persephone

$\mathcal{P}$ersephone

GREECE

Now once there was a time when there was no spring, neither summer nor autumn, nor chilly winter with its black frosts and cruel gales and brief, dark days. Always was there sunshine and warmth, ever were there flowers and corn and fruit, and nowhere did the flowers grow with more dazzling colours and more fragrant perfume than in the fair garden of Sicily.

To Demeter, the Earth Mother, was born a daughter more fair than any flower that grew, and ever more dear to her became her child, the lovely Persephone. By the blue sea, in the Sicilian meadows, Persephone and the fair nymphs who were her companions spent their happy days. Too short were the days for all their joy, and Demeter made the earth yet fairer than it was that she might bring more gladness to her daughter Persephone. Each day the blossoms that the nymphs twined into garlands grew more perfect in form and in hue, but from the anemones of royal purple and crimson, and the riotous red of geraniums, Persephone turned one morning with a cry of gladness, for there stood before her beside a little stream, on one erect, slim stem, a wonderful narcissus, with a hundred blossoms. Her eager hand was stretched out to pluck it, when a sudden black cloud over-shadowed the land, and the nymphs, with shrieks of fear, fled swiftly away. And as the cloud descended, there was heard a terrible sound, as of the rushing of many waters or the roll of the heavy wheels of the chariot of one who comes to slay. Then was the earth cleft open, and from it there arose the four coal-black horses of Pluto, neighing aloud in their eagerness, while the dark-browed god urged them on, standing erect in his car of gold.

In cold, strong arms Pluto seized her—in that mighty grasp that will not be denied, and Persephone wept childish tears as she shivered at his icy touch, and sobbed because she had dropped the flowers she had picked, and had never picked the flower she most desired. While still she saw the fair light of day, the little oddly-shaped rocky hills, the vineyards and olive-groves and flowery meadows of Sicily, she did not lose hope. Surely the King of Terrors could not steal one so young, so happy, and so fair. She had only tasted the joy of living, and fain she would drink deeper in the coming years. Her mother must surely save her—her mother who had never yet failed her—her mother, and the gods.

But ruthless as the mower whose scythe cuts down the seeded grass and the half-opened flower and lays them in swathes on the meadow, Pluto drove on. His iron-coloured reins were loose on the black manes of his horses, and he urged them forward by name till the froth flew from their mouths like the foam that the furious surf of the sea drives before it in a storm. Across the bay and along the bank of the river Anapus they galloped, until, at the river head, they came to the pool of Cyane. He smote the water with his trident, and downward into the blackness of darkness his horses passed, and Persephone knew no more the pleasant light of day.

So, to the great Earth Mother came the pangs that have drawn tears of blood from many a mortal mother's heart for a child borne off to the Shades.

The cry is borne down through the ages, to echo and re-echo so long as mothers love and Death is still unchained.

Over land and sea, from where Dawn, the rosy-fingered, rises in the East, to where Apollo cools the fiery wheels of his chariot in the waters of far western seas, the goddess sought out her daughter. With a black robe over her head and carrying a flaming torch in either hand, for nine dreary days she sought her loved one. And yet, for nine more weary days and nine sleepless nights the goddess, racked by human sorrow, sat in hopeless misery. The hot sun beat upon her by day. By night the silver rays from Diana's car smote her more gently, and the dew drenched her hair and her black garments and mingled with the saltness of her bitter tears. At the grey dawning of the tenth day her elder daughter, Hecate, stood beside her. Queen of ghosts and shades was she, and to her all dark places of the earth were known.

"Let us go to the Sun God," said Hecate. "Surely he hath seen the god who stole away the little Persephone. Soon his chariot will drive across the heavens. Come, let us ask him to guide us to the place where she is hidden."

Thus did they come to the chariot of the glorious Apollo, and standing by the heads of his horses like two grey clouds that bar the passage of the sun, they begged him to tell them the name of him who had stolen fair Persephone.

"No less a thief was he," said Apollo, "than Pluto, King of Darkness and robber of Life itself. Mourn not, Demeter. Thy daughter is safe in his keeping. The little nymph who played in the meadows is now Queen of the Shades. Nor does Pluto love her vainly. She is now in love with Death."

No comfort did the words of the Sun God bring to the longing soul of Demeter. And her wounded heart grew bitter. Because she suffered, others must suffer as well. Because she mourned, all the world must mourn. The fragrant flowers spoke to her only of Persephone, the purple grapes reminded her of a vintage when the white fingers of her child had plucked the fruit. The waving golden grain told her that Persephone was as an ear of wheat that is reaped before its time.

Then upon the earth did there come death and drought and barrenness.

Gods and men alike suffered from the sorrow of Demeter. To her, in pity for the barren earth, Zeus sent an embassy, but in vain it came. Merciless was the great Earth Mother, who had been robbed of what she held most dear.

"Give me back my child!" she said. "Gladly I watch the sufferings of men, for no sorrow is as my sorrow. Give me back my child, and the earth shall grow fertile once more."

Unwillingly Zeus granted the request of Demeter.

"She shall come back," he said at last, "and with thee dwell on earth forever. Yet only on one condition do I grant thy fond request. Persephone must eat no food through all the time of her sojourn in the realm of Pluto, else must thy beseeching be all in vain."

Then did Demeter gladly leave Olympus and hasten down to the darkness of the shadowy land that once again she might hold, in her strong mother's arms, her who had once been her little clinging child.

But in the dark kingdom of Pluto a strange thing had happened. No longer had the pale-faced god, with dark locks, and eyes like the sunless pools of a mountain stream, held any terrors for Persephone. He was strong, and cruel had she thought him, yet now she knew that the touch of his strong, cold hands was a touch of infinite tenderness. When, knowing the fiat of the ruler of Olympus, Pluto gave to his stolen bride a pomegranate, red in heart as the heart of a man, she had taken it from his hand, and, because he willed it, had eaten of the sweet seeds. Then, in truth, it was too late for Demeter to save her child. She "had eaten of Love's seed" and "changed into another."

Dark, dark was the kingdom of Pluto. Its rivers never mirrored a sunbeam, and ever moaned low as an earthly river moans before a coming flood, and the feet that trod the gloomy Cocytus valley were the feet of those who never again would tread on the soft grass and flowers of an earthly meadow. Yet when Demeter had braved all the shadows of Hades, only in part was her end accomplished. In part only was Persephone now her child, for while half her heart was in the sunshine, rejoicing in the beauties of earth, the other half was with the god who had taken her down to the Land of Darkness and there had won her for his own. Back to the flowery island of Sicily her mother brought her, and the peach trees and the almonds blossomed snowily as she passed. The olives decked themselves with their soft grey leaves, the corn sprang up, green and lush and strong. The lemon and orange groves grew golden with luscious fruit, and all the land was carpeted with flowers. For six months of the year she stayed, and gods and men rejoiced at the bringing back of Persephone. For six months she left her green and pleasant land for the dark kingdom of him whom she loved, and through those months the trees were bare, and the earth chill and brown, and under the earth the flowers hid themselves in fear and awaited the return of the fair daughter of Demeter.

And evermore has she come and gone, and seedtime and harvest have never failed, and the cold, sleeping world has awakened and rejoiced, and heralded with the song of birds, and the bursting of green buds and the blooming of flowers, the resurrection from the dead—the coming of spring.

The Sun's Daughter

CHEROKEE, NORTH AMERICA

The Sun lived on the other side of the sky vault, but her daughter lived in the middle of the sky, directly above the earth, and every day as the Sun was climbing along the sky arch to the west she used to stop at her daughter's house for dinner.

Now, the Sun hated the people on the earth, because they could never look straight at her without screwing up their faces. She said to her brother, the Moon, "My grandchildren are ugly; they grin all over their faces when they look at me." But the Moon said, "I like my younger brothers; I think they are very handsome"—because they always smiled pleasantly when they saw him in the sky at night, for his rays were milder.

The Sun was jealous and planned to kill all the people; so every day when she got near her daughter's house she sent down such sultry rays that there was a great fever and the people died by hundreds, until everyone had lost some friend and there was fear that no one would be left. They went for help to the Little Men, who said the only way to save themselves was to kill the Sun.

The Little Men made medicine and changed two men to snakes, the Spreading-adder and the Copperhead, and sent them to watch near the door of the daughter of the Sun to bite the old Sun when she came next day. They went together and hid near the house until the Sun came, but when the Spreading-adder was about to spring, the bright light blinded him and he could only spit out yellow slime, as he does to this day when he tries to bite. She called him a nasty thing and went by into the house, and the Copperhead crawled off without trying to do anything.

So the people still died from the heat, and they went to the Little Men a second time for help. The Little Men made medicine again and changed one man into a great Uktena and another into the Rattlesnake and sent them to watch near the house and kill the old Sun when she came for dinner. They make the Uktena very large, with horns on his head, and everyone thought he would be sure to do the work, but the Rattlesnake was so quick and eager that he got ahead and coiled up just outside the house, and when the Sun's daughter opened the door to look out for her mother, he sprang up and bit her and she fell dead in the doorway. He forgot to wait for the old Sun, but went back to the people, and the Uktena was so very angry that he went back, too. Since then we pray to the rattlesnake and do not kill him, because he is kind and never tries to bite if we do not disturb him. The Uktena grew angrier all the time and very dangerous, so that if he even looked at a man, that man's family would die. After a long time the people held a council and decided that he was too dangerous to be with them, so they sent him up to Galunlati, and he is there now. The Spreading-adder, the Copperhead, the Rattlesnake, and the Uktena were all men.

When the Sun found her daughter dead, she went into the house and grieved, and the people did not die any more, but now the world was dark all the time, because the Sun would not come out. They went again to the Little Men, and these told them that if they wanted the Sun to come out again they must bring back her daughter from Tsusginai, the Ghost country, in Usunhiyi, the Darkening land in the west. They chose seven men to go, and gave each a sourwood rod a hand-breadth long. The Little Men told them they must take a box with them, and when they got to Tsusginai they would find all the ghosts at a dance. They must stand outside the circle, and when the young woman passed in the dance they must strike her with the rods and she would fall to the ground. Then they must put her into the box and bring her back to her mother, but they must be very sure not to open the box, even a little way, until they were home again.

They took the rods and a box and traveled seven days to the west until they came to the Darkening land. There were a great many people there, and they were having a dance just as if they were at home in the settlements. The young woman was in the outside circle, and as she swung around to where the seven men were standing, one struck her with his rod and she turned her head and saw him. As she came around the second time another touched her with his rod, and then another and another, until at the seventh round she fell out of the ring, and they put her into the box and closed the lid fast. The other ghosts seemed never to notice what had happened.

They took up the box and started home toward the east. In a little while the girl came to life again and begged to be let out of the box, but they made no answer and went on. Soon she called again and she said she was hungry, but still they made no answer and went on. After another while she spoke again and called for a drink and pleaded so that it was very hard to listen to her, but the men who carried the box said nothing and still went on. When at last they were very near home, she called again and begged them to raise the lid just a little, because she was smothering. They were afraid she was really dying now, so they lifted the lid a little to give her air, but as they did so there was a fluttering sound inside and something flew past them into the thicket and they heard a redbird cry, "kwish! kwish! kwish!" in the bushes. They shut down the lid and went on again to the settlements, but when they got there and opened the box it was empty.

So we know the Redbird is the daughter of the Sun, and if the men had kept the box closed, as the Little Men told them to do, they would have brought her home safely, and we could bring back our other friends also from the Ghost country, but now when they die we can never bring them back.

The Sun had been glad when they started to the Ghost country, but when they came back without her daughter she grieved and cried, "My daughter, my daughter," and wept until her tears made a flood upon the earth, and the people were afraid the world would be drowned. They held another council, and sent their handsomest young men and women to amuse her so that she would stop crying. They danced before the Sun and sang their best songs, but for a long time she kept her face covered and paid no attention, until at last the drummer suddenly changed the song, when she lifted up her face, and was so pleased at the sight that she forgot her grief and smiled.

Rolando and Brunilde
ITALY

A mother and her daughter lived in a village. The daughter was happy because she was engaged to a boy who lived in the same village, a woodcutter, and they were to be married within a few weeks. So she passed all her time helping her mother a little, working in the fields a little, gathering wood a little; and then in her free time she sat at the window and sang . . . as she spun. She spun and she sang, waiting for her fiancé to return from the forest.

One day, a magician passed through town, and he heard singing; she had a pretty voice. He turned around and saw this girl at the window. Seeing her and falling in love with her was one and the same for the magician. And so he sent . . . he sent someone to ask if she would marry him. This prin . . . this girl said, "No, because I am already engaged to be married. I have a fiancé and I am very fond of him," she replied, "and in a few weeks we are getting married," she said, "so I don't need a magician or these riches," because he had told her that he would make her a rich lady because she was poor.

Then the magician, who had become indignant at her refusal, sent an eagle to kidnap the girl, who was called Brunilde, and it carried her to his castle where he showed her all his riches, all his castles, all his gold, all his money, but she didn't care about any of it. She said, "I will marry Rolando and I want Rolando." The magician then told her, "If you don't marry me then you will never leave this castle." And in fact he locked her up . . . he locked her in a room near his bedroom. Since the magician slept very soundly during the night and snored, for fear that someone would steal her he had an effigy made of himself as big as he was and then he had bells put on it, a thousand tiny bells, so that if anyone bumped into this effigy he would wake up.

Now, her mother and Rolando were worried because the girl didn't come home, and her fiancé wanted to go and kill the magician. But her mother said, "No, wait, let's wait a little." She said, "If not, he could hurt you, too; let's wait a bit." And they tried one night to get into the garden, but the magician had had a wall built that surrounded the garden and it was so tall that it was impossible to enter. And the girl's mother sat all day and cried.

Finally, one day when she was in the forest she came upon a fairy in the form of an old lady who said to her, "Tell me, why are you crying so?" And the girl's mother told the old woman about her Brunilde and how she had been carried off. "Listen," the fairy said, "listen, I don't have much power in this case because the magician is much more powerful than I. I can't do anything," she said. "However, I can help you," and she told her that he had closed the girl in a room and that he had had an effigy made of himself. So she said, "You can't go there because if one of those bells should ring, he'll wake up." She said: "Listen to what you should do. This is the season when the cotton falls from the trees. You should go every day and fill a bag with cotton. In the evening when Rolando comes home from the forest, you have him take the cotton to the castle and I'll help you crawl through a hole." She said: "I get the bag into the garden and you'll get inside the palace . . . into the castle. In the castle you must stuff a few bells each night with cotton. Until you have stuffed them all, so that they will not ring any more, then we'll see what we can do." And, in fact, this poor woman said: "Of course, I'll do it. It will take time but I'll do it gladly."

So they talked to the young man. During the day the mother gathered the cotton while he went to work, and in the evening they took the bag of cotton to the castle, and the mother stuffed the bells. Until one night the bells had finally all been stuffed. She went back to the old woman in the forest and told her that the last bell had been stuffed that same evening. Then the old woman said, "Take Rolando with you." And so the young man was made to enter through the same door that was used to stuff the bells, and the old woman gave him a sword and told him that when they were near enough he should cut off the left ear of the magician. All the power of the magician lies in his left ear, she said . . . In fact they entered the castle and went to get the girl. And the young man went to cut off the magician's ear. After he cut off the ear, the left ear where all his power lay, the entire castle crumbled, everything crumbled. The young couple took all the gold, the silver, and everything that belonged to the magician. They became rich, they got married, and they lived happily ever after.

The Singing Sack

SPAIN

There was once a mother who had an only daughter whom she loved very dearly; and because the girl was very good she had given her a pretty coral necklace. One day the child went to fill her pitcher with water at a fountain near the cottage. When she reached the fountain, she took off her coral necklace and put it down, so that it should not fall into the water as she filled her pitcher. A very hideous old beggar-man with a sack was seated at the fountain, and he gave the child such a terrible look that she was afraid, and scarcely stayed to fill her pitcher before she ran away, quite forgetting the necklace in her fright.

When she reached home the girl remembered her necklace, and ran back to the fountain to seek it; but when she arrived the old beggar, who was still seated there, seized her and thrust her into his sack. He then went on his way begging alms from door to door, saying that he carried a wonderful thing with him, *a sack that could sing.* The folks wished to hear it, so the old rogue cried out with a voice of thunder:

> *"Sing, sack, sing;*
> *Or your neck I will wring!"*

The poor girl, half dead with fear, had no help but to sing, which she weepingly did, as follows:

"I went to the well for water—
   The well near by my home,
And I lost my coral necklace,
   That came from far off Rome.
Alas! my darling mother,
How troubled you will be!

"I went to the well to seek it—
   But could not find it there;
I have lost my coral necklace;
   My necklace rich and rare!
Alas! my darling mother,
How saddened you will be!

"Oh, I could not find my necklace—
   My mother's gift to me!
Oh, I could not find my necklace—
   And I lost my liberty!
Alas! my darling mother,
How wretched you will be!

The poor child sang this so well, that the people were very glad to listen to her; and everywhere much money was given glad to the old man to hear the sack sing.

Going thus from house to house, at last he arrived at the home of the girl's mother, who at once recognized her daughter's voice, and therefore, said to the beggar:

"Father, the weather is very bad; the wind increases and the rain falls; shelter yourself here to-night, and I will give you some supper."

The old rascal was very willing; and the girl's mother gave him so much to eat and drink that he became stupid, and after his supper went to sleep, and slept as sound as a top. Then the mother drew her little darling out of the sack, where she was nearly frozen, and gave her many kisses and a good warm supper, and put her to bed. She then put a dog and a cat into the sack.

The following morning the old beggar thanked her, and went away. On arriving at the next house, he said his usual say of:

"Sing, sack, sing,
   "Or your neck I will wring!"

when the dog answered,

> *"Old rogue, bow-wow;"*

and the cat added,

> *"Old thief, mieau-mieau."*

In a rage, the beggar, thinking it was the girl who said this, opened the sack to punish her, when the dog and cat sprang out furiously; and the cat jumped at his face and clawed out his eyes, whilst the dog bit a piece out of his nose.

· *Conversation* ·

✳

JANE: When I was a child, I loved the story of Persephone. The fierceness of her mother's love seemed extraordinary to me. Would my own mother, I wondered, wreck a world to find me?

Oh, my mother had her own fierce side. When Carl Switzer and his gang of P.S. 93 boys chased me down Central Park West calling names and asking for a kiss, my not-quite-five-foot-tall mother would lean out of the fourth-floor window and shout: "Carl Switzer, you leave Janie alone." The very power of her voice sent those boys running.

My mother was held up once by knife-point in the lobby of our apartment building. She said to the thief, "Now you put that thing away before somebody gets hurt and I will see if I have anything in my purse." When the knife was put away, she took out a dollar and told the young man to buy himself a bowl of soup "and think about your life." Again, the power of her voice sent a miscreant on his way.

But she was still not in Demeter's class. Nor do I think would she have wanted to be. The reason I say this is that as an adult—and a mother and a grandmother—I read the story of Persephone now with a shudder.

There is an obsessiveness at the core of this tale. In psychologist Shari Thurer's wonderful phrase (from her book *The Myths of Motherhood*),

Demeter "literally raised hell (in this case Hades) to repossess her abducted daughter." Demeter in her madness almost destroys the world. This is not mother as nurturer but mother as overprotector. Evelyn Bassoff, in *Mothers and Daughters: Loving and Letting Go,* describes Demeter as demanding "exclusive right to this child." Even the gods come to beg Demeter to calm down; they offer her a bribe, try to talk some sense into her. Bassoff concludes that Demeter then has a chance to "create a personal meaning out of [her] maternal losses."

It depends whether you read the story as a tale of child abuse—in which an overpowering male steals a child away—or as the elopement of two consenting adults. Read the latter way, with Persephone adult enough to "eat the seeds of love," and make the decision to stay with her "husband," and co-rule the underworld with him as his queen, then maybe it's time for mother to butt out.

HEIDI: "We are never so defenseless against suffering as when we love." Freud said it, although not, I think, about motherhood.

I never understood why you refused to watch movies or TV shows about missing children when I was younger. Not even if they had happy endings. I think I saw it as a weakness on your part. When Maddison was born, I finally figured it out. And, with Lexi, I know that I am more strict with her than you were with me. I feel bad about that. But I don't lessen the rules.

That being said, I'd like to point out the interesting differences between the actions of the four mothers in these stories, all of which bring about the return of their daughters, although not always in the way they intended. In "Persephone," the mother appeals to the gods, searches on her own, and—as you mentioned—raises hell. She wins a compromise of sorts, getting her daughter back for half the year. In "The Singing Sack," the mother is not overcome by her emotions; instead she uses her wiles in order to overpower her daughter's abductor. She wins total freedom for her child and even exacts a bit of revenge when the cat and dog claw out the man's eyes and bite off a chunk of his nose. In "Rolando and Brunilde" the mother gets someone else to do the dirty work, like hiring a detective. Finally, in "The Sun's Daughter," the mother is distraught to the point of crippling depression, though it's only fair to mention that in her case, her daughter was dead as opposed to abducted (but retrievable nonetheless). Her depression galvanizes others, but she is less instrumental in the almost-return of her beloved daughter.

A lesson on dealing with grief? Perhaps.

JANE: But is it grief? Or is it anger? Or is it guilt?

I remember the moment after a dinner at your neighbor Jennifer's, when we all discovered that two-year-old Maddison was missing. She had left Jennifer's and run across the cul-de-sac on her own, heading toward your house.

How we all galvanized for the search in the fading light. How we searched Jennifer's house. How we ran out into the street, distraught. But what I felt at that moment was not grief. It was fear compounded by guilt. Why hadn't we watched her more carefully? Why hadn't she been under our eyes, under our hands, the entire time?

Yet if the missing child had been fourteen-year-old Lexi, our reactions would have been different. We would have been ticked off that she had left without saying anything. We would have assumed she was on the phone. Or out with friends. We would have shrugged off her disappearance at first because she was just being a teenager.

What these folk stories don't tell us is the age of the daughter, which is important to our response. Still, I think the mother's reactions are either excessive ("Persephone") or guilt-ridden ("Sun") or extraordinarily brave ("Sack"). However, I would probably have hired the heavy hitter to cut off the magician's ear ("Rolando").

HEIDI: Actually, I had gone home for a little while when Maddison left Jennifer's, so I only knew she was missing when she banged on the back door and I let her in with me.

I do recall, however, the time she decided to hide in the clothing racks at T.J. Maxx. You and Lexi were frantically looking for her but I calmly planted myself in front of the outside door. She might have been lost for the moment, but she was not leaving that store without me.

I have also lost track of Lexi. Scary, but to a different degree. And with a great deal of anger mixed in. But we were lucky. Both girls made it home safely.

Hearing about my grandmother and the knife incident for the first time, I realize I have a lot in common with her. I was also mugged—by three large boys. I was twenty-one at the time and fearless. While the assailants beat up and tried to rob my two male friends, I jumped in the largest guy's face and started yelling at him. The muggers ran away, I'm sure more from shock than fear, but run away they did.

I have calmed considerably since my college days, but I have developed great sharp "mommy claws" which come out when one of my babies (of any age) is threatened.

JANE: My friend Christine Crow, a British poet and novelist, just sent me a Persephone poem she wrote about her mother. Christine is very close to her mother, Stella, who lives in the house next door. The poem goes in part:

Stars, "stellata," oh, all stars!
Only here, living by my side, my mother, Stella, bears that name.
By that same echo of the myth led now in shame back to her life,
I wake in tears to the betrayed, and, grateful spiral from the earth
(remember now that dusty bank on which we lay like some strange birth
the mother from the daughter's younger thigh?)
rise to her lantern there above, Demeter to Persephone restored.

That, of course, reverses the natural order. In her poem, the child gives birth to the mother, loses and seeks the mother, and the mother is finally restored to the child. Christine hears the story of Persephone from a different perspective, as she now mothers her own mother, who has been ill. In the poem, the daughter worries that death will soon be claiming Stella, which is of course the more natural order, mother before child.

What these Persephone stories remind me is that I count on that normal order: that as I outlived my mother, you will outlive me. I think of my Aunt Rose Yolen, who has buried two of her three children—my cousin Burt from an acute asthma attack when he was in his late forties, his sister Michelle a few years afterward from a brain tumor. Aunt Rose has accepted the awful inevitability with a calmness and grace that I do not think I could muster.

My father's mother took to her bed with a smallpox fever, along with her four children. When she got up days later, only one child was still alive. I wrote a poem about it years ago that was published in 1990.

SMALLPOX

My grandmother lay down
in her Russian bed,
two children at her breast,
one child at her back,
and one curled doglike at her feet,
all touched by fire
and the calculus of pain.
They lay in their sweat like herrings in brine.

Ykaterinislav,
Ykaterinislav,
who mourns the children,
who calculates their loss,
the village so halved,
it was beyond crying.
She lay down with four,
arose with one.
How could she get up,
knowing God's casual mathematics,
the subtraction that so divided
her uncountable heart.

If such a thing—God forbid—had happened to me, I guess I would go mad and create a scorched earth policy. So maybe I am Demeter after all.

HEIDI: In both "Persephone" and "The Sun's Daughter," the fertility of the earth is tied to the mother-daughter relationship. Take away the daughter, and the earth suffers a barren fate.

A natural conclusion, I suppose, because it is we daughters who bear grandchildren. It is we daughters who bring ongoing life.

JANE: As your father likes to remind me, according to Darwin what makes us "fit" is not having children, but having grandchildren.

HEIDI: Men traditionally think of their sons as their immortality. I don't think it is a stretch to think that mothers place as much importance on their daughters. Certainly we can read that in these tales as well.

JANE: Another thing you can read in these stories is what psychologists call separation anxiety. Demeter has it the worst, of course. If you think of Persephone as a teenager who has gone off with an unsuitable mate (only unsuitable in Demeter's eyes, of course, since he is a king, after all!), Persephone sure makes a big fuss.

I read somewhere that Demeter focuses so intently on Persephone that she projects onto her daughter her own hopes and aspirations. In other words, Demeter both inflates and smothers the child. I remember reading that with a horrid shock of recognition, realizing suddenly: I am Demeter!

When you went off to college, I had such a big dose of separation blues that I wrote to you every day for the first year. This was before e-mail, of course, which would have made things easier. I don't know if you found the constant mail oppressive, but by the second year, my need to write to you daily had abated. Or else my Demeter side had come to her senses.

Nowadays I find myself jealous of women whose children live close by. Grandmother Demeter lives again! Recently visiting a Chicago friend whose daughter and family live in a downstairs apartment, I was all but gnashing my teeth in envy. A grandbaby within easy reach.

And then suddenly I realized: I have the time—and ability—to visit you and the girls whenever I want. How blessed I am. This could have been a hundred years ago, and you and your husband gone west by oxcart, never to be heard from again. Or like my own grandmothers, come across the ocean from Eastern Europe, leaving the known world behind.

HEIDI: As I keep telling you, move somewhere warm and I'll buy a house down the block. We may not be separated by earth and hell, but by something almost as strong—that seventy-degree comfort level. You can't stand anything above, and I can't live in anything below.

JANE: I suppose that makes the Persephone story an exact metaphor for our lives—you live in a hot place (Hades) and I hate that you live there.

HEIDI: I suppose, although I don't think I live in hell.

But let's turn back for a moment to what you said about a mother focusing so intently on her offspring. I know that I live vicariously though my girls sometimes, especially when I don't have some other project going on. This is true for many mothers, especially ones like myself who stay at home and raise the kids as our job; our motherhood becomes our primary identity.

You may have stayed at home, too, but you were much more the professional than I am. You at least had an office. I, on the other hand, have my computer in the playroom.

JANE: You won't remember this, but my first office as a mom was the playroom in our house in Conway and you stayed happily in your playpen, which was snugged up to my desk.

Whenever you made pick-me-up noises, I was right there. And that's how I wrote through my first two babies. Only when we moved to the other side of the state and I had a third child did I get my own writing room.

HEIDI: Really? Then I feel much better.

Did you know that some past theories went so far as to suggest that women who reject motherhood also reject femininity. This is not to say that we believe that en masse, especially in this country, but even today women who are without children seem to be an anomaly instead of a normal choice.

So do we pressure our children to be all that we want them to be? Yes. And is this justified in the name of a mother's love? Are you more proud of me because I am a writer like you? Would Demeter have been prouder of Persephone if she had followed in her mother's footsteps as the Goddess of Earth instead of becoming the Queen of the Underworld?

JANE: Well, writing as a profession is certainly safer than what you did before—probation officer and then private detective. You handled guns and perps and knew your way around rough neighborhoods. So I am certainly happier now that you are not in immediate and daily danger.

But *more* proud? That's a loaded question.

I think most mothers want their daughters safe, happy, and secure. And certainly, if she is in a work situation to be proud of, any mother would be honored to find the daughter following in her footsteps. But there is, within that pride, also a certain measure of competition. Blythe Danner applauding her daughter Gwyneth Paltrow's win of the Oscar could certainly be excused a moment's pang of jealousy. When you and I submitted poems to the same anthology and my poems were bounced but yours got in, I was proud—and pissed!

Maybe Demeter isn't just upset that her daughter has been torn from her side. Maybe she doesn't want her daughter to be Queen of the Underworld, which is, in itself, as great a position as her own.

HEIDI: These stories can certainly bring a lot of feminist issues to light. In "Persephone" and "The Sun's Daughter," the mothers are all-powerful goddesses. However, in "The Singing Sack" and "Rolando and Brunilde" these mothers aren't in charge of something as important as the earth or sun, yet they show the type of grace under pressure that we all hope for and try to instill in our daughters.

But more interesting to me is a lesson that could be taken from "Persephone" regarding women's place in a man's world. The daughter of a powerful woman is taken by an even more powerful man (with the permission—in some versions of this tale—of the girl's all-powerful father). But an odd, almost Hollywood moment happens. What starts out as an abduction becomes a seduction. The girl, although allowed to return to her mother's world on a part-time basis, is never fully part of that world because she has tasted the seed of the man's world. This loss of virginity forever exiles her from the world created for her by her mother. Once that innocence is gone, she is doomed to live in a man's world no matter how hard her mother tries to re-create the fecund woman's world for her.

JANE: So by extension, leaving the safety of the mother world for the man world (joining the army, the corporation, the academy, etc.) is also a loss of innocence?

Then we daughters best be careful what we eat!

Really Good Mothers

The Mother

LEBANON

This story took place in the north of Lebanon in the village of Hamadin. And the happening, as told, goes like this:

In the village lived a widow and her beautiful daughter, an only child. One day the girl became ill and was ordered to rest. And so she lay on her bed near the window and looked out at the only tree in the yard. Thus, days, weeks, months passed, and the autumn came. But the girl's condition didn't improve. On the contrary, she grew worse. And so, one day, as she looked at the tree, she said weakly, "You see, Mother, see those leaves. When the last leaf falls, I will die." The mother's heart grieved, and she watched anxiously as the leaves fell.

One cold night the wind howled, and the mother's heart was full of despair, as she saw the wind taking the last leaves. With every leaf her heart sank even deeper. At last there was only one leaf left. What could she do?

So the poor woman ran outside, unaware of the cold, the gusts of wind, and the storm. She approached the wall in front of the tree, and there she painted, on that wall, a picture of the last leaf. So good, so accurate was the drawing that it looked like the real leaf itself.

When the girl awoke, she looked out the window, and there she saw one lonely leaf. Days and weeks passed. From time to time she looked out, and always she saw that last leaf, still hanging on to the branch of the tree. A new spirit entered the girl. Slowly, slowly she recovered, and at last she got well.

But the mother, by going out on that windy night, had caught cold. She developed tuberculosis, and soon died.

When the girl was able to leave her bed, she went outside to see the miracle that had occurred: Why had that leaf not fallen?

And what did she see? The painting, done by her mother, which had cost her her life for her child's sake.

Then the girl realized her mother's great love, and grieved greatly for her mother who, in her own death, had given life to her.

The Mirror of Matsuyama

JAPAN

In ancient days there lived in a remote part of Japan a man and his wife, and they were blessed with a little girl, who was the pet and idol of her parents. On one occasion the man was called away on business in distant Kyoto. Before he went he told his daughter that if she were good and dutiful to her mother he would bring her back a present she would prize very highly. Then the good man took his departure, mother and daughter watching him go.

At last he returned to his home, and after his wife and child had taken off his large hat and sandals he sat down upon the white mats and opened a bamboo basket, watching the eager gaze of his little child. He took out a wonderful doll and a lacquer box of cakes and put them into her outstretched hands. Once more he dived into his basket, and presented his wife with a metal mirror. Its convex surface shone brightly, while upon its back there was a design of pine-trees and storks. The good man's wife had never seen a mirror before, and on gazing into it she was under the impression that another woman looked out upon her as she gazed with growing wonder. Her husband explained the mystery and bade her take great care of the mirror.

Not long after this happy home-coming and distribution of presents the woman became very ill. Just before she died she called to her little daughter, and said: "Dear child, when I am dead take every care of your father. You will miss me when I have left you. But take this mirror, and when you feel most lonely look into it, and you will always see me." Having said these words she passed away.

In due time the man married again, and his wife was not at all kind to her stepdaughter. But the little one, remembering her mother's last words, would retire to a corner and eagerly look into the mirror, where it seemed to her she saw her dear mother's face, not drawn in pain as she had seen it on her death-bed, but young and beautiful.

One day this child's stepmother chanced to see her crouching in a corner over an object she could not quite see, murmuring to herself. This ignorant woman, who detested the child and believed that her stepdaughter detested her in return, fancied that this little one was performing some strange magical art—perhaps making an image and sticking pins into it. Full of these notions, the stepmother went to her husband and told him that his wicked child was doing her best to kill her by witchcraft.

When the master of the house had listened to this extraordinary recital he went straight to his daughter's room. He took her by surprise, and immediately the girl saw him she slipped the mirror into her sleeve. For the first time her doting father grew angry, and he feared that there was, after all, truth in what his wife had told him, and he repeated her tale forthwith.

When his daughter had heard this unjust accusation she was amazed at her father's words, and she told him that she loved him far too well ever to attempt or wish to kill his wife, who she knew was dear to him.

"What have you hidden in your sleeve?" said her father, only half convinced and still much puzzled.

"The mirror you gave my mother, and which she on her death-bed gave to me. Every time I look into its shining surface I see the face of my dear mother, young and beautiful. When my heart aches—and oh! it has ached so much lately—I take out the mirror, and Mother's face, with sweet, kind smile, brings me peace, and helps me to bear hard words and cross looks."

Then the man understood and loved his child the more for her filial piety. Even the girl's stepmother, when she knew what had really taken place, was ashamed and asked forgiveness. And this child, who believed she had seen her mother's face in the mirror, forgave, and trouble forever departed from the home.

The Dead Woman and Her Child

SALISHAN (NATIVE AMERICAN), NORTH AMERICA

A woman who had given birth to a daughter died when the child was only a few days old. The people buried the mother, and tried to rear the child by feeding it. The baby, however, was not satisfied, and cried. One night, when it was crying after the people had gone to bed and the fire had gone out, the mother came into the house and suckled it. She remained with it until almost daylight, when she returned to her grave. She did so many nights, and the people wondered that the child was thriving so well and did not cry during the night. They also noticed in the morning that there was dried milk around the child's mouth, and other signs that it had been suckled. They thought this was strange, and asked two old women to watch. About midnight the child cried. Then her mother approached, calling "Tcuxhwî's.ūūū, tcɛx.ū′ūū." The dead woman descended the ladder, calling her child in a low voice. She lay down with it, and remained until near daybreak. The old women told the people that a woman had come in and suckled the child, and they believed that she was its mother. They made preparations to capture her when she should come back the next night. They boiled some medicine, and had a large bucketful of it ready. They tore up some dry cedar-bark, and held it in readiness to make a blaze at any moment. They covered the fire with ashes to keep it alive. They also had split pitchwood ready to start a big fire. Four shamans took their places at the north, south, east, and west, ready to hold the woman. At midnight she came to the top of the ladder, and called to her child as before, but she hesitated a long time before she came down. She seemed to know that something was wrong. However, when her baby continued to cry, she slowly climbed down the ladder. When she reached the child, the four shamans seized her, and held her fast. She (or her soul) tried to escape by going underground and in the air, but the shamans blocked her passage at every point. Others lighted a bright fire, and still others threw medicine on her. At last they tamed her. Her struggles ceased, and finally she became like any other woman. She lay down quietly and suckled her child.

Some years after this, when her daughter was grown up, they went together to bring food from their cellar. The girl sat down at the entrance, while the mother opened the cellar. When she looked in, she saw that it was full of mice, which scampered about in every direction. While she was looking at the mice, she became transformed into one of them, and finally disappeared among them. The girl sat outside and cried, because her mother had become a mouse. The people took her home.

$\mathcal{U}$bazakura

JAPAN

Three hundred years ago, in the village called Asamimura, in the district called Onsengori, in the province of Iyo, there lived a good man named Tokubei. This Tokubei was the richest person in the district and headman of the village as well. In most matters he was fortunate, but he had reached the age of forty without knowing the happiness of becoming a father. Therefore he and his wife, in the affliction of their childlessness, addressed many prayers to the divinity Fudo-Sama, who had a famous temple called Saihoji in Asamimura. At last their prayers were heard. The wife of Tokubei gave birth to a daughter. The child was very pretty, and she received the name of O-Tsuyu. A nurse called O-Sodé was hired for the little one.

O-Tsuyu grew up to be a very beautiful girl, but at the age of fifteen she fell ill and the doctors thought she was going to die. The nurse O-Sodé, who loved O-Tsuyu with a real mother's love, went to the temple Saihoji and fervently prayed to Fudo-Sama on behalf of the girl. Every day for twenty-one days she went to the temple and prayed, and at the end of that time O-Tsuyu suddenly and completely recovered. There was great rejoicing in the house of Tokubei, and he gave a feast to all his friends in celebration of the happy event. But on the night of the feast the nurse O-Sodé was suddenly taken ill, and on the following morning, the doctor who had been summoned to attend her announced that she was dying.

The family in great sorrow gathered about her bed to bid her farewell. But she said to them, "It is time that I should tell you something. My prayer has been heard. I besought Fudo-Sama that I might be permitted to die in the place of O-Tsuyu, and this great favor has been granted to me. Therefore you must not grieve for my death; but I have one request to make. I promised Fudo-Sama that I would have a cherry tree planted in the garden of Saihoji for an offering of thanks and a commemoration. Now I shall nor be able to plant the tree there myself, so I must ask you to fulfill that vow for me. Goodbye, dear friends, and remember that I was happy to die for O-Tsuyu's sake."

After the funeral of O-Sodé, a young cherry tree, the finest that could be found, was planted in the garden of Saihoji by the parents of O-Tsuyu. The tree grew and flourished, and on the sixteenth day of the second month of the following year, the anniversary of O-Sodé's death, it blossomed in a wonderful way. And so it continued to blossom every year on this same date for two hundred and fifty-four years, always upon the sixteenth day of the second month, and its flowers, pink and white, were the most beautiful ever seen.

The people called it *Ubazakura*, the Cherry Tree of the Nurse.

The Three Fairies

PUERTO RICO

There was once a widow who had a very pretty, kind, and good daughter. Being sickly, the woman worried much about dying and leaving her daughter alone in the world. Every night she prayed that the girl would find a good husband who would care for and protect her.

The girl was indeed virtuous and industrious. But not flirtatious at all. Nor yet coy. Nor coquettish. So the young men of the town, being more jocund than judicious, avoided her.

There was in that place a wealthy *señor* who was looking for a girl to marry. A hardworking girl. A comely girl. A good girl. Well, you say, so there's the story. The *señor* married the widow's daughter, and that was that. Nooooo . . . there were complications, and that was *not* that. At least not right away.

True, the *señor* did come to visit the widow. True, he admired the daughter greatly—and said so. True, the widow was most encouraging, pointing out her daughter's attractions: her quietness, her diligence, her tenderness, her flawless complexion, her honey-hued hair, the beauty mark on her chin, and on and on.

"But," inquired the *señor*, who had been pondering, "can she spin? Can she sew? Can she embroider? For in my business there is much of cotton and silk."

"*Por supuesto*, naturally she can sew, spin and embroider to a fare-thee-well. There is nothing that girl cannot do. She spins a thread as fine as a spider's. Her stitches are smaller than the footprints of a fly. She can embroider a bird so you reach to stroke its feathers."

"In that case," announced the *señor*, "it is settled. If she is *that* good a spinner, a sewer, an embroiderer, I will marry her. I shall arrange at once for the wedding." And away he went.

The widow was overjoyed. You would have thought *she* was the one getting married. And what did the daughter have to say? (Though it was by now rather late for her to say anything, even about her own marriage.)

"Mama, I heard what you said. How could you be so foolish? I know little of sewing, nothing of embroidery, and less of spinning. What will that *señor* think of me when we are married?"

"You are the foolish one, daughter. Surely there is a solution to the problem. All you have to do is think of it. I did this for your good, you well know."

When she went to bed that night the poor girl wept a thousand or more tears thinking of the terrible lies her mother had told. Not to speak of what might befall *her* for having deceived the *señor*. She had just resolved to go to him early the next day and confess the truth about herself when she heard a slight noise. Sitting up, she saw three strangers. On top of everything else! The poor girl wept harder than ever.

However, the strangers assured her they were fairies and had come to help her. Their only condition, they said, would be an invitation to her wedding. The girl was only too happy to consent, saying they could come as her dearest relatives. They disappeared, and the girl fell asleep.

Days passed and preparations were made for the wedding. The girl informed her *novio* that she had invited a few of her cousins whom she loved very much to come to the wedding feast.

The day of the celebration arrived, passed and died away. That night all the wedding guests sat down at the table for dinner. Three chairs remained vacant.

"For whom are these reserved?" asked the groom.

At that moment came a knock at the door. It opened and three old horrors entered whom the girl introduced as her cousins.

Dinner was served, and the whole world was content and ate tremendously. When it was over the husband arose and went to speak to the girl's kin, who were now his cousins as well as his wife's.

He asked the first, "Hear me, cousin. Will you tell me why you are so humped and one-eyed?" (A blunt man, the bridegroom.)

"*Ay*, my son! From all the embroidery I did in my life."

The husband whispered to his wife, "From now on I forbid you to embroider. I can pay to have this done and I do not wish you to be so deformed as your unlucky cousin."

Then he asked the second, "And why is it your two arms are so unequal?"

"Because I have spent my whole life spinning."

The *señor* took his wife's hand. "Nevermore will you spin, my love."

And finally he questioned the third of the cousins. "What is the matter with your eyes, that they burst from your head as grapes from their skins?"

"Ah, so would yours if your life had been spent sewing and reviewing tiny stitches."

"This, my dear, shall not happen to you," said the *señor*, turning to his wife. "You are to do no more sewing. None at all."

The very next day the husband gathered up all his wife's sewing equipment and hurled it out the door, since he cared more for his wife's beauty than all the work she could do. The two lived most happily and the girl never had to grieve herself to explain away the lies her poor mother had told.

Habetrot the Spinstress

SCOTLAND

In byegone days, in an old farmhouse which stood by a river, there lived a beautiful girl called Maisie. She was tall and straight, with auburn hair and blue eyes, and she was the prettiest girl in all the valley. And one would have thought that she would have been the pride of her mother's heart.

But, instead of this, her mother used to sigh and shake her head whenever she looked at her. And why?

Because, in those days, all men were sensible: and instead of looking out for pretty girls to be their wives, they looked out for girls who could cook and spin, and who gave promise of becoming notable housewives.

Maisie's mother had been an industrious spinster; but, alas! to her sore grief and disappointment, her daughter did not take after her.

The girl loved to be out of doors, chasing butterflies and plucking wild flowers, far better than sitting at her spinning-wheel. So when her mother saw one after another of Maisie's companions, who were not nearly so pretty as she was, getting rich husbands, she sighed and said:

"Woe's me, child, for methinks no brave wooer will ever pause at our door while they see thee so idle and thoughtless." But Maisie only laughed.

At last her mother grew really angry, and one bright spring morning she laid down three heads of lint on the table, saying sharply, "I will have no more of this dallying. People will say that it is my blame that no wooer comes to seek thee. I cannot have thee left on my hands to be laughed at, as the idle maid who would not marry. So now thou must work; and if thou hast not these heads of lint spun into seven hanks of thread in three days, I will e'en speak to the Mother at St. Mary's Convent, and thou wilt go there and learn to be a nun."

Now, though Maisie was an idle girl, she had no wish to be shut up in a nunnery; so she tried not to think of the sunshine outside, but sat down soberly with her distaff.

But, alas! she was so little accustomed to work that she made but slow progress; and although she sat at the spinning-wheel all day, and never once went out of doors, she found at night that she had only spun half a hank of yarn.

The next day it was even worse, for her arms ached so much she could only work very slowly. That night she cried herself to sleep; and next morning, seeing that it was quite hopeless to expect to get her task finished, she threw down her distaff in despair, and ran out of doors.

Near the house was a deep dell, through which ran a tiny stream. Maisie loved this dell, the flowers grew so abundantly there.

This morning she ran down to the edge of the stream, and seated herself on a large stone. It was a glorious morning, the hazel trees were newly covered with leaves, and the branches nodded over her head, and showed like delicate tracery against the blue sky. The primroses and sweet-scented violets peeped out from among the grass, and a little water wagtail came and perched on a stone in the middle of the stream, and bobbed up and down, till it seemed as if he were nodding to Maisie, and as if he were trying to say to her, "Never mind, cheer up."

But the poor girl was in no mood that morning to enjoy the flowers and the birds. Instead of watching them, as she generally did, she hid her face in her hands, and wondered what would become of her. She rocked herself to and fro, as she thought how terrible it would be if her mother fulfilled her threat and shut her up in the Convent of St. Mary, with the grave, solemn-faced sisters, who seemed as if they had completely forgotten what it was like to be young, and run about in the sunshine, and laugh, and pick the fresh spring flowers.

"Oh, I could not do it, I could not do it," she cried at last. "It would kill me to be a nun."

"And who wants to make a pretty wench like thee into a nun?" asked a queer, cracked voice quite close to her.

Maisie jumped up, and stood staring in front of her as if she had been moonstruck. For, just across the stream from where she had been sitting, there was a curious boulder, with a round hole in the middle of it—for all the world like a big apple with the core taken out.

Maisie knew it well; she had often sat upon it, and wondered how the funny hole came to be there.

It was no wonder that she stared, for seated on this stone was the queerest little old woman that she had ever seen in her life. Indeed, had it not been for her silver hair, and the white mutch with the big frill that she wore on her head, Maisie would have taken her for a little girl, she wore such a very short skirt, only reaching down to her knees.

Her face, inside the frill of her cap, was round, and her cheeks were rosy, and she had little black eyes, which twinkled merrily as she looked at the startled maiden. On her shoulders was a black and white checked shawl, and on her legs, which she dangled over the edge of the boulder, she wore black silk stockings, and the neatest little shoes, with great silver buckles.

In fact, she would have been quite a pretty old lady had it not been for her lips, which were very long and very thick, and made her look quite ugly, in spite of her rosy cheeks and black eyes. Maisie stood and looked at her for such a long time in silence that she repeated her question.

"And who wants to make a pretty wench like thee into a nun? More likely that some gallant gentleman should want to make a bride of thee."

"Oh, no," answered Maisie, "my mother says no gentleman would look at me because I cannot spin."

"Nonsense," said the tiny woman. "Spinning is all very well for old folks like me my lips, as thou seest, are long and ugly because I have spun so much, for I always wet my fingers with them, the easier to draw the thread from the distaff. No, no, take care of thy beauty, child; do not waste it over the spinning-wheel, nor yet in a nunnery."

"If my mother only thought as thou dost," replied the girl sadly; and, encouraged by the old woman's kindly face, she told her the whole story.

"Well," said the old Dame, "I do not like to see pretty girls weep; what if I were to help thee, and spin the lint for thee?"

Maisie thought that this offer was too good to be true; but her new friend bade her run home and fetch the lint; and I need not tell you that she required no second bidding.

When she returned she handed the bundle to the little lady, and was about to ask her where she should meet her in order to get the thread from her when it was spun, when a sudden noise behind her made her look round.

She saw nothing; but what was her horror and surprise, when she turned back again, to find that the old woman had vanished entirely, lint and all.

She rubbed her eyes, and looked all round, but she was nowhere to be seen. The girl was utterly bewildered. She wondered if she could have been dreaming, but no, that could not be, there were her footprints leading up the bank and down again, where she had gone for the lint, and brought it back, and there was the mark of her foot, wet with dew, on a stone in the middle of the stream, where she had stood when she had handed the lint up to the mysterious little stranger.

What was she to do now? What would her mother say when, in addition to not having finished the task that had been given her, she had to confess to having lost the greater part of the lint also? She ran up and down the little dell, hunting amongst the bushes, and peeping into every nook and cranny of the bank where the little old woman might have hidden herself. It was all in vain; and at last, tired out with the search, she sat down on the stone once more, and presently fell fast asleep.

When she awoke it was evening. The sun had set, and the yellow glow on the western horizon was fast giving place to the silvery light of the moon. She was sitting thinking of the curious events of the day, and gazing at the great boulder opposite, when it seemed to her as if a distant murmur of voices came from it.

With one bound she crossed the stream, and clambered on to the stone. She was right.

Someone was talking underneath it, far down in the ground. She put her ear close to the stone, and listened.

The voice of the queer little old woman came up through the hole. "Ho, ho, my pretty little wench little knows that my name is Habetrot."

Full of curiosity, Maisie put her eye to the opening, and the strangest sight that she had ever seen met her gaze. She seemed to be looking through a telescope into a wonderful little valley. The trees there were brighter and greener than any that she had ever seen before; and there were beautiful flowers, quite different from the flowers that grew in her country. The little valley was carpeted with the most exquisite moss, and up and down it walked her tiny friend, busily engaged in spinning.

She was not alone, for round her were a circle of other little old women, who were seated on large white stones, and they were all spinning away as fast as they could.

Occasionally one would look up, and then Maisie saw that they all seemed to have the same long, thick lips that her friend had. She really felt very sorry, as they all looked exceedingly kind, and might have been pretty had it not been for this defect.

One of the Spinstresses sat by herself, and was engaged in winding the thread, which the others had spun, into hanks. Maisie did not think that this little lady looked so nice as the others. She was dressed entirely in grey, and had a big hooked nose, and great horn spectacles. She seemed to be called Slantlie Mab, for Maisie heard Habetrot address her by that name, telling her to make haste and tie up all the thread, for it was getting late, and it was time that the young girl had it to carry home to her mother.

Maisie did not quite know what to do, or how she was to get the thread, for she did not like to shout down the hole in case the queer little old woman should be angry at being watched.

However, Habetrot, as she had called herself, suddenly appeared on the path beside her, with the hanks of thread in her hand.

"Oh, thank you, thank you," cried Maisie. "What can I do to show you how grateful I am?"

"Nothing," answered the Fairy. "For I do not work for reward. Only do not tell your mother who spun the thread for thee."

It was now late, and Maisie lost no time in running home with the precious thread upon her shoulder. When she walked into the kitchen she found that her mother had gone to bed. She seemed to have had a busy day, for there, hanging up in the wide chimney in order to dry, were seven large black puddings.

The fire was low, but bright and clear; and the sight of it and the sight of the puddings suggested to Maisie that she was very hungry, and that fried black puddings were very good.

Flinging the thread down on the table, she hastily pulled off her shoes, so as not to make a noise and awake her mother; and, getting down the frying-pan from the wall, she took one of the black puddings from the chimney, and fried it, and ate it.

Still she felt hungry, so she took another, and then another, till they were all gone. Then she crept upstairs to her little bed and fell fast asleep.

Next morning her mother came downstairs before Maisie was awake. In fact, she had not been able to sleep much for thinking of her daughter's careless ways, and had been sorrowfully making up her mind that she must lose no time in speaking to the Abbess of St. Mary's about this idle girl of hers.

What was her surprise to see on the table the seven beautiful hanks of thread, while, on going to the chimney to take down a black pudding to fry for breakfast, she found that every one of them had been eaten. She did not know whether to laugh for joy that her daughter had been so industrious, or to cry for vexation because all her lovely black puddings—which she had expected would last for a week at least—were gone. In her bewilderment she sang out:

> "My daughter's spun se'en, se'en, se'en,
> My daughter's eaten se'en, se'en, se'en,
> And all before daylight."

Now I forgot to tell you that, about half a mile from where the old farmhouse stood, there was a beautiful castle, where a very rich young nobleman lived. He was both good and brave, as well as rich; and all the mothers who had pretty daughters used to wish that he would come their way, some day, and fall in love with one of them. But he had never done so, and everyone said, "He is too grand to marry any country girl. One day he will go away to London Town and marry a Duke's daughter."

Well, this fine spring morning it chanced that this young nobleman's favourite horse had lost a shoe, and he was so afraid that any of the grooms might ride it along the hard road, and not on the soft grass at the side, that he said that he would take it to the smithy himself.

So it happened that he was riding along by Maisie's garden gate as her mother came into the garden singing these strange lines.

He stopped his horse, and said good-naturedly, "Good day, Madam; and may I ask why you sing such a strange song?"

Maisie's mother made no answer, but turned and walked into the house; and the young nobleman, being very anxious to know what it all meant, hung his bridle over the garden gate, and followed her.

She pointed to the seven hanks of thread lying on the table, and said, "This hath my daughter done before breakfast."

Then the young man asked to see the Maiden who was so industrious, and her mother went and pulled Maisie from behind the door, where she had hidden herself when the stranger came in; for she had come downstairs while her mother was in the garden.

She looked so lovely in her fresh morning gown of blue gingham, with her auburn hair curling softly round her brow, and her face all over blushes at the sight of such a gallant young man, that he quite lost his heart, and fell in love with her on the spot.

"Ah," said he, "my dear mother always told me to try and find a wife who was both pretty and useful, and I have succeeded beyond my expectations. Do not let our marriage, I pray thee, good Dame, be too long deferred."

Maisie's mother was overjoyed, as you may imagine, at this piece of unexpected good fortune, and busied herself in getting everything ready for the wedding; but Maisie herself was a little perplexed.

She was afraid that she would be expected to spin a great deal when she was married and lived at the castle, and if that were so, her husband was sure to find out that she was not really such a good spinstress as he thought she was.

In her trouble she went down, the night before her wedding, to the great boulder by the stream in the glen, and, climbing up on it, she laid her head against the stone, and called softly down the hole, "Habetrot, dear Habetrot."

The little old woman soon appeared, and, with twinkling eyes, asked her what was troubling her so much just when she should have been so happy. And Maisie told her.

"Trouble not thy pretty head about that," answered the Fairy, "but come here with thy bridegroom next week, when the moon is full, and I warrant that he will never ask thee to sit at a spinning-wheel again."

Accordingly, after all the wedding festivities were over and the couple had settled down at the Castle, on the appointed evening Maisie suggested to her husband that they should take a walk together in the moonlight.

She was very anxious to see what the little fairy would do to help her; for that very day he had been showing her all over her new home, and he had pointed out to her the beautiful new spinning wheel made of ebony, which had belonged to his mother, saying proudly, "To-morrow, little one, I shall bring some lint from the town, and then the maids will see what clever little fingers my wife has."

Maisie had blushed as red as a rose as she bent over the lovely wheel, and then felt quite sick, as she wondered whatever she would do if Habetrot did not help her.

So on this particular evening, after they had walked in the garden, she said that she should like to go down to the little dell and see how the stream looked by moonlight. So to the dell they went.

As soon as they came to the boulder Maisie put her head against it and whispered, "Habetrot, dear Habetrot"; and in an instant the little old woman appeared.

She bowed in a stately way, as if they were both strangers to her, and said, "Welcome, Sir and Madam, to the Spinsters' Dell." And then she tapped on the root of a great oak tree with a tiny wand which she held in her hand, and a green door, which Maisie never remembered having noticed before, flew open, and they followed the fairy through it into the other valley which Maisie had seen through the hole in the great stone.

All the little old women were sitting on their white chucky stones busy at work, only they seemed far uglier than they had seemed at first; and Maisie noticed that the reason for this was, that, instead of wearing red skirts and white mutches as they had done before, they now wore caps and dresses of dull grey, and instead of looking happy, they all seemed to be trying who could look most miserable, and who could push out their long lips furthest, as they wet their fingers to draw the thread from their distaffs.

"Save us and help us! What a lot of hideous old witches," exclaimed her husband. "Whatever could this funny old woman mean by bringing a pretty child like thee to look at them? Thou wilt dream of them for a week and a day. Just look at their lips"; and, pushing Maisie behind him, he went up to one of them and asked her what had made her mouth grow so ugly.

She tried to tell him, but all the sound that he could hear was something that sounded like SPIN-N-N.

He asked another one, and her answer sounded like this: SPAN-N-N. He tried a third, and hers sounded like SPUN-N-N.

He seized Maisie by the hand and hurried her through the green door. "By my troth," he said, "my mother's spinning-wheel may turn to gold ere I let thee touch it, if this is what spinning leads to. Rather than that thy pretty face would be spoilt, the linen chests at the castle may get empty, and remain so for ever!"

So it came to pass that Maisie could be out of doors all day wandering about with her husband, and laughing and singing to her heart's content. And whenever there was lint at the castle to be spun, it was carried down to the big boulder in the dell and left there, and Habetrot and her companions spun it, and there was no more trouble about the matter.

· Conversation ·

JANE: Reading some of these stories, I feel as if I am being told that the only way to be a really good mother is to die. And not only to die, but to do so as a sacrifice for the beloved child.

And while I love you a lot . . .

That wound the death of a mother leaves may scab over, but it never really heals. I still think of my mother all the time. Maybe not daily, but certainly several times a week. And especially when I think about the pleasure my granddaughters give me, I realize how much she missed dying at fifty-nine. I am determined to live forever.

What I have missed most was having access to her mother-wisdom. All I had left to help me through my days of young mothering was that distilled stuff—the mother lines—which are the jokes made from old truths. I missed being able to call her up and ask her advice. I missed being able to ask her about my own childhood. Not having my mother to teach me mothering, I am left only with memory.

Journalist Cokie Roberts was recently on a tour supporting her book *We Are Our Mothers' Daughters*. She spoke about how women received sustenance—and even courage—from one another, as well as wisdom from earlier generations.

It is that thread of continuity that I miss—from my mother to her mother to the great-grandmother whose name I do not even know.

HEIDI: While I see your point about dying as a way to be a good mother, I would like to state that this is generally a way to become a good anything. We see this time and time again especially with public figures. Think of Princess Diana. We, the public, fed daily on tales of her misery. And of her silly twit boyfriends and her bad behaviors. As long as she was alive we could criticize her. And simultaneously many of us took the stance that we didn't really read that stuff anyway. But her tragic death raised her to an almost saintly status. We feel guilty for our public scrutiny and criticism of her life and we make up for it in her death.

I'm not implying that the mothers in these stories were subjects for tabloid fodder, but even the average relationships with their daughters pre-death were, I'm sure, marked with the usual problems, all forgotten postmortem. "Don't speak ill of the dead"—an all-encompassing rule of our society.

JANE: At least dead mothers get to miss those moments when daughters are embarrassed by them, as you were by me when I hummed in public. As I was by my mother when she walked hand-in-hand with my father along the sidewalks of Westport, Connecticut. As my mother was of her mother who took long walks every evening and could be seen by all the neighbors. (I think it was my grandmother's only escape from six children.)

I believe we each loved our mothers, but during adolescence we are struck with contradictory emotions, which Mary Pipher describes in *Reviving Ophelia* as "I respected her and mocked her, felt ashamed and proud of her, laughed with her and felt irritated by her smallest flaws." Interesting that while she is talking here about her mother, the mother might have said the same of her teenage daughter.

So much easier to make a saint or martyr out of a dead mother than live—at least through adolescence—with an embarrassment.

HEIDI: While it may be true that dead mothers are easier for adolescents to live with, I find it refreshing in "The Mirror of Matsuyama" that the sainted mother's gift is what brings the girl and her stepmother together. The second mother became "ashamed and asked forgiveness"—actually admitting to being wrong, something you don't see every day in fairy tales, let alone in life. In the longer versions of this tale we read, the stepmother even states that she will think of her stepdaughter as a child that she has borne herself, which forever moves her out of the evil-stepmother stereotype. I think the real story here is one of repentance and forgiveness.

On the other hand, "The Mother" reflects the horrors of possibly having to bury one's child. Most mothers feel that they would trade their own life for that of their child. I have often said that I would step in front of a bullet, a speeding bus, and any other fatal trajectory for my kids, and I mean it.

JANE: Yes, and I suppose—like the nurse who loved the daughter "with a real mother's love" in "Ubazakura"—we both would ask to be permitted to die in the child's place.

But here's a slightly different way to look at "The Mother": *Why didn't she bundle up?*

Of course my initial feeling on reading that story was one of pathos. I wept and thought, "I would have done the same." (By the way, I had first come across the tale in a complete book of O. Henry stories my mother gave me for my thirteenth birthday. Whether O. Henry took it from the Middle Eastern tale or his work has become incorporated into the oral tradition of Lebanon, I don't know.)

But by the second time I read it, all I could think was that the sick girl is still going to need her mother. So put a scarf on, lady. And earmuffs. A heavy coat. Nothing says you can't do your painting in the storm while properly dressed.

Dying is not a good mother's only option. It's her last one.

HEIDI: Does she protest too much?

But here's an interesting (and sad) note. There is a case going on as I write this involving a little girl whose body has rejected a transplanted kidney and her father, who gave her his first, has offered to donate his last kidney. He is a longtime prisoner and has no hope of getting out. However, there is no doctor who will operate, since it would most likely end the father's life. So, in essence, the law—or at least the Hippocratic oath—is preventing this parent from keeping one of the most basic promises we make to our children.

JANE: None of us is going to be able to come back from death and help our daughters (or our sons) literally, unless it is to donate an organ or leave money in a will. Not like the dead mother in the Salishan story nursing her baby when no one else can do the job. But we do come back in the family stories that are passed down, and in the photos and films of birthday parties, vacation trips, and other milestones. We see our mothers when we look in the mirror as the girl in Kyoto does. Is it enough to sustain us when our mothers are gone? It better be.

HEIDI: Since we're on the topic of death, I'd like to bring up Elisabeth Kübler-Ross, who is the best known authority in this field. She states that dealing with death (your mother's, your own impending death, as well as things less fatal such as the "death" of a relationship—really any kind of great loss) is marked by five stages.

I first read her book *On Death and Dying* in college just months before one of my dearest friends was killed in a helicopter crash. The book was instrumental in getting me through a tough time, and I lent it to so many friends that I finally lost it for good and had to purchase another copy in order to quote it here.

Kübler-Ross's five stages of grief consist of Denial and Isolation, Anger, Bargaining, Depression, and finally Acceptance. As a former grief counselor, I asked myself: At what stage are the girls in these stories? There seems to be an awful lot of denial going on. Will they come through to an acceptance of their mother's deaths? Does one ever?

JANE: There are days, almost thirty years later, when I am not sure I have come to accept my mother's death. I rarely see her sisters—my aunts Cicely, Lilian, Madeline—as if I blame them for still being alive and into their nineties when she has been gone so long.

These stories seem to me to miss what I know most about a mother's death, and that is its permanence. Good mother or bad mother, gone is gone. No mirror, no dry cedar bark, no painted wall is a good enough substitute. Just as none of my books will be compensation to you or your daughters when I'm gone. We remember both the good mothers and bad. Bad with relief. Good with continued grief, though that grief abates in time.

HEIDI: But what about the other stories, where the mother surrogates don't die, but they do lie to help their daughters? Is that a better choice?

JANE: A better choice? I think about the real-life stories I have heard: the mother who lies to the police about her child's whereabouts, the mothers who steal their daughters away from a reputed abusing husband, the mothers who take on school authorities even in the face of overwhelming evidence against their children.

Supposedly folktales carry a harder and truer morality. The great wisdom of stories from the old tradition. G. K. Chesterton wrote (and I used to quote it all the time), "If you really read the fairy-tales, you will observe that one idea runs from one end of them to the other—the idea that peace and happiness can only exist on some condition. This idea, which is the core of ethics, is the core of the nursery-tales."

But sometimes these stories surprise by their amorality. Even immorality.

Some of the tales in this section are prize examples. In each a lie or deception is practiced by a really good mother or mother substitute. The husband guiled by the three old spinners ("Habetrot") in order to spare a selfish and lazy girl. A bridegroom fooled by three shape-shifters ("The Three Fairies") to save a girl from having to explain her mother's lies. Morality's castle! It is often built on shifting sands.

Still, I remember the many times as a mother—or as a surrogate mother to the many young friends you and your brothers brought home—I battled with teachers, administrators, even police to try to make things easier for all of you. I am a product of the sixties sensibility that believed that there should be no punishment for what was not really a crime. I look back now and wonder if I should have been harder, colder, cooler, less willing to take the bullet for you all, like some Secret Service agent mother.

HEIDI: Trust me. You were tough enough.

I'm tougher. Just ask Maddison and Lexi.

These stories appeal to me both as a birth mother and as a foster mother, a surrogate for a biological mother who is unable—for whatever reason—to care for her child. As of this writing, I am legally Lexi's foster mother (the adoption is not final yet), but I'm not speaking of her here. I have fostered another teenage girl in our home, as well as given a shoulder, advice, and lots of free meals to dozens of teenagers. I even harbored a pair of short-term runaways.

Laughingly, I often say that I have more teenage friends than I do adult friends. All right, they're not really friends, but I certainly know more teenagers than I ever thought I would want to since graduating from high school myself.

Whether it is the primary caregiver—as the nurse in "Ubazakura"—or token aunts who may be fairies, the nonmother mother figures in these stories (and I add the snakes in "The Serpent Mother," which I wanted to be placed in this grouping as well) give to the girls what the mother cannot: family, advice, problem solving, and even life.

I was watching a TV movie last week while doing the dishes, or folding clothes, which means I watched it with half a mind. It was about two mothers, one biological and one not, who were fighting over their daughter. One of these women had a stepmother who reminisced about a neighbor to whom she went in times of trouble. She concluded by saying that everyone picks their own mother.

These stories brought that to the front of my mind. I think that most girls have a woman in their life whom they look up to in a motherly way, someone who can give them what their mother cannot. This in no way takes away from the girl's feelings for her actual mother. But the surrogate fills in the gaps. When you could do nothing about my choice of taboo subjects, I took those things to a teacher at school. Sally Ingram was my surrogate mom in my teen years.

JANE: As I had my cousin, Honey Knopp.

HEIDI: I have tried to steer Lexi and Maddison in the right direction when it comes to their fill-in-the-gap moms. Their godmothers are sisters: Andrea, who is a take-no-prisoners manager in a male-dominated field, and Tracy, who is a neonatal nurse with strong life goals and is continuing her education to achieve them. I'm hoping since they are such good role models that my girls will go to them when they feel they cannot come to me. Lexi already does this with Tracy, her godmother. Maddison will likely do this also when it's her time.

JANE: I used Honey as my political and spiritual godmother. She gave me a copy of *George Fox's Journal* when I was sixteen, which set me on the path toward Quakerism. She modeled pacifism and social activism, both of which became a part of my adult life. Though my own mother was a political liberal and mouthed good works, hers was a passive attitude. Honey taught me by doing.

HEIDI: Although our lives today are significantly different from the lives of the mothers and daughters in these tales, there is still a battle going on for women to find role models, mentors, or sponsors. Generally, we no longer find that this is needed within the family, but we speak of it when we talk of women in job and career situations bonding together against the traditional good-old-boy networks. Women are creating their own networks, sisterhoods, sororities.

✦

Hero Mother

✦

The Wife of the Monkey

CHINA

Once a very beautiful girl disappeared. Her mother was unable to eat or sleep for worry, and went about the whole day asking where her daughter was.

One day she was sitting in the yard bemoaning her loss when a sparrow flew down on the roof and began to twitter. "Dear sparrow," the mother said, "if you know where my daughter is and can lead me to her, I will give you a bushel of roasted beans."

The sparrow agreed. So the mother tied a red string on to the bird's tail as a sign, and they set off on their search. But the bird flew much quicker than the woman and was always waiting for her. Finally, it flew to a cave in the mountains, where it sat down on a stone and chirruped.

A girl came out of the cave, and was much surprised to see the red string on the sparrow's tail. "Where did you get the red string from our house?" she asked. "Your mother gave it to me," said the bird. "She will soon be here herself." While they were speaking, the mother arrived.

"What are you doing here, my child?" she asked. The daughter answered, "I was going for a walk in the village when a monkey came up and carried me off. He will be here in a moment. You must hide, because if he sees you he will eat you up!"

The mother had just time to hide under a jar before the monkey appeared. He sniffed and said, "Why is there such a smell of human flesh?" His wife tried to conceal it from him, but eventually, seeing there was nothing to be done, she told him the truth, "My mother is here but, fearing you would eat her, she hid under a jar." The monkey, however, was very pleased. "Your mother has come?" he said. "Tell her to come out quickly. I want to meet her," and he went and turned up the jar. The daughter said to him, "That is your mother-in-law," whereupon they embraced, and were very happy. The monkey then said, "Today, we have nothing good to eat. I will buy some meat and wine." He went out.

The mother and daughter decided to take this opportunity to run away.

First, the daughter told her mother to cook a pot of lime. When the little monkeys saw it, they asked, "Grandmother, what is that?" "It is a good eye medicine," she said, "but it isn't for children." "But we want some," said all the little monkeys. So she covered their eyes with lime, and then said to them, "Go in to the sun and let it dry." When it was dry, they could not open their eyes. Then the mother and daughter fled, taking with them all the gold and silver that the monkey had stored away.

When the old monkey came back and saw the little ones could not open their eyes, he asked them what had happened. They told him the whole story. He boiled a great pot of water and told the children to wash their eyes, but afterward there was a red rim around their eyes.

From then on, every morning the old monkey took the children down to the house of their mother. He sat down on the millstone in front of the house, and in a sad voice began to sing his song, "Monkey wife. Monkey wife. It is unnatural to leave your children. Your children weep, your husband is sad."

The girl began to be frightened as well as affected by the tragic song. She evolved a plan with her mother. One night they made the millstone red hot. In the morning the monkey came as usual with his children. When the little ones sat down on the stone they jumped up with a scream. "What's the matter?" cried the monkey. "I will sit down." He also leaped up with a scream of pain, and they all fled home together. When they looked at each other, all the hair was burned off their buttocks.

They never returned to look for their mother again. From that time, all monkeys have bare buttocks.

The Old Woman and the Giant
PHILIPPINES

In a cave near the village of Umang, there once lived a wicked and greedy giant. He would kill and eat anyone who happened to pass by the cave. That was why everybody tried to avoid the place.

But one day, an old woman, who had gone to the woods to gather fuel, lost her way and found herself near the giant's cave. Seeing her, the giant shouted, "Now, I'm going to kill and eat you, unless you can show me that you can make a louder noise than I."

This frightened the old woman. But being wise and shrewd, she kept her head.

"What good will it do you if you eat a skinny old woman like me?" she asked the giant. "But if you let me go, I'll fetch my daughter, who's young and stout. Then, if you can make more noise than the two of us together, you may kill both of us. And you'll really have something good to eat."

The giant's greed was aroused. And so he told the old woman, "All right, you may go. But be sure to come back and bring your stout daughter with you."

The old woman went home and returned as she had promised, bringing her daughter with her. She had a drum with her, while her daughter had a bronze gong.

As soon as they neared the cave, the old woman began to beat her drum. At the same time, the daughter beat her gong. The noise that they made was so great that the giant could not hear his own voice, no matter how hard he shouted.

When he could no longer stand the noise, the giant covered his ears with his hands. Then he dashed blindly out of the cave. And he fell into a great big hole.

That was the end of the wicked and greedy giant. And the people of the whole countryside rejoiced at his death.

· *Conversation* ·

JANE: I have written stories about strong women and mothers who have stood up for their children, but I have always wondered how I might act in similar circumstances. Would I—like the old woman against the giant—use my wits and get my daughter's help in defeating an overwhelming enemy? Could I—like the monkey's mother-in-law—find my child against all odds and rescue her from a brutal marriage?

Do any of us mothers truly know how we will react in bad situations? Only twice have I been even slightly tested with you. Once when I rescued you from a difficult relationship, sending you down to Florida to escape a seriously disturbed boyfriend. And once when you were sick with meningitis and I had to fly down while on crutches myself to nurse you, since your husband had his hands full with two children.

But it is in story that I act out the truly awful possibilities and come out of them a hero. Reading mysteries—my one guilty pleasure—I drink from the cup of borrowed courage. These two folk stories remind me how glad I am not to have to face the reality of a Littleton, Colorado, or an Auschwitz, or a Kosovo or Rwandan massacre, where daughters are taken from their mothers and slaughtered before their eyes.

I remember being twelve when a man approached me and asked me a question I did not quite understand. He even began to unbutton his fly. That, at least, I knew was wrong. Gathering my brother and my best friend with me, I ran screaming all the way home.

When we got to our apartment, my mother kept saying, "Did he do anything? Did he do anything?" while I wept on her big bed. But I didn't know what he was supposed to have done, only knew it was something frightening. *He* was something frightening.

I gulped and cried, "He said . . . he said . . ." But I could not say the words he had said.

My mother must have been terrified, but she never showed it. She remained strong and calm, which gave me strength and calmed me. It was years before I understood what could have happened, and what hadn't happened.

HEIDI: I'm glad you mentioned the Littleton, Colorado, school shooting because you and I have written half of our conversations for this book before the tragedy and half after.

So here I sit, the armchair critic, glued to the television. The condemner of bad parenting. I ask myself: Are the Littleton killers' parents responsible? Are the parents blameless?

All the kids involved—both killers and victims—are Lexi's age. Two shock-and-horror-filled teary days after the shooting, I picked Lexi up at school and told her I was revising my parenting. I said that I had been too lax.

No, I cannot stop stray bullets. I am not Superman, or even Supermom. But I can be a better protector—the only kind of hero that I know how to be—by making rules ("More rules, Mom?") that I hope will help protect my children. These rules include no going places with two or more boys without a female friend along. Lexi hates that.

JANE: You would have hated that, too. Your best friends in high school were boys. I was the same. I was the only girl in a group of five teenagers. They were really my friends, not romantic interests.

HEIDI: Different times, Mommy. You didn't have teenage boys shooting up their schools or giving their girlfriends the date-rape drug. And neither did I.

Another rule: I have to meet the boy Lexi plans to go somewhere with before she leaves the house—this works even better when my husband, Brandon, is home to scare the boy a bit.

Does this make me a hero? I've never had to rescue my daughters from a giant wanting to eat them or a crazed monkey kidnapper. But I'd like to think that if these two things represent the hidden dangers out there, I would do what I have to, be it mixing lime or banging a loud drum.

And the best start I can think of is to limit my daughters' exposure to those dangers, real or imagined. While this does not make me popular at home, it does keep the monkeys and giants of the world a little farther away from my girls.

JANE: A mother's job is not to win the Miss Congeniality contest. Still, we all want our daughters to love us, to admire us, to think we are the best mom in the entire universe.

But making rules and being a hero mom are two different things. We can warn and warn about such things as violence. Yet one study cited in *For All Our Daughters,* by Pegine Echevarria, reported that 18 percent of girls in grades five through twelve reported some form of physical or sexual abuse. We can warn about drugs, or alcohol abuse, or AIDS. We can make curfews and curtail allowances. But none of this helps when the giants threaten or the monkeys steal our daughters away.

I think of a colleague of mine, Lois Duncan, who has written many award-winning children's novels. She had a warm and open relationship with her daughter. And then her daughter was brutally murdered. The police basically gave up on the case. Lois has spent the last few years following leads herself, trying to solve the unsolvable, because she had not been able to save her daughter.

And I think of the mothers who put their children's faces on milk cartons and post office walls. Or follow brutal ex-husbands to foreign countries to try to win their children back. (Have you read *Mothers on Trial* by Phyllis Chesler? It was a landmark book back in 1986 when it was first published and it's now updated. All about the custodial rights of mothers, which is still an ongoing issue.)

Being a hero mom may not be possible. We simply aren't there all the time. We cannot take the bullet for our daughters in a high school massacre, or save them from date rape, or keep them from starving under a tree in Kosovso. But we can make rules. We can issue warnings. We can tell stories. And we can hope that it will be enough.

HEIDI: I have to point out that in both of these stories the daughter is an integral part of the plan to defeat the enemy. So it's actually the mother and daughter working together to defeat a common foe.

I like the working together part. Some mothers and daughters can never become a team like that. I wasn't sure we could. But after four books, half a dozen short stories, and this huge project, I suppose I can stop wondering.

JANE: I am not sure writing a book is the same as defeating an enemy. But maybe we can save one mother. Maybe we can save one child.

HEIDI: Now you sound like a cliché—"If I can just reach one child, it will all be worth it."

Maybe we shouldn't reach quite so high. Maybe the best we can hope for is to get some mothers and daughters talking.

✦

Grandmother

✦

Tuglik and Her Granddaughter

ESKIMO

Once there was a big narwhal hunt to which everyone went but an old woman named Tuglik and her granddaughter Qujapik. The two of them were getting rather hungry, but they hadn't any idea of how to hunt for their food. Yet old Tuglik knew a few magical words, which she uttered during a trance. All of a sudden she changed into a man. She had a seal-bone for a penis and chunk of *mataq* for testicles. Her vagina became a sledge. She said to her granddaughter:

"Now I can travel to the fjords and get some food for us."

The girl replied. "But what about dogs to pull your sledge?"

And so strong was the old woman's magic that she was able to create a team of dogs from her own lice. The dogs were barking and yelping and ready to go, so Tuglik cracked her whip and off she went with them to the fjords. Day after day she went off like this, and she would always return in the evening with some sort of game, even if it was only a ptarmigan or two. Once, while she was away hunting, a man came to their hut. He looked around and said:

"Whose harpoon is this, little girl?"

"Oh," said Qujapik, "it is only my grandmother's."

"And whose kayak is this?"

"Just my grandmother's."

"You seem to be pregnant. Who is your husband?"

"My grandmother is my husband."

"Well, I know someone who would make a better husband for you . . ."

Now the old woman returned home with a walrus thrown over her sledge. "Qujapik!" she called out, "Qujapik!" But there was no Qujapik at all. The girl had gathered up all her things and left the village with her new husband.

Tuglik saw no point in being a man any more—man or woman, it's all the same when a person is alone. So she uttered her magic words and once again she was a wrinkled old hag with a vagina instead of a sledge.

· Conversation ·

JANE: I had the most bizarre response to this story, which I found both repellent and fascinating. So I have tried to understand what bothers me about it—beyond the sex change and the genitalia. (Understand—I am not repelled by the mere fact of these things. I know at least three actual transsexuals and I do have my very own genitalia.)

I think what bothers me is threefold. First, the grandmother is a magic maker and a shape changer, yet she feels she cannot go and hunt for food unless she becomes a man. As a twentieth-century American woman, I find this annoying at best, and mortifying at worst. While I am not a hunter—and have an abhorrence for guns—one of my West Virginia sisters-in-law is a hunter and a state bow-and-arrow champion. One of our close neighbors was your father's hunting partner for years, and she was even keener than he to go out and sit in cold, dark, wet places in the forest.

At the same time, I am very aware that I am putting my own cultural biases first. Most likely the culture from which this story comes banned women from hunting.

But I am also appalled at the relationship of the grandmother and granddaughter in the story. The casual acceptance of what is, after all, incest really bothers me. I long ago learned that even in small subsistence cultures, the taboo against incest is exceedingly strong. Maybe that's incorrect?

Again, am I putting my own cultural perspective above the story-teller's? I can think of almost nothing worse than the sexual abuse of one's own children or grandchildren, so there is little likelihood that I can get rid of that mind-set.

Finally, there is the story's tacit assumption that the loss of the child/grandchild to marriage equals loneliness and incapacity. The grandmother is suddenly a "wrinkled old hag" where before she had been assertive, inventive, and strong. As both a mother and grandmother, I can tell you that having a daughter grow up to be independent is a wonderful thing. It did not make me enter worthless hagdom.

But all that being said, I have to admit I also have a spectacular knee-jerk reaction to words for genitals, even when they are as clinical as "vagina" and "penis."

The other words—the slang you can hear every day in R-rated movies, rap music, or the impeachment hearings—I cannot bear to say aloud, and certainly not write down with any ease.

HEIDI: Well, thank goodness for small favors! I tend not to use those words myself if I can help it. And although I can swear like any good trucker, I find myself in full mother mode here. Nothing will stop a mom from swearing (and I'm talking specifically about the anatomical swear words) faster than her cherubic three-year-old saying, "Mommy, these are my boobs!" And I'd like to note for the record that while she did learn "damn" and "hell" (two of my personal favorites) from my mouth, she did not hear "boobs" from me.

It's not too difficult to explain why we, as women, are embarrassed by this story. It is very blunt about the female body—using some of the words we don't like to say, even in the presence of our doctors. We were brought up to keep these body parts secret.

Even as infants little girls are treated differently. I have never had a friend with a baby boy—mother or father—who hasn't commented on the size of the newborn's genitalia. But I have never heard this from any girl's parents, myself included. I didn't set out to make Maddison ashamed of her body, but I think it's almost inevitable. My favorite quote is from her preschool teacher, who tells the girls to "put your goodies in your basket" before exiting the little girls' room. I think that says a lot about how we treat our girls.

JANE: I think it says a lot about living in the South. I cannot imagine a Massachusetts nursery school teacher saying that.

HEIDI: In researching this matter, I found a book called *Growing a Girl* by Dr. Barbara Mackoff. She writes: "We can teach [a daughter] to celebrate—rather than critique—her body." She goes on to suggest beginning with vocabulary.

But how can I make my daughter comfortable with words that I am not comfortable with? Now, although I cringe at the thought of even typing these words, I think it's important to mention here that, as Dr.

Mackoff points out, everyone knows that a boy has a penis, but the female counterpart, the vagina, is an internal organ, and not the entire area (which is externally made up of the clitoris and vulva—words I am *sure* I have never mentioned to Maddison).

My huge gap in vocabulary was especially evident the other day when Lexi was telling me of an injury a friend sustained and she used a slang term that she then felt she needed to define for me. I had to assure her that I *did* know what she meant.

JANE: The power that certain sexual words have over women is enormous. We are simply made mute by them. Some my mouth won't form; some actually hurt my ears. I didn't even say the f-word until I was in my early forties and you were about sixteen. In fact, it sprang from my lips as a curse, and you and your brothers were so excited that I finally said it, you wrote on a piece of paper: "Mommy said Fuck on December 20, 1982." Then the three of you—with great ceremony—pinned it to the bulletin-board wall in the TV room.

I don't think I have ever said the c-word for female genitals out loud, though when I play Boggle with my friend Andrew, I will sometimes use it in the Boggle pattern. The written word—so important to me as an author—does not have the embarrassment factor of the spoken word.

But do we learn to be at ease with certain words from our mothers or our peers? I think we are all bilingual in that way. We have our mother tongue, a vocabulary and grammar we speak with our parents, and another we speak with our friends. (And perhaps a third we speak on the job if we work outside the home.)

HEIDI: I agree with you that the vocabulary is only one thing that is difficult in this story. I also have a problem with the "women can't hunt" aspect to this story. But I guess I see it differently because I was brought up in a world that considers women as more equal (although not entirely) to men than the world you grew up in. I don't feel all sorts of pressure to defend myself or women in general, because there is less sexism now. I was never told I couldn't do something because of my gender, or at least not from anyone I took seriously.

As for dealing with incest, I suppose that I have seen far too much of it up close and personal, working for the Department of Corrections, a halfway house for felony boys, and as a foster mother. So I am not as stunned by it as you are. Where you see incest as this big horrible aberration, I have known too many people who have been there and survived—or not. I am not happy about the fact that incest no longer shocks me. And you certainly raised me as far away from the horrors of real life as you could. But I immersed myself fully in them as an adult because you also raised me to make a difference.

So I try.

Rapunzel

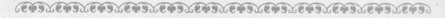

Rapunzel

GERMANY

There once lived a man and his wife who had long wished for a child, but in vain. Now there was at the back of their house a little window which overlooked a beautiful garden full of the finest vegetables and flowers; but there was a high wall all round it, and no one ventured into it, for it belonged to a witch of great might, and of whom all the world was afraid. One day when the wife was standing at the window, and looking into the garden, she saw a bed filled with the finest lettuce; and it looked so fresh and green that she began to wish for some; and at length she longed for it greatly. This went on for days, and as she knew she could not get the lettuce, she pined away, and grew pale and miserable.

Then the man was uneasy, and asked, "What is the matter, dear wife?" "Oh," answered she, "I shall die unless I can have some of that lettuce to eat that grows in the garden at the back of our house." The man, who loved her very much, thought to himself, "Rather than lose my wife I will get some lettuce, cost what it will."

So in the twilight he climbed over the wall into the witch's garden, plucked hastily a handful of lettuce and brought it to his wife. She made a salad of it at once, and ate of it to her heart's content. But she liked it so much, and it tasted so good, that the next day she longed for it thrice as much as she had done before; if she was to have any rest the man must climb over the wall once more. So he went in the twilight again; and as he was climbing back, he saw, all at once, the witch standing before him, and was terribly frightened, as she cried, with angry eyes, "How dare you climb over into my garden like a thief, and steal my lettuce! It shall be the worse for you!"

"Oh," answered he, "be merciful rather than just; I have only done it through necessity; for my wife saw your lettuce out of the window, and became possessed with so great a longing that she would have died if she could not have had some to eat."

Then the witch said, "If it is all as you say, you may have as much lettuce as you like, on one condition—the child that will come into the world must be given to me. It shall go well with the child, and I will care for it like a mother."

In his distress of mind the man promised everything; and when the time came when the child was born the witch appeared, and, giving the child the name of Rapunzel (which is the same as lettuce), she took it away with her.

Rapunzel was the most beautiful child in the world. When she was twelve years old the witch shut her up in a tower in the midst of a wood, and it had neither steps nor door, only a small window above. When the witch wished to be let in, she would stand below and would cry, "Rapunzel, Rapunzel! Let down your hair!"

Rapunzel had beautiful long hair that shone like gold. When she heard the voice of the witch she would undo the fastening of the upper window, unbind the plaits of her hair, and let it down twenty ells below, and the witch would climb up by it.

After they had lived thus a few years it happened that as the King's son was riding through the wood, he came to the tower; and as he drew near he heard a voice singing so sweetly that he stood still and listened. It was Rapunzel in her loneliness trying to pass away the time with sweet songs. The King's son wished to go in to her, and sought to find a door in the tower, but there was none. So he rode home, but the song had entered into his heart, and every day he went into the wood and listened to it.

Once, as he was standing there under a tree, he saw the witch come up, and listened while she called out, "Oh Rapunzel, Rapunzel! Let down your hair."

Then he saw how Rapunzel let down her long tresses, and how the witch climbed up by them and went in to her, and he said to himself, "Since that is the ladder, I will climb it, and seek my fortune." And the next day, as soon as it began to grow dusk, he went to the tower and cried, "Oh Rapunzel, Rapunzel! Let down your hair." And she let down her hair, and the King's son climbed up by it.

Rapunzel was greatly terrified when she saw that a man had come in to her, for she had never seen one before; but the King's son began speaking so kindly to her, and told how her singing had entered into his heart, so that he could have no peace until he had seen her herself. Then Rapunzel forgot her terror, and when he asked her to take him for her husband, and she saw that he was young and beautiful, she thought to herself, "I certainly like him much better than old mother Gothel," and she put her hand into his hand, saying, "I would willingly go with you, but I do not know how I shall get out. When you come, bring each time a silken rope, and I will make a ladder, and when it is quite ready I will get down by it out of the tower, and you shall take me away on your horse."

They agreed that he should come to her every evening, as the old woman came in the daytime. So the witch knew nothing of all this until once Rapunzel said to her unwittingly, "Mother Gothel, how is it that you climb up here so slowly, and the King's son is with me in a moment?"

"O wicked child," cried the witch, "what is this I hear! I thought I had hidden you from all the world, and you have betrayed me!"

In her anger she seized Rapunzel by her beautiful hair, struck her several times with her left hand, and then grasping a pair of shears in her right— snip, snap—the beautiful locks lay on the ground. And she was so hard-hearted that she took Rapunzel and put her in a waste and desert place, where she lived in great woe and misery.

The same day on which she took Rapunzel away she went back to the tower in the evening and made fast the severed locks of hair to the window hasp, and the King's son came and cried, "Rapunzel, Rapunzel! Let down your hair."

Then she let the hair down, and the King's son climbed up, but instead of his dearest Rapunzel he found the witch looking at him with wicked, glittering eyes.

"Aha!" cried she, mocking him, "you came for your darling, but the sweet bird sits no longer in the nest, and sings no more; the cat has got her, and will scratch out your eyes as well! Rapunzel is lost to you; you will see her no more."

The King's son was beside himself with grief, and in his agony he sprang from the tower; he escaped with life, but the thorns on which he fell put out his eyes. Then he wandered blind through the wood, eating nothing but roots and berries, and doing nothing but lament and weep for the loss of his dearest wife.

So he wandered several years in misery until at last he came to the desert place where Rapunzel lived with her twin children that she had borne, a boy and a girl. At first he heard a voice that he thought he knew, and when he reached the place from which it seemed to come, Rapunzel knew him, and fell on his neck and wept. And when her tears touched his eyes they became clear again, and he could see with them as well as ever.

Then he took her to his kingdom, where he was received with great joy, and there they lived long and happily.

ℒanjeh

MOROCCO

Once there was a monster who, every day, would go off into the forest to hunt for food, and there devour plants, animals, anything it could.

Now, this monster had a home, set deep in the forest near a grazing pasture, as large and luxurious as the home of a wealthy person. It lacked for nothing. And, upon arriving home each day, the monster would chant a certain spell, then to be transformed into a beautiful woman, and, thus, enjoy the luxury of her palatial home, while, outside the house, it remained a ferocious beast.

One day, while rummaging about in some ancient ruins hidden in a deep cave in the forest, the monster came upon a cradle, shaped like an egg. From the cradle came a weak, thin voice. "Please, please don't eat me."

Greatly frightened, the monster asked, "Who are you? Where do you come from, the land of demons or the land of humans?"

"From the land of humans," squeaked the voice.

So then the monster slowly opened the cradle, and behold! There within lay a beautiful girl, whom the monster took home and adopted as a daughter. The girl was called Lanjeh.

Now, when the mother went out to hunt, she locked the girl in the last and highest room of the many rooms in that house, so that Lanjeh was out-of-sight, should anyone by chance come upon that house. And, every morning, before leaving, the monster would wash and clean the girl's lovely black hair, which seemed to become even more beautiful as she grew. In the evening the mother would check and count the girl's lovely hair to make sure that no one had touched it but she. Thus the days and years passed until the girl reached the age of ten. And her sparkling beauty grew even greater with time.

One day, when the king's shepherd had brought his flock to the pasture to graze, his own horse lifted its head and beheld an amazing sight. There in the window of a huge house was a young girl of radiant beauty. "How can God bestow so much beauty upon one person?" thought the horse.

And every day, as it grazed, the horse looked up at that window. Soon it could think of nothing else, not of grass, not of drink, until it became thin and gaunt.

Now it so happened that one day the king himself came to inspect his flock and inquired about the reason for the horse being so thin. "May my soul live, I know only one thing," replied the shepherd. "Every day, when the horse grazes, it lifts its head and stares intensely at a nearby house."

"Silly shepherd," retorted the king, "you too must lift your head and see what the horse sees." The shepherd, greatly embarrassed, begged forgiveness for his foolishness, and did as the king bade. And when he saw the face of the beautiful girl, he too wondered, "How could God bestow so much beauty on one person? Why, she is surely fit for no one other than the prince."

And, before long, the king had received this suggestion, and sent his son to the forest to look upon the girl. The prince stood beside the shepherd's horse, and when the animal lifted its head, the prince did likewise, casting his eyes at the radiant girl. His heart went out to her at once, and, the very next day, determined to speak to her, he approached the walls of the house and whistled—one long, shrill sound.

"What is that?" asked the girl as she looked out the window, and, seeing the face of the youthful prince, she fell in love with him as well.

"Can you, perhaps, give me some water?" asked the prince. "My journey has been a long one and I am quite thirsty."

"Oh, I gladly would," she answered, "but I have no way to get it down to you."

"Well, you have a long braid," advised the prince. "Tie the water bucket to your hair and, in that way, lower it down." This the girl did, but soon afterwards, she became worried. "My monster mother will soon be home. Leave at once, or your end will be bitter." And soon afterward, upon her return, as the monster mother counted the girl's hair, as usual, she did indeed find one missing.

"Who has been here?" she demanded in an angry voice.

"No one, Mother. As I looked out, the passing birds must have plucked one hair from my head." Thus the girl told her mother a lie.

The woman was quiet, but the girl spoke deviously. "Tell me, Mother, how could a person succeed in escaping from an enemy?"

The mother's heart sank. She took these words as a bad omen. "Lanjeh," she asked, "are you planning to leave me?"

"How can you think such a thought? Where would I go, Mother? Who has even seen me here?"

So the monster mother answered the girl's question. "You would take with you a comb, a mirror, and black *kahal* for the eyes. When the enemy approaches, throw down the comb. At once the road will be covered with thorns. As the enemy succeeds again, throw down the mirror. At once the woods will be filled with water. And if the enemy succeeds again, throw down the *kahal*. At once the road will be clouded in darkness, and you will be able to make your escape." The girl listened and remembered the words of her mother in her heart.

The very next morning, after the monster mother had brushed the girl's hair and left on her daily hunt, the prince came for the lovely girl. Lowering herself down on a rope, Lanjeh made sure to take with her a comb, a mirror, and a small quantity of *kahal*. Then the prince mounted his horse and rode off like a thundering storm. But the monster, hearing the great noise, dashed through the forest to overcome them.

"Lanjeh! Lanjeh! Lanjeh!" she called. The girl did not stop. "Lanjeh! Lanjeh! Lanjeh!" the mother begged, cried, pleaded. She almost came upon the horse, when the girl threw down her comb, and, in an instant, the entire road was covered with thorns. The monster, in her anguish, made her way through this obstacle and almost came upon the horse once again, when Lanjeh lifted the mirror and threw it down upon the road. Deep lakes filled the road. But the monster mother made her way through these as well, and just as she was about to overtake the horse, Lanjeh threw down the *kahal*, black as coal. In an instant the fog and darkness blocked her way. The monster mother, unable to continue, cried and wept at the loss of her daughter.

As loudly as she could, she called, "Lanjeh, Lanjeh, listen to my words, which I tell you for your own good. Heed my words and no harm will come to you, I promise. At the crossroads you will find two spools of thread: one white; the other, black, and where the white spool rolls, take that path. Remember, Lanjeh, don't take the black road. Farewell, Lanjeh, farewell."

Soon Lanjeh and the prince came to the crossroad, and Lanjeh did as her mother's words told her. She prepared to follow the path of the white thread.

"No, no, no," objected the prince, "your mother means only to trick us. If she told us to follow the white path, it is there that she will catch us. It is the other road we must take."

And no amount of the girl's pleading would dissuade the prince. So, putting spurs to the horse, they rode off down the path of black. There, in front of them, swooped a powerful eagle of enormous size, whose feathers were a palette of color as if they were enchanted. "Who wants my special feathers?" it cried. "Come forth and pluck them!" The colors were so beautiful that at first the girl was tempted, but then she thought, "No, no, we don't need them."

But the prince insisted, "I must have those feathers," and so he dismounted and put his hands on the eagle's back. At that moment he felt himself lifted up, up, up as the eagle swept away into the sky. "Lanjeh, Lanjeh, ride to my parent's palace. The horse knows the way," he cried. And so, as her beloved prince was carried away, out of sight, she rode to the palace, where the whinny of the horse brought the king and queen at once. "And where is our son?" they asked, as they recognized the horse. The girl was thrown into a prison room. "This is my punishment," she thought, "for the way I treated my monster mother, who adopted me and cared for me with great love."

That night the eagle descended to the roof of the prison, the prince upon its back.

"Lanjeh, Lanjeh, where did you sleep tonight?" he asked.

"In a warehouse of straw," she replied.

"Lanjeh, Lanjeh, what did you eat tonight?"

"Only water and crusts of bread."

"My God," thought the prince, "this is my bad luck for not heeding your voice."

On the second night the eagle reappeared, the prince again upon its back.

"Lanjeh, Lanjeh, where did you sleep tonight?"

"In a warehouse of animals."

"Lanjeh, Lanjeh, what did you eat tonight?"

"Crusts of bread from dishes filled with dirt."

"My God," thought the prince, "why did I not heed your voice?"

Meanwhile the people of the house were awakened by the voices. "Whom were you speaking to?" they inquired of the girl.

"Only to your son, the prince."

Upon uttering these words, the girl was taken to the palace, there fed and garmented, as befits a royal princess.

That night the eagle and the prince descended again.

"Lanjeh, Lanjeh, where did you sleep tonight?"

"In the palace in a warm bed."

"Lanjeh, Lanjeh, what did you eat tonight?"

"The finest of foods on dishes of gold."

"Be happy, my heart," called the prince, "for at last you are in the trusty hands of my parents."

At all this talk the king and queen were most alarmed, and quickly summoned the most trusted advisors to find a way to rescue the prince.

"Only the rabbi, the teacher of the Jews, can help you," they were told.

And so the rabbi was summoned. "Find a way to save our son or your people will be expelled!" The king's demand was curt and clear.

"The solution is simple," stated the rabbi. "Order your servants to bring forth a wide, deep bowl filled with boiling tar. Spread this on the roof on the very spot where the eagle lands."

And so the rabbi's advice was carried out at once. That night when the eagle landed, its feet indeed stuck to the hot tar, and the prince, weakened and almost dead from thirst and hunger, was rescued.

Of course, he was quickly nursed back to health, after which preparations were made for a wedding feast of great luxury, never before seen in that kingdom.

And the prince and his bride lived together in health and in wealth all the remaining days of their lives.

So may we as well!

Katanya
TURKEY

Once upon a time there was a poor old woman. All her life she had wished for a child of her own. But though she wished and wished, she never had any children.

Her husband died, and still she wanted a child. "Oh, how wonderful it would be if only I had a little boy or girl," she said. So she prayed to God to help her.

God saw how lonely the old woman was and sent Elijah to visit her. Elijah is a prophet who often returns to earth in the form of an old man to help his people, the Jews, when they are in trouble. But no one knows who he is. Sometimes he disguises himself as a beggar, and sometimes he dresses like a merchant. And sometimes he uses the powers of God to work his magic.

Now this old woman had worked hard all of her life, but she had no money left and nothing to sell for food. So each day she went to the market to ask the merchants for what they could spare: one peach, one apricot, one little olive. Sometimes they took pity on her and gave her a piece of fruit. And some days that was all she had to eat.

But one day all the merchants were in a bad mood because the king had raised their taxes. And when the old woman begged for fruit, each and every one of them shooed her away. She did not get anything—not one peach, not one apricot, not one little olive. The old woman was very sad, for it looked as if she would go hungry all day long.

Just as she was about to leave the market, she noticed a merchant she had never seen before, an old man who looked as poor as she was. As she walked over to the old man, she saw that all he had left were six brown dates, drying in the sun.

"Could you spare just one?" she asked.

"Surely," said the old man (who was really Elijah). "Take the one you want."

Now five of the dates were very little, but one was big, and that is the one she chose. "Thank you, kind sir," she said, and went on her way.

When she got home, the old woman placed the date on the windowsill, where sunlight shone on it. "You know," that old woman said to herself, "this is such a beautiful date, I don't have the heart to eat it." So she left it there, even though she was hungry, and went out to see if she could find something else to eat.

The sun continued to shine on the date until it was quite warm. Soon the date began to stir, as if something were inside. All at once it broke open—and out popped a little girl. She was no bigger than a little finger, and she wore a pretty dress of many colors. The little girl stood up on the windowsill and looked around. The house was quite bare—only a bed and a table and a chair stood in the room—and it wasn't very clean, for the old woman's broom had only a few straws left.

The first thing the little girl did was to climb out the window. She saw a ball of string hanging on the wall and, grabbing one end of the string, she lowered herself down to the ground. There she picked some of the short grasses, because she was very short herself, and she tied the bundle together with another piece of straw. "Oh, what a perfect broom for me!" she cried.

Back up the string and onto the windowsill she climbed, and then she started to clean the house. She swept from corner to corner, until the floor sparkled like new.

Meanwhile, the old woman was still walking on the road, searching for some food, when whom should she meet but the old man who had given her the date! The old man smiled and this time he gave her a large shiny olive. She thanked him and he continued on his way. When the old woman bit into the olive, what did she find inside but a golden coin! She hurried after the old man to give it back, but he was nowhere to be found. The golden coin was hers to keep. What a lucky day for me! she thought.

But she was even more surprised when she got home, for there was her house, all neat and clean! She couldn't believe her eyes. "Who did this?" she asked out loud.

"I did, Mother," said a tiny voice.

The old woman looked around. There on the windowsill, where the old woman had left the date, was the tiniest girl in the world, a girl no bigger than the woman's little finger. The old woman blinked to see if she was dreaming. "Did you call me Mother?"

"Yes, Mother," said the girl. And at that moment the old woman realized that the kind old man must have been Elijah the prophet. And she hugged the tiny girl very carefully, so as not to hurt her.

Then she asked the girl her name. But the girl did not answer. "No one has given me a name," she said at last.

"Then I will name you!" said the old woman. She thought and thought. "I will call you Katanya, the little one," she said. And so it was that her name became Katanya.

Katanya and the old woman lived together happily in that little hut. With the help of the golden coin they never had to go hungry. And the first thing the old woman did with the money was to pay back every merchant who had given her fruit to eat.

The old woman loved Katanya with all her heart. She made a little bed for her inside a teacup, She fashioned a fur hat for her from a bunny's tail, shoes out of tiny nutshells, and dresses made of rose petals. But of all her clothes, Katanya loved best her dress of many colors, the one she had been wearing when she first popped out of the date.

Katanya helped her mother by sweeping out the house with her tiny broom. She even cleaned between the boards of the floor—an easy task for her, since she was so small. While she did her chores, Katanya sang. She had a beautiful voice that sounded as if a full-grown girl were singing. Katanya's voice filled the city with gladness, bringing joy to everyone who heard it.

One day a prince was riding down the street, when he heard a lovely song drifting from an open window. The voice was so beautiful that he fell instantly in love. When he returned to the palace, he told his father, the king: "Father, I have found a lovely bride, and I wish to be married."

"Very well, my son," said the king in surprise, "but who is the bride?"

"I wish to marry the girl whose beautiful singing I heard today," said the prince.

The king sent a servant at once to the house of the old woman and invited her to come with her daughter to the palace. The servant told the woman: "I have brought a tailor with me who will sew dresses for you both."

But when the old woman told Katanya this, the girl shook her head. "No, no, no! I love my dress of many colors, and that's what I will wear." So the tailor fitted the old woman, but when he asked to see the girl, he was told that she already had a pretty dress.

A few days later, the old woman put on her new dress and went to the palace, with Katanya hiding inside the pocket. The king welcomed her, but the prince was very sad. "Your daughter was invited to join us too," he said. "Why has she not come?"

All at once a tiny voice came from the pocket: "Here I am!" Then Katanya's head peeked out.

"Is it you I heard singing?" asked the prince, much amazed.

"Perhaps," she answered.

"In that case," said the prince, "could you sing for us now? If you are the girl I heard, then it is you I want to marry, even though you are small."

Katanya smiled, for what the prince said was very nice indeed. And she sang a song more beautiful than any he had ever heard.

So it was that Katanya married the prince and became Princess Katanya. At her wedding she wore her favorite dress of many colors. And the old woman came to live at the palace along with her. And all of them—the prince, Katanya, and her mother—lived happily ever after.

· Conversation ·

JANE: When I was a girl I read "Rapunzel" simply as a tale of an adoptive/foster mother trying to keep her teenager locked away from life. Repressing all independence. Disapproving. As Anne Sexton says at the beginning of her Rapunzel poem in *Transformations*:

> *Many a girl*
> *had an old aunt*
> *who locked her in the study*
> *to keep the boys away.*

But when that poem is read in its entirety, it is clearly about the seduction of the girl by the older woman. Youth by age. Innocence by knowledge.

> *A woman*
> *who loves a woman*
> *is forever young.*

I read that story differently now.

HEIDI: I think the Rapunzel stories appeal to women differently during different stages of life.

First, for children, "Rapunzel" has all the elements of an adventure story: a beautiful princess, a terrific villain, rescue by Prince Charming, and a happily-ever-after. At least that's what Maddison looks for in a story.

Then, in the teen and early adult years, it is a story of love won at all costs from an overprotective (read evil) parent. That's the way I remembered it, and I'm sure Lexi would read it this way.

But for me now, as a mother—especially the mother of an adopted teenager—the witch is the hero. I see the prince as a villain, a young and horny man who sneaks in (and then out) to sully the virginal beauty of the mother's young innocent daughter. In "Rapunzel," he actually gets her pregnant. With twins! Putting his eyes out should be the least of his punishment.

However, there are many other issues in these Rapunzel stories that interested me. First, one of the most basic slippery slopes of parenting is how to respond to lies. Both girl-children in "Rapunzel" and "Lanjeh" lie to their mothers. Such a difficult subject. Where is the line between lying and tattling? When do you hold a confidence with your child? If I say to my daughters that they can tell me everything, do I really mean it? Is knowing what they're doing better than ignorant bliss?

JANE: I think I was happier finding out about some of your adolescent escapades years later. Of course if you had been in serious trouble—hard drugs, excessive drinking, abusive sex, theft, murder—I would have wanted to know at the time so I could help. But I didn't need to know about every little kiss, every time you had a drink or took a toke or counseled a friend with problems.

I remember when you were about fourteen, and I was picking up your room—mainly to rescue glasses and plates left there. I found an open notebook in which you had been practicing dirty words. They shocked me thoroughly. But I closed the notebook, tucked it away, and never spoke to you about it. Adolescents need their secrets. And their little lies. It is one of the ways they begin to separate from their parents. But it is, as you say, a very slippery slope.

Somehow, each time I caught you out in a small lie (and they were small, though they loomed large at the time), it seemed to bring us closer. Like the time Billy Lacey crashed your grandfather's car and you took the blame because he was an underage driver. Or the time a bunch of your friends got drunk and slept in tents on our lawn. But I think you wanted to be caught so you could talk about what was bothering you.

Your brothers were different. They definitely did not want to be caught. And they both denied any bad behavior until well into their twenties, when it was safe to tell us how awful they'd been as teenagers.

You, though, needed to confess and thereby get forgiveness.

HEIDI: Well, I have to say, I didn't see it that way back then. But I can neither confirm nor deny that I had a need to confess.

And, in my defense, I told you immediately that Billy Lacey was driving. It was the police I lied to.

At least he didn't climb up my hair and into my bedroom.

JANE: I recently re-read portions of Marina Warner's incredibly rich book, *From the Beast to the Blonde,* and she has this to say about Rapunzel's hair and the prince's climb: "There is a German proverb, 'A woman's hair pulls stronger than a bell rope' or, 'A woman's hair is stronger than a hempen rope,' and in the story, in the punning manner of dreams, Rapunzel enacts this belief literally." Warner also reminds the reader that such a bush of maidenhair can also symbolize the maidenhead—or virginity—and its loss (when the witch cuts off Rapunzel's hair).

In other words, the story is a metaphor for Rapunzel's initiation into sexuality. Since fairy tales can often be read as extended metaphors, I don't think it's much of a stretch to read "Rapunzel" this way.

So I am glad indeed that Billy didn't climb up your hair into the bedroom! Though I must confess that when I met your father, he had just climbed through the window of the first-floor apartment I shared with two other girls. He came in that way because we were throwing a party and the doorway was blocked by too many other people. He walked over to where I was standing in the middle of the living room, my thigh-length braid over one shoulder. He kissed me on the neck and said, "Hi, I'm friends with one of the girls in the apartment." And I replied . . .

HEIDI: [Laughing.] I know this story. You replied "I *am* one of the girls in the apartment, and you're no friend of mine."

JANE: As an aside, when we were in the middle of revising this conversation, I visited Long Island to give a speech at a librarians' convention, and on the way from the hotel passed a hair salon called Rapunzel's which offered "hair extensions." I laughed out loud. Fairy tales seem to come into our lives even at funny turns in the road.

HEIDI: Perhaps I am not stretching when I see in "Lanjeh" the early-warning signs of a man who becomes an abuser. This is not to say that the prince in this story is irredeemably on his way to beating his wife, just that he manifests one of the classic signals. He makes Lanjeh choose between her mother and her love for him. This attempt at isolation could mark the beginning of an abusive relationship.

I have been asked repeatedly by mothers with daughters in abusive relationships (both physical and emotional) what they can do about the situation, especially when they have been told to mind their own business by both parties. Should they write off their daughter and the abusing spouse? Since I had one boyfriend who backhanded me so hard I hit the wall on the other side of the room (and I went back to him) and another who grabbed me by the throat and jacked me up against a wall (just to get my attention?), I consider myself a formerly abused woman. So my advice comes from experience (more so, of course, than from these two separate incidences, but we don't have all day to quote chapter and verse of my "stupid years"). I counsel that a mother has to be strong, ignoring her own hurt feelings, and always leave a door open for her daughter in such a relationship. No abused wife will leave until she is ready, but as long as she knows there is someplace to go, that's where she'll head as soon as she finds her own strength.

You did this for me. Did I ever thank you?

JANE: Often.

Though I have to add that until this moment, I didn't know about those two incidents. Just that you had a boyfriend (not two) who had hit you. Once. Had I known, I would have been over there with the police. Your father would have been there even sooner.

I didn't catch those possible warning signs in "Lanjeh" until you alerted me to them. Just as I didn't really know about the abusive boyfriend till you told me. Growing up in the fifties, I was conditioned not to notice that sort of thing.

In fact, a dear friend of mine was in a longtime abusive marriage, and until she finally confessed to a group of her friends, of which I was one, I had thought her husband charming and an original. That he was moody, I put down to his being a musician. That she was occasionally depressed, or whey-faced, or broke dates with me I took as a sign of her artistic nature.

Abuse? That belonged in trailer parks or slums or in bad TV movies. You would probably say I led a very sheltered life.

But you are certainly not alone in wondering about the prince's role. My friend, storyteller and poet Milbre Burch, recently sent me a poem of hers about Rapunzel in which she writes:

> *the witch had been hard of hearing*
> *and the prince was not a good listener*

And later on she says of him:

> *Her tears of joy at seeing him, cured his blindness*
> *but they could not heal his heart*

where it had been pricked
by thorns of many kinds in the years before.

Her take on the prince is slightly different from yours. She understands his darkness. So I have taken your response and added it to Milbre's and given my own more tepid understanding of the story a shaking up.

HEIDI: Neither of the princes in the Rapunzel stories actually becomes an abusive spouse, at least as far as we see in the actual tale.

However, all the stories end happily ever after. The front door to the castle is shut in our faces. So how can we possibly know how these marriages unfold? I just wanted to point out that at least one danger sign is present. I may be overly sensitive to these things.

And, while the idea of being an abused wife is horrible, just think what we pass on to our children. We teach our boys that it is the norm to treat women in this way. And we teach our daughters how not to be strong. We allow for a cycle of abuse through our non-actions. It's not an exact science, but strong women grow strong daughters more easily than mothers who are perceived (rightly or otherwise) as victims.

To take this theory one step further, psychologist and author Abraham Maslow believes that in order to reach self-actualization, one has to have all the basic needs met first, beginning with basic physiological needs (food, air, and shelter) and moving through safety and security. Then on through love and belonging. Once these needs (as if climbing a ladder) are met, a person can truly move on to his or her growth needs and live a fulfilled life. When we cannot meet these needs in ourselves as mothers, we cannot grow. If we cannot give our daughters this, how can they move on to healthy adulthood?

JANE: That's an interesting theory, but it puzzles me. It doesn't fit facts as I know them.

For example, my mother did not have a particularly good self-image. She saw my father as the one everyone loved. She forgave him over and over. Yet I grew up strong and unwilling to be walked over. When a college boyfriend tried that, I broke off our engagement, though I must admit that what I told him was that I needed to be free to explore my chances in the world of writing and publishing.

You grew up in a stable household. Your father and I are certainly in an equal partnership. We have hardly ever fought, never yelled at one another, have always been supportive of choices we each made. Yet you allowed a boyfriend to emotionally abuse you for quite some time.

Coincidentally, the other day I came upon an article in *Newsday* in which T. M. Whitney talks about her relationship with her daughter Tressa. She writes that Tressa had inadvertently revealed she'd been "slapped more than once last semester by one of her teen boyfriends." Now Ms. Whitney, a tough-minded executive, had a first reaction (as did I), which was to get the "boy's name and mailing address for the letter bomb" she thought of sending. Boy, did I relate to that column! Sometimes a strong woman as a role model is not enough.

And to be honest—even unhealthy mothers can make healthy daughters. Look at Lexi. A jewel so long unpolished can still shimmer under a master jeweler's cloth.

There are simply some young women who make themselves healthy. They repudiate and refute their own pasts. Like Snow White, who grows up beautifully away from the envious mother figure, like Cinderella in her new gown, like the girl speaking rare gems in "Diamonds and Toads." They are entire firmaments of goodness despite their ghastly mothers or stepmothers.

So I will have to think on Maslow further. But then I always tend to go to the particular, away from the general anyway.

HEIDI: Ah, but you missed that this is an *imperfect* science. These are the exceptions that prove the rule. After all, we all go through bad relationships and deal with them in our own ways. You are a strong woman and you raised me, a strong woman, even though I haven't been that way from birth to adulthood. I took a pit stop at doormat status.

But I stand by my point, since it reads, "Strong women grow strong girls *more easily,*" not "every time."

JANE: Meanwhile, I wanted to mention something that jumped out at me in "Rapunzel" this reading, something that made me extremely uncomfortable—the shallow reason the birth mother uses to give up her child. Pregnant, she has a craving for lettuce and she swears that without a bowl of her favorite food, she will die.

Now when I was pregnant with you, we were on a year-long camping trip in Europe and the Middle East. We were in Florence for a couple of weeks and there was nothing I wanted more than a chicken salad sandwich. Italy. November 1965. A chicken salad sandwich was a hopeless desire. But would I have promised you to a local cook for a bite? It never entered my mind.

Now, I know there are many legitimate reasons for giving up a child. They include an inability to mother, unfortunate monetary circumstances, rape, psychological infirmities, addictions, extreme youth, and so on. However, trading a child for a bowl of lettuce or a chicken salad sandwich—or even chocolate—seems to me to be as stupid a reason as I have ever heard.

At least in "Lanjeh" we never hear the reason for the child's abandonment. No reason is certainly better than abandonment by reason of lettuce. And in "Katanya" the adoptive mother has been wanting a child for a very long time, so the fact that the child is minuscule never matters to her.

HEIDI: When I was pregnant I wanted anything with salt—but that's another bloated story.

And you are being naive. We have all seen the news reports of mothers who have abandoned their babies because of postpartum depression, zero population controls, drugs.

In my opinion, there is no good excuse, lettuce or otherwise, to abandon a child.

At least Rapunzel's mother didn't leave her newborn baby in the high school rest room during her prom.

JANE: No good reason to abandon one. And every good reason to take one in.

Reading "Rapunzel" as an adult, I am actually relieved that the so-called witch gets the charge of the child. She is clearly willing to do the hard work of mothering. And mothering, as we both know, is extremely hard work. As the old Jewish proverb goes: "Because God could not be everywhere, He made mothers."

That old witch works her fingers to the bone for Rapunzel the first twelve years and, when the girl reaches puberty, the witch works even harder climbing up that hair-case every day. (The monster in "Lanjeh" works equally as hard—hunting for food, washing and cleaning the girl's lovely hair, generally guarding her.)

I couldn't have climbed a hair stair when you were a teen. (Hell—I couldn't have done it when *I* was a teen) But then, when you were a teen I not only had you at home, but your two brothers, your father going through tenure at the university, my father sick with Parkinson's, and his round-the-clock nurses to organize and deal with. Being a meal delivery service to a rebellious, sex-obsessed child in an inaccessible tower would have killed me.

HEIDI: And the tower didn't even do any good. Those hormonal teenage boys—ever resourceful.

The two Rapunzel stories seemed unfinished to me. I'll grant you the fact that neither foster mother is perfect. One is a monster and one a witch. But they both do their best. Where are they at the end of the story? They just disappear. Unloved. Unappreciated. Unthanked.

How many mothers does it take to change a light bulb? None. I'll just sit here in the dark.

JANE: Thanks? I'll give you thanks. One foster mother gets a runaway preteen, the other an unwed pregnant adolescent. Seen from the perspective of the fosterer, these stories both have the same dark moral: After years of obsessive and careful mothering, neither one ever gets to see her beloved daughter again. Only the old woman in "Katanya," who loves without overprotecting, without judging, gets to live with her daughter in the prince's palace. I hope—for all their sakes—that it is a very large palace indeed.

Caring Daughters

Achol and Her Wild Mother

SUDAN, DINKA

Achol, Lanchichor (The Blind Beast) and Adhalchingeeny (The Exceedingly Brave One) were living with their mother. Their mother would go to fetch firewood. She gathered many pieces of wood and then put her hands behind her back and said, "O dear, who will help me lift this heavy load?"

A lion came passing by and said, "If I help you lift the load, what will you give me?"

"I will give you one hand," she said.

She gave him a hand; he helped her lift the load and she went home. Her daughter, Achol, said, "Mother, why is your hand like that?"

"My daughter, it is nothing," she answered.

Then she left again to fetch firewood. She gathered many pieces of wood and then put her hand behind her back and said, "O dear, who will now help me lift this heavy load?"

The lion came and said, "If I help you lift the load, what will you give me?"

"I will give you my other hand!" And she gave him the other hand. He lifted the load on to her head and she went home without a hand.

Her daughter saw her and said, "Mother, what has happened to your hands? You should not go to fetch firewood again! You must stop!"

But she insisted that there was nothing wrong and went to fetch firewood. Again she collected many pieces of firewood, put her arms behind her back and said, "Who will now help me lift this heavy load?"

Again the lion came and said, "If I help you lift the load, what will you give me?"

She said, "I will give you one foot!"

She gave him her foot; he helped her, and she went home.

Her daughter said, "Mother, this time, I insist that you do not go for the firewood! Why is all this happening? Why are your hands and your foot like this?"

"My daughter, it is nothing to worry about," she said. "It is my nature."

She went back to the forest another time and collected many pieces of firewood. Then she put her arms behind her back and said, "Who will now help me lift this load?"

The lion came and said, "What will you now give me?"

She said, "I will give you my other foot!"

So she gave him the other foot; he helped her, and she went home.

This time she became wild and turned into a lioness. She would not eat cooked meat; she would only have raw meat.

Achol's brothers went to the cattle camp with their mother's relatives. So only Achol remained at home with her mother. When her mother turned wild, she went into the forest, leaving Achol alone. She would only return for a short time in the evening to look for food. Achol would prepare something for her and put it on the platform in the courtyard. Her mother would come at night and sing in a dialogue with Achol,

> *"Achol, Achol, where is your father?"*
> *"My father is still in the cattle camp!"*
> *"And where is Lanchichor?"*
> *"Lanchichor is still in the cattle camp!"*
> *"And where is Adhalchingeeny?"*
> *"Adhalchingeeny is still in the cattle camp."*
> *"And where is the food?"*
> *"Mother, scrape the insides of our ancient gourds."*

She would eat and leave. The following night, she would return and sing. Achol would reply; her mother would eat and return to the forest. This went on for a long time.

Meanwhile, Lanchichor came from the cattle camp to visit his mother and sister. When he arrived home, he found his mother absent. He also found a large pot over the cooking fire. He wondered about these things and asked Achol, "Where is Mother gone, and why are you cooking in such a big pot?"

She replied, "I am cooking in this big pot because our mother has turned wild and is in the forest, but she comes at night for food."

"Take that pot off the fire," he said.

"I cannot," she replied, "I must cook for her."

He let her. She cooked and put the food on the platform before they went to bed. Their mother came at night and sang. Achol replied as usual.

Her mother ate and left. Achol's brother got very frightened. He emptied his bowels and left the next morning.

When he was asked in the cattle camp about the people at home, he was too embarrassed to tell the truth; so he said they were well.

Then Achol's father decided to come home to visit his wife and his daughter. He found the big pot on the fire and his wife away. When he asked Achol, she explained everything to him. He also told her to take the pot off the fire, but she would not. She put the food on the platform, and they went to bed. Achol's father told her to let him take care of the situation. Achol agreed. Her mother came and sang as usual. Achol replied. Then her mother ate. But her father was so frightened that he returned to the camp.

Then came Adhalchingeeny (The Exceedingly Brave One) and brought with him a very strong rope. He came and found Achol cooking with the large pot, and when Achol explained to him their mother's condition, he told her to take the pot off the fire, but she would not give in. He let her proceed with her usual plan. He placed the rope near the food in a way that would trap his mother when she took the food. He tied the other end to his foot.

Their mother came and sang as usual. Achol replied. As their mother went towards the food, Adhalchingeeny pulled the rope, gagged her and tied her to a pole. He then went and beat her with part of the heavy rope. He beat her and beat her and beat her. Then he gave her a piece of raw meat, and when she ate it, he beat her again. He beat her and beat her and beat her. Then he gave her two pieces of meat, one raw and one roasted. She refused the raw one and took the roasted one, saying, "My son, I have now become human, so please stop beating me."

They then reunited and lived happily.

How Sun, Moon, and Wind Went Out to Dinner

INDIA

One day, Sun, Moon, and Wind went out to dine with their uncle and aunts Thunder and Lightning. Their mother (one of the most distant Stars you see far up in the sky) waited alone for her children's return.

Now both Sun and Wind were greedy and selfish. They enjoyed the great feast that had been prepared for them, without a thought of saving any of it to take home to their mother—but the gentle Moon did not forget her. Of every dainty dish that was brought round, she placed a small portion under one of her beautiful long finger-nails, that Star might also have a share in the treat.

On their return, their mother, who had kept watch for them all night long with her little bright eye, said, "Well, children, what have you brought home for me?" Then Sun (who was eldest) said, "I have brought nothing home for you. I went out to enjoy myself with my friends—not to fetch a dinner for my mother!" And Wind said, "Neither have I brought anything home for you, Mother. You could hardly expect me to bring a collection of good things for you, when I merely went out for my own pleasure." But Moon said, "Mother, fetch a plate, see what I have brought you." And shaking her hands she showered down such a choice dinner as never was seen before.

Then Star turned to Sun and spoke thus, "Because you went out to amuse yourself with your friends, and feasted and enjoyed yourself, without any thought of your mother at home—you shall be cursed. Henceforth, your rays shall ever be hot and scorching, and shall burn all that they touch. And men shall hate you, and cover their heads when you appear."

(And that is why the Sun is so hot to this day.)

Then she turned to Wind and said, "You also who forgot you mother in the midst of your selfish pleasures—hear your doom. You shall always blow in the hot dry weather, and shall parch and shrivel all living things. And men shall detest and avoid you from this very time."

(And that is why the Wind in the hot weather is still so disagreeable.)

But to Moon she said, "Daughter, because you remembered your mother, and kept for her a share in your own enjoyment, from henceforth you shall be ever cool, and calm, and bright. No noxious glare shall accompany your pure rays, and men shall always call you 'blessed.' "

(And that is why the moon's light is so soft, and cool, and beautiful even to this day.)

· *Conversation* ·

JANE: The first time I really understood how time turns the tables on mother-daughter relationships was on my honeymoon. Your father and I took what we called the "Two Dying Grandmothers" trip to Virginia and then West Virginia.

In Hampton Roads we visited my grandmother, who—when I had last seen her—had been an active, strong-minded octogenarian, walking over a mile every evening around the long block where her house sat. Now she was small, cowed, quiet, vacant-eyed. Though she had a full-time nurse, her daughter Cecily and her daughter-in-law Ruth, both of whom lived nearby, had become caretakers. Luckily for them, Grandma had not turned wild in her old age, like Achol's lion mother.

When I read the "Sun, Moon, and Wind" story, I thought immediately of the time I had nursed my father through his four-year final bout with Parkinson's. At the time I fully recognized that it would have been so much easier nursing my mother, had she lived so long. For she was, like Moon, "cool, calm, and bright." He was more the selfish Sun, greedy and self-involved.

But then I also remembered going to a Smith College reunion and sitting down with a number of women from my class at a panel about being a member of the "tween generation"—sandwiched in between the demands of one's teenagers and the demands of one's increasingly frail parents. What we all said to one another, first in hushed and then in rising tones, was: "Why me?" Because even those of us with brothers found that the work of taking care of aging parents fell squarely on our shoulders. My brother had a perfect excuse—he lived in Brazil, a little far to do any casual nursing. But others in my reunion class had close-by brothers, and still they had the entire care and feeding (and sometimes diapering) of their elderly parents.

The American Association of Retired Persons has estimated that three-quarters of the people who do elder care and sick care for family members are women. There are, it is estimated, some twenty-five million households where the woman does the tending. In fact, I remember reading in one bulletin that more than one-third of these women are destined to spend more of their lives parenting their parents than they ever did caring for their children.

HEIDI: Another bad subject for me. If I could make you promise me never to get old and die, I would. You've made me promise that I would send both you and Daddy to a nursing home when the time comes. But, although I promised under the threat of making us (me and my brothers) sign legal papers, I crossed my fingers behind my back. I look at such things the same way I look at day care. I'm sure the majority of places doing preschool and postretirement care are wonderful, but if I'm not the one doing the caring, how will I know it's being done right? Control freak. That's me.

JANE: Having visited friends in nursing homes the last few years, we have changed our minds on that subject. The Federal General Accounting Office recently reported that one in four—*one in four!*—of the nation's seventeen thousand nursing homes has problems that cause, in their own words, "immediate jeopardy or actual harm" to the residents. And President Clinton said in a radio address that we need special legislation to protect those residents because they "cannot lock the door against abuse and neglect by the people paid to care for them."

So now we have insurance that should cover complete home care for us. You can relax on that front.

But most people cannot afford that kind of insurance. Or they do not want to pay for it. Theirs is a roulette attitude. Or else they really do want to be cared for by their kids, or their particular culture demands such a role. A sort of "I-took-care-of-you, now-it's-your-turn" attitude.

However, I have this serious worry about being a burden. I want to be loved, not tolerated. I want to be remembered with fondness, not thought of with a loud sigh.

HEIDI: I'd like to speak to something that Achol's mother says after losing both her hands to the lion: "My daughter, it is nothing to worry about . . . It is my nature." This, to me, is the key. A mother's nature is to protect her children. For example, you didn't like to tell me when there was something medically wrong with you, until I blew up at you during a conversation that started, "Oh by the way, I found a lump in my breast, but the tests came back negative." How could you do that to me? Telling me only after the fact. I was an adult and should have known about the lump so that I could worry with you. But it's in your nature to shield me from those little details.

I do the same with my girls, of course. I didn't want them to visit me in the hospital when I had meningitis. Brandon finally sneaked Lexi in just before I was discharged, but only because she really wanted to. He did it for her, not for me. If asked, I would have said absolutely not. She didn't need to see me like that, whey-colored and full of IVs. But then, my kids are not adults yet.

When do we cross the line where it's not only appropriate but expected for an adult daughter to start caring for her mother?

On a recent trip to Florida for a visit, I encountered this same problem. My friends Andrea and Tracy had their mother, Shirley, visiting at the same time. Andrea—the older sister—confided in me that she was worried about her mom's health and that her mom laughed it off anytime the subject was broached. I told her I had to get tough with you and she would have to do the same.

It must be so difficult to see your baby become an adult. To allow her the responsibility to care for you even in a small way. I guess I'll find out about that soon enough.

JANE: I am not sure the problem is a difficulty in seeing my baby grow up. I am perfectly willing to let you take care of your own children. But once you start taking care of me, I have lost something precious—my independence, my authority, my control.

You are not the only control freak in the family.

HEIDI: Ah, but then you have missed my saying "worry *with* you." Not for you. Not even so much about you. But *with* you. I do not want to take over, I want to share. Because taking over would not only diminish your role, it would mean giving up my daughterly role. Something I still need to hang on to.

Enough of that. May I male-bash? I love that Achol's brother is literally scared shitless. All right, maybe I find so much joy in this because in the end of the story the other brother—the brave one—eventually is the one who, through tough love, I guess, brings back the mother to human form. The daughter's love and gentle devotion is not enough. Big brave man has to come in and pound the wild beast into submission.

Jealous of my brothers? Maybe.

Of course, in the "Sun, Moon, and Wind" story, the opposite is true. The quiet devotion of the Moon daughter is rewarded by Mother Star.

JANE: I want to quickly point out that when you and the boys were young, it was your little brother Jason who did the tender nursing. You were always too busy with friends to bring me a glass of water or a cup of tea. Adam was always nose-down in a book and didn't even notice I was sick. But Jason would come in, place his hand on my forehead, and ask what I wanted.

So these things are not necessarily gender-dictated all the time.

HEIDI: I'd like to mention an interesting point made by Francis Mading and Angela Carter on the Achol story, in which they explain that the lion in the tale is likely to be a personification of the crime/sin of adultery. If this is true, then it immediately changes the dynamic of the mother-daughter relationship and the roles of the father and sons.

Does the daughter relate differently than the males in the story because she identifies with her mother more than her brothers and father? Could it be that the reason for the adultery was an abusive relationship with the father, who leaves when confronted by a situation he is no longer in control of?

Could the "brave" son have learned violence at the hands of his father and again abused the mother, giving her nowhere else to turn but back to the abusive home? Or has my work with abused women made me supersensitive to this issue?

JANE: It seems to me that the one part of the Achol story which has always made me uncomfortable—the beating of the mother—is more than adequately explained by your questions. And it reminds us again that these stories have more in them than simple narrative. We do not always understand them by a single reading, or by ourselves. But by talking about the tales, sharing them, we can open up both the external and internal meanings of the stories—and our own lives.

Mothers-in-Law

The Story of Ruth

HEBREW, THE BIBLE

It happened in the days when the great judges of Israel lived, that there was a famine in the land. So a man from Bethlehem named Elimelech came with his wife Naomi and their two sons to sojourn in the fields of Moab.

Elimelech died suddenly and Naomi was left with only her two sons. When they were old enough, they married Moabite women, one named Orpah and the other Ruth, both lovely young women, full of honor and without deceit. For ten years they dwelled in Moab and there was enough to eat.

But death comes to all, and some sooner than later. The two sons died, one after another, and Naomi was left without either husband or sons. It was a desperate time, for both Naomi and her daughters-in-law were poor now and without means.

Then Naomi recalled that in her home in Judah, poor women were dealt with far better than in Moab. She was determined to make the long trip back. But she told her daughters-in-law—Orpah and Ruth—to return to the homes of their fathers.

"I have no more sons in my womb to be husbands for thee," she said. "Go to thy old homes and there thou wilt find new husbands and raise families and be happy." She kissed them both, and they wept.

"Let us come with thee, mother," they cried. "We will return with thee to thy people."

But Naomi shook her head. Seeing that the old woman was determined, Orpah kissed her one last time and started down the road back to her own father.

However, Ruth would not go. She clung to Naomi, saying, "Do not entreat me to leave thee, for wherever thou goest, I will go. Wherever thou lodgest, I will lodge. Thy people will be my people, and thy God my God. Nothing but death will separate me from thee."

When Naomi saw how set Ruth was, she stopped arguing, and the two of them packed their few belongings and went down the road until they came at last to Bethlehem just at the beginning of the barley harvest.

When they entered the city, there was a great cry over them, for Naomi was recognized wherever they went.

"Do not call me Naomi," the old woman answered. "Call me Mara, which means embittered, for the Almighty has dealt bitterly with me. I was full when I went away, but now I am full only with misfortune."

Ruth said to the old woman, "We may yet turn misfortune into something else. Let me go into the fields and glean among the ears of grain, for then we will be able to eat well. But rest now, my mother, for the walk was long and thou art tired."

"Go, my daughter," said Naomi. "I shall await thy return."

So Ruth went and gleaned behind the harvesters, and her fate made her happen upon a parcel of land that belonged to Boaz, a man of substance who was also a relative of Naomi's through her husband.

When Boaz came at noon into the fields, he noticed Ruth at once. Speaking quietly to his servant who was overseeing the harvest, Boaz asked, "Who is that young woman? I do not recognize her."

The servant answered, "She is a Moabite woman who returned with old Naomi. Though she is the old woman's daughter-in-law, she treats her as one would a mother. I have given her permission to glean and she is such a good worker, she has been on her feet since early morning."

Boaz nodded and went over to Ruth. "Hear me well, young Moabite, do not glean in any other field but stay here and close to my maidens. I have ordered the young men to leave thee alone. Shouldst thou get thirsty, go to the jugs that have been set aside for the workers."

In gratitude, Ruth fell down on her knees. "Why hast thou taken note of me, though I am a foreigner?"

Boaz lifted her up by the hands and said, "I have heard all that thou hast done for thy mother-in-law, and that is good. May the Almighty reward thy actions."

Ruth looked down, suddenly shy. "May I continue to find favor in thine eyes, my lord." Then she turned and went back to her gleaning.

At mealtime, Boaz called to Ruth. "Come here, young Moabite, and partake of this bread. Dip thy morsel into the vinegar." This was showing her great favor and she came over eagerly to sit beside the harvesters.

Then Boaz told his harvesters, "Let the Moabite woman glean even among the sheaves. And even deliberately pull out some for her from the heaps and leave them for her. Do not rebuke her in any way." For he wanted to be certain she had enough grain to take back to old Naomi so that they could make a solid meal that night.

So Ruth continued to glean until evening, and when she beat out what she had gleaned, she had enough barley for both Ruth and her to have a goodly meal.

"Where didst thou work today?" Naomi asked when Ruth had returned from the fields. "May the one who took such generous notice of thee be blessed."

"In the fields of Boaz," Ruth said.

"Ah, Boaz," Naomi said, nodding. "He is a relative of ours. One of our redeeming kinsmen."

"More than kin and much more than kind," Ruth replied, "for he told me to stay close to his workers until they finish the harvest."

And so it was.

But after the meal, Naomi thought to herself, *What will happen to us when the harvest is done?* She knew that Ruth needed security after the gleaning was over. For herself, she cared little. But for Ruth she made a plan.

"My daughter," she said to Ruth, "Boaz and his harvesters will be winnowing the barley tonight on the threshing floor. Therefore, I would have thee bathe and anoint thyself with oil and perfume. Don thy good gown. Then go down to the threshing floor but do not make thyself known to Boaz until he has finished eating and drinking. When he lies down to sleep, note where he lies. Go over and uncover his feet and lie down there." And she told her even more, all of which was in accordance to the customs of that place which Ruth did not know.

"I will do thy bidding," Ruth said.

And so she did.

In the middle of the night Boaz awoke suddenly, startled, and saw someone at his feet. "Who art thou who lies at my feet?"

"I am thy handmaid Ruth," she said. "Spread thy robe over me for I am cold. Thou art a redeemer."

And he answered, "Blessed is the Almighty indeed. Thy last act of kindness is greater than thy first, for thou hast not gone after younger men, be they poor or rich."

Ruth was silent, as Naomi had cautioned.

"While it is true I am a redeemer—which is to say one who is related to thee through thy husband's line and can therefore marry thee and thus carry on thy husband's name—there is another redeemer who stands closer than I. Stay here at my feet the night. And if in the morning he will redeem thee—fine. But if he does not want to be thy husband, I shall take on that role."

So Ruth lay at Boaz's feet all the night long and in the morning she arose before anyone could recognize her, and went back to the house she shared with Naomi.

Naomi was waiting at the door. "How did it go, my daughter?" she asked.

Ruth told her everything, then opened her shawl. "He gave me these six measures of barley before I left, saying, 'Do not go empty-handed to thy mother-in-law.' "

Naomi smiled. "Boaz is a good man. And he knows the law. He will not rest until the matter is settled today."

Now Boaz had already gone up to the gate of the city and sat down there, with some of the elders of Judah, waiting.

When at last the sun was high overhead, the other redeemer passed by and Boaz waved to him.

"Come and sit with me," Boaz called out. "I have business to transact with thee."

The other man came and sat and Boaz said, "The parcel of land which belonged to our brother Elimelech is being offered for sale by Naomi, who has returned from the fields of Moab. If thou wish to redeem it, then re-deem it. But if thou art not interested, tell me, for I am willing if thou art not."

The other man looked thoughtful. "Is the land free and clear?"

Boaz shook his head. "Thou must also acquire Ruth the Moabite, the wife of Mahlon, with it."

"No, no—this I cannot do. It would imperil my own inheritance should I marry a Moabite," the man said. "Buy it thyself." He took off his shoe and gave it to Boaz, which was what was done in those days to transact business.

Holding the shoe up, Boaz then turned to the elders. "Thou art all wit-nesses that this day I have bought all that was Elimelech's and all that was Chilion's and Mahlon's from the widow Naomi. And what is more, I have acquired Ruth the Moabite as my wife, to perpetuate the name of the de-ceased and his inheritance."

Then all the people who were there at the gate cried, "We are wit-nesses!"

And so Boaz took Ruth and she became his wife and she bore him a son.

Old Naomi held the child and became his nurse, for neither she nor

Ruth would have any other woman care for the baby. In fact, the neighborhood women all smiled, saying, "A son is born to Naomi as well as to Ruth."

And that son was Obed, the father of Jesse, who was the father of David who became king over all Israel.

The Serpent Mother

INDIA

An old couple had seven married sons. All the sons and their wives lived with their old parents. The six senior daughters-in-law were well regarded because they had rich relatives. But the seventh one was ignored and despised, for she had no relatives at her father's place. She was an orphan. Everyone in her father-in-law's house took to calling her "the one who has no one at her father's place."

Every day the whole family would eat their meals joyously. The youngest daughter-in-law had to wait till everyone else was finished and then collect the scraps of food left in the bottom of the earthen pots and eat them. Then she had to clean the whole heap of pots.

Things went on this way till the season came for offering food to dead ancestors. They made sweet *khir*, rice pudding, with the milk of buffaloes. The youngest wife was pregnant and had a craving for the *khir*, but who would give her any? The others ate it with relish and left her nothing but half-burned crusts at the bottom of the earthen pot. She looked at them and said, "Half-burned crusts of *khir*—well, that'll do for me." She carefully scraped the crusts into a piece of cloth and decided to eat them somewhere where no one would see her. It was time to fetch water from the well. The well site was overcrowded with the women of the village. The young daughter-in-law thought she would eat her *khir* crusts after everyone else was gone. When her turn came to fetch water, she put her little bundle of *khir* near a snake-hole. She drew her pitcher of water from the well. She thought she would eat her *khir* after a bath.

While she was bathing, a female serpent came out of the hole unseen. She too was pregnant, and the smell of *khir* drew her. She craved to eat it, and she ate it all up and went back to her hole. She had decided that she would bite the owner of the *khir* if he or she used abusive language and cursed the thief who had taken it.

The young daughter-in-law returned eagerly after her bath to pick up her bundle. She found that the cloth was there but all the crusts of *khir* were gone. Not even a crumb was left.

"Oh," she cried, almost aloud, "I didn't get to eat any *khir* in the house and I didn't get to eat it even here. Maybe there's another unhappy woman like me somewhere around, and she may have eaten it. Whoever she is, let her be satisfied, as I would have been."

On hearing this, the female serpent came out of the hole and asked her, "Who are you, young woman?"

"Mother, I'm just an unhappy woman. I'm pregnant, and I craved to eat *khir.* I had some crusts here, but when I went for my bath, someone ate them up. Well, she must be someone unhappy like myself and may have been hungry. I'm glad that someone was made happy by my *khir.*"

"Oh, I was the one who ate your *khir,*" said the serpent. "If you had cursed me and abused me, I'd have bitten you. But you have blessed me. Now tell me why you're so miserable."

"Mother, I've no one to call mine in my father's place. The ceremony for my first pregnancy will be due soon. My parental relatives are supposed to perform it, and there's no one to do it," she said. As she spoke, her eyes filled with tears.

The serpent said, "Daughter, do not worry. From today on, just think of me and my kin as your parental relatives. We all live in this hole. When it's time to celebrate your first pregnancy, just put an invitation near the hole. It's a happy, auspicious occasion and should not go uncelebrated." Thus she became the young woman's foster mother. The young daughter-in-law went home, astonished at the turn of events.

When the auspicious day for celebrating the first pregnancy was near, the mother-in-law said, "This last daughter-in-law of mine has no brothers, nobody. Who's going to celebrate her first pregnancy?" The young wife said, "Mother-in-law, give me a letter of invitation for the ceremony."

"You brotherless woman, whom do you have at your father's or mother's place? Nobody! To whom will you give the letter of invitation?"

"I have a distant relative. Please give me a letter for her."

"Look, everybody! Our brotherless lady is out of her mind. She has suddenly found a relative."

At that point, a neighbor woman spoke up: "Oh, come along! Give the poor thing a piece of paper. What do you have to lose?"

The young daughter-in-law went to the snake-hole at the outskirts of the village, put the letter near it, and came back home.

The day for celebrating the first pregnancy came. The wives of the elder brothers and the mother-in-law ganged up on the young woman and began to mock her: "Just wait. Our daughter-in-law's relatives will come now from her father's place, her mother's place, from everywhere. They'll bring her presents and trunks full of clothes. Put pots of water on the stove to boil and bring wheat to make *lapasi*. Hurry, they'll all be here any minute!"

Even as they were teasing her and making jokes, guests arrived wearing festive red turbans. They looked like Moghul grandees. A noblewoman, looking like a Rajput, was among them. The young daughter-in-law knew at once that the noblewoman was none other that the serpent mother. Her mother-in-law and sisters-in-law were all astonished at the sight and began to mutter, "Where did these people come from? She has no one, not even a father or a mother or a brother. Where did all these relatives come from? And so rich!"

Then they began to welcome the guests: "Welcome, make yourselves at home. We have been waiting all this time for our young daughter-in-law's relatives." The pots for cooking *lapasi* for the festive occasion were actually placed on the stoves and preparations began.

Now the serpent mother called the young woman aside and whispered in her ear, "Daughter, tell them not to cook anything. Just put pots of spiced and boiled milk in this room. We'll drink it after we shut the door. We belong to the serpent community, as you know, and we can't eat ordinary food."

The young woman went to her mother-in-law and told her not to cook anything because her parental relatives belonged to a caste that drank only spiced milk—that was their prescribed food.

It was time for the meal. Vessels full of milk boiled with spices were put in the room. As soon as the door was shut, the guests resumed their original form as snakes, put their mouths to the vessels, and drank up the milk in no time at all.

The first pregnancy of the daughter was celebrated with all due ceremony. The guests gave gold and silver and silk to the husband and his relatives, who were wonderstruck and said, "Oh, look how much they've brought! They've given her such a rich dowry!"

The guests said at the end of it all, "Now give all of us leave to go and take our sister to our house for the delivery."

"Oh surely, surely! Please. After all, this is the daughter of your house. How can we refuse?" said the mother-in-law.

"And you don't have to send anyone to bring her back. We will come and bring our sister back to you," said the guests.

All the husband's relatives came out to bid good-bye to the young daughter-in-law and her relatives. The guests said, with great courtesy, "Now please go back in. We'll find our way." When all of them had gone back into the house, the serpents led the young woman to the hole on the outskirts of the village. There they said to her, "Sister, don't be afraid. We'll now assume our original forms. And we'll take you into the hole." The girl said, "I'm not afraid." Then they all entered the hole, taking the young woman with them.

As they went inside, she found spacious rooms. They were as beautiful as the datura flower. There were beautiful beds and swings. The serpent mother, the matron of the family, sat on a swinging bed that made noises like *kikaduka, kikaduka.* The snake god had jewels on his head and a big mustache. He was sitting on a soft, satin-cushioned seat.

The snake god treated the young woman as his daughter and looked after her every need in that underground world. She enjoyed the swinging bed made of gold and silver. Her new parents and the entire clan treated her with love and care.

Now the serpent mother was also ready to deliver. She told the young daughter-in-law, "Look here, Daughter, I want to tell you something, and don't be shocked. We are a community of snakes. We know that if all our babies survived, then we would disturb the balance in the world. There would be no place for any other creature, no place for people to walk, even. Therefore, we eat our babies as they are born, and only those that escape will live on. Don't be upset when you see me doing this."

When the time came, the young woman stood near the serpent mother with an earthen lamp in her hand. The serpent went on devouring the eggs as they were laid. Seeing this, the young mother-to-be was filled with disgust. Her hands shook and the lamp dropped from her hand. In the darkness two eggs hatched and escaped. The serpent mother could bite off only the tails of the two babies before they got away. So there were two tailless snakes.

When the young daughter-in-law was nine months pregnant, she went into labor and delivered a son, beautiful as the ring on the finger of a god. The son grew bigger day by day. When he began to crawl on his knees, she told her serpent mother, "Mother, you've done a lot for me. Now please take me to my house."

The serpent mother gave her mattresses, a cradle, necklaces, anklets, all sorts of ornaments, and overwhelmed her with gifts. Then she said, "Daughter, I want you to do something. Put your hand into the mouth of your grandfather sitting here. Don't be afraid. He won't bite you."

The young woman shook with fear but put her hand into the old snake's mouth. The hand and the whole arm went into his mouth, and when she took it out, shaking all the while, the arm was covered with bracelets of gold.

"Now put in the other hand, all the way," said the serpent mother. The young woman, less afraid this time, put her other arm all the way into the mouth of the snake, and when she withdrew it, it too was covered with bracelets of gold. Then two brothers in human form went with her and left her at the outskirts of her husband's village. When she arrived at her door, both mother and son, surrounded by all the relatives, shouted with joy, "The young daughter-in-law has come! The young daughter-in-law has come! She has brought a big dowry. But nobody knows where her relatives' village is."

The young woman said nothing.

Her son grew. One day the wife of the eldest son of the family was cleaning grain and getting it ready for grinding. The little boy picked up fistfuls of the grain and began scattering it. The eldest daughter-in-law shouted, "Son, don't do that. Why do you want to scatter the grain? We are poor people and can't afford to waste it." This was meant to taunt the young daughter-in-law about her dowry. She was hurt by the taunt. She went to the outskirts of the village, stood near the snake-hole, and wept. When she came back, a number of bulls arrived, carrying bags full of grain to her husband's house. The husband's relatives were put to shame.

Once her son spilled some milk. The eldest daughter-in-law threw him a taunt: "Son, don't do that. Your mother's relatives are rich. They will send you a herd of buffalo. But we are poor people. Don't spill our milk."

Again, the young daughter-in-law went to the snake-hole and wept there. The serpent mother came out and said to her, "We'll take care of it. Go home now, but when you go, do not look behind you. Do not give buttermilk to a juggler. Say *Nagel, nagel* and a herd of buffalo will come to your house." The woman returned to her house, saying *Nagel, nagel* all the way, and a herd of buffalo followed her. When she reached home, she called out to her in-laws and said, "We must clean the buffalo shed." All the relatives came out and were amazed to see countless buffalo with white marks on their foreheads.

Now what was happening in the snake-hole? The two young snakes without tails were unhappy because no one wanted to play with them. Their playmates said:

> Go away, Tailless. I won't let you play!
> Go away, Minus-Tail. I won't let you play!

The two young snakes went to their mother and asked her, "Mother, Mother, tell us. Who made us without tails?"

She said, "Sons, you have a sister who lives out there on the earth. When you were born, the earthen lamp accidentally fell from her hand. So, you have no tails."

"Then we'll both go and bite her for doing this to us."

"No, no! How can you bite your sister? She is a good girl. She'll bless you."

"If she blesses us, we'll give her a sari and a blouse for a gift and come back. But if she says nasty things about us, we'll bite her."

Before the mother could say anything, the two tailless snakes crept away and went to the sister's house. It was evening. One hid himself near the threshold, the other one lay hidden in the watershed. They thought, "If she comes here, we'll bite her."

When the sister came to the threshold, she stumbled and her foot struck something. She said, "I'm the one without a parent. May my paternal relatives be pleased to forgive me if I've struck something. The serpent god is my father and the serpent mother is my mother. They've given me silk and jewels for my dowry."

When he heard these words, the tailless snake thought, "Oh, this sister is blessing me. How can I bite her?"

The sister went then to the watershed. There also, she stumbled and her foot hit something. Again she said, "I'm the one without parents. May my paternal relatives be pleased to forgive me if I've struck something. The serpent god is my father and the serpent mother is my mother. They've given me silk and jewels for my dowry."

The second tailless snake also thought, "This sister is blessing me. How can I bite her?"

Then both the brothers assumed human form, met their sister, gave her a sari and a blouse, her son golden anklets, and went home to their hole.

May the Serpent Mother be good to us all as she was good to her!

JANE: Bad mothers-in-law are the stuff of Borscht Belt comics. Don't most stand-ups tell those jokes? Yet my first knowledge of mothers-in-law came from my father's reaction to my mother's mother. They seemed happily suited. He would tell stories and she would laugh and applaud. Since he always loved an audience, it was an in-law match made in heaven.

When Grandma came to visit—which was not very often, because she lived in Virginia and we lived in New York—my father seemed genuinely delighted to see her. The only one discommoded was me. Grandma slept in my room, sucked on lemons at night, took out her teeth and set them in a glass on my dresser, and snored.

Since I was quite young when my father's mother died, I have no memory of her at all, and no clue as to how she and my mother responded to one another. However, she was called "The Duchess" and "The General" by her own children, so I do have to wonder.

Whenever I thought about mothers-in-law in real life, I took my lesson from the story of Ruth, which I knew from Sunday school. I guess I expected that kind of relationship when I grew up.

And indeed, when your father and I got married, I received love and respect from his mother, Betty—after she got over the shock of her Catholic son marrying a Jewish girl, that is. (She said on the phone, "Well, if you aren't marrying a Catholic girl, at least you are marrying a Jew. After all, they are the most intelligent race!" Which is the nicest kind of racism, don't you think? Though like most racist statements, inaccurate as all get-out.)

So I was ready for the Ruth-and-Naomi life.

But Betty died even before you were born, and one of my lasting sorrows is that you never got to meet her. She was a loving, gentle, humorous, warm, saintly woman. I only knew her when she was sick with the bone cancer that would kill her at fifty-eight. But I admired her grace under the greatest of physical pressures.

And then a year later, my father-in-law married again. She was as different from your grandmother as chalk is from cheese. Oh, she had a peculiar sense of humor and was quite a beauty in her day. She adored her own daughter and could not do enough for her. But your father and his three brothers were ignored from the moment she walked into that house. She never once—in the twenty-plus years she and my father-in-law were married—came to visit us. Never (except once) sent Christmas presents for the grandchildren. Never (except once and that a year late) sent a present at the birth of our children.

I went from Ruth-and-Naomi to the ignored daughter-in-law in a single year.

Now I am a mother-in-law myself, not once but twice. I expect that I—like most mothers-in-law—fall somewhere between Naomi and the awful greedy woman of the Indian story. When I visit, I try not to overstay my welcome at either house. And I always come bearing gifts. In the back of my mind is the picture of that poor young woman sitting near the well with only a few crusts to eat being pitied only by a snake.

HEIDI: Well, I cannot speak for Betsy, your only daughter-in-law to date, but my husband—your son-in-law—adores you.

My introduction to mothers-in-law came not from you or Daddy, since both of your mothers-in-law died before I could understand the complexities of that relationship. Instead I found out about them from television. As you said, mothers-in-law are a bad joke, or the butt of the joke, but always a joke. It may be just TV humor, but I can understand why this happens.

In theory, a man has two important women in his life: his mother and his wife. I say "in theory" since in today's society of complex family relationships, a man is actually more likely to also have a stepmother, or be raised by his grandmother, or a single father, or any number of other variables. Since, in our perfect theoretical world, the mother is the primary woman in a man's life, the wife then has to compete with that. This can manifest in clichés like "It's not as good as my mother's meatloaf" or "Now you are sounding like my mother." So good or bad, we will always be compared to our husbands' moms.

I have to say, I have a kind of a strange relationship with my mother-in-law, Mimi. She had Brandon (her only child) at a very early age. It was a struggle for her to raise her son; at times it was the two of them against the world. So Mimi is not only much younger than you, but she is practically living in her childhood now. We have an almost sisterly relationship. She allows me to call or e-mail her about the stupid things her son does and she invariably comes back with the answer "Well, I didn't teach him that!" And then we laugh because we are the two women who truly know what a pain and a joy our Brandon is.

When Mimi moved in with us for a while, while she was getting her life back together, the two of us had to gang up on Brandon to let her get her own apartment. He has an overwhelming urge to protect his mom and it was smothering her. Whereas neither one of us could have won this argument alone, Brandon was overpowered by the two women he loved most in the world and finally gave in.

JANE: While I worried about the dynamics of your mother-in-law living with you, I was extremely jealous too. It reminded me of how little I had known my own two mothers-in-law, the one because she died early and the other because she withheld herself—and my father-in-law—from the family.

In these two folktales, though, the relationships of the mothers to their sons' wives is exaggerated to the right and to the left. On the one hand, Ruth and Naomi seem preternaturally loving to one another. (However, a recent conversation with a college professor friend made me realize such relationships do exist. She was taking care of her ninety-year-old mother-in-law out of a sense of deep devotion, even though her own husband had died several years previously.) On the other hand, the mother-in-law in the Indian story seems pathological.

HEIDI: Well, "The Serpent Mother" has been a bit of a bone of contention between us. You felt it needed to be grouped with "Ruth," whereas I thought it was less about a bad mother-in-law and more about a foster or surrogate mother—the snake. I wanted to place it elsewhere and discuss "Ruth" alone. Please, readers, notice who won this argument.

JANE: I think I wanted these two stories together because they represent for me the mother-in-law I wanted and the one I eventually got. There are any number of destructive mothers-in-law in fairy tales: the ogress who tries to kill her son's wife in order to eat the babies, for example, a motif that seems to have appeared in European tales from the thirteenth century on. Or mothers-in-law who steal the children away and have the poor wife accused of the deed. Or the classic Greek myth in which Venus persecutes poor Psyche partly because she is beautiful (shades of "Snow White") and partly because she dares to marry a goddess's son, Cupid.

Daring to marry the son—that's one of the keys, I guess. Does the mother see the son as a possession and resent the intrusion?

But it isn't the only key. With my second mother-in-law it was more a feeling of "Good, she has taken him off our hands and we needn't bother anymore."

I guess I am still looking for a Naomi—without having to marry again to get one! Though at sixty, I will probably have to settle for Ruth instead.

HEIDI: Brandon has said to me that if I die, he will move closer to you so that our daughters will be raised as I was raised. So if we can change the gender of Ruth, there he is.

JANE: I am stunned. Really. He certainly has never said any such thing to me. And I am terrifically moved. Though I do remember that after Maddison was born, and I stayed with you the first week and a half to help out, he actually said as the taxi pulled up to the house, "Are you really going so soon?" Next time I see him, I shall have to address him as Ruth. Do you think he'll understand?

HEIDI: No, but what a great segue—thanks.

There is another take on the Ruth/Naomi story that I have seen discussed at length on the Internet. It has been suggested that these two women do not have a motherly/daughterly relationship at all. It is thought by some fringe groups that the reason they were so close was that the death of their husbands freed them to become lesbians. I love this version and I hate it.

First, I love the thought that there could be a positive portrayal of homosexuals in the Bible. Since so many people use the Bible to preach against things, it would open up new avenues to preach tolerance and love—sometimes forgotten lessons in my opinion.

But I hate it as well because it says to me that some people find that love and devotion between two women have to be motivated by something other than just that, if they are not related by blood.

JANE: Xena and Gabrielle on television provide another example of this. And Emily Dickinson and her sister-in-law. Passionate friendships can be without sexual content. Woman to woman, man to man, woman to man. Even Adrienne Rich has mentioned, in *Of Woman Born,* the "close, sometimes explicitly sensual, long-lasting female friendships characteristic of the [1760s–1880s.]" And she also writes that such friendships were "tender, devoted" and lasted "through separations caused by the marriage of one or both women."

HEIDI: What is the matter with loving someone who didn't give birth to you as a mother? Why is that threatening? Women have bonds like this all the time. We share more of ourselves than men do and therefore are open to stronger ties. Friendships between men are often on a less intimate level. And although not familial, these female relationships take on a sister-to-sister or mother-to-daughter feeling. Like Ruth to Naomi.

JANE: Like you to me.

HEIDI: Ah, but we share a blood tie, so no one ever questions our love and devotion, mother to daughter, daughter to mother.

Snow White

Snow White

GERMANY

It was the middle of winter, and the snowflakes were falling like feathers from the sky, and a queen sat at her window working, and her embroidery frame was of ebony. And as she worked, gazing at times out on the snow, she pricked her finger, and there fell from it three drops of blood on the snow. And when she saw how bright and red it looked, she said to herself, "Oh, that I had a child as white as snow, as red as blood, and as black as the wood of the embroidery frame!"

Not very long after she had a daughter, with skin as white as snow, lips as red as blood, and hair as black as ebony, and she was named Snow White. And when she was born the Queen died.

After a year had gone by the King took another wife, a beautiful woman, but proud and overbearing, and she could not bear to be surpassed in beauty by anyone. She had a magic looking glass, and she used to stand before it, and look in it, and say:

> *"Looking glass upon the wall,*
> *Who is fairest of us all?"*

And the looking glass would answer:

> *"You are fairest of them all."*

And she was contented, for she knew that the looking glass spoke the truth.

Now, Snow White was growing prettier and prettier, and when she was seven years old she was as beautiful as day, far more so than the Queen herself. So one day when the Queen went to her mirror and said:

> "Looking glass upon the wall,
> Who is fairest of us all?"

It answered:

> "Queen, you are full fair, 'tis true,
> But Snow White fairer is than you."

This gave the Queen a great shock, and she became yellow and green with envy, and from that hour her heart turned against Snow White and she hated her. And envy and pride like ill weeds grew in her heart higher every day, until she had no peace day or night. At last she sent for a huntsman, and said:

"Take the child out into the woods, so that I may set eyes on her no more. You must put her to death, and bring me her heart for a token."

The huntsman consented, and led her away; but when he drew his cutlass to pierce Snow White's innocent heart, she began to weep, and to say:

"Oh, dear huntsman, do not take my life; I will go away into the wild wood, and never come home again."

And as she was so lovely the huntsman had pity on her, and said,

"Away with you then, poor child"; for he thought the wild animals would be sure to devour her, and it was as if a stone had been rolled away from his heart when he spared to put her to death. Just at that moment a young wild boar came running by, so he caught and killed it, and taking out its heart, he brought it to the Queen for a token. And it was salted and cooked, and the wicked woman ate it up, thinking that there was an end of Snow White.

Now, when the poor child found herself quite alone in the wild woods, she felt full of terror, even of the very leaves on the trees, and she did not know what to do for fright. Then she began to run over the sharp stones and through the thornbushes, and the wild beasts after her, but they did her no harm. She ran as long as her feet would carry her; and when the evening drew near she came to a little house, and she went inside to rest. Everything there was very small, but as pretty and clean as possible. There stood the little table ready laid, and covered with a white cloth, and seven little plates, and seven knives and forks, and drinking cups. By the wall stood seven little beds, side by side, covered with clean white quilts. Snow White, being very hungry and thirsty, ate from each plate a little porridge and bread, and drank out of each little cup a drop of wine, so as not to finish up one portion alone. After that she felt so tired that she lay down on one of the beds, but it did not seem to suit her; one was too long, another too short, but at last the seventh was quite right; and so she lay down upon it, committed herself to heaven, and fell asleep.

When it was quite dark, the masters of the house came home. They were seven dwarfs, whose occupation was to dig underground among the mountains. When they had lighted their seven candles, and it was quite light in the little house, they saw that someone must have been in, as everything was not in the same order in which they left it. The first said:

"Who has been sitting in my little chair?"

The second said:

"Who has been eating from my little plate?"

The third said:

"Who has been taking my little loaf?"

The fourth said:

"Who has been tasting my porridge?"

The fifth said:

"Who has been using my little fork?"

The sixth said:

"Who has been cutting with my little knife?"

The seventh said:

"Who has been drinking from my little cup?"

Then the first one, looking round, saw a hollow in his bed, and cried: "Who has been lying on my bed?"

And the others came running, and cried:

"Someone has been on our beds too!"

But when the seventh looked at his bed, he saw little Snow White lying there asleep. Then he told the others, who came running up, crying out in their astonishment, and holding up their seven little candles to throw a light upon Snow White.

"O goodness! O gracious!" cried they, "what beautiful child is this?" and were so full of joy to see her that they did not wake her, but let her sleep on. And the seventh dwarf slept with his comrades, an hour at a time with each, until the night had passed.

When it was morning, and Snow White awoke and saw the seven dwarfs, she was very frightened; but they seemed quite friendly, and asked her what her name was, and she told them; and then they asked how she came to be in their house. And she related to them how her stepmother had wished her to be put to death, and how the huntsman had spared her life, and how she had run the whole day long, until at last she had found their little house. Then the dwarfs said:

"If you will keep our house for us, and cook, and wash, and make the beds, and sew and knit, and keep everything tidy and clean, you may stay with us, and you shall lack nothing."

"With all my heart," said Snow White; and so she stayed, and kept the house in good order. In the morning the dwarfs went to the mountain to dig for gold; in the evening they came home, and their supper had to be ready for them. All the day long the maiden was left alone, and the good little dwarfs warned her, saying:

"Beware of your stepmother, she will soon know you are here. Let no one into the house."

Now the Queen, having eaten Snow White's heart, as she supposed, felt quite sure that now she was the first and fairest, and so she came to her mirror, and said:

"Looking glass upon the wall,
Who is fairest of us all?"

And the glass answered:

"Queen, thou art of beauty rare,
But Snow White living in the glen
With the seven little men
Is a thousand times more fair."

Then she was very angry, for the glass always spoke the truth, and she knew that the huntsman must have deceived her, and that Snow White must still be living. And she thought and thought how she could manage to make an end of her, for as long as she was not the fairest in the land, envy left her no rest. At last she thought of a plan; she painted her face and dressed herself like an old peddler woman, so that no one would have known her. In this disguise she went across the seven mountains, until she came to the house of the seven little dwarfs, and she knocked at the door and cried:

"Fine wares to sell! fine wares to sell!"

Snow White peeped out of the window and cried:

"Good day, good woman, what have you to sell?"

"Good wares, fine wares," answered she, "laces of all colors"; and she held up a piece that was woven of variegated silk.

"I need not be afraid of letting in this good woman," thought Snow White, and she unbarred the door and bought the pretty lace.

"What a figure you are, child!" said the old woman, "come and let me lace you properly for once."

Snow White, suspecting nothing, stood up before her, and let her lace her with the new lace; but the old woman laced so quick and tight that it took Snow White's breath away, and she fell down as dead.

"Now you have done with being the fairest," said the old woman as she hastened away.

Not long after that, toward evening, the seven dwarfs came home, and were terrified to see their dear Snow White lying on the ground, without life or motion; they raised her up, and when they saw how tightly she was laced they cut the lace in two; then she began to draw breath, and little by little she returned to life. When the dwarfs heard what had happened they said:

"The old peddler woman was no other than the wicked queen; you must beware of letting anyone in when we are not here!"

And when the wicked woman got home she went to her glass and said:

> *"Looking glass against the wall,*
> *Who is fairest of us all?"*

And it answered as before:

> *"Queen, thou art of beauty rare,*
> *But Snow White living in the glen*
> *With the seven little men*
> *Is a thousand times more fair."*

When she heard that she was so struck with surprise that all the blood left her heart, for she knew that Snow White must still be living.

"But now," said she, "I will think of something that will be her ruin." And by witchcraft she made a poisoned comb. Then she dressed herself up to look like another different sort of old woman. So she went across the seven mountains and came to the house of the seven dwarfs and knocked at the door and cried:

"Good wares to sell! good wares to sell!"

Snow White looked out and said:

"Go away, I must not let anybody in."

"But you are not forbidden to look," said the old woman, taking out the poisoned comb and holding it up. It pleased the poor child so much that she was tempted to open the door; and when the bargain was made the old woman said:

"Now, for once your hair shall be properly combed."

Poor Snow White, thinking no harm, let the old woman do as she would, but no sooner was the comb put in her hair than the poison began to work, and the poor girl fell down senseless.

"Now, you paragon of beauty," said the wicked woman, "this is the end of you," and went off. By good luck it was now near evening, and the seven little dwarfs came home. When they saw Snow White lying on the ground as dead, they thought directly that it was the stepmother's doing, and looked about, found the poisoned comb, and no sooner had they drawn it out of her hair than Snow White came to herself, and related all that had passed. Then they warned her once more to be on her guard, and never again to let anyone in at the door.

And the Queen went home and stood before the looking glass and said:

> *"Looking glass against the wall,*
> *Who is fairest of us all?"*

And the looking glass answered as before:

> *"Queen, thou art of beauty rare,*
> *But Snow White living in the glen*
> *With the seven little men*
> *Is a thousand times more fair."*

When she heard the looking glass speak thus she trembled and shook with anger.

"Snow White shall die," cried she, "though it should cost me my own life!" And then she went to a secret lonely chamber, where no one was likely to come, and there she made a poisonous apple. It was beautiful to look upon, being white with red cheeks, so that anyone who should see it must long for it, but whoever ate even a little bit of it must die. When the apple was ready she painted her face and clothed herself like a peasant woman, and went across the seven mountains to where the seven dwarfs lived. And when she knocked at the door Snow White put her head out of the window and said:

"I dare not let anybody in; the seven dwarfs told me not."

"All right," answered the woman; "I can easily get rid of my apples else-where. There, I will give you one."

"No," answered Snow White, "I dare not take anything."

"Are you afraid of poison?" said the woman. "Look here, I will cut the apple in two pieces; you shall have the red side, I will have the white one." For the apple was so cunningly made, that all the poison was in the rosy half of it. Snow White longed for the beautiful apple, and as she saw the peasant woman eating a piece of it she could no longer refrain, but stretched out her hand and took the poisoned half. But no sooner had she taken a morsel of it into her mouth than she fell to the earth as dead. And the Queen, casting on her a terrible glance, laughed aloud and cried:

"As white as snow, as red as blood, as black as ebony! this time the dwarfs will not be able to bring you to life again."

And when she went home and asked the looking glass:

> *"Looking glass against the wall,*
> *Who is fairest of us all?"*

at last it answered:

> *"You are the fairest now of all."*

Then her envious heart had peace, as much as an envious heart can have.

The dwarfs, when they came home in the evening, found Snow White lying on the ground, and there came no breath out of her mouth, and she was dead. They lifted her up, sought if anything poisonous was to be found, cut her laces, combed her hair, washed her with water and wine, but all was of no avail, the poor child was dead, and remained dead. Then they laid her on a bier, and sat all seven of them around it, and wept and lamented three whole days. And then they would have buried her, but that she looked still as if she were living, with her beautiful blooming cheeks. So they said:

"We cannot hide her away in the black ground." And they had made a coffin of clear glass, so as to be looked into from all sides, and they laid her in it, and wrote in golden letters upon it her name, and that she was a king's daughter. Then they set the coffin out upon the mountain, and one of them always remained by it to watch. And the birds came too, and mourned for Snow White, first an owl, then a raven, and lastly, a dove.

Now, for a long while Snow White lay in the coffin and never changed, but looked as if she were asleep, for she was still as white as snow, as red as blood, and her hair was as black as ebony. It happened, however, that one day a king's son rode through the wood and up to the dwarfs' house, which was near it. He saw on the mountain the coffin, and beautiful Snow White within it, and he read what was written in golden letters upon it. Then he said to the dwarfs:

"Let me have the coffin, and I will give you whatever you like to ask for it."

But the dwarfs told him that they could not part with it for all the gold in the world. But he said:

"I beseech you to give it me, for I cannot live without looking upon Snow White; if you consent I will bring you to great honor, and care for you as if you were my brethren."

When he so spoke the good little dwarfs had pity upon him and gave him the coffin, and the King's son called his servants and bid them carry it away on their shoulders. Now it happened that as they were going along they stumbled over a bush, and with the shaking the bit of poisoned apple flew out of her throat. It was not long before she opened her eyes, threw up the cover of the coffin, and sat up, alive and well.

"Oh dear! where am I?" cried she. The King's son answered, full of joy, "You are near me," and, relating all that had happened, he said:

"I would rather have you than anything in the world; come with me to my father's castle and you shall be my bride."

And Snow White was kind, and went with him, and their wedding was held with pomp and great splendor.

But Snow White's wicked stepmother was also bidden to the feast, and when she had dressed herself in beautiful clothes she went to her looking glass and said:

> *"Looking glass against the wall,*
> *Who is fairest of us all?"*

The looking glass answered:

> *"O Queen, although you are of beauty rare,*
> *The young bride is a thousand times more fair."*

Then she railed and cursed, and was beside herself with disappointment and anger. First she thought she would not go to the wedding; but then she felt she should have no peace until she went and saw the bride. And when she saw her she knew her for Snow White, and could not stir from the place for anger and terror. For they had ready red-hot iron shoes, in which she had to dance until she fell down dead.

$\mathcal{N}$ourie Hadig

ARMENIA

There was once a rich man who had a very beautiful wife and a beautiful daughter known as Nourie Hadig [tiny piece of pomegranate]. Every month when the moon appeared in the sky, the wife asked: "New moon, am I the most beautiful or are you?" And every month the moon replied, "You are the most beautiful."

But when Nourie Hadig came to be fourteen years of age, she was so much more beautiful than her mother that the moon was forced to change her answer. One day when the mother asked the moon her constant question, the moon answered: "I am not the most beautiful, nor are you. The father's and mother's only child, Nourie Hadig, is the most beautiful of all." Nourie Hadig was ideally named because her skin was perfectly white and she had rosy cheeks. And if you have ever seen a pomegranate, you know that it has red pulpy seeds with a red skin which has a pure white lining.

The mother was very jealous—so jealous in fact, that she fell sick and went to bed. When Nourie Hadig returned from school that day, her mother refused to see her or speak to her. "My mother is very sick today," Nourie Hadig said to herself. When her father returned home, she told him that her mother was sick and refused to speak to her. The father went to see his wife and asked kindly, "What is the matter, wife? What ails you?"

"Something has happened which is so important that I must tell you immediately. Who is more necessary to you, your child or myself? You cannot have both of us."

"How can you speak in this way?" he asked her. "You are not a stepmother. How can you say such things about your own flesh and blood? How can I get rid of my own child?"

"I don't care what you do," the woman said. "You must get rid of her so that I will never see her again. Kill her and bring me her bloody shirt."

"She is your child as much as she is mine. But if you say I must kill her, then she will be killed," the father sadly answered. Then he went to his daughter and said, "Come, Nourie Hadig, we are going for a visit. Take some of your clothes and come with me."

The two of them went far away until finally it began to get dark. "You wait here while I go down to the brook to get some water for us to drink with our lunch," the father told his daughter.

Nourie Hadig waited and waited for her father to return, but he did not return. Not knowing what to do, she cried and walked through the woods trying to find a shelter. At last she saw a light in the distance, and approaching it, she came upon a large house. "Perhaps these people will take me in tonight," she said to herself. But as she put her hand on the door, it opened by itself, and as she passed inside, the door closed behind her immediately. She tried opening it again, but it would not open.

She walked through the house and saw many treasures. One room was full of gold; another was full of silver; one was full of fur; one was full of chicken feathers; one was full of pearls; and one was full of rugs. She opened the door to another room and found a handsome youth sleeping. She called out to him, but he did not answer.

Suddenly she heard a voice tell her that she must look after this boy and prepare his food. She must place the food by his bedside and then leave; when she returned, the food would be gone. She was to do this for seven years, for the youth was under a spell for that length of time. So, every day she cooked and took care of the boy. At the first new moon after Nourie Hadig had left home, her mother asked, "New Moon, am I the most beautiful or are you?"

"I am not the most beautiful and neither are you," the new moon replied. "The father's and mother's only child, Nourie Hadig, is the most beautiful of all."

"Oh, that means that my husband has not killed her after all," the wicked woman said to herself. She was so angry that she went to bed again and pretended to be sick. "What did you do to our beautiful child?" she asked her husband. "Whatever did you do to her?"

"You told me to get rid of her. So I got rid of her. You asked me to bring you her bloody shirt, and I did," her husband answered.

"When I told you that, I was ill. I didn't know what I was saying," his wife said. "Now I am sorry about it and plan to turn you over to the authorities as the murderer of your own child."

"Wife, what are you saying? You were the one who told me what to do, and now you want to hand me over to the authorities?"

"You must tell me what you did with our child!" the wife cried. Although the husband did not want to tell his wife that he had not killed their daughter, he was compelled to do so to save himself. "I did not kill her, wife. I killed a bird instead and dipped Nourie Hadig's shirt in its blood."

"You must bring her back, or you know what will happen to you," the wife threatened.

"I left her in the forest, but I don't know what happened to her after that."

"Very well, then, I will find her," the wife said. She traveled to distant places but could not find Nourie Hadig. Every new moon she asked her question and was assured that Nourie Hadig was the most beautiful of all. So on she went, searching for her daughter.

One day when Nourie Hadig had been at the bewitched house for four years, she looked out the window and saw a group of gypsies camping nearby. "I am lonely up here. Can you send up a pretty girl of about my own age?" she called to them. When they agreed to do so, she ran to the golden room and took a handful of golden pieces. These she threw down to the gypsies who, in turn, threw up the end of a rope to her. Then a girl started climbing at the other end of the rope and quickly reached her new mistress.

Nourie Hadig and the gypsy soon became good friends and decided to share the burden of taking care of the sleeping boy. One day, one would serve him; and the next day, the other would serve him. They continued in this way for three years. One warm summer day the gypsy was fanning the youth when he suddenly awoke. As he thought that the gypsy had served him for the entire seven years, he said to her: "I am a prince, and you are to be my princess for having cared for me such a long time." The gypsy said, "If you say it, so shall it be."

Nourie Hadig, who had heard what was said by the two, felt very bitter. She had been in the house alone for four years before the gypsy came and had served three years with her friend, and yet the other girl was to marry the handsome prince. Neither girl told the prince the truth about the arrangement.

Everything was being prepared for the wedding, and the prince was making arrangements to go to town and buy the bridal dress. Before he left, however, he told Nourie Hadig: "You must have served me a little while at least. Tell me what you would like me to bring back for you."

"Bring me a Stone of Patience," Nourie Hadig answered.

"What else do you want?" he asked, surprised at the modest request.

"Your happiness."

The prince went into town and purchased the bridal gown, then went to a stone cutter and asked for a Stone of Patience.

"Who is this for?" the stonecutter asked.

"For my servant," the prince replied.

"This is a Stone of Patience," the stonecutter said. "If one has great troubles and tells it to the Stone of Patience, certain changes will occur. If one's troubles are great, so great that the Stone of Patience cannot bear the sorrow, it will swell and burst. If, on the other hand, one makes much of only slight grievances, the Stone of Patience will not swell, but the speaker will. And if there is no one there to save this person, he will burst. So listen outside your servant's door. Not everyone knows of the Stone of Patience, and your servant, who is a very unusual person, must have a valuable story to tell. Be ready to run in and save her from bursting if she is in danger of doing so."

When the prince reached home, he gave his betrothed the dress and gave Nourie Hadig the Stone of Patience. That night the prince listened outside Nourie Hadig's door. The beautiful girl placed the Stone of Patience before her and started telling her story:

"Stone of Patience," she said, "I was the only child of a well-to-do family. My mother was very beautiful, but it was my misfortune to be even more beautiful than she. At every new moon my mother asked who was the most beautiful one in the world. And the new moon always answered that my mother was the most beautiful. One day my mother asked again, and the moon told her that Nourie Hadig was the most beautiful one in the whole world. My mother became very jealous and told my father to take me somewhere, to kill me and bring her my bloody shirt. My father could not do this, so he permitted me to go free," Nourie Hadig said. "Tell me, Stone of Patience, am I more patient or are you?"

The Stone of Patience began to swell.

The girl continued, "When my father left me, I walked until I saw this house in the distance. I walked toward it, and when I touched the door, it opened magically by itself. Once I was inside, the door closed behind me and never opened again until seven years later. Inside I found a handsome youth. A voice told me to prepare his food and take care of him. I did this for four years, day after day, night after night, living alone in a strange place, with no one to hear my voice. Stone of Patience tell me, am I more patient or are you?"

The Stone of Patience swelled a little more.

"One day a group of gypsies camped right beneath my window. As I had been lonely all these years, I bought a gypsy girl and pulled her up on a rope to the place where I was confined. Now, she and I took turns in serving the young boy who was under a magic spell. One day she cooked for him and the next day I cooked for him. One day, three years later, while the gypsy was fanning him, the youth awoke and saw her. He thought that she had served him through all those years and took her as his betrothed. And the gypsy, whom I had bought and considered my friend, did not say one word to him about me. Stone of Patience, tell me, am I more patient or are you?"

The Stone of Patience swelled and swelled and swelled. The prince, meanwhile, had heard this most unusual story and rushed in to keep the girl from bursting. But just as he stepped into the room, it was the Stone of Patience which burst.

"Nourie Hadig," the prince said, "it is not my fault that I chose the gypsy for my wife instead of you. I didn't know the whole story. You are to be my wife, and the gypsy will be our servant."

"No, since you are betrothed to her and all the preparations for the wedding are made, you must marry the gypsy," Nourie Hadig said.

"That will not do. You must be my wife and her mistress." So Nourie Hadig and the prince were married.

Nourie Hadig's mother, in the meanwhile, had never stopped searching for her daughter. One day she again asked the new moon, "New moon, am I the most beautiful or are you?"

"I am not the most beautiful nor are you. The princess of Adana is the most beautiful of all," the new moon said. The mother knew immediately that Nourie Hadig was now married and lived in Adana. So she had a very beautiful ring made, so beautiful and brilliant that no one could resist it. But she put a potion in the ring that would make the wearer sleep. When she had finished her work, she called an old witch who traveled on a broomstick. "Witch, if you will take this ring and give it to the princess of Adana as a gift from her devoted mother, I will grant you your heart's desire."

So the mother gave the ring to the witch, who set out for Adana immediately. The prince was not home when the witch arrived, and she was able to talk to Nourie Hadig and the gypsy alone. Said the witch, "Princess, this beautiful ring is a gift from your devoted mother. She was ill at the time you left home and said some angry words, but your father should not have paid attention to her since she was suffering from such pain." So she left the ring with Nourie Hadig and departed.

"My mother does not want me to be happy. Why should she send me such a beautiful ring?" Nourie Hadig asked the gypsy.

"What harm can a ring do?" the gypsy asked.

So Nourie Hadig slipped the ring on her finger. No sooner was it on her finger than she became unconscious. The gypsy put her in bed but could do nothing further.

Soon the prince came home and found his wife in a deep sleep. No matter how much they shook her, she would not awaken; yet she had a pleasant smile on her face, and anyone who looked at her could not believe that she was in a trance. She was breathing, yet she did not open her eyes. No one was successful in awakening her.

"Nourie Hadig, you took care of me all those long years," the prince said. "Now I will look after you. I will not let them bury you. You are always to lie here, and the gypsy will guard you by night while I guard you by day," he said. So the prince stayed with her by day, and the gypsy guarded her by night. Nourie Hadig did not open her eyes once in three years. Healer after healer came and went, but none could help the beautiful girl.

One day the prince brought another healer to see Nourie Hadig, and although he could not help her in the least, he did not want to say so. When he was alone with the enchanted girl, he noticed her beautiful ring. "She is wearing so many rings and necklaces that no one will notice if I take this ring to my wife," he said to himself. As he slipped the ring off her finger, she opened her eyes and sat up. The healer immediately returned the ring to her finger. "Aha! I have discovered the secret!"

The next day he exacted many promises of wealth from the prince for his wife's cure. "I will give you anything you want if you can cure my wife," the prince said.

The healer, the prince and the gypsy went to the side of Nourie Hadig. "What are all those necklaces and ornaments? Is it fitting that a sick woman should wear such finery? Quick," he said to the gypsy, "remove them!" The gypsy removed all the jewelry except the ring, "Take that ring off, too," the healer ordered.

"But that ring was sent to her by her mother, and it is a dear remembrance," the gypsy said.

"What do you say? When did her mother send her a ring?" asked the prince. Before the gypsy could answer him, the healer took the ring off Nourie Hadig's finger. The princess immediately sat up and began to talk. They were all very happy: the healer, the prince, the princess and the gypsy, who was now a real friend of Nourie Hadig.

Meanwhile, during all these years, whenever the mother had asked the moon her eternal question, it had replied, "You are the most beautiful!" But when Nourie Hadig was well again, the moon said, "I am not the most beautiful, neither are you. The father's and mother's only daughter, Nourie

Hadig, the princess of Adana, is the most beautiful of all." The mother was so surprised and so angry that her daughter was alive that she died of rage there and then.

From the sky fell three apples: one to me, one to the storyteller and one to the person who has entertained you.

Mirabella
PORTUGAL

The trees were pines, old and lovely, and the ground was a soft mixture of pine needles and sand and felt cool to the feet of the young girl who walked there. Through a gap in the trees she could see a stretch of shore and beyond it the sea, sparkling in the bright sunshine. The girl, Mirabella, would have liked to have gone down to the shore and watched the waves and played among the pools and rocks, but she remembered that her father had once told her that it was dangerous for little girls to go on to the beach alone. And she remembered, too, that her father was dead and, also, that she was hungry.

Mirabella's father had been king of the Silver Isles, a good man whom all his subjects loved. Mirabella was his only child, but he had died and her mother had married again. Now she had a little boy, Gliglu, and in order that he might inherit the kingdom, she had ordered one of her servants to take Mirabella deep into the forest and leave her there, hoping that the wolves would find her and eat her. But when Mirabella was born, her aunt, who was a fairy, had placed round her neck a fairy chain on which was a silver bell, and though Mirabella's mother had often tried to get it off, she had never been able to do so. Somehow the chain would not slip over her head, no scissors could cut it, nor could her mother or any of the servants break it with the strength of their hands; as a result Mirabella still had her silver bell which tinkled gaily wherever she went.

That evening, as Mirabella walked along feeling hungrier and sadder than ever, she happened to stumble and her bell tinkled more loudly than

usual, so that a wolf heard it on its way through the forest and came running. When Mirabella saw the wolf, she was very frightened, because she
had heard such horrid tales about wolves, but this wolf just said:

> *"Silver bell, silver bell, I am here.*
> *Tell me what you wish and I shall do it,*
> *Never fear."*

At first, Mirabella could not believe her ears, but when the wolf repeated his offer of help, she decided that he looked rather kind and said:
"Dear Mr. Wolf, if you could go and fetch my mother, I should be most
grateful."

Mirabella, of course, did not know that it was on her mother's orders
she had been taken into the forest and left. The wolf turned and ran off
without saying another word, but Mirabella knew that he was going to do
as she asked and she began jumping about for joy, making the bell tinkle
more loudly than ever. A fox heard the silvery sound and came lolloping
up; then it sat back on its haunches and said:

> *"Silver bell, silver bell, I am here.*
> *Tell me what you wish and I shall do it,*
> *Never fear."*

Mirabella clapped her hands in delight and said:
"Oh, kind Mr. Fox, I am *so* hungry. Do you think you could get me
something to eat?"

Away went the fox, but in a few minutes he was back again carrying a
basket inside which Mirabella found a roast chicken and a loaf of bread, a
plate and knife and fork, all wrapped up in a clean white napkin. She was
delighted with her friend the fox and patted his head and stroked his back,
making him wag his thick brush. Then she spread the napkin and began to
eat. When she had finished her meal, which she enjoyed very much, the fox
picked up the basket and ran off.

Only now, however, did Mirabella realize that she had been thirsty as
well as hungry. Having been so successful with her bell, she decided to try
it again. No sooner had its silvery tinkle rung out than she heard the tin-
kling of another bell in the distance, coming nearer and nearer. Standing
on tiptoe to crane over some bushes, she saw a stream of water flowing
towards her, and sailing on it a small canoe. When it came near, she saw
that the canoe had a silver bell like hers fixed to its bows. The canoe

stopped beside her, and looking in she saw a silver mug. The canoe was singing a little song:

"Silver bell, silver bell, here I be.
When your mother comes, step in me."

Mirabella was very puzzled. She still thought that her mother loved her and could not understand why she should get into the canoe when her mother came. But she was too thirsty to worry, and taking the mug she stooped down, filled it with water and drank.

All at once she heard screams in the distance, the screams of a woman who was both frightened and angry. Nearer and nearer the sounds came, growing louder and louder as they did so, till Mirabella could distinctly hear: "Help! Help! Let me down, you brute." Then she saw the wolf come trotting into the clearing and on its back her mother. Every time her mother tried to jump down, the wolf turned its head and bared its teeth, so she stayed where she was. The wolf came running up to Mirabella and deposited her mother at her feet.

Mirabella's mother jumped up and began calling her daughter names and scolding her for having sent the wolf for her. She said that as soon as she got back to her palace she was going to make a law that all wolves were to be killed and that, if Mirabella ever dared show her nose anywhere near the palace again, she would have her put to death, too. Poor Mirabella was horrified to discover that her mother did not love her, and perhaps never had, and there was such a wicked look in the queen's eyes that Mirabella stepped into the canoe. "Where to?" asked the canoe. "Take me to where my father is," said Mirabella. At once the canoe began to move, gliding forward so smoothly and steadily that Mirabella was able to stand up and call good-bye to the fox and the wolf. She was just about to call to her mother too, when she saw the queen turn into a tree.

Soon the canoe had reached the coast and sailed on out across the sea. On and on it sailed for four whole days, and then at last land came in sight and Mirabella saw that they were approaching a beautiful island, on which were lots of the kind of palm-tree known as sacred palms. The grass was greener than any grass she could remember, and the sun seemed brighter, though warm rather than hot. As the canoe touched the sand on the shore she saw her father and, stepping out, they fell into each other's arms.

They walked up from the shore together, arm-in-arm. Mirabella thought how lovely it was to be loved and know she was loved. The fronds of the palms waved greetings, humming-birds flitted to and fro: everything seemed to be welcoming her. Her father looked younger and more hand-some than she remembered. And so they walked on till they came to a lovely house, not big enough to be called a palace, but a place of light and many windows, set in a wonderful garden in which were beds ablaze with the loveliest and strangest flowers, and there Mirabella lived with her father most happily.

One day, when Mirabella was walking along the shore of this enchanted island, she heard the familiar ringing of a silver bell and, looking out to sea, saw a canoe approaching in which sat her friend the wolf. Gently the canoe ran up on to the wet sand and, jumping out, the wolf told her that her aunt, the fairy, had sent him to fetch her. The prince of the neighbour-ing country, with whom she had often played when they were both chil-dren, wanted her to marry him and help him rule his country wisely and well. Mirabella remembered the prince, of whom she had been very fond, and readily agreed to go back to the world of ordinary mortals. So, having said good-bye to her father and her friends and companions, she went back to the shore and got into the canoe beside the wolf.

As they sailed along across the sparkling sea, the wolf told her what a commotion there had been in the Silver Isles when her mother the queen, who had been turned into a tree, had not come back. Search parties had been sent out, and when she could not be found people had said that the wolves must have eaten her, as the queen had hoped they would eat Mirabella, and the men had all taken their guns and bows and arrows and gone off into the forest intending to kill all the wolves or else drive them out of the country. But then they had come to the place where the oak tree stood, into which the queen had been turned, and someone had seen the queen's golden bracelet round one of the branches. Try as they would, they had been unable to get the bracelet off, so they had fetched a saw and sawn through the branch. As it fell, they had heard a loud shriek, like a cry of pain, and the tree had collapsed and fallen to the ground. Then they knew what had happened and realized that the queen must have been a wicked woman, so they had called off the wolf-hunt and the men had all gone back to their homes to get on with their work. And they had made Gliglu king and, although he was still just a youth, he was being a good king be-cause he took the advice of his aunt, the fairy.

When they reached the mainland there was Gliglu waiting for her with two lovely horses, one with a side-saddle which Mirabella mounted, and together they rode to the palace of the Silver Isles, the wolf trotting along beside them.

There was a great banquet to celebrate Mirabella's return. She sat between her brother and the prince who wanted to marry her, while underneath the table, with its head in her lap, sat the wolf. If ever she felt afraid or doubtful about the future, she had only to look into the wolf's kind brown eyes to be reassured. She fed him scraps and once he smacked his lips so loudly that the prince heard and, looking down, saw the wolf. Then Mirabella had to tell all about the wolf and she asked if the wolf might come and live with them, to which the prince at once agreed. But the wolf said that he thought he would rather stay in the forest, where his real home was; but that if Mirabella should ever need help, she had only to tinkle her silver bell and he would hear it and come to her aid as fast as four enchanted paws could take him, which was very fast indeed.

· *Conversation* ·

JANE: The first time I remember reading the Grimm's "Snow White" I was six years old, a native New Yorker, living in Manhattan. My mother had warned and warned both my brother and me not to open the door to strangers. In fact she spelled out in some detail why not.

So when Snow White—despite a similar warning from the dwarfs— let the old witch woman in, I knew that she deserved what she got. With that peculiar moral certainty that six-year-olds (and certain Republican congressmen and religious groups such as the Taliban) have, I was not at all surprised or horrified at what happened to Snow White. In fact, I believe I was somewhat miffed that she was rescued in the end. She seemed much stupider than my real literary heroine of the day, Alice, who knew that "if you drink much from a bottle marked 'poison,' it is almost certain to disagree with you, sooner or later."

The next time I read "Snow White" seriously, I was preparing to teach it at Smith College in a children's literature course. You were sixteen then, and all sorts of impossible young men were sniffing about. I realized with a shock that the story was not Snow White's story at all, but rather it was about the old queen who saw in her beautiful stepchild proof positive that time was passing her by. I did not need a mirror to hear in my ear the words whispered, "More beautiful than thou, oh Queen." Though in fact I was never as beautiful at sixteen as you were.

That was the moment I would have loved to build a glass coffin to put you in, and let you sleep there till the right college acceptance came along instead of your impossible boyfriends.

Never mind a prince.

HEIDI: My first reaction upon reading "Snow White" was "It's a good thing she is so beautiful since she is *so* stupid." Although the degree of her stupidity waxes and wanes in the retelling of stories through the ages and countries, it remains the one constant. The old saying that pops into my head is "Fool me once, shame on you. Fool me twice, shame on me." No one even touches upon that third time. Yikes.

While you grew up in a metropolitan area, I was raised in a small town (Hatfield, Massachusetts, population 3,000). I'm sure you gave me the whole "stranger danger" speech, but I don't remember it. I never felt unsafe since I knew everyone. I remember that even when we were young, my brothers and I used to be allowed to go on long walkabouts on our own, through the fifteen acres of our property.

These days, with my own girls, I am extremely overprotective. Where we live may not be the murder-and-kidnapping capital of the world, but even in our cul-de-sac, my four-year-old is not allowed to play outside without a grown-up around. Times are changing, and no one knows whom to trust.

There is presently a lot of talk about how to raise our children to be knowledgeable about the types of danger without frightening and crippling them. It's a fine line to be sure. And don't get me started on the whole issue of children on a leash (which I find a better option than a lost or stolen child). Independence versus safety. There are as many opinions as there are mothers.

Oh, and I think you should apologize to all of my ex-boyfriends for calling them "impossible," which I have to admit is pretty nice compared to some of the other things I have heard you say. Most of them are now married, fathers, entirely respectable men. Fifteen years can make an enormous difference.

I understand now why you couldn't stand them. To the mother of a teenage girl, teenage boys often seem the enemy. I know because I talk to teenage boys on the phone now, feed them dinner, and try to convince my daughter (and myself) that they get marginally better with age. But at least none of them have asked to take Lexi away to watch over her every day in her coffin.

JANE: Those princes in the two Snow White stories really are a piece of work. One is a necrophiliac and the other is stupid; but then he has been asleep for seven long years, so perhaps we can excuse him by reason of coma.

Has no one ever pointed out that Snow White's prince falls in love with a dead girl? (Or at least she is dead so far as he knows.) I have never seen it discussed in any of the literature about the story I have read. The prince wants to "collect" her and take her home. In fact he is remarkably insistent upon it, saying, "I cannot live without looking upon Snow White" and promises the dwarfs all kinds of things for her body in its glass coffin.

Now I know we should be reading that as metaphor. And I had one boyfriend in college who—because I wouldn't sleep with him—wrote a poem to me called "To Snow White." I think he felt that I had encased myself in a glass casket. But even as a child I had the heebie-jeebies at this part of the story. Of course, growing up Jewish in New York meant I didn't know about saintly relics and the worship of mummified bodies. (Though I admit that as an eight-year-old I was fascinated by the shrunken heads at the Museum of Natural History.)

However, there are always men who "collect dead girls," and I am not talking about serial killers. Rather, I mean men who want a girlfriend/wife/daughter who is a passive, decorative conversation piece. Someone to be talked about, not talked with. The Mick Jagger model syndrome, I suppose you might call it.

HEIDI: I have a theory that might explain why Snow White's prince felt this way. Once Lexi asked me if I believed in love at first sight. That was in response to my husband telling her that he fell in love with me instantly when he saw me win a limbo contest in a pair of very short shorts with strategically placed holes. (Don't ask.)

My theory is that everyone falls in love at first sight about ten times a day—with the man on a TV commercial, the guy in the grocery store, a teacher, the mailman, the weather girl—anyone he or she finds attractive. But normally we don't really have the opportunity to meet that person, nor do we have any chance to possess him or her, except with our imaginations.

Maybe this helps explain Snow White's obsessive suitor. He is instantly and physically attracted and—because he is a prince and obviously very rich—he is able to arrange a more permanent association with the girl of his dreams.

JANE: That doesn't make it any less creepy. Needing to possess the beloved in such a way seems to me dysfunction at the highest level. And no amount of interpretational gobbledygook (one text has it that "Snow White" is "a story of successful initiation of a young woman into patriarchal culture") can make me like that obsessive prince.

If the story were turned around—with the prince in the coffin and the forest girl purchasing him as a keepsake—I think we would find it just as disturbing. And in fact, there are elements of that turnaround in the "Nourie Hadig" variant. It is the prince, not the heroine, who lies comatose, needing tending. But we know that he is sleeping. Coma is marginally more acceptable in a partner than death, I suppose.

I think only in "Mirabella" is there a reasonable ending and a possible happily-ever-after.

HEIDI: But let's get back to the mother-daughter relationship in the story for a moment. "Snow White" has the classic evil stepmother, while in "Nourie Hadig" and "Mirabella" the antagonist is the actual biological mom.

JANE: And there is not a whit of difference among them. The Snow White moms are both bloodthirsty, vain, envious harridans. But there is something even more cold-blooded about Mirabella's mom, who simply wants the kingdom for her own son. She could as easily have married the girl off to a foreign king, but she pursues her relentlessly.

But as for those Snow White moms: The simple fact that a mother can look in the mirror and realize that time has stamped its little crow's-feet at the corners of her eyes and that her sixteen-year-old daughter still has the gorgeous lambent skin of childhood, does not mean Mom pulls out a knife. The older women portrayed in the these two stories are sociopaths, and not to be confused with a regular mother or stepmother, who may have occasional moments of vanity. Iona and Peter Opie, whose *Classic Fairy Tales* was a core text in the children's literature class I taught at Smith, says of the story that it is a "morality, perhaps, on the spitefulness of which beauty queens are capable," but I think rather the two women in these stories are beyond mere spitefulness and have raised themselves to true psychopathy. As does Mirabella's mother, but for different reasons.

Roger Sale, in his book *Fairy Tales and After,* wrote: "There is . . . no suggestion that the queen's absorption in her beauty gives her pleasure."

That, I think, is the key. She has set up in her mind a world in which only she and the daughter exist: eternal opposites, implacable enemies.

However, here is something else to think about: it's somewhat sly on the part of the Snow White tellers that the three things that tempt the child into opening the door to the old witch are either vanity toys—the comb and the laces—or that old forbidden apple trick, which we can assume means sexual knowledge. In fact, one critic of the story, Dr. Evelyn Bassoff, goes so far as to say, "What the fairy tales teaches us is that a mother's marketing of her daughter's sexuality exploits her."

I came from a mother-daughter relationship that was supportive, not set in that awful dyad of foe against foe. My mother didn't resent my youth. But I know many women who have just that continuing, antagonistic Nourie Hadig relationship with their mothers. They call their mothers names like "Old Bitch" and "She Who Must Be Obeyed." They shiver at the thought of having to spend a single moment in their mother's company. They pass that antagonism down to their own children. It makes me unutterably sad.

Please note that Nourie Hadig is—at least momentarily—a poor starving Armenian. My mother would be so pleased.

HEIDI: I believe that I called you a couple of those names when I was Snow White's age, but I certainly don't anymore. In fact, I had to explain to a nine-year-old friend just last night that I was not in the least offended that Lexi called me (in the presence of this young friend) all sorts of nasty names. The child was torn between telling me the offending words and keeping a secret for Lexi, whom she holds in the highest regard. I had to tell her that such name-calling was perfectly normal and that she would no doubt call her mother similar things soon.

I don't think her mother (my friend Jennifer) was amused.

But such is the often rocky relationship between mother and teenage daughter.

JANE: Rocky? Rather it's what one editor friend of mine (a stepmother herself) calls "as embattled an area as I can imagine." In fact, when you were a teen, I suddenly became a teen too, or at least that's what it looked like to your father. You and I would squabble like two sixteen-year-olds, slamming doors and getting huffy, and making large pronouncements.

"I'm not going to live here anymore."

"I can't live this way anymore."

"Why can't you leave me alone?"

"Why can't she just do what I say?"

Why. Why. Why.

Mostly it was a tug-of-war. You wanting to grow up and away. And me wanting you to grow up the way I'd planned.

I had these snapshots of you in my head. One minute you were a squalling colicky baby, totally dependent on me. Then an active toddler, engaged with the world. Next an eight-, nine-, ten-year-old who was a bright, charming, loving, book-centered gymnastics star. Then a preteen whose scrubbed beauty and athletic body did not disguise an inquiring intelligence that loved poetry, music, bird watching, and little babies. You were the fulcrum around which an entire galaxy of young girls spun. You were kind to unfortunates, and always ready to help out friends. And then . . .

And then you became a teenager. All those wonderful traits became engorged. Your brightness became brittle backtalk. Your kindness to unfortunates extended to dating criminals. The poetry and music you loved were in impossibly bad taste. Your beauty became artificial. I could not see this as a passage through to adulthood. I was scared you were going to dead-end that way.

As a father in *Reviving Ophelia* asks plaintively: "Does my daughter need to be hospitalized, or is she just acting like a fifteen-year-old?" It's the question all parents ask. In fact I used to call adolescence the "arsenic hour." Only it was never clear whether I wanted to feed it to you or take it myself.

I think as a mother I internalized that question even more, because as I asked it, I remembered how I had been as a teen. I don't mean whether I was a good teen or a bad teen, but I remembered all those feelings of resentment, obligation, cultural expectations, and the overwhelming hopes of my own parents that weighed heavily on me.

All you heard, of course, was the nagging.

HEIDI: Nagging is one thing. At least I had had a good childhood. A solid foundation.

Jennifer told me that she not only had nasty things to say about her own mother at that age, but had even said them to her mom's face, something I don't recall ever doing.

Actually, Jennifer's childhood sounds a bit like a bad fairy tale. Raised by her father until his sudden death when she was a teen, she was then shipped off to her mother, a sort of biological stepmother. Her mother never tried to poison her or have her banished, but she certainly never taught her fabulous parenting skills either.

What saved Jennifer was not seven dwarfs or a kind-hearted woodsman or a Stone of Patience. She saved herself because she is smart and sharp-tongued and has a sense of humor and proportion.

Maybe Snow White could have learned a thing or two from Jennifer, who would have never accepted that first gift, let alone two others. She probably would have sent the old witch away in tears.

Of course now, like the jealous mothers (step or otherwise) in the stories, I find myself raising a gorgeous daughter. Two actually, but a four-year-old's beauty is a source of pride, not something anyone could be jealous of.

I don't think I am jealous of Lexi's beauty. In fact, I freely admit that her looks far surpass mine at her age.

There are nights when Jennifer and I cook together while our kids play. We share a bottle of wine and show each other photos of ourselves pre-pregnancy—our skinny, sexy pictures. We bemoan the loss of our waistlines, grayless hair, carefree attitudes. But we do it with humor, not obsessive jealousy.

JANE: I came upon a photograph of myself the other day, from the time when your father and I were first engaged. What startled me was that, for a moment, I thought it was a photo of you. And that made me proud—not envious or sad or full of longing.

Ten years ago, my mother's brother saw me after a long separation. For a moment he stared, and then said in his Virginia drawl that is larded over with a Harvard-Cambridge accent, "My gawd, woman, you look just like your mother."

Now that's a compliment that goes both ways—to my past, and to my future. I cannot imagine being jealous to the point of psychosis about either point of the scale.

But some of the fairy-tale critics also point tellingly to the fact that the "Snow White" stepmother is jealous because she fears her husband's eye might be straying to the younger girl. She wants to test the man in her life (the huntsman in "Snow White," the father in "Nourie Hadig") by getting him to kill the child.

And that made me think back to a moment when both your father and I clearly realized you had grown into a sexual being, no longer just a lovely child. You were sitting on the hood of his car in shorts and a

T-shirt and around you, like sharks in a feeding frenzy, were about ten of the boys in your class. Your father looked out of the kitchen window and remarked to me: "I didn't know she was in heat!"

Was I jealous? Did I see you as a threat? I honestly think your father's sense of humor about the situation defused for all time any such possibility.

Did I want to eat your heart and liver? I'm not that good a cook.

HEIDI: Let me slip back into my old Psychology 101 textbooks for a moment and point out that Eric Erikson created a model of "eight ages of man" in which he calls the growth from adolescence to early adulthood "identity vs. role confusion" and early adulthood "intimacy vs. isolation." And this made me wonder if those fairy tales with sleeping or comatose heroines had some connection with that move from child to adult. And then I began reading an interesting book, *In a Different Voice: Psychological Theory and Women's Development,* by Carol Gilligan. In it I came upon Bruno Bettelheim's theories about women's development in fairy tales. He says that in these fairy tales "the girl's first bleeding is followed by a period of intense passivity in which nothing seems to be happening." Yet Bettelheim believes that the deep sleeps of Snow White and Sleeping Beauty are a kind of inner concentration that he considers to be the necessary counterpart to the activity of adventure. In her book Gilligan writes: "Since the adolescent heroines awake from their sleep, not to conquer the world, but to marry the prince, their identity is inwardly and interpersonally defined. For women, in Bettelheim's as in Erikson's account, identity and intimacy are intricately conjoined."

JANE: Ah yes!—Bettelheim. I guess you can't get through a discussion of fairy tales—especially the Grimm's stories—without citing Dr. Brutal Bettelheim (as one friend's malaprop daughter called him) at least once.

But Bettelheim was a Freudian and he was mostly dealing with the stories as he used them with psychologically damaged children. I always read his book *The Uses of Enchantment* (which I called *The Abuses of Enchantment*) with a great big grain of salt. A salt lick, actually. I tend to fall into the Jungian camp when talking about fairy tales.

But what if he—and Erickson—are right? That most girls go through adolescence in a deep sleep. Maybe it's time to wake them up.

Mixed Messages

The Wood Maiden

CZECHOSLOVAKIA

Betushka was a little girl. Her mother was a poor widow with nothing but a tumble-down cottage and two little nanny-goats. But poor as they were Betushka was always cheerful. From spring till autumn she pastured the goats in the birch wood. Every morning when she left home her mother gave her a little basket with a slice of bread and a spindle.

"See that you bring home a full spindle," her mother always said.

Betushka had no distaff, so she wound the flax around her head. Then she took the little basket and went romping and singing behind the goats to the birch wood. When they got there she sat down under a tree and pulled the fibers of the flax from her head with her left hand, and with her right hand let down the spindle so that it went humming along the ground. All the while she sang until the woods echoed and the little goats nibbled away at the leaves and grass.

When the sun showed midday, she put the spindle aside, called the goats and gave them a mouthful of bread so that they wouldn't stray, and ran off into the woods to hunt berries or any other wild fruit that was in season. Then when she had finished her bread and fruit, she jumped up, folded her arms, and danced and sang.

The sun smiled at her through the green of the trees and the little goats, resting on the grass, thought: "What a merry little shepherdess we have!"

After her dance she went back to her spinning and worked industriously. In the evening when she got home her mother never had to scold her because the spindle was empty.

One day at noon just after she had eaten and, as usual, was going to dance, there suddenly stood before her a most beautiful maiden. She was dressed in white gauze that was fine as a spider's web. Long golden hair fell down to her waist and on her head she wore a wreath of woodland flowers.

Betushka was speechless with surprise and alarm.

The maiden smiled at her and said in a sweet voice:

"Betushka, do you like to dance?"

Her manner was so gracious that Betushka no longer felt afraid, and answered:

"Oh, I could dance all day long!"

"Come, then, let us dance together," said the maiden. "I'll teach you."

With that she tucked up her skirt, put her arm about Betushka's waist, and they began to dance. At once such enchanting music sounded over their heads that Betushka's heart went one-two with the dancing. The musicians sat on the branches of the birch trees. They were clad in little frock coats, black and gray and many-colored. It was a carefully chosen orchestra that had gathered at the bidding of the beautiful maiden: larks, nightingales, finches, linnets, thrushes, blackbirds, and showy mocking-birds.

Betushka's cheeks burned, her eyes shone. She forgot her spinning, she forgot her goats. All she could do was gaze at her partner who was moving with such grace and lightness that the grass didn't seem to bend under her slender feet.

They danced from noon till sundown and yet Betushka wasn't the least bit tired. Then they stopped dancing, the music ceased, and the maiden disappeared as suddenly as she had come.

Betushka looked around. The sun was sinking behind the wood. She put her hands to the unspun flax on her head and remembered the spindle that was lying unfilled on the grass. She took down the flax and laid it with the spindle in the little basket. Then she called the goats and started home.

She reproached herself bitterly that she had allowed the beautiful maiden to beguile her and she told herself that another time she would not listen to her. She was so quiet that the little goats, missing her merry song, looked around to see whether it was really their own little shepherdess who was following them. Her mother, too, wondered why she didn't sing and questioned her.

"Are you sick, Betushka?"

"No, dear mother, I'm not sick, but I've been singing too much and my throat is dry."

She knew that her mother did not reel the yarn at once, so she hid the spindle and the unspun flax, hoping to make up tomorrow what she had not done today. She did not tell her mother one word about the beautiful maiden.

The next day she felt cheerful again and as she drove the goats to pasture she sang merrily. At the birch wood she sat down to her spinning, singing all the while, for with a song on the lips work falls from the hands more easily.

Noonday came. Betushka gave a bit of bread to each of the goats and ran off to the woods for her berries. Then she ate her luncheon.

"Ah, my little goats," she sighed, as she brushed up the crumbs for the birds, "I mustn't dance today."

"Why mustn't you dance today?" a sweet voice asked, and there stood the beautiful maiden as though she had fallen from the clouds.

Betushka was worse frightened than before and she closed her eyes tight. When the maiden repeated her question, Betushka answered timidly:

"Forgive me, beautiful lady, for not dancing with you. If I dance with you I cannot spin my stint and then my mother will scold me. Today before the sun sets I must make up for what I lost yesterday."

"Come, child, and dance," the maiden said. "Before the sun sets we'll find some way of getting that spinning done!"

She tucked up her skirt, put her arm about Betushka, the musicians in the treetops struck up, and off they whirled. The maiden danced more beautifully than ever. Betushka couldn't take her eyes from her. She forgot her goats, she forgot her spinning. All she wanted to do was to dance on forever.

At sundown the maiden paused and the music stopped. Then Betushka, clasping her hands to her head, where the unspun flax was twined, burst into tears. The beautiful maiden took the flax from her head, wound it round the stem of a slender birch, grasped the spindle, and began to spin. The spindle hummed along the ground and filled in no time. Before the sun sank behind the woods all the flax was spun, even that which was left over from the day before. The maiden handed Betushka the full spindle and said:

"Remember my words:

Reel and grumble not!
Reel and grumble not!"

When she said this, she vanished as if the earth had swallowed her.

Betushka was very happy now and she thought to herself on her way home: "Since she is so good and kind, I'll dance with her again if she asks me. Oh, how I hope she does!"

She sang her merry little song as usual and the goats trotted cheerfully along.

She found her mother vexed with her, for she had wanted to reel yesterday's yarn and had discovered that the spindle was not full.

"What were you doing yesterday," she scolded, "that you didn't spin your stint?"

Betushka hung her head. "Forgive me, mother. I danced too long." Then she showed her mother today's spindle and said: "See, today I more than made up for yesterday."

Her mother said no more but went to milk the goats and Betushka put away the spindle. She wanted to tell her mother her adventure, but she thought to herself: "No, I'll wait. If the beautiful lady comes again, I'll ask her who she is and then I'll tell mother." So she said nothing.

On the third morning she drove the goats as usual to the birch wood. The goats went to pasture and Betushka, sitting down under a tree, began to spin and sing. When the sun pointed to noon, she laid her spindle on the grass, gave the goats a mouthful of bread, gathered some strawberries, ate her luncheon, and then, giving the crumbs to the birds, she said cheerily:

"Today, my little goats, I will dance for you!"

She jumped up, folded her arms, and was about to see whether she could move as gracefully as the beautiful maiden, when the maiden herself stood before her.

"Let us dance together," she said. She smiled at Betushka, put her arm about her, and as the music above their heads began to play, they whirled round and round with flying feet. Again Betushka forgot the spindle and the goats. Again she saw nothing but the beautiful maiden whose body was lithe as a willow shoot. Again she heard nothing but the enchanting music to which her feet danced of themselves.

They danced from noon till sundown. Then the maiden paused and the music ceased. Betushka looked around. The sun was already set behind the woods. She clasped her hands to her head and looking down at the unfilled spindle she burst into tears.

"Oh, what will my mother say?" she cried.

"Give me your little basket," the maiden said, and I will put something in it that will more than make up for today's stint."

Betushka handed her the basket and the maiden took it and vanished. In a moment she was back. She returned the basket and said:

"Look not inside until you're home!
Look not inside until you're home!"

As she said these words she was gone as if a wind had blown her away.

Betushka wanted awfully to peep inside but she was afraid to. The basket was so light that she wondered whether there was anything at all in it. Was the lovely lady only fooling her? Halfway home she peeped in to see.

Imagine her feelings when she found the basket was full of birch leaves! Then indeed did Betushka burst into tears and reproach herself for being so simple. In her vexation she threw out a handful of leaves and was going to empty the basket when she thought to herself:

"No, I'll keep what's left as litter for the goats."

She was almost afraid to go home. She was so quiet that again the little goats wondered what ailed their shepherdess.

Her mother was waiting for her in great excitement.

"For heaven's sake, Betushka, what kind of a spool did you bring home yesterday?"

"Why?" Betushka faltered.

"When you went away this morning I started to reel that yarn. I reeled and reeled and the spool remained full. One skein, two skeins, three skeins, and still the spool was full. 'What evil spirit has spun that?' I cried out impatiently, and instantly the yarn disappeared from the spindle as if blown away. Tell me, what does it mean?"

So Betushka confessed and told her mother all she knew about the beautiful maiden.

"Oh," cried her mother in amazement, "that was a wood maiden! At noon and midnight the wood maidens dance. It is well you are not a little boy or she might have danced you to death! But they are often kind to little girls and sometimes make them rich presents. Why didn't you tell me? If I hadn't grumbled, I could have had yarn enough to fill the house!"

Betushka thought of the little basket and wondered if there might be something under the leaves. She took out the spindle and unspun flax and looked in once more.

"Mother!" she cried. "Come here and see!"

Her mother looked and clapped her hands. The birch leaves were all turned to gold!

Betushka reproached herself bitterly: "She told me not to look inside until I got home, but I didn't obey."

"It's lucky you didn't empty the whole basket," her mother said.

The next morning she herself went to look for the handful of leaves that Betushka had thrown away. She found them still lying in the road but they were only birch leaves.

But the riches which Betushka brought home were enough. Her mother bought a farm with fields and cattle. Betushka had pretty clothes and no longer had to pasture goats.

But no matter what she did, no matter how cheerful and happy she was, still nothing ever again gave her quite so much pleasure as the dance with the wood maiden. She often went to the birch wood in the hope of seeing the maiden again. But she never did.

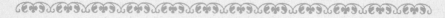

Tunjur, Tunjur

PALESTINIAN ARAB

TELLER: Testify that God is One!
AUDIENCE: There is no god but God.

There was once a woman who could not get pregnant and have children. Once upon a day she had an urge; she wanted babies. "O Lord!" she cried out, "why of all women am I like this? Would that I could get pregnant and have a baby, and may Allah grant me a girl even if she is only a cooking pot!"

One day she became pregnant. A day came and a day went, and behold! she was ready to deliver. She went into labour and delivered, giving birth to a cooking pot. What was the poor woman to do? She washed it, cleaning it well, put the lid on it, and placed it on the shelf.

One day the pot started to talk. "Mother," she said, "take me down from this shelf!"

"Alas, daughter!" replied the mother, "where am I going to put you?"

"What do you care?" said the daughter. "Just bring me down, and I will make you rich for generations to come."

The mother brought her down. "Now put my lid on," said the pot, "and leave me outside the door." Putting the lid on, the mother took her outside the door.

The pot started to roll, singing as she went, "Tunjur, tunjur, clink, clink, O my mama!" She rolled until she came to a place where people usually gather. In a while people were passing by. A man came and found the pot all settled in its place. "Eh!" he exclaimed, "who has put this pot in the middle of the path? I'll be damned! What a beautiful pot! It's probably made of silver." He looked it over well. "Hey, people!" he called, "whose pot is this? Who put it here?" No one claimed it. "By Allah," he said, "I'm going to take it home with me."

On his way home, he went by the honey vendor. He had the pot filled with honey and brought it home to his wife. "Look, wife," he said, "how beautiful is this pot!" The whole family was greatly pleased with it.

In two or three days they had guests, and they wanted to offer them some honey. The woman of the house brought the pot down from the shelf. Push and pull on the lid, but the pot would not open! She called her husband over. Pull and push, but open it he could not. His guests pitched in. Lifting the pot and dropping it, the man tried to break it open with hammer and chisel. He tried everything, but it was no use.

They sent for the blacksmith, and he tried and tried, to no avail. What was the man to do?

"Damn your owners!" he cursed the pot. "Did you think you were going to make us wealthy?" And, taking it up, he threw it out the window.

When they turned their back and could no longer see it, she started to roll, saying as she went:

> *"Tunjur, tunjur, O my mama.*
> *In my mouth I brought the honey.*
> *Clink, clink, O my mama.*
> *In my mouth I brought the honey."*

"Bring me up the stairs!" she said to her mother when she reached home.

"Yee!" exclaimed the mother. "I thought you had disappeared, that someone had taken you."

"Pick me up!" said the daughter.

Picking her up, my little darlings, the mother took the lid off and found the pot full of honey. Oh! How pleased she was!

"Empty me!" said the pot.

The mother emptied the honey into a jar, and put the pot back on the shelf.

"Mother," said the daughter the next day, "take me down!"

The mother brought her down from the shelf.

"Mother, put me outside the door!"

The mother placed her outside the door, and she started rolling—tunjur, tunjur, clink, clink—until she reached a place where people were gathered, and then she stopped. A man passing by found her.

"Eh!" he thought, "what kind of a pot is this?" He looked it over. How beautiful he found it! "To whom does this belong?" he asked. "Hey, people! Who are the owners of this pot?" He waited, but no one said, "It's mine." Then he said, "By Allah, I'm going to take it."

He took it, and on his way home stopped by the butcher and had it filled with meat. Bringing it home to his wife, he said, "Look, wife, how beautiful is this pot I've found! By Allah, I found it so pleasing I bought meat and filled it and brought it home."

"Yee!" they all cheered, "how lucky we are! What a beautiful pot!" They put it away.

Towards evening they wanted to cook the meat. Push and pull on the pot, it would not open! What was the woman to do? She called her husband over and her children. Lift, drop, strike—no use. They took it to the blacksmith, but with no result.

The husband became angry. "God damn your owners!" he cursed it. "What in the world are you?" And he threw it as far as his arm would reach.

As soon as he turned his back, she started rolling, and singing:

> *"Tunjur, tunjur. O my mama,*
> *In my mouth I brought the meat.*
> *Tunjur, tunjur, O my mama,*
> *In my mouth I brought the meat."*

She kept repeating that till she reached home.

"Lift me up!" she said to her mother. The mother lifted her up, took the meat, washed the pot, and put it away on the shelf.

"Bring me out of the house!" said the daughter the next day. The mother brought her out, and she said, "Tunjur, tunjur, clink, clink" as she was rolling until she reached a spot close by the king's house, where she came to a stop. In the morning, it is said, the son of the king was on his way out, and behold! there was the pot settled in its place.

"Eh! What's this? Whose pot is it?" No one answered. "By Allah," he said, "I'm going to take it." He took it inside and called his wife over.

"Wife," he said, "take this pot! I brought it home for you. It's the most beautiful pot!"

The wife took the pot. "Yee! How beautiful it is! By Allah, I'm going to put my jewelery in it." Taking the pot with her, she gathered all her jewelery, even that which she was wearing, and put it in the pot. She also brought all their gold and money and stuffed them in the pot till it was full to the brim, then she covered it and put it away in the wardrobe.

Two or three days went by, and it was time for the wedding of her brother. She put on her velvet dress and brought the pot out so that she could wear her jewelery. Push and pull, but the pot would not open. She called to her husband, and he could not open it either. All the people who were there tried to open it, lifting and dropping. They took it to the blacksmith, and he tried but could not open it.

The husband felt defeated, "God damn your owners!" he cursed it, "what use are you to us?" Taking it up, he threw it out the window. Of course he was not all that anxious to let it go, so he went to catch it from the side of the house. No sooner did he turn around than she started to run:

"Tunjur, tunjur, O my mama,
In my mouth I brought the treasure.
Tunjur, tunjur, O my mama,
In my mouth I brought this treasure."

"Lift me up!" she said to her mother when she reached home. Lifting her up, the mother removed the lid.

"Yee! May your reputation be blackened!" she cried out. "Wherever did you get this? What in the world is it?" The mother was now rich. She became very, very happy.

"It's enough now," she said to her daughter, taking away the treasure. "You shouldn't go out any more. People will recognise you."

"No, no!" begged the daughter. "Let me go out just one last time."

The next day, my darlings, she went out, saying "Tunjur, tunjur, O my mama." The man who found her the first time saw her again.

"Eh! What in the world is this thing?" he exclaimed. "It must have some magic in it, since it's always tricking people. God damn its owners! By Allah the Great, I'm going to sit and shit in it." He went ahead, my darlings, and shat right in it. Closing the lid on him, she rolled along:

"Tunjur, tunjur, O my mama
In my mouth I brought the caca.
Tunjur, tunjur, O my mama,
In my mouth I brought the caca."

"Lift me up!" she said to her mother when she reached home. The mother lifted her up.

"You naughty thing, you!" said the mother. "I told you not to go out again, that people would recognise you. Don't you think it's enough now?"

The mother then washed the pot with soap, put perfume on it, and placed it on the shelf.

This is my story, I've told it, and in your hands I leave it.

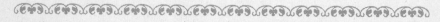

The Well o' the World's End

SCOTLAND

There was once an old widow woman, who lived in a little cottage with her only daughter, who was such a bonnie lassie that everyone liked to look at her.

One day the old woman took a notion into her head to bake a girdleful of cakes. So she took down her bake-board, and went to the girnel and fetched a basinful of meal; but when she went to seek a jug of water to mix the meal with, she found that there was none in the house.

So she called to her daughter, who was in the garden; and when the girl came she held out the empty jug to her, saying, "Run, like a good lassie, to the Well o' the World's End and bring me a jug of water, for I have long found that water from the Well o' the World's End makes the best cakes."

So the lassie took the jug and set out on her errand.

Now, as its name shows, it is a long road to that well, and many a weary mile had the poor maid to go ere she reached it.

But she arrived there at last; and what was her disappointment to find it dry.

She was so tired and so vexed that she sat down beside it and began to cry; for she did not know where to get any more water, and she felt that she could not go back to her mother with an empty jug.

While she was crying, a nice yellow Paddock, with very bright eyes, came jump-jump-jumping over the stones of the well, and squatted down at her feet, looking up into her face.

"And why are ye greeting, my bonnie maid?" he asked. "Is there aught that I can do to help thee?"

"I am greeting because the well is empty," she answered, "and I cannot get any water to carry home to my mother."

"Listen," said the Paddock softly. "I can get thee water in plenty, if so be thou wilt promise to be my wife."

Now the lassie had but one thought in her head, and that was to get the water for her mother's oat-cakes, and she never for a moment thought that the Paddock was in earnest, so she promised gladly enough to be his wife, if he would get her a jug of water.

No sooner had the words passed her lips than the beastie jumped down the mouth of the well, and in another moment it was full to the brim with water.

The lassie filled her jug and carried it home, without troubling any more about the matter. But late that night, just as her mother and she were going to bed, something came with a faint "thud, thud," against the cottage door, and then they heard a tiny little wee voice singing:—

> *"Oh open the door, my hinnie, my heart,*
> *Oh, open the door, my ain true love;*
> *Remember the promise that you and I made*
> *Down i' the meadow, where we two met."*

"Wheesht," said the old woman, raising her head. "What noise is that at the door?"

"Oh," said her daughter, who was feeling rather frightened, "it's only a yellow Paddock."

"Poor bit beastie," said the kind-hearted old mother. "Open the door and let him in. It's cold work sitting on the doorstep."

So the lassie, very unwillingly, opened the door, and the Paddock came jump-jump-jumping across the kitchen, and sat down at the fireside.

And while he sat there he began to sing this song:

> *"Oh, gie me my supper, my hinnie, my heart,*
> *Oh, gie me my supper, my ain true love;*
> *Remember the promise that you and I made*
> *Down i' the meadow, where we two met."*

"Gie the poor beast his supper," said the old woman. "He's an uncommon Paddock that can sing like that."

"Tut," replied her daughter crossly, for she was growing more and more frightened as she saw the creature's bright black eyes fixed on her face. "I'm not going to be so silly as to feed a wet, sticky Paddock."

"Don't be ill-natured and cruel," said her mother. "Who knows how far the little beastie has travelled? And I warrant that it would like a saucerful of milk."

Now, the lassie could have told her that the Paddock had travelled from the Well o' the World's End; but she held her tongue, and went ben to the milk-house, and brought back a saucerful of milk, which she set down before the strange little visitor.

> "Now chap off my head, my hinnie, my heart,
> Now chap off my head, my ain true love;
> Remember the promise that you and I made
> Down i' the meadow, where we two met."

"Hout, havers, pay no heed, the creature's daft," exclaimed the old woman, running forward to stop her daughter, who was raising the axe to chop off the Paddock's head. But she was too late; down came the axe, off went the head; and, lo and behold! on the spot where the little creature had sat, stood the handsomest young Prince that had ever been seen.

He wore such a noble air, and was so richly dressed, that the astonished girl and her mother would have fallen on their knees before him had he not prevented them by a movement of his hand.

"'Tis I that should kneel to thee, Sweetheart," he said, turning to the blushing girl, "for thou hast delivered me from a fearful spell, which was cast over me in my infancy by a wicked Fairy, who at the same time slew my father. For long years I have lived in that well, the Well o' the World's End, waiting for a maiden to appear, who should take pity on me, even in my loathesome disguise, and promise to be my wife, and who would also have the kindness to let me into her house, and the courage, at my bidding, to cut off my head."

"Now I can return and claim my father's Kingdom, and thou, most gracious maiden, will go with me, and be my bride, for thou well deserv'st the honour."

And this was how the lassie who went to fetch water from the Well o' the World's End became a Princess.

· *Conversation* ·

JANE: Folktales are often called moral tales. Well, yes and no. There are some very mixed-message tales in the folk canon. The Eskimo grandmother story is one. Another is "Rumpelstiltskin," in which a miller lies, his daughter is complicitous in the lie, the king is in it for the gold only, and the only character who does what he says he is going to do is the little man. And look where it gets him in the end!

Or think of "Puss in Boots," in which the cat happily lies, cheats, steals—and murders—for his master.

Yet "Rumpelstiltskin" and "Puss in Boots" are very popular stories and often used with little children. Gorgeous picture-book renditions of both were recent Caldecott Award Honor Books, one of the two most prestigious awards in children's books.

And what do the three mother-daughter tales we have just read tell us? Among other things, that lying to your mother can win you gold, that stealing from your neighbors is okay unless you get caught, and that a promise enforced will win you a prince (as long as you cut off his head in time). If this is the core of ethics, I'll eat my Brothers Grimm.

What do we make of all these messages?

HEIDI: If there was one right answer to every question, if there was black and white with no shades of gray, if the line we were not supposed to cross was clearly inked into the ground, then we'd have it made. But they aren't, and we don't.

Ethics. Legal, moral, spiritual, maternal.

When it comes to happiness existing without conditions, well, even the most simple pleasures come with a cost—hidden or otherwise. Take chocolate, for example. It's all the things good in this world, wrapped up in one bite. But it is fattening and can rot your teeth.

JANE: Not to mention giving me reflux. Growing older has many things to answer for, but the one I am least forgiving of is that I can no longer eat chocolate. And it's not a question of guilt but of pain!

HEIDI: I find it a bit strange that the two things missing from most of the tales we've read are guilt and remorse. Either the women and girls don't feel them or the tale tellers are simply not interested in exploring these responses further.

Not that I'm complaining—neither are favorite emotions of mine, though as a mom I dole out Jewish guilt regularly and feel remorse constantly. As a daughter, I feel these two emotions less now that I'm grown, but I remember them clearly from my youth.

JANE: There's a line in a Robert Herrick poem about the three fatal sisters waiting on a sin. He names them: "Fear and Shame without, then Guilt within." Herrick was a seventeenth-century poet and one of the so-called London wits of his day. His little poem proves that guilt is not merely a Jewish trait.

But of course I have a major share of guilt and remorse in my life. It's hard to reach sixty without it, regardless of race, religion, or national culture.

For example, I will always feel guilty about not being able to visit my mother the last few months of her life, for I was hugely pregnant with your brother Jason. The doctor warned me that driving the three hours down to see her might easily precipitate an early birth and then my father would have had to deal with her death and my new life. (Though, as it was, Jason was seventeen days overdue and had to be induced. My mother died nine days later.) We spoke every day on the phone, but it was not the same. Huge guilt!

And I will always feel bad about not sending the three of you to one of the many fine private schools around, though at the time it was as much a money decision as an educational choice.

These should-haves can load up a lot of guilt on a person. But you are right—guilt and remorse are almost entirely missing in fairy tales, which are stripped down, compacted, compressed stories. Real emotions—other than happiness or fear—are left out, to be supplied by the readers or listeners.

HEIDI: In legal terms, guilt is something we punish for and remorse is a key mitigating factor in both sentencing and paroling. But these are steps taken, apparently, far after the happily-ever-afters of these stories. There is no need for guilt if your laziness or lying or greed are rewarded instead of punished. I tend to prefer the tales with an ending that teaches rather than stories that finish with mixed messages.

In old tales and new, or even old tales adapted into new ones (here I mean the Disney movies of same), I often see the lessons I am trying to teach my daughters being negated: outer beauty equals good girl; if we don't do our work, the fairy or frog or bunnies or birds (or, God forbid, the man) will do that work for us just as long as we cry, dance, or try to be clever. Or if you are the lovely heroine, no matter how bad the act, Mommy (or those ever present magical creatures) will bail you out.

However as a mother, I will keep the stories that say: "Do whatever it takes." That message is as true in today's society as in the folk stories, even if the monsters of the stories are no longer around. After all, I have never seen an omelet-cooking wolf, a lustful God of the underworld, or a vain witch stepmother. But the Ira Einhorns and the Ted Bundys are certainly out there. "Mothers," those non-mixed message stories seem to say to me, "Keep your daughters safe at all costs."

One of the reasons I love the story "Tunjur, Tunjur" so much is that it has a clear message in the end as to what will happen if you don't listen to your mom.

JANE: Someone will leave a hefty deposit in your little jar.

BEYOND THE MAGIC MIRROR: AN EPILOGUE

JANE: So what have we learned? Not that folktales simply teach us "lessons" about life. Rather that they can offer us platforms upon which we can play out our inner conflicts. They are starting places for the stories that are our own lives. Sheldon Cashdan, in *The Witch Must Die,* calls them "psychodramas of childhood." I think they are psychodramas in adulthood as well.

But do not be beguiled by the magic in these stories. Sometimes what they seem to be saying and what they actually "teach" are very different.

HEIDI: I've long held that the story "Beauty and the Beast" teaches our daughters exactly how to become battered wives. Its message—to me—states clearly that no matter how beastly and cruel the monster you live with is, somewhere there is a prince hidden, and that if you just love him enough during his "nice" periods, that prince will appear. Not the message I am trying to get across to my girls.

But when Maddison wants to watch that video, I always make sure we talk about the issues afterward.

"Do you think that she should have allowed the Beast to be that mean?" I ask. "What should she do?"

Maddison at three told me, "She should go away. He is mean." And I felt my job was done.

But it isn't done. Those mothering strings remain firmly attached, like the leashes on little children at the mall.

JANE: They call those "leading strings" in Britain.

HEIDI: I like that. "Leading strings." Because mothers need to lead their children.

Every tale has a hidden message that children (young and old) can learn from. I'm an old child, and you—my mother—can still teach me a few things.

Perhaps in working on this book, I have taught you a few things, too. Discussing these tales and the hidden and sometimes quite mixed messages has opened up much conversation between us.

Even about sex.

Even about death.

JANE: For me, these conversations have been a gift of time. As mothers, as daughters, we rarely take the time to hold such conversations, preferring the safety of the shorthand speech. Those coded messages that often carry much more emotional weight than we realize.

I would have loved to have shared these stories and had these conversations with my own mother. Recently reading Caledonia Kearns's anthology of Irish American women's writing, *Motherland*, I came upon this paragraph in a piece by Anna Quindlen:

> "When I was younger and saw the world in black and white, I believed the woman my mother was was determined by her character, not by social conditions. Now that I see only shades of gray, I know this is nonsense. She would have gotten her second wind in the seventies. She would have wanted the things I have come to take for granted: work, money, a say in the matter, a voice of her own. She would have wanted to run her life, too."

And I thought: Quindlen could have been describing my Jewish mother. My mother who forgave her errant husband. Who wanted to be a writer but never quite made it. Who had worked for a while as a social worker, but gave it all up forever to be a wife and stay-at-home mom.

What I could have said to her, using these stories as permission to speak. What layers of meaning in our lives we could have uncovered together.

For you and I have done just that. Using these folktales as starting places, we have been forced to go where we have not gone before. (Look out William Shatner, be careful Jean-Luc!) Not just into conversations about sex and death, but into other forbidden places in our shared histories as well.

We have held the magic mirrors up and seen not just the self but the many mothers before us, the many daughters after us. Each folktale it-self has been a repeating glass.

You and I have taken steps to look into—and then beyond—the magic mirror. And when we close the pages of this book, we will have been changed for good by what we have said to one another.

Really—for the good of both of us.

BIBLIOGRAPHY

Abrahams, Roger D. *Afro-American Folktales.* New York: Pantheon, 1985.

Asala, Joanne. *Fairy Tales of the Slav Peasants and Herdsmen.* Iowa City, Iowa: Penfield Press, 1994.

Bacchilega, Cristinae. *Postmodern Fairy Tales: Gender and Narrative Strategies.* Philadelphia: University of Pennsylvania Press, 1997.

Barchers, Suzanne I. *Wise Women: Folk and Fairy Tales from Around the World.* Englewood, Colo.: Libraries Unlimited, 1990.

Bassoff, Evelyn. *Mothers and Daughters: Loving and Letting Go.* New York: Penguin, 1989.

Belkin, Gary S. *Contemporary Psychotherapies.* 2d ed. Monterey, Calif.: Brooks/Cole, 1987.

Bettelheim, Bruno. *The Uses of Enchantment: The Meaning and Importance of Fairy Tales.* New York: Knopf, 1976.

Boggs, Ralph Steele, and Mary Gould Davis. *Three Golden Oranges and Other Spanish Folktales.* Longmans, Green & Co., n.p. 1936. Reprint, 1964.

Bottigheimer, Ruth. *Fairy Tales and Society: Illusion, Allusion and Paradigm.* Philadelphia: University of Philadelphia Press, 1986.

Burch, Milbre. "Rapunzel." Unpublished poem © by the author, 1996.

Carter, Angela, ed. *The Old Wives Fairy Tale Book.* New York: Pantheon, 1990.

Carter, Dorothy Sharp. *Greedy Mariani and Other Folktales of the Antilles.* New York: Atheneum, Margaret K. McElderry Book, 1974.

Cashdan, Sheldon. *The Witch Must Die: How Fairy Tales Shape Our Lives.* New York: Basic Books, 1999.

Chesler, Phyllis. *Mothers on Trial: The Battle for Children and Custody.* New York: Harcourt Brace Jovanovich, 1986. Reprint 1987.

Clifton, Lucille. "To My Last Period," in *Quilting: Poems 1987–1990.* Brockport, N.Y.: BOA Editions.

Cohen-Sandler, Roni, and Michelle Silver. *I'm Not Mad, I Just Hate You: A New Understanding of Mother-Daughter Conflicts.* New York: Viking, 1999.

Cole, Joanna. *Best-Loved Folk Tales of the World*. New York: Anchor Press/Doubleday, 1983.

Creeden, Sharon. *In Full Bloom: Tales of Women in Their Prime*. Little Rock, Ark.: August House, 1999.

Crow, Christine. "Poem for Stella's 80th Birthday." Unpublished poem.

Deng, Francis Mading. *Dinka Folktales: African Stories from Sudan*. New York: Holmes & Meier, Africana Publishing Company, 1974.

Doyle, James A. *Sex and Gender: The Human Experience*. Dubuque, Iowa: Wm. C. Brown, 1985.

Dundes, Alan, ed. *Cinderella: A Casebook*. New York: Wildman Press, 1983.

Eberhard, Wolfram, ed. *Folktales of China*. Folktales of the World Series, ed. Richard Dorson. Chicago: University of Chicago Press, 1965.

Echevarria, Pegine. *For All Our Daughters*. Worcester, Mass.: Chandler House Press, 1998.

Estes, Clarissa Pinkola. *Women Who Run with the Wolves: Contracting the Power of the Wild Woman*. London: Random House Group, Rider, 1992.

Fraser, Kennedy. *Ornament and Silence*. New York: Random House, Vintage Books, 1998.

Freud, Sigmund. *The Ego and the Id*. New York: W. W. Norton, 1960.

Gale, Steven H. *West African Folktales*. Lincolnwood, Ill.: NTC Publishing Group, 1995.

Gilligan, Carol. *In a Different Voice: Psychological Theory and Women's Development*. Cambridge: Harvard University Press, 1983.

Gleitman, Henry. *Basic Psychology*. New York: W. W. Norton, 1983.

Glenn, Evelyn Nakano, Grace Chang, and Linda Rennie Forcey. *Mothering: Ideology, Experience, and Agency*. New York: Routledge, 1994.

Grierson, Elizabeth W. *The Scottish Fairy Book*. London: Fischer, Unwin, n.d.

Hoogasian-Villa, Susie. *100 Armenian Tales*. Wayne State University Press, 1966.

Hunt, Margaret, trans. *Grimm's Fairy Tales*. New York: Cupples and Leon, 1914.

Inciardi, James A. *Criminal Justice*. 2d ed. San Diego: Harcourt Brace Jovanovich, 1987.

Inness, Sherrie A. *Tough Girls: Women Warriors and Wonder Women in Popular Culture*. Philadelphia: University of Pennsylvania Press, 1999.

Jacobs, Joseph. *Indian Fairy Tales*. London: David Nutt, 1892.

Kast, Verena. *Through Emotions to Maturity: Psychological Readings of Fairy Tales*, trans. Douglas Whitcher. New York: International Publishing Corporation, 1993.

Kearns, Caledonia. *Motherland: Writings by Irish American Women About Mothers and Daughters*. New York: William Morrow, 1999.

Knoppflmacher, U. C. *Ventures into Childland: Victorian Fairy Tales, and Femininity*. Chicago: University of Chicago Press, 1998.

Kübler-Ross, Elisabeth. *On Death and Dying*. New York: Simon & Schuster, 1969.

Lang, Andrew. *The Red Fairy Book*. London: Longmans, Green, and Co., 1890.

Lang, Jean. *Myths from Around the World*. London: Random House UK, Bracken Books, 1915. Reprint, 1996.

Lee, F. H. *Folk Tales of All Nations*. New York: Coward McCann, 1932.

Mackoff, Barbara. *Growing a Girl: Seven Strategies for Raising a Strong, Spirited Daughter*. New York: Dell, 1996.

Megas, Georgios A. *Folktales of Greece*. Folktales of the World Series, ed. Richard Dorson. Chicago: University of Chicago Press, 1970.

Michael, Maurice, and Pamela Michael. *Portuguese Fairy Tales*. Chicago: Follett, 1965.

Miller, Jean Baker. *Toward a New Psychology of Women*. Boston: Beacon Press, 1976.

Mueller, Lisel. "The Need to Hold Still," in *The Voice from Under the Hazel Bush*. Baton Rouge: Louisiana State Press, 1980.

Muhawi, Ibrahim, and Sharif Kanann. *Speak Bird, Speak Again: Palestinian Arab Folktales*. University of California Press, 1988.

Narayan, Kirin, and Urmil Devi Sood. *Mondays on the Dark Night of the Moon: Himalayan Foothills Folktales*. New York: Oxford University Press, 1997.

Newman, Leslea. "One Hundred Years of Gratitude." *Lilith* 23, no. 4 (Winter 1998–99):

Opie, Iona, and Peter Opie. *The Classic Fairy Tales*. New York: Oxford University Press, 1974.

Paley, Grace. *Grace Paley: The Collected Stories*. New York: The Noonday Press, 1994.

Pipher, Mary. *Reviving Ophelia: Saving the Selves of Adolescent Girls,* New York: Ballantine Books, 1994.

Ralston, W. R. S. *Russian Folk-Tales*. New York: Lovell, Adam, Wesson & Company, nd.

Ramanujan, A. K. *Folktales from India*. New York: Pantheon, 1991.

Randolph, Vance. *The Devil's Pretty Daughter and Other Ozark Folk Tales*. 1955.

Rich, Adrienne. *Of Woman Born: Motherhood as Experience and Institution*. New York: W. W. Norton, 1976. Tenth Anniversary Edition, 1986.

Rush, Barbara. *The Book of Jewish Women's Tales*. Northvale, N.J.: Jason Aronson Inc.

Russo, Nancy. "The Motherhood Mandate." *Journal of Social Issues* 32 (1976): 143–53.

Sale, Roger. *Fairy Tales and After: From Snow White to E. B. White*. Cambridge, Mass.: Harvard University Press, 1978.

Schwartz, Howard, and Barbara Rush. *The Diamond Tree: Jewish Tales from Around the World*. New York: HarperCollins, 1991.

Secunda, Victoria. *When You and Your Mother Can't Be Friends: Resolving the Most Complicated Relationship of Your Life*. New York: Dell, 1990.

Sexton, Anne. *Transformations*. Boston: Houghton Mifflin, 1971.

———. "Mother and Daughter," in *The Complete Poems*. Boston: Houghton Mifflin, 1981.

Shandler, Sara. *Ophelia Speaks: Adolescent Girls Write about Their Search for Self.* New York: HarperPerennial, 1999.

Stone, Kay. *Burning Brightly: New Light on Old Tales Told Today.* Peterborough, Ontario: Broadview Press, 1998.

Tatar, Maria. *Off with Their Heads: Fairy Tales and the Culture of Childhood.* Princeton, N.J.: Princeton University Press, 1992.

Thompson, Stith, selector. *Tales of the North American Indians*. Bloomington: Indiana University Press, 1929.

Thurer, Shari L. *The Myths of Motherhood: How Culture Reinvents the Good Mother.* New York: Penguin, 1994.

Van Buren, Jane Silverman. *The Modernist Madonna: Semiotics of the Maternal Metaphor.* Bloomington: Indiana University Press, 1989.

Verdier, Yvonne. "Little Red Riding Hood in Oral Tradition." *Marvels & Tales, Journal of Fairy-Tale Studies* 11, nos. 1–2 (1997):

Von Franz, Maria. *The Feminine in Fairytales*. Dallas, Tex.: Spring Publications, 1972.

Warner, Marina. *From the Beast to the Blonde: On Fairy Tales and Their Tellers.* New York: Farrar, Straus and Giroux, 1994.

Whitney, T. M. "A Blessing: Some Values Are Ageless." *Newsday,* 27 March 1999, B3.

Wilson, Laurence L. *Tales from the Mountain Province.* Manila, Phillipines: Philippine Education Co., 1958.

INDEX

Sources and Acknowledgments

"The Voice from Under the Hazel Bush" from *The Need to Hold Still* by Lisel Mueller. Copyright © 1980 by Lisel Mueller. Reprinted by permission of Louisiana State University Press.

"Cinderella (Germany)" and "One-eye, Two-eyes, and Three-eyes" from *Grimm's Fairy Tales* translated by Margaret Hunt (New York: Cupples and Leon Company, 1914).

"Cinderella" from *Perrault's Complete Fairy Tales* translated by A. E. Johnson (New York: Dodd, Mead, 1961).

"Rapunzel" and "Snow White" from *Best Loved Folk-Tales of the World* edited by Joanna Cole (New York: Doubleday, 1983).

"The Wonderful Birch" from *The Red Fairy Book* edited by Andrew Lang (London: Longmans, Green, and Co., 1890).

"The Good Girl and the Ornery Girl" from *The Devil's Pretty Daughter and Other Ozark Folk Tales* by Vance Randolph (Columbia University Press, 1955). Copyright © Vance Randolph, 1955. Copyright renewed Frances B. Lott, 1983. Reprinted by permission of the Estate of Vance Randolph.

"Sukhu and Dukhu" from *Folktales from India* selected and edited by A. K. Ramanujan. Copyright © 1991 by A. K. Ramanujan. Reprinted by permission of Pantheon Books, a division of Random House, Inc.

"The City Where People Are Mended" and "Gboloto, the River Demon" from *West African Folktales* by Steven H. Gale (NTC Publishing Group). © 1995 Steven H. Gale. Reprinted by permission of the author.

"The Fairy" (herein titled "Diamonds and Toads") from *The Classic Fairy Tales* by Iona and Peter Opie. © Iona and Peter Opie 1974. Reprinted by permission of Oxford University Press (UK).

"The Greedy Daughter," "The Singing Sack," and "The Mirror of Matsuyama" from *Folk Tales of All Nations* edited by F. H. Lee (New York: Coward-McCann, 1930).

"The King of the Mineral Kingdom" from *Fairy Tales of the Slav Peasants and Herdsmen* retold by Joanne Asala, selected from the 1896 classic written and illustrated by Emily J. Harding. © 1994 Joanne Asala. By permission of Penfield Press.

"Maroula" from *Folktales of Greece* edited by Georgios A. Megas, translated by Helen Colaclides. © 1970 by The University of Chicago. By permission of The University of Chicago Press.

"The Water Snake" from *Russian Folk-Tales* by W.R.S. Ralston (New York: Lovell, Adam, Wesson & Company).

"Daughter, My Little Bread" from *Mondays on the Dark Night of the Moon: Himalayan Foothill Folktales* by Kirin Narayan in collaboration with Urmila Devi Sood. Copyright © 1997 by Kirin Narayan. Used by permission of Oxford University Press, Inc.

"The Girl Made of Butter" from "Folk Tales of Andros Island, Bahamas" by Elsie Clews Parsons, *Memoirs of the American Folklore Society*, volume 13.

"Persephone" from *Myths from Around the World* by Jean Lang (London: Bracken Books, 1915).

"Orpheus" (herein titled "The Sun's Daughter"), *Report of the Bureau of American Ethnology*, xix, 252, no. 5.

"Rolando and Brunilde" from *The Second Virago Book of Fairy Tales* edited by Angela Carter (London: Virago Press Limited, 1992).

"The Mother" and "Lanjeh" from *The Book of Jewish Women's Tales* retold by Barbara Rush. Copyright © 1994 by Barbara Rush. Reprinted by permission of the publisher, Jason Aronson Inc., Northvale, New Jersey.

"The Dead Woman and Her Child" from *Folk-Tales of Salishan and Sahamptin Tribes* edited by Franz Boas (Lancaster, Pa: The American Folklore Society, 1917).

"Ubazakura" from *Fairy Tales of the Orient* selected by Pearl S. Buck (Simon & Schuster). Copyright © 1965 by Pearl S. Buck and Lyle Kenyon Engel. Reprinted by permission of Harold Ober Associates Incorporated.

"The Three Fairies" from *Greedy Mariani and Other Folktales of the Antilles* selected and adapted by Dorothy Sharp Carter (New York: Atheneum, 1974).

"Habetrot the Spinstress" and "The Well o' the World's End" from *The Scottish Fairy Book* by Elizabeth W. Grierson (London: Fischer, Unwin).

"The Wife of the Monkey" from *Folktales of China* edited by Wolfram Eberhard. Revised edition © 1965 by Wolfram Eberhard. By permission of The University of Chicago Press.

"The Old Woman and the Giant" from *Tales from the Mountain Province* by Laurence L. Wilson (Manila: Philippine Education Co., 1958).

"Tuglik and Her Granddaughter" from *The Old Wives' Fairy Tale Book* edited by Angela Carter. Collection, introduction and notes copyright © 1990 by Angela Carter. Reprinted by permission of Pantheon Books, a division of Random House, Inc.

"Katanya" from *The Diamond Tree: Jewish Tales from Around the World* selected and retold by Howard Schwartz and Barbara Rush. Copyright © 1991 by Howard Schwartz and Barbara Rush. Used by permission of HarperCollins Publishers.

"Achol and Her Wild Mother" from *Dinka Folktales: African Stories from the Sudan* by Francis Mading Deng (New York: Africana Publishing Co., a division of Holmes & Meier, 1974). Copyright © 1974 by Francis Mading Deng. Reprinted by permission of the publisher and the author.

"How Sun, Moon, and Wind Went Out to Dinner" from *Indian Fairy Tales* by Joseph Jacobs (London: David Nutt, 1892).

"The Serpent Mother" from *Folktales Told Around the World* edited by Richard M. Dorson. By permission of The University of Chicago Press.

"Nourie Hadig" from *100 Armenian Tales* collected and edited by Susie Hoogasian-Villa. By permission of Wayne State University Press.

"Mirabella" from *Portuguese Folk Tales* retold by Maurice and Pamela Michael (Chicago: Follett Publishing Company, 1967).

"The Wood Maiden" from *Czechoslovak Fairy Tales* by Parker Fillmore (New York: Harcourt, Brace & Co., 1919).

"Tunjur, Tunjur" from *Speak, Bird, Speak Again: Palestinian Arab Folktales* edited and translated by Ibrahim Muhawi and Sharif Kanaana. Copyright © 1988 The Regents of the University of California. By permission of the University of California Press.